The
Rabbi
of Lud

The
Rabbi
of Lud

a novel

by STANLEY ELKIN

Charles Scribner's Sons

NEW YORK

Charles Scribner's Sons
Macmillan Publishing Company
866 Third Avenue, New York, NY 10022
Collier Macmillan Canada, Inc.

Library of Congress Cataloging-in-Publication Data
Elkin, Stanley. 1930–
    The Rabbi of Lud : a novel / by Stanley Elkin.
      p. cm.
    ISBN 0-684-18902-X
    I. Title.
PS3555.L47R3   1987   87–17821
813'.54—dc19   CIP

10 9 8 7 6 5 4 3 2 1

Printed in the United States of America

For Joan as always.

But for Bill Whitehead too.

The author wishes to thank Rabbi James S. Diamond and Rabbi Devorah Jacobson of the Hillel Foundation for their generous assistance whenever he asked for it. He would also like to thank Kaye Norton, Leanna Boysko and Millie Hoerner, and all the folks in the coffee room.

The
Rabbi
of Lud

one

THEY SAY IT'S FLAT as sea level and, so far as the eye can tell, it sure looks like it—some great, blunt stub of the earth, level as a table, as if the Creator had meant to mimic in dirt and pure planes of real estate the dark ascensions and black declinations of space, all His monotonous deep celestials. Heaven on earth, so to speak. Or, to hear me tell it—I'm Jerry Goldkorn, the Rabbi of Lud—under earth, either.

Well, this part of Jersey's not known for its mountains. The Jersey flats, they call it, that stretch between Hoboken and Newark, the upper reaches of the Garden State Parkway and the Hudson River, and though it's built up now, condos and malls, industrial parks and factory outlet stores, and the skyscrapers of New York in the middle distance like another country altogether, it must once have looked like scorched earth or the kind of terrain where two opposing civilizations came to grips, just the sort of undistinguished, insignificant but bloodied parcel where the battle park goes or historic field where important papers were signed.

Which doesn't, when it comes right down, preclude. Ain't it bloodied? That bunch of our dead, I mean. And at least legal if not out-and-out historical? I mean all those contracts, notarized papers, the official documents, certificates and reciprocal pledges.

Legend has it—this would have been sometime in the
tenderloin of the seventeenth century, pre-Colonial times, New
Amsterdam days—that some founding Jew lost his wife and all
his male and female children to one of those cyclical miniplagues
that used to hit the New World from time to time. (Listen,
usually the missionaries and imperialists take the rap, the troops
and camp followers good for the fall. But pox is a two-way
street. Disease is just as often a tradeoff. I've got nothing against
the red man per se, but all you hear about is the white guy's
syphilis and TB, smallpox on the blankets, typhoid in the
orange juice, and other assorted germs of the paleface. Let's be
frank here. The Indians dished it out pretty good themselves.
There was your maize, there were your bark and berry poison-
ings. There was your bad peace pipe, your war-paint cosmetics
and other fatal allergies. Death by the digestive and the killer
contact rashes.) Forgive and forget, I say. Live and let live, why
not? But the fact remains, the van Feldmaans and van Gildbergs,
or whoever, came to grief along with other of their Dutch
neighbors. So, sooner or later, the need arose. Say what you
will, pioneers are generally rotten city planners. Many are the
reasons for this, but in the case of the Jewish peoples, living on
the leading edge of the Diaspora, there's usually so much else on
their minds. They have to pick out a ghetto, they have to put a
reliable minyan together. In a radically new environment like
New Amsterdam must have been, they probably had to do a
whole classification number on the flora and fauna, checking the
trayf factors in the deer and the turkeys, in the catfish and
tortoises, in the newfangled salads, the pumpkin pies and cran-
berry candies. (I'm no expert in the matter—I don't say I
shouldn't be, I say I'm not—but it's a pretty good bet that those
founding Jews were probably a very choosy chosen people,
more Orthodox than anything we see today, if not hounded
then at least closely questioned, at least scrutinized, and *maybe*
hounded, even by their old Old World coreligionists, who would
have looked on them, even in those old gabardine times, as a
separate branch or sect or even cult, or otherwise why would
they have bothered to make the trip in the first place? So who
knows what must have been on their minds or what they would
have made of all the what-have-you of the buckskin life?)

Anyway, when the sickness—we'll call it New World fever—broke out and made its way under the pales and pickets and over the posts of their little Jewish stockade, and the Angel of Death took off with most of his family, the founding Jew guy was probably caught short. Not only didn't he have a family plot, there wasn't a consecrated cemetery on all Manhattan Island. What did he see? His gentile neighbors taking their particular dead off in canoes to Queens. (Because the New Amsterdam Jews were only a small contingent and were not as prepared as their Christian brothers and sisters who, outnumbering them probably a hundredfold in life, quite naturally were way ahead of them in death, too, and were already in possession of a place to bury their dead.)

Which is when, it's said, someone—the name is lost to history—crossed the Hudson and discovered Lud— the vast, once and future compound of departed Jews to come. Maybe it was the treeless soil, maybe just the brown, dead look of the place, or it could be he saw a correspondence between the blank, fresh page of that open plain and the charged, historic enterprise of making something out of what wasn't just a new country this time but a new continent too.

Though the latter, I'm the first to admit, is probably just the rabbi in me talking, the opportune poetry of my sacramental, laureate occasions. I'm leaving a couple of things out here anyway— the mounds and the grief. Hey, I'm no expert. Maybe I'm thinking of a different tribe altogether. Maybe the Mounds Indians never even came East. But the subject is still savages, people buried upright or sitting in the earth like schoolchildren at their lessons, in mass graves, or left out to dry like laundry on platforms in trees. But, whatever, interfacing, impacting on a people who came from Holland by way of Poland out of Prussia and from Prussia by way of Spain out of North Africa. The whole Jew thing a wandering minstrelsy. Assimilated a dozen times before they were chewed up and spit out, covered in cultures like a snowball rolling downhill, fattening. Except that these couldn't even have been Jews as we know them, a cult, a clan, a sect, a faction, their beliefs—I'm a rabbi, I should know these things but here I'm speculating—on the lintels of their log cabins and on their gates, and as frontlets in their beards, say, and even their skullcaps—no disrespect—improvised, improbable as the headdress of the Indians themselves. But, whatever, by this time so culture-shocked out, and outraged, too, that they—he, the founder Jew, or maybe the lookout, shotgun-riding, scout-emissary-agent Jew for him—felt strong enough about it to shove off in the old birchbark and out into the wide and whelming Hudson—this would have been after the winter thaw, during the spring plagues—not just to seek out Lud but to get their dead as far away from the redskin dead as possible. And from the Dutchmen dead too, all those borough-of-Queens-grounded Katrinkas and Jans, Wilhelminas and Hauke Pjeters, as if they needed to put not just one but *two* rivers between their different theologies, almost, I mean, as though life is one thing and it's all right to walk around on the surface of the earth together without losing any sleep over it or doing any lasting damage, but death, which lasts longer, and isn't just any only make-do, temporary arrangement, is another thing entirely, and you have to do whatever you have to do in order to defend your remains against their remains.

On the grief side the ground is less shaky.

That founding Jew, the one who lost his whole family. His grief, at least, is documented.

Well, documented. I say "documented," but you want to know something? Not even their names have come down to us. (Now, as you know, the whole graven-image business is a Jewish thing— the idol taboos, the no-other-gods-before-Me arrangements, all that forbidden working-model, doll-and-dummy iconography that so exercised Moses when he came down the mountain and found the Jews disporting with the golden calves.) And that's the key to it— those missing names.

There's this old joke. In front of the whole congregation the rabbi knocks his breast and proclaims, "I'm nothing, I'm nothing." Then the president of the synagogue starts smacking himself around the bema and says *he's* as insignificant as lint. They're really beating up on themselves, these two, and the temple's janitor is very moved that two such holy, scrupulous men should get up in front of everyone and carry on like that, so he too gets up in the shul and starts to rap himself in the heart. "O God," he says, "I'm unworthy, I'm beneath notice, I'm nothing," and the rabbi turns to the president of the synagogue, nudges him, points to the janitor, and whispers, "Look who says he's nothing."

You get around, you know what I'm talking about. You've been to the hospitals and must surely have noticed those names sandblasted into the marble over the entrance to the nifty new wings, or seen the plaques in the temples, under every window in the sanctuary. The *sanctuary*? The toilets— the stalls and the urinals. Trees in Israel, waves in Waikiki, moonlight in Vermont. For a people wary of blowing God's horn—saying His name, I mean—we're not so reluctant to memorialize the monikers and to-do's of our loved ones. Not a sparrow falls, as it were. We're the backbone of the customized CAT-scan industry, the personalized Intensive Care Unit one. So right there's the clue. To his knocked-down-dragged-out, solid-gold, championship, world-class grief. Because what are we dealing with here, Arlington National, Flanders Field? The military rows, lanes and aisles of some close-order-drilled death with Stars of David and simple white wooden crosses like a kind of punctuation? Lud International—my little joke—is as makeshift finally as any other project of pioneers. It's zoned for death, sure, but otherwise as gerrymandered and catch-as-catch-can as any boardwalk or world's fair. Did you ever try to find someone in one of these places? They're mazes. Vaults and sepulchers, tombs, cairns, barrows and mausoleums all mixed in with each other. Obelisks and grave pits. Indiscriminate. There seem to be no codes or ordinances. A cemetery is kind of like a boom town, I think. Anyway, the point is that usually everything in one of these places is as carefully marked and labeled as your kid's socks when he goes off to camp. Which is *why* I suspect what we're dealing with is some really spectacular grief.

So this is the thing. Buckskin or no buckskin, pales and pickets or no pales and pickets, they had some incredible artisans back in those days. You think they couldn't build a monument? They could *build* a monument. And when they wanted to they could build a monument like nobody's business! It would be a match for anything in the Old World. So this fellow, this founder Jew I'm talking about, sends out the word, gets all the best craftsmen in the city together, the best draughtsmen, the best architects and engineers, and commissions a mausoleum that practically looks at you it says, "Money's no object."

You get around. (Ain't Newark Airport a stone's throw? Ain't LaGuardia a hop and a skip? JFK?) I'm talking about humility. Sure. I'm speaking in my rabbi mode here, and I'm telling you. This is a nice theological point. That joke I told you? That's an unrighteous joke. You heard me. Most people, they get a kick out of that story they have no more idea what they're laughing at than the man in the moon. Because the point ain't that the rabbi's puffed up, or that the big-shot president of the congregation is. And it's not on the janitor, either. No. That's a joke that mocks God. Because where, in Torah, is God's name? *Where is it written?* God, Jehovah, Lord and Yahweh. All aliases— the nicknames, noms de plume and a.k.a.'s of Agency, your basic top-secret, undercover, cloak-and-dagger, off-the-record, ambush-laying Pussyfoot. Peekaboo to you from the burning bush! God likes to make a big deal of this sort of thing. So in the view of the Rabbi of Lud, that joke is a commentary on God's humility. Look, a Jew isn't a Christian. Jesus says, "Follow me," and the church makes a big thing out of the imitation of Christ. Not by us. On an individual level, by us there's a real distinction between church and state. We're supposed to keep the dishes for meat and the dishes for dairy strictly separate. What do you think *that's* all about? It's about place, that's what that's all about. So "Look who says he's nothing" is, to a Jew, just about the most serious charge you could bring against him. You're accusing him of playing God, and what's so wicked about that old joke is that it accuses *God* of playing God, too! (I'm wasting my time in New Jersey.)

So, given the background, can you at least begin to understand the grief of that founding New Amsterdam Jew with the fancy tomb, that marble miracle of seventeenth-century know-how with its state-of-the-art arches, piers, cantilevers, columns, finials and traves? He had to have been beside himself! He must have been! Not a mark on it anywhere to indicate who was who! Nowhere the family name! Not a Sarah, not a Joe! Nowhere a Darling Daughter! No place a Beloved Son! As if God, God forbid, Himself had died! Grief so great it didn't matter anymore about keeping the appearances up. An out-and-out proclamation that not only am *I* nothing, but that my wife is nothing too, my sons and my daughters. All. All nothing. Denying the Creator. Denying Creation. I'll tell you something. Grief that immense has got to be a lesson to me. Yes, and a comfort, too. Because whenever I'm feeling sorry for myself, whenever I'm blue or feeling down because I'm only the Rabbi of Lud and haven't a real congregation but am just this pickup rabbi, God's little Hebrew stringer in New Jersey, I like to wander out by our seminal, primal monument, that ahead-of-its-time memorial to nothing, just to get my bearings again and put things in the proper perspective.

I'll be frank with you. If I don't sound to you like the Rabbi of even Lud, maybe it's because I never had a true calling in the conventional sense. Sue me. The fact is our Christian friends have the music and that's half the battle right there. I'm not even thinking about plainsong, Gregorian chants, the hard-core liturgical stuff. I discount madrigals, chimes, ding-dongs from the carillon. I'm not even thinking of the dirges, dead marches, oratorios and canticles. Just ordinary *hymns*! Forget the "Hallelujah Chorus." Where in the Judaic tradition do you get an "Amazing Grace"? A "Rock of Ages," a "Just a Closer Walk With Thee"? So never *mind* hymns. Where are your Jewish Christmas carols? We don't *have* "The Little Drummer Boy." We don't *have* an "Angels We Have Heard on High." And did you ever hear of a *Jewish* spiritual? Of course not, even though the Jordan is our river, Jewish water from the word go. We don't even have good chants. There are saffron-robed kids in the airports with better. What do we have, "Bei Mir Bist Du Schön"? So if it isn't the calling, the compelling musical inspiration, I mean, maybe it's because I've always been just a little bit more spiritual then the next guy.

•   •   •   •   •

Take away the cemeteries, here's what Lud looks like:

I'm not a world traveler and don't put myself forward as an expert in these matters, but ever since I first saw it it's always struck me that downtown Lud is a lot like the buildings and stores that line the highways of western towns like a peddler's fruit stands, garment racks and card tables. It's a, what-do-you-call-it, a strip, and Lud, like Las Vegas or Hollywood or Washington, D.C., is essentially a one-industry town. Only it's even less diversified than those other places, and though there's nothing to see, it's even something of a tourist town. It's amazing how it's all linked together. The cemetery came first and was out here on its own for a good many years like, oh, say, the Valley of the Kings in Egypt, but then somebody had the bright idea of bringing all death's service-related industries together under one roof, so the town's long main street has two monument companies where they cut and engrave the monuments. It has two funeral homes, a nursery, a landscaper, Pamella's flower shop and a dry cleaner's.

Let's see, there's a barber, a notary and a PIP instant printer that does a land-office business in death certificates. There are a couple of lawyers, a limo wash, a draper, a tiny hotel and coffee shop, a post office, and an office with a telex machine that can send obituary notices to any newspaper in the country. There's also a gas station that has a wrecker on twenty-four-hour call and a trucker named Pete who hauls stone from the quarries. We have a little Jewish notions shop that stocks greeting cards, prayer books, yarmulkes and yahrtzeit candles for the funeral homes, and an agency that provides day laborers to the town's cemeteries. Also there's a small office, not connected with either the cemeteries or the funeral homes, that deals in the buying and selling of deeds, graves, plots and all the rest of the real estate of death. And everything done in that brick and white-trim style designed to make you think you're back in Colonial Williamsburg or Federal Philadelphia during the Revolution. The rest is residential, a staggered half-dozen houses on either side of Route 43—we live in one ourselves—with big backyards and swimming pools and the town's two leading cemeteries behind them like farms. (There are smaller graveyards in Lud, pockets of consecrated land that touch the town like suburbs.)

•　　•　　•　　•

So here I am, representing—the merchants and the other rabbis don't live here, don't or won't, and drive in from Ridgewood and other places in northern Jersey, and the houses are either unoccupied or turned into rooming houses for Lud's transient gardeners and gravediggers—oh, virtually the entire Jewish population, effectively, as I say, the Rabbi of Lud. The rabbi, the mayor, the chief of police. Whatever I say I am. Because of *course* there's no mayor and, except for that post office, no civil services. No police unless you count the security people who work the traffic for the funerals. No school board, no health department, no tax collector, no department of streets. We're this company town. (There's no company.) We're this ghost town. (No ghosts either, but lots of potential.) And not even the Rabbi of Lud finally, because, to tell you the truth, when it comes right down to it, except for my immediate family, there's not any Jews who live here. And every so often, in my rabbi mode again, I have to ask, How could this happen? Who shapes discrepancy? I understand about Leviathan, I know about the treasuries of the sky, but what's responsible for our Luds, those perfectly logical closed systems outside connection? God doesn't usually do anomaly. I'm not saying He couldn't if He wanted, but it's against His nature.

I say "every so often" but it's more frequent than that. On a nice morning I might be having my breakfast on the red cedar table in my backyard and I'll look up from my newspaper and coffee and see it spread out before me, cemetery as far as the eye can see. The earth-drowned Jews of Lud, New Jersey. Our crowd. How did there get to be so many? There are grave-yards in New York now, of course, in every borough except Manhattan, and new places opening up in Connecticut all the time, in Stamford and other poshy venues and climes even farther out, but Lud still gets more than its fair share. It doesn't take a back seat even to the cemeteries you see out your taxi window coming in from the airport through Queens. You know what land is like in New York. They look that crowded because they're so close together. We're more spread out and, according to the *Journal of the American Funeral Association*, we have fewer people but more families. My God, I sound like a booster!

·   ·   ·   ·

How could this happen? *I'll* tell you how this could happen. As the twig is bent, that's how it could happen. There I am, a kid in Chicago. Not from a particularly religious family. On top of the world, in the middle of the middle class. Ten years old and an only child. The war over half a decade and the good guys winners. Absolutely content. Not looking for trouble—and where could I find it if I was?—and coming into consciousness postwar. This is the end of the 1940s, before the X-ray machines in shoe stores could irradiate your toe bones, before cigarettes could kill you with cancer, before blacks, before projects, ghettos and changing neighborhoods, before juvenile delinquency even. This was a golden age when wholesale was wholesale and your edge was real. I'm living the good life on Chicago's South Side. My daddy's rich and my ma is good lookin'.

Let me interrupt myself here a minute. You know what's largely responsible for the increased popularity of Judaism in America? In America. Not closing the camps, not the new state of Israel. What's largely responsible for the increased popularity of Judaism in America was the development of the printed invitation. I mean things like when raised lettering came within the price range of the middle classes. I mean when they perfected that transparent tissue paper. Because it isn't only necessity that's the mother of invention. Sometimes it's boom and amplitude. Take Miami, that town's flush days when they were throwing up buildings right and left and they'd advertise, "Come to the Fabulous Such-and-So— This Year's Hotel." It was like that back at the end of the forties. Money relatively easy to come by and the printed invitation revolution moving in to take up the slack, people excited and trying to outdo one another with celebrations, with their weddings and bar mitzvahs and what-have-you's.

Which goes toward explaining how I'm reading comic books one minute and studying in the cheder the next. Plucked and translated out of my customary ways and haunts by parents who were already thinking about what the invitations would look like three years down the road when it was time for their only son to be bar mitzvah'd, what wondrous concoctions would be coming onstream to amaze the neighbors and confound the relatives.

I *don't* scorn them. I *don't* cast aspersion. This isn't any easy satire I do. Because God does *too* move in mysterious ways, and ain't *that* the truth, wonders the Rabbi of Lud from his plain in New Jersey. Mysterious? Byzantine. He wants me in Jersey, He arranges raised lettering and transparent tissue paper spinoffs from Second World War R & D. (I've got to think I'm doing the work of the Lord or I'll plotz. —Excuse me. Bust. This other is still a second language to me. I don't have it right, the rhythms, the Yiddish singsong ways.)

But that ain't the half of it. Taking a secular kid from a secular family in Chicago and throwing him into Hebrew school ain't the half of it. Here's the miraculous, mysterious part. *I'd never been more bored!* I stuttered and hemmed and hawed myself through those lessons like a dyslexic, like someone disadvantaged, Job Corps material, volunteer Army, Operation Headstart— all broke-will, underfunded, bust-hope beneficiary. God's little own welfare cheat. I had no aptitude for what was finally just another inscrutably foreign language to me and not the ordinary, conversational vulgate of God Himself. The superheroes in those comic books had more reality for me than all the biblical luminaries and shoguns in Pentateuch. And this is who He chooses to ride shotgun for Him in New Jersey?

As my thirteenth birthday approached my teachers started to sweat. My haphtarah, the passage from Prophets that bar mitzvah boys read for their bar mitzvahs, was too long for my poor skills, and they postponed the ceremony for three months, finding another haphtarah for me, the shortest of the year. All the time plotting, conspiring with His sense of the dramatic, arranging His improbable, mysterious scenarios, having taken the secular kid from the secular Chicago family—which, when it came right down to it, was probably more Chicago than Jewish— and putting him through paces that he never understood— that he was never interested enough to understand— finally bar mitzvahing the kid, the bozo Jew, to less than rave reviews, and getting ready to uncork the real and final miracle— to give me, just *me*, a calling, passing over my classmates, the bona fide buchers, those little ten-, eleven- and twelve-year-old keepers of the flame to whom Hebrew script did not look like the business end of so many heavy, old-fashioned keys. (Let alone worry about the problem of God, being at that stage in my

theological development where whether He sported a long white
beard was still an issue.)

So I became a man on the Shabbes of the year's shortest
haphtarah passage, and if I felt any different it was strictly in a
material way. The newfangled invitations had done their job.
My bar mitzvah attracted over two hundred and fifty people.
Family and close friends, of course, but a sort of papered house
of the more distantly connected—the rabbi, big shots from the
temple, my dad's bosses and colleagues, his competitors and
customers, certain featured gentiles (you could not, in those
days, even *think* of throwing a big affair without their little
ecumenical presence), my ma's cleaning lady, everyone, possibly, for whom they could obtain a good address. I did all right.
I did better than all right. I cleaned up. Because now, in those
boom times, a spinoff of the spinoff, checks and money began to
come in envelopes tricked out like little paper billfolds and later,
in the hotel, it was practically de rigueur to slip a bar mitzvah
kid—or a bridegroom, or a bride—his gift in one of them, working it into a handshake or a pocket of the kid's suit, throwing maybe a wink into the mix and making the cloak-and-dagger
razzle-dazzler's or card sharp's or pickpocket-in-reverse's almost
invisible feints. It was a sight to see. Really. A sight to see. The
way one moment some guy you weren't even sure you knew
might be brushing your lapel for you and the next you felt the
flap on a pocket of your suitcoat lifted and heard the soft
susurrus of money changing not hands but actual clothing. It
might have looked vulgar for a freshly decreed all-grown-up
man to go around like that, paper hanging from him like the tags
on new ready-to-wear, except that every so often my mother or
father came up to take my envelopes to hold for me. I pulled in
over eight hundred 1949 dollars. (Question, Rabbi: Which is
more vulgar, if the proceeds from a bar mitzvah exceed or do
not meet expenses? Answer: I'm here to tell you this isn't even a
good question. First of all, a man who throws an affair with a
view toward making money from it has to be out of his head.
Consider the price of the hall, the cost of the catering. Don't
forget what they charge for flowers, don't forget what you give
for a band. And what about those fancy invitations, what about
the postage to send them, the stamps for the RSVPs? Plus you

have to remember the incidentals. Also there's an ostentatious element that takes pleasure in outspending the guests. That's only happy if the numbers make no sense at all, if the very idea of cost effectiveness is thrown out altogether. Admittedly, this has always been a distinct minority, never higher than a couple of percent. For the vast majority of us, the money outlay is only the necessary expense of doing business and the real payoff and genuine pleasure come from showcasing the kid. It's the kid's day, his or hers, he or she, whoever's up to bat that Saturday. I'll go out on a limb here. I'll tell you that maybe not the majority but many of us, many of us would just as soon put by showbiz and do away with the shindig part of it entirely and close down after the kid says his piece in the temple. So *vulgar*? Sure, if love is vulgar. —And *this* is the lesson of the rabbi!

(Who was not a rabbi yet and who's still trying to explain the roundabouts of his mysterious calling.)

Speaking of whom, well, it was the rabbi himself who came up to me, us, me and the older cousin with whom I was slow dancing, the parents and grandparents watching, taking it all in how yesterday's klutz and this morning's man had lickety-split discovered sex, beaming, getting their money's worth from the showcased kid. First I thought he wanted to move us apart, then that he meant to cut in. Then—oh, youth's tender, indiscriminate imperialism that assumes such tribute—merely that he had forgotten to give me my present and couldn't wait for the band to stop playing to make amends. Which would he be, I wondered in the split second he'd left me to consider the question, a handshake stuffer or a mock valet?

"Jerry," he said. "Miss," he told the girl, "please. Excuse us."

"Oh, Rabbi Wolfblock," I said, "you didn't have to. Don't you remember? You already gave me *The Illustrated History of the Tallith*."

He guided me to a chair at an unoccupied table. "Jerome, you impressed me this morning. The broches could have melted in your mouth."

"Thank you, Rabbi."

"No, I mean it. I think you could have done it even if I hadn't written it all out for you in English."

"Thank you, Rabbi."

"You used your extra months to advantage."

"Thank you, Rabbi."

"One good turn deserves another. You know this expression?"

"Of course, Rabbi."

"Good boy," Rabbi Wolfblock said. The band finished a set and some of the people whose table we occupied had started to drift back but were pulled up short when Wolfblock held up his hand. "A moment, friends," he said, and turned back and lowered his voice. "What you have to understand, Jerry, is that I'm the fellow who found that eensy miniscripture for you that we waited for it to come round like people waiting on a solstice."

"I know that, Rabbi."

"Jerry," he said, "that some thirteen-year-old pisher becomes a man when he's bar mitzvah is only a legalism. With all due respect it's probably a holdover from the time before penicillin when most people didn't have a Chinaman's chance of making it past twenty-nine and were already middle-aged by the time they were eighteen. Methuselah lived nine hundred years? Days is more like it. *Weeks!* Listen, Jerry, Jewish people practically invented cancer and heart conditions. And what about anti-Semitism? That had to shave *something* off the life expectancy. And those momzers weren't fooling around. I'm not talking about country clubs you couldn't get into or nasty jokes in the observation car with 'kike' in the punchline. They violated the women and children and shot to kill. So of *course* little boys got to go around like their seniors. Of *course* they did. A legal fiction. —In a minute, friends.

"Rabbi Wolfblock doesn't say these things to make you feel bad. To make you feel bad? When he scoured Torah to find your itty-bitty portion? Was that to make you feel bad? No, it was so an ignorant, backward boy could be bar mitzvah like anybody else and have a nice affair with a band and lovely presents and a bunch of strangers to cheer him on to remember all his life. Jerry, promise me."

He recruited me, a thing someone with my record of rotten attendance and demonstrably lousy skills could never, had no right ever to, have expected, for his minyan.

In addition to our attendance on people just bereaved who were supposed to stay in their homes during the mourning period, the compulsory seven days of shiva, we had additional assignments.

You have to understand something. This was Chicago at the end of the forties, the war over four years and the terrors of the Holocaust still fresh. In those days certain older people wouldn't leave their apartments at first light or walk abroad at dusk to go to synagogue for the sunrise and sunset services. They believed that Jew-haters, familiar with the broad outlines of our religious practices, waited and watched for a lone Jew to leave his home and come into the streets, where they would be hiding themselves, posing behind kiosks perhaps, where they sold newspapers, or skulking about the gangways between apartment buildings. It was a familiar nightmare, a common delusion among old people. So these old Jews, some of them even Orthodox, wouldn't or couldn't get to shul. And it wasn't that long after the war, remember. The agencies still verifying the identities of death camp victims and the Defense Department still closing the books on MIAs, each day making grief official. So it wasn't as if there was any shortage of relatives to mourn. And they were old, infirm, handicapped. A lot of these people couldn't have gotten to temple even if they'd wanted to. (And, let's face it, they didn't all want to. The invitation revolution just didn't have the kick that some of these old IWWs and Trotskyites and ILGWUs were accustomed to.) So we delivered. Rabbi Wolfblock's Traveling Minyan. We were like Meals-on-Wheels. Like the Postal Service. It was neither rain nor snow nor dark of night by us too.

We were not comforters, not eulogizers—most of the time we didn't even know the people whose souls we were commending to God, vouchsafing to God as if we were cosigning their loans—and I wish I could say there was something embarrassing about sweeping into the homes of people who had just been widowed or lost a father, say, a mother, a brother, a sister, a child, who hadn't yet had time to take in the implications of their ceremonial or blood bond so surprisingly destroyed, and inviting them to override their grief not only with ritual but with ritual made suspect by having it served up by mere legalisms, a troupe—that's what we were—of thirteen-year-old bar mitzvah pishers. We were, what? Rabbi Wolfblock's Children's

Crusaders. Ten little men, thirteen to fifteen years old, ten little Infants for Orthodoxy against a background of the new calligraphy—so ornate it might itself have been a kind of Hebrew—on the new invitations, who minstreled the South Shore of the South Side, Shachris to Marev, administering Sh'ma, administering Shemoneh Esray, administering Kaddish, administering, that is, what any *grown* quorum of ten bar mitzvah'd Jews—God does not hear the prayers of nine Jews—would administer. I wish I could say I was embarrassed. There was certainly enough opportunity— the mirrors covered with sheets, the mourners' stools and low, hard, makeshift benches, the rumpled clothing, bad breath and sour smells of the bereaved, as if a little at least of death were contagious, its sloven, unshaven, caught-short essence. I wish I could say I was embarrassed, but the fact is, I loved it, and loved the articles about us in the weekend supplements. I ate it all up like a Hitler Youth and loved saying prayers for the dead and guiding people five and six times my age through the mazes of Jewish death. I wish I could say I was embarrassed, but I was more embarrassed on the bema reading my haphtarah.

And anyway you don't look a calling in the face. For this was it, the real, genuine, miracle calling— me, Jerry Goldkorn, God's little card trick, His will, take it or leave it, revealed. Working, as ever, with chaff, His by-this-time familiar, boring, inferior materials, His . . . Ech, to hell with it. And if we're going to plumb the depths of all this, untangle the ironies, is it really, come to think of it, such a wonder after all? Is it the first time someone has found himself in too deep, out of his league, out of his depth, in over his head? Corruption—don't get me wrong, it's an example, I'm not corrupt—almost goes with the public trust. Even a starting pitcher who can go the full nine innings is a rarity. So why should I carry on just because I happen to read a halting Hebrew and am a little rusty in the ritual and custom departments? Isn't my heart in the right place?

All right, you're going to find out sooner or later, so I'll make a clean breast right now and be done with it. You're asking yourselves, if his Hebrew is so bad how did this improbable guy ever get to be a licensed rabbi? Well, you know those offshore medical schools where people sometimes go if they haven't got the best grades in the world? Places like Grenada and St. Lucia and along the Pacific rim? All right, I attended an offshore yeshiva. It was on this tiny atoll in the Maldive Islands a few hundred miles southwest of India. What are you going to do, arrest me? I'm a person whose calling came about, at least indirectly, through a postwar boom in the engraved bar mitzvah invitation industry. Don't be so quick to judge. (I'm speaking in my rabbi mode here.) Isn't it only fitting I received most of my religious training abroad, among Sikhs and Hindus— all the queer castes with their sacred cows and trayf human beings? Only fitting that an almost charter member of Rabbi Herschel Wolfblock's all-boy minyan and original Little League davening society should pick up his Hebrew lore somewhere closer to the road to Mandalay than the Wailing Wall? My God, my brothers, my God, my sisters, we were like the von Trapp Family Singers, Quiz Kids, famed vaudeville chimps.

Norman Sachs, Donny Levine, Ray Haas, Billy Guggenheim, Sam Bluweiss, Marv Baskin, Stanley Bloom, Jake Heldshaft, Al Harry Richmond and I were Wolfblock's first team, and though we had understudies, kids who could be called upon to stand in if one of us was out of commission, the odd thing was we never got sick. Once we signed with Wolfblock's special forces we never came down with flu or fell victim to the kid diseases.

Now maybe *you* can explain this, but at the time it was as difficult to account for—and Wolfblock the first to point out what was happening, not crying miracle, understand, just underscoring our strange run of good health—as it was for us to fathom the wonders of the Ouija board or the dynamics that worked the little pendulum that hung from a thread which we used to swing above one another's palms in circles or verticals and that it never occurred to us we controlled.

So why *not* New Jersey? Why *not* Lud?

The world isn't plotted like a model city, isn't laid out on a neat grid for the convenience of tourists and postal employees. There really was a Diaspora, you know, and shipwrecks and castaways, folks lost in deep woods and in the higher elevations and not everywhere filled up with the symmetrical quotas of Caracas and Paris, London, São Paulo, Cape Town, New York.

Anomalies abound. The Ten Lost Tribes of Israel weren't all found. Or weren't found where you might expect. There are frontiers, outposts if not of empire then at least of likelihood. I'm speaking of queer parishes on the high seas, congregations in the wilderness. And this *isn't* my rabbi mode. I'm not being mystical here, I'm not suggesting martyrs slugging it out with the elements and with themselves in the jungles and along the frozen wastes, and I'm not being glamorous either, only practical. I'm speaking, I mean, of accepting what's left after the plummy assignments have all been awarded. Practical, we're practical men we rabbis of Lud, compliant, comers to terms with our oblique, improbable lives. Yes, and if you troubled to press us you'd find that there isn't a man among us who doesn't dream of the splashy yellow architecture of some temple in Cleveland. Hey, I know a rabbi who conducts services on a cruise ship that often happens to find itself in the Caribbean of a Friday evening. (Well, you say, but *that's* glamorous. Oh? He's hooked on Dramamine and, though he's not yet forty, the ship's doctor informs him his beautiful tan is only an early stage of skin cancer.) And wasn't I myself once Chief Rabbi of the Alaska Pipeline?

Because there isn't a place that *ain't* covered, or at least that a man of the cloth couldn't get to on six or seven hours' notice given good weather and the right bush pilot.

So why not Lud? Why not Lud, New Jersey? Why not this funerary, sepulchral, thanatopsical town?

two

SO I'M WALKING DOWN Lud's main street one fine Tuesday morning figuring I'll pop by Sal's, see can I hear anything worth listening to. I'm fresh from my prayers, the modified Shachris I do on my own about nine or nine-thirty, after my shower, before my breakfast. To keep myself honest, if you take my meaning. Because, in case I haven't made myself clear, theologically speaking this is the sticks— ultima Thule. God— and I'm talking in my rabbi mode here—forsaken. I don't even bother with the phylacteries anymore and haven't since maybe my second or third year in Lud, since, that is, what was supposed to be temporary began to feel permanent. My wife, Shelley, thinks I still lay t'phillim every morning, but Shelley's a little eccentric in her ways and doesn't question me too closely about Jewish practices anymore— not since she saw those leather straps bound about my forearm and head and confessed they were a turn-on for her.

"You know what you're saying? There are parchments inside these boxes with sacred quotations from the Holy Scriptures."

"I can't help it," Shelley said, "I think you look sexy in them."

"If that stays fair it's blasphemous, Shelley," I a little relented. Shelley always knew how to get to me.

"Well, you *do*," she said, and tried to get me to promise I'd wear my tallith when I came to bed that night.

"Shelley!"

"It's the fringes, Jerry. They do something to me."

"Cut it out, Shelley."

"If you'd taken a post in Williamsburg I'd get to see you in those swell hats and long gabardine coats all the time," idiosyncratic Shelley pouted.

"You don't even keep kosher."

"Would you put your yarmulke on?"

I'll tell you the truth, now I think of it, maybe my backsliding had more to do with Shelley's preposterous attitudes than with my growing awareness that I was playing to an empty house. I'm no Graham Greene rabbi, I never was. I don't burn out so easy. What, because I have a lousy job and I'm stuck in the sticks, there's no God? Who am I to say? I'm not even good at what I do. But even I have to admit it's futile. What, it isn't futile? In this travesty of a community? It's futile. And face it, who's to say if that extra hour or so of sleep I get by modifying the morning prayers to my own specifications doesn't put me in a better mood for the day and make me not only a better husband to my wife but a better father to my daughter, Constance? Surely it does. Because, frankly, you have to be in a good mood to deal with some of Shelley's idiosyncrasies. Although there's never been any question in my mind of *not* dealing with them.

Do declarations of love embarrass you? I suppose it *is* difficult to accommodate to other people's passion. Rapture's the only feeling state that looks silly from the outside. Even, I guess, the other person's absorption, your own partner's in the bed. Listen, did *I* make the world? Was I around when they poured the foundations of the earth? Did I command the morn or cause dawn to know its place? I can't draw out Leviathan with a fishhook, run a rope through his nose or put him on a leash for my maidens. The wild ox never spent the night at my crib. I never bound the chains of the Pleiades, I never loosed the cords of O'Brian. You've got no quarrel with *me*, what I'm saying. Close your eyes, shut your ears— I'm nuts about my wife. It's a federal case, almost pathological, *past* pathological.

I'll lay my cards on the table. I'm a licensed, professional rabbi, a certified, bonded spiritual counselor. Good and evil are my stock in trade. I carp and I hector, or would if I had anything like a real congregation and not just a bunch of dead people. I cavil, crab, deprecate and reprove. I chalk talk temperament like a coach of character. Yet despite what it says in the job description, and that for all my faults I'm no hypocrite, I tell you that if, on Rosh Hashanah, on Yom Kippur, I were to catch some fellow merely glance in my wife's direction, at her legs or her figure, in what I construed as a lascivious, concupiscent manner, on the highest holiday, the *highest* holiday, I would stop whatever I was doing, it could be the holiest prayer on the most sacred day of the year, and beat the son of a bitch over the head with a Torah.

So past pathological. *Way* past.

I don't care she's eccentric, what I'm saying, I don't care she's idiosyncratic— I'm nuts about my wife. Smitten. Smited, I sometimes think. Yes, a visitation from the Lord, love like the Plague of Lud.

No, really. I get this bolus of lust whenever I look at her, in my throat, in my gut. Well, she's a looker, of course, enough to drive even a high-minded religious like myself to apostasy. Great big bedroom eyes and this really sultry mouth and smashing, come-hither schnoz and hair. If I'd known her back on the atoll it'd have been curtains for this rebbe's concentration. And, believe me, her face is the least of it. I don't much care for locker-room tales or the men who tell them. Smut isn't my métier, and even the mildest suggestiveness or whispered, low-key insinuation passed among the good old boys like loose change laid down on a table for a tip gets my Irish up and makes me want to sock somebody and do righteous things, but if I'm to be honest I have to admit that Shelley's figure, even now, at thirty-seven, makes me think that the Creator has got to be at least part pornographer. She's got these really incredible knockers and these long hubba-hubba legs and thighs. She's built like a brick shithouse, my Shelley is, and has a behind on her, God bless, could make old Solomon sing all over again. Her scarlet lips and the halved pomegranates of her cheeks and those twin-fawn, lily-fed titties and her wheat-heaped belly and all those

apple exhalations . . . So when I warned her about blasphemy
that time she caught me in my phylacteries, in my prayer shawl
and leathers, it wasn't *her* soul I was trying to save, it was my
own. Shelley, for all she's the rabbi's wife or speaks longingly
about ultra-Orthodox Williamsburg, is essentially soulless. But
does that bother me? It does not. What bothers me is something
else entirely.

I swear it on the Bible, Shelley today is even lovelier than
when we married. Her hair is longer and softer, her figure is
shapelier, her breath sweeter in the mornings. She's *taller!* I'm
crazy about her. Do you know what this can do to a man?
Always to go around like some goony, love-struck schoolboy? I
could be burying somebody, no kidding, I could actually be
saying Kaddish over some poor sap's fresh grave, and all I have
to do is see, oh, say, a dress that Shelley might have had once in
a similar shade and that's it, I'm a goner, my concentration is
shot and I lose my place, not just in the text but literally. It's as
if I'm not in Lud anymore, not in New Jersey, and I'm horny as
hell and off somewhere in fantasy cuckooland, and all I can
think of is how soon it will be before I'm with Shelley again,
grazing in my head her varied parts and wondering which
square inch of her to nuzzle first.

And, as I say, she only gets lovelier. And has ever since
she gave birth to Constance, our first child. It wasn't that, like
any woman, she sloughed off her pregnancy. No, she left the
hospital slimmer, firmer, not just than when she went in but
than before she got pregnant. And her *features* had changed,
molded into gorgeous new Scandinavian planes and angles on
her face. After Shelley gave birth it was as if she merely *resembled*
Shelley, and don't think it didn't occur to me for a minute that,
my God, what a place *this* is, they don't switch the babies on
you, they switch the *mothers!* I mentioned she's taller? Here's
what I think happened. I don't say this lightly. It goes against
nature, and I'm enough of a scholar to know what God thinks
about *that* sort of thing. I think her stretched-out belly not only
snapped back into place and readjusted itself but was somehow
recast in inches of actual height. Crazy, huh? Tell me about it.
Because the same thing happened her *second* pregnancy!

And growing lovelier, always lovelier, and here am I, the
humble Rabbi of Lud, a slave to my passions, married almost

seventeen years to the same woman and practically a sex ma-
niac, certainly a lunatic, taking what I take, accepting what I
accept. All, I mean, the fair Shelley's mishegoss and enthusi-
asms. Her obsession with playing the rebbitzin, for example,
the rabbi's wife. Of course we're starved for community here,
but some of the lengths Shelley goes to are absolutely potty. By
nature she's a warm and generous woman, compassionate and
kind, but I grow fearful if I see her standing at the back of the
room when I'm delivering a eulogy. I know that before I even
began the service, that while the organ music was still playing
and the chief mourners were gathering in the front benches to
accept with their nods and all the authority of their grief the
condolent, embarrassed sympathy of their relatives and friends,
my Shelley has already been by to offer her solicitude on behalf
of herself and her husband, the rabbi. If there's *any*thing she can
do . . . she tells them, or invites them, transients in Lud,
arrivals from out of town, people, many of them, bound for the
Newark airport when they're through at the cemetery, over to
our house for "coffee and."

Or there's the business of the car pool.

Because there's no school in Lud, Constance, who's in the
ninth grade at the high school in Fairlawn, is entitled to be
bussed. Since it's about an eleven-mile ride, it only makes sense
to take advantage of what we're paying taxes for anyway, but
Shelley won't hear of it. Shelley insists the kid should be driven
in a car pool. As I said, I don't see the sense myself, and
neither, for that matter, did the other moms Shelley approached
to share the ride. When they declined, Shelley volunteered to
take their kids anyway, to drive *both* ways in fact, not twenty-
two miles every day but more like thirty or thirty-five when you
take into account the doglegs she has to make, the distance she
goes out of her way each time to pick up or deliver the shirkers'
children. When I ask her why she goes to this trouble, she
reminds me she's the rabbi's wife and it's the duty of the rabbi's
wife to be useful. I'd say it's got at least something to do with
staying busy, with helping to keep her from going nuts. I'd say
that, but she *is* nuts.

You need better evidence?

"Oh, Jerry," she tells me after the stillbirth of our second
child, a son, whose right leg would have been almost two inches

shorter than his left, "Oh, Jerry," she says, this beautiful woman in her late twenties who'd grown still another inch since the one she'd put on when Connie was born, "I don't want to be tall if it's to be at the expense of my children. Some of my height is rightfully the baby's. I feel so guilty. I stole a piece of my stature from his poor little life. I'm not fit to be a mother. I must never allow myself to become pregnant again."

She was serious, but I'm not so innocent in the matter myself. By now she was *so* beautiful I didn't need anyone in the house who would make extra demands on her time or distract her attentions. I was too compliant. To my shame, I agreed. Sometimes I think I'm too uxorious for my own good.

You know she thinks she's a frump? She actually believes she's this dowdy, inelegant woman, some humble blind spot in her like the anorexic's phantom weight. This is one of the reasons she stands by me, I think, why she's the first to back off if we quarrel. I could take advantage here, never let on, cover the mirrors, keep her benighted, and I wouldn't be the first, I bet, to withhold valuable information, but do I know my Shelley or do I know my Shelley? Every chance I get I'm all over her with the evidence, Johnny-on-the-Spot with the facts and the figures, Shelley's advance man, Shelley's flack. And I acknowledge up front I benefit from this, that Shelley believes I'm only being supportive and loyal. I even own up it could be some bread-on-the-waters, New Testament thing. So what if it is? Am I not supposed to do the right thing just because I stand to gain? I can just hear the disputations. "It depends," says the one, "whether you do what's right because it's right or *only* because you stand to gain." "No," objects the other, "a world pleasing to God, a proper world, a good world, a successful world, is put together by piling right action upon right action." Then a third puts in about intention and will. Another county heard from! Oh, please. I'm the rabbi, but you tell *me*, is it *all* religious? It makes my brains breathless to think of the possibilities. Let the Talmud stay put in the Talmud.

Anyway, I'm bringing all this in just to let you know what's on the mind of a lowly man of God, a humble servant of the Lord, Yahweh's instrument in New Jersey, as he ambles down Lud's main drag of a beautiful Tuesday morning, fresh

from his shower and his breakfast Shachris on his way to see
Sal, codependent of Shull and Tober, Funeral Directors, and
barber to the dead.

Sal's is just about one of the swellest barbershops I've ever
seen, the building itself in that neat Federal style, like a trim,
salmon-brick Acropolis, three chairs, no waiting. There's one of
those heavy brass eagles over the entrance and a wooden barber
pole next to the door like an antique in a restaurant. The minute
you walk in you're bathed in the sweet, crisp atmospherics of
wonderful shampoos from the hair-oil orchards.

"Hey," Sal said over the easy-listening station on the FM,
"it's Mr. G. What can I do you for, Rabbi?"

"I'm up for a trim, please, Sal," I said.

"Take a chair. Any chair. Any chair at all," he intones
like someone setting up a card trick. I almost don't have to
hear him to hear him. It's what he always says, a reference to
his situation. Which is not unlike my own, for if I'm the Rabbi,
then Sal is the Barber of Lud, la Figaro Figaro la, Figaro la.
Because for all it's one of the world's swell barbershops, it's
only, like practically everything else in this town, a front. I'm
not even certain it belongs to Sal. Perhaps Shull and Tober
hold the paper on it, or Art Klein or John Charney of Lud
Realty, or all of them perhaps, the whole entire complicated
interlocking directorate behind the operation here. And except
for myself and the pool Sal can draw from of maybe fifty or so
people who live in Lud or work for one of the town's businesses,
he has no regulars. Sal is the contract barber for the two
funeral parlors—he calls them "business parlors"—and tells me
he doesn't do badly. Not a soul goes into the ground, Sal
says, until he gives them that final haircut. "I'm just like
you, Father," he tells me. "Here's a mirror, see is it all right
in the back."

As usual, I'm a little saddened that my haircut's finished,
for it makes me realize how underemployed I am. I should
challenge Sal with weird stylistic demands— to move my part
from one side of my head to the other, or request dye jobs,
layered sideburns, a more interestingly shaped nape. If I left
now I'd have to kill time till lunch. I would be unwelcome at
Seels, the stonecutter, who, though he works for a Jew and

makes his living chiseling Jewish names and perfectly formed Stars of David and scraps of prayer in astonishingly fine Hebrew lettering, is a vicious anti-Semite. And I'd feel foolish poring over the greeting cards in the little Jewish notions shop. The flower shop is out. I see enough flowers. And I have no desire to kibitz the gravediggers or the guys scrubbing down the hearses and limos. And to be perfectly frank, dropping by the cleaner's or the funeral home to see what's up just isn't the treat it once was. Of course I could always go home and shtup my wife thirty minutes before we have lunch, but I just shtupped her thirty minutes after we had breakfast.

"Sal," I said, "I could do with a shave."

"You're clean-shaven."

"A manicure."

Sal gave me a funny look. "You know," he said, "you say something like that to the ordinary barber, he'd probably tell you to get lost. It happens because of the nature of my work I *do* hand care. Head care *and* hand care.

"You know what else?" He'd lowered his voice.

"You apply their cosmetics."

"You knew that?"

"You already told me."

"I talk too much, don't I?"

"Of course not."

"Yeah," Sal said, "I talk too much. Occupational what-do-you-call-it."

"Hazard."

"Yeah, but it's interesting. If I had anything like a regular clientele instead of those stiffs on the preparation table over in Shull and Tober's basement, they'd be popeyed at some of my tales."

He'd taken a manicurist's dish and emery board from a kind of doctor's bag he kept stashed inside one of the cabinets under a shelf that held some of his razors and combs.

"You talk about cosmetics," he said, "but most folks got no idea what that entails. I mean when you're making up a corpse after it's embalmed. You know we're talking of at *least* one lipstick? Probably half of another. And a whole *dish* of rouge. And pancake and moisturizers? Forget it. Way too prohibitive.

You could make up the entire cast of a Broadway musical for what pancake would cost you. And moisturizers, you start moisturizers into these folks they'll drink you under the table. It's because their skin's so dry. You have to go to special tinted powders, slap on some fixative and hope the wind don't blow.

"But I'll tell you something," Sal confided, "the haircut, that's the *real* challenge. I got to wear gloves. Otherwise I'd prick myself on their hair. So spiky, so sharp. Like iron filings. And *heavy*? You wouldn't believe it. Because hair is dead weight too. Even a kid's. Even a baby's."

So we talked about our mutual trade, or Sal talked while I soaked in his warm, soft, soapy water, between us encompassing just about all there was to say about death, Sal speaking up for the long-term metabolisms, those gone-gray-overnight details of canceled flesh, rhapsodies of death gossip, intimate as singing—gore, juice—a little saliva, Sal said, always lay puddled under the tongue—life's lymphs and ichors and gassy residuals, the finger and toenail legacies—the thin, keratinous plates lengthening, thickening, curling like the horns of a kudu—matter's fabulous displacements, lividity, and all the other evidences from death's black boxes. Pacemakers, implanted in the chest, Sal reminded me on the morning of my manicure, went on tick tick ticking for years.

"Brr, Sal. Brr."

"Ain't *that* the truth?" said Sal.

So I spoke up now too. A little. Coming round to meet him from the other side. Lighting up the spook house with the ineffable and sublime. We're not just these bruises in the winding sheets, I told him, and the proof of a life and an identity ain't only X rays and dental records. There's good deeds, I told him in my rabbi mode, and almost mentioned that I'd fucked old Shelley that morning but said something instead about the wonderful memories we make for the people who love us and whom we love. What's a few yards of gnarled toenail compared to that?

"I talk to them," Sal said. "On the prep table. Just as if they were a regular customer. I ain't scared. That ain't it. It's more, I don't know, lonely like. It ain't just that nobody's there, it's like they've gone away. I mean, I never even knew them but.

Still, in their carcasses, it's like they just stepped into the cab
that will take them off to the airport. Bingo, they're gone. I talk
to keep my mind occupied. I'm not afraid of the dead. Though
you know yourself, Rabbi, we probably got a right."

"That's crapola, Sal."

"You say that because you're so holy. We ain't everyone a
man of the cloth."

Sal was making a veiled allusion to the rumors of bad
things that get whispered by all help everywhere, but that are
particularly nasty in the graveyard business. We have these
blockbuster imaginations, my brothers, that truckles to disaster
and caves in at the merest whiff of evil. I'd been in Lud almost
twenty years, almost twenty years a pillar of this—to me—still
frontierlike community, a limited, Noah's Ark sort of town with
its representative, time-capsule exemplaries and instances, its
cornerstone samples and specimens, heavy on death but with
certain greening shoots of the possible— lawyers, a nursery, the
draper's, Lud's day laborers, the gravediggers who at any moment could beat their shovels into hoes and spades, all the rakes
and irons of a proper agriculture. For almost twenty years an
objective but finally unsympathetic ear, put upon by those wild
stories—tales, legends—of illicit burials so grievous (and we're
Jewish, not subject to most of the strictures and taboos of other
religions: drunkards we bury, suicides and incesters, atheists
and excommunicados, blasphemers and trayf gluttons) that to
shove one of these customers under Lud's dirt would be like
tarnishing the barrel with that one rotten apple that spoils all the
rest, blemishing forever our consecrated ground. Outrageous
tales of the secret disposal of great villains, outscale brutes and
monsters, so that it was made out—I'm talking about what the
natives heard, insiders like Sal, myself, even Mr. Shull, even
Mr. Tober—that the cemetery was a blind, the eternal resting
place of big-time mafiosi, executed and dumped under phony
names in a Jewish cemetery in Jersey where no one would ever
think to look for them.

Even, or so ran the scuttlebutt, famous Nazis were buried
there, savage celebrities from the more infamous camps. One
story had it that Doctor Josef Mengele may have been interred
in Lud, unknowingly buried under the guise of a Morris

Feldman, a hat salesman from Garden City, Long Island.

Which goes to show how silly these fables can get. Because it wasn't unknowingly, and I was the guy who was supposed to have buried him and, at least at the time, I thought I knew what I was doing.

It was our second or third year in Lud, Shelley and I into what would have been the third or fourth year of our honeymoon, our first child not born yet and, if not exactly newcomers to Lud, then still in that state of innocence which encourages and then embraces what it perceives to be novelty, still, I mean, outsiders and enjoying those fervent sexual perks and practices of our first blooming, three and possibly four years—time itself blurred here, living in one long smudge of the now, the memorial, anniversary instincts as yet unkindled—running, not only not socialized but so protected by that innocence and the novelty of things we didn't even know we weren't being snubbed, that the town—this a novelty, too—was only the makings of a town, that that draper, that lawyer and those gravediggers were just signs, like a cowpoke's pouch, tobacco and cigarette papers are signs, of some still-to-be-fired destiny. We observed nothing, knew nothing, thought—if we even took time out to think—we lived in a booming metropolis and not only did not resent—the new rabbi, his young rebbitzin—the fact that we were being ignored but, God help us, actually believed that all the world loved a lover as much as we did, and actually appreciated people's thoughtfulness—shameless, a rakehell, his hoyden—in leaving us free to fuck each other's brains out. Our heads in our beds and still getting, we thought, settled.

"My," I might tell my Shelley as we promenaded Lud's main avenue not only hand-in-hand but arm-in-arm too, and looking, I guess, like some fierce special team, "but I do so love it when an entire city looks like a mall. Oh, look, dear," I might say with a snide, blue snicker, "it's that little Jewish notions shop," and elbow her ribs, blow in her ear, chew on her lobe, turning her round in the direction we'd just come, leaving no doubt what little Jewish notions had cropped up in this Jew's head.

The astonishing thing is that they stood for it. Charney and Klein. Pete, the stone hauler. Seels the vicious, anti-Semite

tombstone carver. Any *normal* Luddian. Though their tolerance
could have been an honest mistake. Shull and Tober, who
employed me, whose funerals I officiated, reciting last words,
drawing the characters of the dead from inference, the chancy
observations of the bereft like witnesses to a crime, like the
paltry consensus portrait of a police artist, say, cheerfully running one Jew after the other into the New Jersey ground, hadn't
even bothered to interview me but had hired me by return mail
when I'd responded to their notice clipped from *The Rabbinical
Assembly Newsletter* tacked to a bulletin board in the placement
office of the old alma mama back in the Maldives. Maybe they
assumed my gaga flirtation with my wife some arcane, peculiar
heterodoxy. The others, Lud's *Fortune* two dozen, probably
took our open sexuality as an extreme example of Jewish clan-
nishness. Whatever, it was live and let live in that little community of death.

So if I say it wasn't unknowingly you have to consider the
source, and judge for yourself what does and doesn't constitute
knowing when the so-called knower is a horny, love-struck mooncalf.

It was Shelley who took the call. In the screened breezeway—
I won't forget this, it's as good an indication as any of the way
we were—both of us called "the rabbi's study." (This wasn't
cynicism. We weren't cynical. We weren't smug or disenchanted
or cocksure. I remembered everything Wolfblock ever taught
me. I knew who was a pisher and who wasn't. If we called the
breezeway where we watched television and read the papers and
sometimes made love the rabbi's study, we had good reasons.
We were three or four years into our marriage and still playing
house. We had good hearts.)

"It's Mr. Pamella," my wife said, holding the phone out
and covering the mouthpiece. (You see? You see how good? It
embarrassed me whenever she covered the mouthpiece on the
telephone. I was mortified for the person on the other end. You
see? You see how good she was, how good I had it? I thought
this her worst flaw!)

The florist wanted to know if I could take a funeral service
the next day. This was strange enough on its own merit. I
worked for Shull and Tober. They were the ones who contacted
me for a service.

"Lou," I said, "tomorrow's Saturday."

"Hey," he said, "I didn't ask for a weather report."

"It's Shabbes. Jews don't bury on the Shabbes."

"Maybe these people ain't so religious," Pamella hinted quietly. "Maybe these people are desperate characters."

Tober seemed nervous when I called, and asked if I'd stop by the funeral home so we could talk.

Tober is one of those big, slack, gray-faced men in a black wool suit, a shambler in a vest and gold watch chain who, though he doesn't smoke, looks like someone with cigar ash on his clothes. He has the peculiar frailty of certain bearish men, some loose, dusty, posthibernative excess about him of meat and fabric.

He closed the door to his office. "What did he tell you?"

"That the family wants it over and done with. A party named Feldman."

Tober nodded. "Almost a year a vigil by the bedside. A long, drawn-out cancer. The worst kind."

"But it's the Sabbath."

"You know, Rabbi," he said, "all these religious considerations are beating our brains into crap. You provide a service, I provide a service. It's not always at our convenience that people die. Or even at their own. If we could, we'd all pass away after the holidays. We'd hold on till graduation was over. Till the kids got back from the honeymoon and were already set up in the new apartment. But who has a choice? We're poor, weak creatures, Rabbi. Do I have to tell you?"

"It's the Sabbath," I repeated.

"We lose a lot of business because of these ultra-Orthodox arrangements," Tober reflected.

"Ultra-Orthodox? This is common practice five thousand years."

"Listen," Tober said. "I'm not telling you your business, but suppose, just suppose, that this 'Feldman'—or whoever he *really* is—was such a nonstop, no-good s.o.b. that being buried on Saturday was just one more thing to tick God off. If that's the case then maybe we ought to bury the s.o. bitch in the name of justice and civil rights. Have done with the son o.b. Throw the s. of b. right down the toilet!"

"Manipulate Lord of the Universe? Manipulate Blessed-Be-He?"

You mustn't think I'm the spoony I make myself out here. This was back when most things seemed novel and picturesque to me. My views of marriage you already know, but maybe the other side of that idyllic picture of the sweet, hand-holding life, the supersensitive, hold-your-nose-Dearheart, someone-just-cut-one-in-Europe one, is gloomy and sour to just the degree that the recto is bright. All Jersey I thought corrupt, not put off by the prospect of working there, never wincing at the idea of men on the take, not shying at the thought of whatever violent, even darker acts lay behind the bribes that co-opted those who so casually sold their witness to the baddies. On the contrary, I thought I'd just stumbled into life, as, had I been given a pulpit in Los Angeles, say, I might have supposed I'd come to live among the less than serious. I was governed, I mean, by clichés.

Of course I didn't bury Feldman on a Saturday. And I didn't believe for a minute that Tober expected me to. Pamella's call is the key to what I thought. Lou Pamella was the floral guy, the nurseryman and landscaper for Lud's two big cemeteries—Pineoaks and Masada Plains, the names pleasant and euphonious as the labels on aftershave. I worked for Tober, I worked for Shull. Not only was Pamella's call to me unprecedented, it was impossible to conceive he could even have made it if Tober or Shull hadn't asked him to. I didn't know why, but they were covering ass. For reasons unknown they wanted me in on it, widening witness, spreading complicity. These were the novel, picturesque notions I had in those days.

You don't want to look rushed. It's best if the rabbi is on the scene before the family and friends of the deceased. It seems a strange, dark thing to say, but I'm the host on these occasions. Everyone else—the wife, the children, the brothers and sisters, even the parents—is a guest. Tober, Shull, and all their assistants, from the drivers to the men who work the hydraulics at the graveside, are just the caterers. The rabbi's the host. It's his fellowship, tact and hospitality they go out whistling. I've too many responsibilities, I can't afford to be late. And I wasn't. I was at the chapel better than half an hour before my first guests might reasonably have been expected, and a full hour before we were scheduled to begin. I even had my key in case Tober, Shull, or whoever else was on duty that morning hadn't arrived yet. But when I came in Sunday, the casket was closed and the family already gathered. So, though the chapel was less than a quarter full, had the guests. I knew from the way they sat, facing forward, not talking to each other, quiet, even rapt, all eyes fixed on the casket, that no one else would be coming. It was as if—no small children played about the drinking fountain in the foyer (no children were there at all), no one smoked in the lounge—the service had already begun. Maybe what Pamella had told me was true, maybe they *did* want it over and done with.

When he saw me, Tober moved away from the side wall where he'd been standing and went to one of the people in the front and whispered something. The man looked at me for a moment, adjusted the yarmulke, black and shiny as a patent-leather button, he'd taken from the open box at the entrance to the sanctuary, and nodded. As he came up the aisle toward me he'd tip first one hand then the other to his skullcap like some-one maintaining balance as he rushed along a tightrope. Tober, looming large and clutching the documents I would have to sign, followed wretchedly in his wake, distraught as a hand-wringer. "Not here," Tober whispered and handed me the papers as we stepped out of the auditorium. "Rabbi Goldkorn," he introduced, "Mr.—er—Levine."

"I'm sorry for your loss," I told him.

"The casket stays closed," Levine said in a faint German accent.

"Well, of course," I said. "The family's wishes, the ravages of the cancer. I perfectly understand."

"The cancer?"

"Please," big Tober said nervously, "can we just get on with it, Rabbi, please?"

"Of course I never had the pleasure of knowing the deceased personally. Could you tell me about your . . . For the eulogy," I said. "I'll need to know a little something about your—"

"Second cousin," he said.

"I see. Your second cousin. Yes. Well, can you tell me something about him for my eulogy?"

"He was a hat salesman." Though he stood still, he was still doing his balancing act with the skullcap.

"It's just that I might be of some comfort to the widow," I said. "The sons and the daughters. Sometimes it helps even if they only hear a list of characteristics, outstanding traits."

"Jerry," Tober said, "*please.*"

"You mean was he a left-handed hat salesman?"

"No, no, that's all right," I said, as if Tober had objected or the wise guy apologized. "Our teachers back in the Maldives used to remind us that men of the cloth are often God's first line of defense. Ours is the contemplative, spiritual life, so naturally, people assume we're His agents. We take the gibes and blows meant for Him. We're quite used to it by now. His holy punching bags. Really. Particularly when Master-of-the-Universe sees fit to pull your loved ones up short."

"Oh, Goldkorn, Goldkorn," Tober chanted under his breath.

Even as he glared at me the man continued to position his skullcap.

It was true. Far from being angry, I had somewhat softened my opinion of him. I put my hand out to comfort him. "I can tell," I said, "that you are only recently beneath the yarmulke. Don't worry, they don't fall off so easy."

"Goldkorn, Goldkorn."

"All right," he said, "he was married. But circumstances—there's no reason to go into them—prevent the wife and kids from being here today. My cousin"—he lowered his voice—"well, my cousin wasn't everyone's cup of tea. People didn't always understand him."

I did, I thought. And just then, just there, I knew it was Mengele in that closed casket. My reasons? I had no reasons. I was a man of faith, wasn't I? All right then, this was faith. The Nazi, Mengele, had happened in death to tumble into my theological jurisdiction. It came like a bolt from the blue. Which was all the more reason a man of faith didn't need reasons.

"He was very well organized," the guy was saying. "People who worked with him, his customers, may have thought he was obsessed. They never realized what drove him was his devotion to his job. That was unrelenting. If he'd been in medical research instead of a hat salesman they'd have called it scientific curiosity. He was an immensely *passionate* man. *Immensely* passionate."

"I see," I said. "Organized, passionate, misunderstood. Like a scientist when it came to his work. This was some hat salesman we're talking about here."

"*Goldkorn!*" Tober growled.

Levine, passionate himself now, had warmed to his theme and went on with his character reading like a handwriting expert or an astrologer on the radio. I wasn't even listening anymore. The man in the casket was Mengele.

Or some other high-up Nazi.

I didn't bat an eye. I nodded at the Levine character, winked at Tober, and indicated it was time we start back to the chapel.

As I moved down the aisle to take my place behind the plain, free-standing lectern that was the only pulpit I'd ever known, I could see that all the male mourners, *all* of them, not only sat under one of those Shull and Tober, in-house yarmulkes, at once as well-behaved and smug as tourists at a ritual of natives, but were as new to the skullcap as the phony Levine. A whole entire coven of Nazis!

Of course it was Mengele. Sure it was. Though I didn't understand it. (But why would I? How could all that good death gossip have filtered down through all those layers of concentrated, unmediated lust, my four-year-long hard-on? Unless my marriage had sprung a leak. Was something awry? I'd heard things. I hadn't known I'd heard them but I had, and maybe wasn't so far gone in my boobery and bumbledom and all-thumbs, Tom Fool mooncalfery as I'd thought.) I'm not paranoid. Anyway, a rabbi's got to be very careful about death. What do you think all that documentation is about? Those seals and death certificates? All mortality's red tape? Why is death law—murder, probate—law's biggest portion? It's because the dead are potential contraband. (They are. Consider the pharaohs stashed in all those old bank vaults and safety deposit boxes. Saints' relics come to mind. Old bones, the fossil record. And a skull-and-crossbones is still your dark signal of poison and stolen treasure!)

So there I was, Mengele or that other high-up Nazi behind me in the box. There I was, reciting the prayers, buttering up

God, carrying on. And getting as big a kick out of it as when I was one of Wolfblock's wandering minstrels in the minyan back on Chicago's South Side. I could see big, gray Tober standing off to the side toward the back. He seemed to be hiding out right there in the open. Shull, on the other hand, I spotted sitting bold as you please smack in the middle of my little congregation just as if he were one of the mourners. Or spotted his smile rather. That strange broad beaming which complemented and set off the depleted energies of the grievers and seemed in its stubborn joy rather more like the exaltation of Christians assured of Heaven than the woe of a Jew. It wasn't the first time I'd seen him plunk himself down right in the midst of the customers. It always made a big hit.

And me? I wasn't doing too badly, but there were tears in the eyes of the Nazis and some were openly sobbing, the bastards. That had taken me by surprise and made me more than a little furious too, the idea that this riffraff were not only moved by the loss of a world-class putz like the guy laid out in the casket but could be moved even in Hebe by a representative of a religion they hated. I poured it on, turned up the feeling and the temperature, chanting the prayers as if I were standing before the Wailing Wall and banging my breast like a rabbi in heat. Tober looked alarmed and Shull's grin widened, but the S.S. only moaned the louder. No matter what I did there wasn't a dry eye in the house. I threw extra trills into my broches, all the trills the traffic would bear. More. Tober stared at me, curiosity and frank, sober astonishment gradually replacing apoplexy. Shull's grin, appraising me, seemed impressed.

I was excited. I was keen. Whatever might yet happen to me, whatever civil laws I was breaking, as well as whichever of God's commandments I was violating—His injunction against false witness and, in view of my hammed-up prayers in front of the Nazis, probably the one about taking the Lord's name in vain—and whatever arrangements had been arranged—I was sure now that Shull was the mischief-maker, that big, craven Tober was only his frightened, maybe even unwilling, accomplice—and which I in my anger and eagerness was determined to upset, I was resolved to deliver this day in New Jersey such a eulogy as had never before been heard.

I took a breath. You don't fly off the handle, I cautioned myself. You control yourself. You don't slander.

"I don't know this Morris personally," I began, "but don't I hear your sobs and catarrhs? Copious, copious. I'm in the business, I'm a professional, and I'm telling you, you get to bury somebody pulls this much grief maybe once in an entire career. If that. This is probably it for me, I should think. I mean, what the heck, I'm a relative youngster. If, kayn aynhoreh, my health holds up, I suppose I can expect to bury maybe another six or seven thousand dead people. How do *I* know what lies in store, what mensches have yet to give up the ghost? But, the way I see it, it doesn't matter. Let those six or seven thousand be six or seven *times* six or seven thousand, sorrow like yours knocks the needle out of the red and right off the grief-o-meter!

"What can one say about such a man? We see how loved he was all the way down the line. *A second cousin is his chief mourner!*

"Yes, and Cousin Levine tells me our beloved friend was a passionate, organized, misunderstood, scientific sort of man. Passionate. Organized. Scientific. Misunderstood. Ask yourselves, what does Talmud tell us it means when a man is passionate and scientific? When he's well-organized and misunderstood? It tells us," I told them, "it tells us that what we're dealing with here is a super Jew, maybe the Messiah.

"That's right, you heard me. The Messiah. Messiah Himself!"

It was, I recall thinking, the perfect touch. They were outraged. They stared at me in disbelief and wanted, I saw, to knock me down. They still wept, but now their tears were angry, furious in fact, so intense they might have scalded their retinas and burned through their cheeks.

"God takes," I said, not through with them yet, "a Moses, He takes an Abraham and throws in an Isaac. He adds a Jacob and adds a Joshua. He takes an Elijah and stirs in a David. He folds in a Solomon and a Daniel, you homemakers and balebostes. He takes the First and Second Isaiahs and adds a dash of Noah, a pinch of Job. He separates your Maccabees, First and Second, and mixes with an Ezekiel.

"He takes," I said, glaring at them and leaning forward, "He takes a *Josef . . .*"

I broke off and slipped into the Kaddish. It was just one
more thing. They wouldn't know. You say Kaddish at the
graveside. Also, a lone man may lay t'phillim, but it takes a
minyan of ten Jewish males to make a Kaddish. Me, Shull and
Tober were the only Jews in the room. All my wailing, breast-
knocking and trilled broches didn't mean a thing. In God's eyes
the Kaddish not only didn't count, it never happened! This is a
Jewish mystery.

Shull's grin had disappeared. I was pretty sure he was aware
I knew what was up. What difference did it make? Nothing would
happen. They kept me on because I was their stooge. They thought
they could manipulate me. They knew I'd look the other way. It
was all right with me. Why would I want to be in a Pittsburgh?
Why would I care to go to a New York? My Shelley was here.

On the way to the cemetery I sat between Shull and
Tober. We rode along in silence for a while. Then Shull chuckled. "That was one hell of a job you did back there," he said and
patted my thigh. "One *hell* of a job!"

"It was," Tober agreed.

"I never heard anything like it."

"Neither did I," said Tober.

"You gave them a real run for their money, a real, what-do-
you-call-it, catharsis."

"You sure did," Tober said.

"What an idea," said Shull, shaking his head. "What a
thing to do."

"Messiah recipes."

"Mocking their dead."

"Making them feel guilty."

"Having them eat their misery like pie."

"Lick their loss like a lollipop. A catharsis. A real
catharsis."

"They'll owe you forever. They'll never forget it."

"None of us will. Though you might have added," Tober
added, "about how they loan him all that money to open his hat
place in Garden City, then, after he's sick, when his visitors leave
and his painkillers kick in, he turns around and jimmies the books
on them right from his hospital room. Or how his widow wouldn't
come to his funeral because she was too humiliated."

My God, a widow-humiliating book-jimmier! How could I have thought he was Mengele? Or any other high-up or low-down Nazi either? How could I? Because. Because you want to believe. Because you want to believe all the high jinks, all the back-room, front-page, deep-throat kinkery and irregularity, all the rumor, all the talk. Because you want to believe there's all-out, anything-goes evil in the world, conspiracy, Armageddon moving in like a cold front, anything, whatever keeps you engaged. Like you want to believe there's a God.

How *could* I? Because the honeymoon was starting to wind down, the three or four years of desert-isle lust and abandon beginning to feel more like four than three. She wasn't there that morning and I hadn't even realized she was missing, and both of us, me with the distractions that my work sometimes offered or that I could invent, and Shelley with her visits and Lady Bountiful routines, were just beginning to look around.

      •   •   •   •

"I stay open," Sal said, "in the hopes that Lud will grow and I can turn this place into a real barbershop one day." He was brushing loose hairs from my jacket with one of those yellow, short-handled whisk brooms you don't see anymore or you'd buy one.

"Nice job, Sal," I told him, admiring myself in the mirror. "The wife's been after me to get this done." I handed him his money and waved off the change.

"Thanks," Sal said, then made his voice lower than ever. I had to strain to hear him. "The gangland killing in that restaurant over in Brooklyn? Joe 'Black Olives' Benapisco that they shot bullets in his eyes?"

"Yes?"

"I think I may have to style his hair."

"Sal," I said, "come on."

"No shit," he said. "And Rabbi?"

"What is it?"

"There's some bones and ashes I'm supposed to put into his pockets with him. Some ground-up teeth."

"What?"

I couldn't hear him.

"What's that?" I said. "Who?"

"Jimmy Hoffa," he whispered.

three

IN LUD, on the night before a funeral, you used to be able to see, through the wide plate glass of the funeral homes, the dead laid out in their caskets. The practice was discontinued when the oversight committee that passes on such things, that determines the height of the buildings you can put up and rules on the color of the bricks you may use, decided that however convenient it was for the old and infirm to be driven past their loved ones lying in state behind the mortuary's big windows and view them from their cars, it never quite made up for a certain lapse in taste, that the deceased always looked too much like the lobsters one picks out for one's dinner at the bottom of the tanks in seafood restaurants.

It was before her time, so I'd been explaining this to my daughter, Constance, filling her in on the history and heritage of Old Lud.

During the school year Connie was off in Fairlawn much of the day, but recently I'd begun to notice that the kid was behaving a little uneasily, that she'd go to her room as soon as she came home and bury herself in homework, most of it for extra credit. Connie had never been what you'd call a grind, but now she asked her mother to drive her to the libraries over in Wyckoff or Ridgewood almost every day for the books she used for those seemingly endless research projects she was working on that year. She'd return with armloads, entire shelves, but soon complained that the public libraries in those smaller towns had limited holdings and that only the main library in Newark could serve her learned purposes.

"Oy," Shelley would kvell, pointing after Connie as she disappeared into her room, proudly beaming and breaking out into her broken, makeshift Yiddish. "Look at the daughter-le, the scholar-le. Just like the papa-le!"

And now she came back with two times the books, three. Shelley checked books out for her on *her* card.

We started to worry she wasn't getting enough fresh air, we began to fret about her eyes.

But when school was out that year Connie's grades were about the same as they'd always been, maybe a little poorer. We'd seen the books she was always reading, the pens she used up, the pencils she wore down.

And now, in summer, she wouldn't leave the house at all, but, having discovered term papers, continued to write them, to take on abstruse, incredible, impossible topics— how the discovery of rubber and the invention of the bouncing ball were responsible for the idea of points in sports, what, given the notion of the diatonic scale, the first tune would have had to have been.

We couldn't tell her to go out and find a friend to play with. She was Lud's only living child. And that's when it occurred to me that my daughter was terrified of her hometown. And how I came to speak to her of the history of the place, to explain its odd sociology, and even, to get her out of the house and out into what we had for a world, to go strolling with her in the graveyards, reading the headstones with her and, when they belonged to people I had buried, trying to explain, to the limited extent I could, what I knew of them, their families, trying to show Connie that they weren't just dead people, the abundant ghosts that haunted her imagination, but as real as the kings and heroes whose histories she'd been taking notes on in her copybooks all year.

"Dov Peretz Fish, Daddy?"

I peered at the dates on the stone. "1821 to 1847, Connie?"

"Sorry. Samuel Shargel. Ira Kiefer."

"There was a Shargel in the slipcover business. Was his name Samuel?"

"1973."

"Too early," I said.

"You weren't here in 1973?"

"I was here. The Shargel I'm thinking of couldn't have died more than two or three years ago. They're probably related. What was that other name?"

"Ira Kiefer?"

"Ira Kiefer, Ira Kiefer."

"1982, Dad."

"Oh, sure," I said, "*Ira* Kiefer." I shut my eyes. "Beloved, loved, oved, ed . . . Brother! Beloved *brother* of . . . I forget their names. There were four boys. In their forties, in their fifties. Ira was the youngest. A single man. Divorced, I think. I could be wrong about that, but I don't recall any surviving children. There were nephews and nieces. That's right, I remember. That's what it was. He was their uncle. He had all these nephews and nieces. There must have been at least ten of them. Mom told them that if they had their bathing suits they could drop by afterwards for a dip. Sure," I said, "Ira Kiefer."

We'd leave little stones on the tops of the monuments. "Out of respect," I told her, "a signal to the families that others have been here." Though once in a while I'd catch my daughter take six or seven stones at a time out of the deep pockets in her jumper where they rattled like bones, and carefully arrange them on a gravestone, ordering them in rows or neat bunches that were meant, I supposed, to suggest—not to the family but possibly to the dead themselves, fooling the dead themselves—not just individual callers but whole groups, making it up to them, placating the dead for their isolation and loneliness.

"Lewis Elkins," my daughter said.

"How is it," I asked, "you never read off the names of females?"

It was true. The thought of the distaff dead was more troubling to her than any idea of a dead *man* could have been. I assumed she was only protecting herself. For Connie, Lud was a bog, a heath, a moor. She didn't know about her brother and had only the examples of her complacent mother and unborn sisters. Her ghosts were girls.

"Jacob Heldshaft," Connie said, "1937 to 1968."

"Who?"

"Jacob Heldshaft, 1937 to 1968."

I read the details on the headstone.

The slipcover Shargel had been a myth. Also Uncle Ira Kiefer, but Jake Heldshaft I knew. He'd been one of my old minyan buddies from the Wolfblock contingent back in Chicago, and I hadn't known he was buried in Lud or even that he'd died. A man by dint of bar mitzvah, his voice had never changed and he was still singing soprano at fifteen and sixteen and seventeen when he went off to college and when I last saw him. He was our songbird—whom he somewhat resembled with his short, stubby body and puffed-up chest—our thrush. Jake Heldshaft, the Jewish Nightingale. Jacob Heldshaft, the Puffy Pisher. The Kike Canary, we called him, and Hebe Heldshaft, the Yiddish Mockeybird. And hid in the bushes to spy on him. Ambushing him in Jackson Park where we held imaginary binoculars to our eyes or caught each other up short, pretend blocking each other's way with an extended arm and hushing each other with great, exaggerated pantomime as if we really *were* birders and Jake some rare, prized sighting. Calling after him when he broke cover. "It's Heldshaft," we'd call, "it's Hebe Heldshaft, the Puffy Pisher!"

"Oh, Connie," I told my little girl, "here was a man! I *knew* him, darling! He was your daddy's pal in Chicago in the old days when we were boys. What a voice he had! I didn't know he died, I hadn't heard. In sixty-eight? Was he killed in Vietnam? But what could he have been doing there? He'd have been too old to go for a soldier, though he might have been an officer. What a waste, *what* a waste! A voice like that! A gift straight from God, as your mother might say. Stilled now forever!"

My voice, more suspect than ever our old falsetto mimicry in the park when we called out after Hebe Heldshaft, the Yiddish Mockeybird, hung about my ears. And right then and there I let loose with an impromptu Kaddish and sent my solo keening, meant for Jake Heldshaft, who, could he but hear it,

might have broken cover one last time and run for his life, out
through the air of the Jersey summer and across the eternal
resting places of the strangers, Dov Peretz Fish, Sam Shargel,
Ira Kiefer and Lewis Elkins.

"We miss you, Jake," I told him. "Norman Sachs, Ray
Haas, Donny Levine, Billy Guggenheim, Sam Bluweiss, Marv
Baskin, Stan Bloom, Al Harry Richmond and myself miss you,"
I said, calling off his colleagues for him from Wolfblock's long-
ago, first-team minyan.

Connie stared at me, nervously paying out stones onto
Jake's monument like someone who does not know the currency
of the country in which she finds herself.

"Lobsters, Daddy?" she asked later, after our walking
tours of the graveyard ceased and I'd started her in on her
"Know Thy Lud" lessons. "May rabbis eat lobster?"

"Well," I said, "I wasn't always a rabbi. Was I?"

And it was a little, I thought, like giving up the past of a
priest, always more mysterious, at least to me, than the known
proscriptions of his circumscribed life, all that last-fling riot and
disorder, the whirlwind sexual spree and rampage of his ladies'-
man, precelibate years. Maybe it was melodramatic, but I'd felt
a little like that back in the cemetery explaining Jake Heldshaft
to Connie, mentioning Sachs and Haas and Stan Bloom and the
others to her for the first time. Now, with my remark that I
hadn't always been a rabbi, and my gratuitous digs about her
mom, it seemed to me that it was as if I'd told Connie she was
adopted or suggested, boasting, some prepriestly, wild-oats past.
It was a wrong footing, clumsy, almost drunken.

I'd felt rotten since the Kaddish at the Puffy Pisher's
graveside and had been trying to call Al Harry Richmond in
Chicago. Al Harry was the sort who kept up. If anyone did,
he'd know what happened. But when you're a professional grief
administrator like myself you're always running into problems
of measurement, issues of proportion. You have to give them
their money's worth over a eulogy, touch their hearts without
breaking them, as one of the holy men back in the Maldives put
it. Also, you never know how much anybody knows. It's the
beginning of politics. So when I finally reached Al Harry I was
all bluff, hail-fellow congeniality and cautious, red-alert pussyfoot.

"Son of a gun," I told him, "it's a blessing from Eternal-Our-God just to hear your voice again. Your voice is a sight for sore eyes, Al Harry. It's been way too long. *Way* too long. Remember the South Side? Remember the minyan? Remember old Wolfblock? Those were the days, hah? Carefree and gay. Not like today with all our responsibilities and what-with-one-thing-and-anothers. Say," I said, "I'm something of a Wolfblock myself now. Our-God-and-God-of-Our-Fathers saw fit to make me a rabbi in Lud, New Jersey. Maybe you knew that. Well, the other day, the strangest thing. I was walking through this graveyard and I came across a marker for a Jacob Heldshaft. Remember Hebe Heldshaft, the Yiddish Mockeybird? Well, this one out here has a birth year that would be just about the same as Jake's and I was wondering, well, do you think it could be the same fella? You hear any talk about He-Who-Is-Most-Merciful taking him out?"

"That'd be Jake all right," he said. "Throat cancer."

"Throat cancer? The thrush?"

"His falsetto did him in."

And went on to tell me that Sachs, Haas and Marv Baskin were also history.

"What? No!"

Stan Bloom, who was still alive, he said, had been diagnosed as having a rare and dangerous blood disease. The trouble with people who keep up is just that. They get the bad news first. I felt awful. I was even a little jealous, if you want to know. I was the rabbi here, I was supposed to be the guy with the backstage access. Hearing all this gave me the same sense I sometimes get in Sal's about how underemployed I am. Never mind that four of us were already out of the picture, never mind that Stan Bloom was apparently down for the count. Other things troubled me. I'd turned into this hick. Sowing my indifferent dead into the ground like a sort of truck farmer.

"Listen," I told my old friend, "I'm glad we had this talk. Your news is terrible. It's hard to take it all in. Jesus, Al Harry, the Jewish Nightingale was a falsetto? The Puffy Pisher wasn't a natural soprano?"

"Heldshaft? He wasn't even a natural tenor."

"I'm going to pray for Stan Bloom's blood count," I told him.

"Sure," he said.

"I'm going straight to Creator-of-the-World with this one."

"Do what you have to."

"I'm the Rabbi of Lud!"

"Kayn aynhoreh."

"What, you think Gracious God is just going to stand by when He hears about this one? In the old days, in the minyan, in the old days He wouldn't even let us catch a cold!"

"Tell Him."

And I did. I dug out my phylacteries and prayer shawl and squeezed my eyes tight shut during an entire unmodified Shachris, conjuring God and praying and praying for the restoration of Stan Bloom's blood. Though the image I had behind my boarded-up eyelids was the leather box blossoming from my forehead like the horn on a Jewish unicorn.

Because I was a little spooked myself now, just like my little girl, on the defensive in the upper reaches of the Garden State, hard by Pineoaks and Masada Plains, those big Jewish graveyards in the Jersey flats where Jake Heldshaft was buried and which death and Perpetual Care had made bloom like a desert in Israel. Hence the sociology, all the worked-up learning and high academics of my lessons, my scholarly observations on Lud and Judaism. Which I was actually preparing, writing down now, like Connie on a homework tear, rehearsing and delivering to the kid just as if, Lord save us, she were a living, breathing, fleshed-out, honest-to-God congregation instead of only just a by-blood, captive audience of one.

"Since coming to Lud," I told her in my discourse upon Civilization and the Jews, "which, to be quite frank with you, Connie dear, has too many people under it not to be classified as a sort of Jewish death farm, I have had ample opportunity to observe our gentile, American neighbors. They're handymen and artisans. They not only putter, these people, they flat-out *build*! And they do this with an ease that belies simple competence or skill. Now I put it to you that what's happening here is that many of even the Yankee waspiest of our Christian friends are simply presenting—I use the word in its medical sense—not so much traditional values as racial traits and characteristics, the drives, I mean, of the peasant! And *now* I put it to you—I speak in my rabbi mode here—that most Jews don't know their wrenches, are board-foot illiterates and are behind in their band saws. We're often heavy smokers but generally nondrinkers, good husbands and loving, doting daddies who worship our kiddies. We leave them philosophy, talmudic quease and quibble, leave them, that is, history, culture and civilization. But for all that we practically invented the city, there are very few Jewish architects, and for all that a gemütlich notion of our families is the popular and conventional one, or that our drawing rooms frequently smell like comfortable old quilts or the fixings for soup, it's the Wasp pop who's loved. —And I'll *never* understand how we ever got our reputation as a desert people!"

"I love you, Daddy," Constance said.

"Then why are you so troubled?"

"I have no one to play with."

This wasn't, in the strictest sense, true.

As Lud's only living child it would have been unusual if Connie weren't at least a *little* spoiled. She could have had, had she wanted them (as once she did, on first-name terms with the gravediggers and, when she'd been small, Sal's happy little helper, his assistant—I hadn't known this—coffinside, bumping up bouffants, shaping corpses' hairdos with her little hands and picking the odd thread from the burial clothes they lay in, smoothing the lapels of the men and punching up the big, puff sleeves on the women's dresses, playing dolly with the dead), all the town's day laborers at her beck and call, all its clerks, landscapers, stonecutters, morticians, and small shopkeepers.

And me. She had *me*. I was still giving her instruction, coaching her in her theosophics, rabbinics and doxologicals.

"When Hear-O-Israel wants—"

"Why do you use those names?"

"What names?"

"Hear-O-Israel. Holy One, Blessed-Is-He. Whole-Kit-and-Kaboodle. Master-of-the-Fruit-and-Vegetables. Those names you call God."

And I tried to explain to her that it wasn't mockery but I/Thou, only a little tit for tat. "He likes it," I said. "He likes the way I do business."

"Really?"

"Sure," I said, "He don't mind. He's got a terrific sense of humor."

"Really?"

"Hey," I said, "didn't He hang some monikers on the Jews? Why, your own name is Goldkorn. Your mother was a Guttman. Or take a look at the names on those stones out there. Schwartz and Fishbloom, Cohen, Lebowitz and Prumm and Stein. Steins fore and aft. Steinberg. Rothstein. *All* the Steins— Goldstein, Rubenstein, Finklestein, Finestein. Feigenbaum, Wiedenbaum, Teitelbaum. Weinberg, Goldberg, Rosenberg. The Baums and the Bergs. The Baums and the Bergs and the Blooms. Goldbloom, Rosenbloom, Blumbloom. You see? He stuck us with Plotkin and Popkin. He stuck us with Krochmalnik and Eppel.

"Even first names. Names you'd have every right to expect would be denomination-neutral. What did Old Nachas-Giver give *us*? Irving and Sam, Jake and Izzy. Moe and Meyer. Are these proper Christian names? Names out of jokes, Connie. Tailors' names, names from the rag trade. Of peddlers, diamond merchants, the owners of discount appliance stores.

"And what about Jew itself? *Jew*ish?"

"Oh, Daddy!"

"Papa."

"*Fa*-ther!"

"Pop."

Because, as I told my Connie, we're not a chosen people so much as a marked one. Handles on us like signs over pubs. A called attention. This way to the Jews! The sounds of our titulars like cleared sinuses, the intimate throat and nose catarrhs. This way to the Jew! The blums, blooms, baums and bergs, the steins and itzes like a periodic table of the percussive, all the booms, snares and rimshots of baggy pants and low comedy. *This way*, *this* way to the Jew! All the landmarks, signposts, milestones. Our banners and gonfalons. The heraldry of our hair. The footprint of our faces. Something in our mien and countenance, at large in the lineaments like handwriting. The spectacle of the schnoz, the shrug like a broken code and an accent like a visible scar. Our outsize pores and busted profiles like difficult coastline. Some faint sweat and kasha scent and feel in the ambiance. And all the rest. Our farpotshkets, zaftigs,

zhlubs, and shlumperdiks. The loksh's unleavened life. Genug!
Who said genug? *Not* genug! Step right up, right this way,
ladies and gentlemen. *This* way to the Jew! The ghetto and
mezuzah. The menorah, the yarmulke, the golden chai. The
inscribed gates, I mean, the lintels and frontlets— all the blood
plagues, all the frog, the vermin and beasts and marred cattle,
the boils, the hail, the locusts and darkness and smiting of the
firstborn— the Angel-of-Death-blessed, God-fingered children of
Israel with their bloodied, odd-and-even, apotropaically marked
doors. This way, *this* way to the Jews!

So don't talk to *me* about designation and nomenclature,
don't tell *me* about the shrill, brassy mouthfuls, the racket of roll
call. Because if I feel like mixing it up with Him once in a way
now and again or, as I was laying it right out for my daughter, if
I take Him at His Word and choose to engage Him in the
I/Thou's and Me/You's, it ain't only any testy Old Testament
God we're dealing with here, it's a testy Old Testament rabbi,
too! Don't go screaming Mocker! Heresiarch! Blasphemer! Apos-
tate! Pagan! at *me*. I'm in a game two can play, and am only
living the quid pro quo, turn-table, give and get, measure-
for-measure life. Ain't that so, Blessed-Art-Thou? Do I have
the range, All-Including-I-Am-the-One-and-Not-the-Other? Do
I, Messiah-Scheduler? Am I at least in the ballpark, Sabbath-
Sanctifier? How about it, Eternal-Our-God, Ruler-of-the-
Universe? How about it, King-of-the-King-of-the-Kings?

Now genug! Basta! Ge*nug* already!

Anyway, Shelley came in at this point in the discussion
and threw me one of those quick little as-you-were headshakes,
sloughing her existence with some don't-mind-me squint and
grovel of the eyes, all her voluntary, I'm-not-here subordinatives
and Cheshire meltdowns of being. She may even have put a
finger to her lips. They were like salutes, selfless Shelley's
sinuous sloughings and shruggings, and I'm here to tell you you
wouldn't be*lieve* what one of my wife's elaborate downcast-eyes
gestures could do to this little man of God.

Or I, apparently, in my rabbi mode, to her.

"Go, doll," I told my daughter, "go play."

"No," Shelley said in what I can't help but think of as her
piggy Jew Latin, "go on with the lessons-e-le. Don't mind-a-le me."

"It's all right, Shelley. We were through anyway."

"Oy, I'm interrupting," Shelley said, pouting obeisance.

"Really," I said, "we're finished. Aren't we, Connie?"

"I guess."

"Sure," I said. "Go on, sweetheart. Go and play."

"Who with?"

"What about Robert? Go find Robert and keep him company."

"That's so *grisly*, Daddy. Robert's crazy."

"Robert is *not* crazy. Don't say Robert is crazy. Robert has a touch of Alzheimer's."

I don't know what it is Shelley does to me. Or vice versa either. Some mutual sucker punch to the wayward randoms of our drifting sexuals, I guess. A shove in the frictions, the rubbed chilblains of our underground plates and riled, misunderstood tectonics of all low nature's abrasive underbite, I suppose. The attractions and curious customaries—tits, testicles, elbows and armdown, great gams, fleshy cocks, muscles and eyebrows, kneecaps, jawlines and hairlines, the heft of an ass or tone of a tooth—in us converted to stuff lifted above conventional flesh and blood and bone, lifted beyond fact or even ordinary aberrant deviation, the quotidian fabrics and metals, I mean— your leathers, your irons, I do declare! In us converted to stuff beyond parsing, mysteries, enchantments, beyond, in fact, my rabbi's mode to understand, all my offshore learning notwithstanding, all that talmudic quease and quibble I was telling our Connie about. Our aphrodisiacs, our spice and pick-me-ups, sorcerous endearings, something amiss in the character perhaps. In Shelley a thing—though I wear none—for beards. (Didn't I *say* lifted above the conventional flesh and blood and bone?) The gray and unkempt beard she cartoons in on me in her imagination to her only some necessary high sign of spirit. God the turn-on and the rabbi, in her mind, merely the conductor or maybe the buffer or just the good grounding that will keep her from harm. Or in love, could be, with the dark Jew gabardines of the head and heart. And in me—the attraction—to quirkiness itself, Shell's forlorn, fussy, pseudo-baleboste ways. I don't *know* what it is Shelley does to me. Well, of course I know *what*. It's *how* that sends me to the encyclopedias.

Meanwhile I'm growing a hard-on as big as the Ritz and Shelley is filling up with wet like you could let in a tub from her. She's probably raining on herself. I know this. I can tell. It's urgent. We've got to dispose of Connie. And it's Shelley who's going to handle it.

"Sha," she says. "Let-e-le me. I'll talk-e-le to her."

"I under*stand* Yiddish, Ma!" Connie, exasperated, said.

"I know that, darling. We're just so *proud* of you. But you know," she said, "Daddy's right. Robert's always been so fond of you. It cheers him up just to look at you. I know it does. And I'll tell you the truth, I've been meaning to send over some of that bread of mine he loves so much. You could do Mommy a favor and take it over for her."

Connie rolled her eyes, but Shelley had already turned her back and was headed into the kitchen. When she returned she was holding a loaf of Wonder Bread. She held it out to our daughter. "Tell Robert he's always in our thoughts and that I'm going to get over myself just as soon as I can make time-e-le."

"Sure," Connie said, and left.

"Oh, oh!" Shelley exclaimed as I danced around her and shook my head and snapped my fingers like a naked Tevya. "Oh! Oh!"

"In Yiddish," I groaned, coming.

"Oy!" she said. "Oy!"

We lay back, breathless, spent.

"Maybe," Shelley said after a while, "I should have sent over some of my jelly too."

"Your Welch's?"

"My Smucker's," she said. "It's Robert's favorite."

Robert Hershorn couldn't have been in his sixties but presented symptoms everyone regarded as the onset of Alzheimer's. (It's surprising how little we knew in Lud about disease, what with its being a cemetery town, I mean.) The stuff we got from the papers, the cover stories in the newsmagazines— a spotty and, in Hershorn's case, loosely reasoned paranoia, a memory in visible retreat, sliding, that is, off the tip of his tongue (in most people his age there's still this tension at least, this urgent, clumsy reach and stretch for forgotten words and names as for badly fielded ground balls, some nervous working of the visible will to hold on and draw up, like an inexperienced fisherman, say, with a bite on his line) and out of sight, slipped through the cracks forever. Robert hadn't only surrendered the words and names but had almost absently, and quite possibly with some relief, agreed to the surrender terms. The struggle had gone out of him, I mean. Abandoning even his confusion. (That other big symptom in the inventory we all recognized.)

As far as we knew all his autonomics were still in place. He didn't appear incontinent. He didn't smell of urine or the telltale clays. If he felt a sneeze coming on he reached into the pocket where he kept his handkerchief.

He even drove an automobile, negotiating the distance between his home in Ridgewood twelve miles off, and managing the correct turns on the half-dozen streets in his hometown that would take him the seventeen blocks to the one state, then one federal, then one state highway again that brought him to the first of the three-and-a-quarter blocks to Seels, the vicious, anti-Semitic tombstone carver and Jewish monument names chiseler who figured that a jew buried was a jew nailed (and who probably *thought* "jew," in lower case, as if it were a verb or adjective, and once remarked in my hearing that the pebbles and stones people placed on jew gravestones wasn't a kind of calling card, or for remembrance, it was for the extra weight, to keep them down, in the earth), and who, at least officially, was still on Hershorn's payroll, though anyone would have thought it was the other way around, that it was Seels who kept Hershorn on the books, for the humiliation of the thing, for the pleasure it gave him to see a Jew in decline.

Robert even remembered how to use his tools, all that crisp cutlery of his profession— the variously weighted ball peens, chisels, bevels and gauged nibs. But had forgotten the Hebrew alphabet he worked in, and no longer knew how to use even the apprentice beginner's open-windowed stencil, even for the least complicated Star of David or simplest ornamental menorah flame.

So Seels gave him buffers, rags and smoothers, the employee turning the employer into some benignly tolerated Jack-of-all-trades-master-of-none sort, a kind of gofer-cum-handyman, and set him to work polishing markers and sopping up and breathing into his already defiled lungs the harsh marble dust and grating stone powders. I guess we wanted Seels to buy him out and fire him already.

They'd been pals. Hershorn and Connie. When she was small, and even after he no longer recognized her and Connie had to remind him who she was every time she went over.

As I say, a town's only child has got to be at least a little spoiled, pulling the attentions of its laborers and artisans and taking the benefit of its folklore. The lunch-pail insights and time-clock wisdoms. It was Hershorn, for example, not me, who taught my daughter to read Hebrew. But now she visited only on assignment, Shelley's silly, envoyed charities, my own wanton occasions.

She was crying when she returned.

"Tears?" Shelley said. "What's-e-le wrong-e-le?"

Connie scarcely glanced in our direction but moved through the hall to the stairs.

"Hold it right there, young layd-e-le. I asked you a question."

"Ma, *please.*"

"Connie," I said.

"She always does this to me, Daddy."

"Connie, shh."

"What did I do-de-le? I asked her a question. Did-e-le I do-de-le something so terrible?"

"Shelley, please, she's upset. Connie, what happened?"

"I don't know she's upset? Who saw her tears-e-le? Who heard her sobs-e-le? I don't know she's upset?"

The thicker Shelley lays it on the thicker I get. (And pose myself a question, not my style, though well, I suppose, within the parameters of my mode. Am I a heavier man, I ask myself, with an erection than without? I realize it's just a displacement of the blood, but the explanation feels wrong. I feel this perceptible increase of my meats, the sluice and slosh of barbarous, heavy chemicals. And is it a sin, I worry, to consider these questions with my daughter in the room?) But no matter. Nothing's to be done. Connie, who has taken the offensive, has stopped crying and her mother has begun. There is anger and dejection in the room. War and wailing. (And desire petering out like the diminuendo of a siren.)

"She always does this," Connie complained.

"*What? What* do I always do-de-le? My daughter comes back crying from that fascist palooka-le, I'm expected to hold my tongue?"

"Who sent me to him? *You* sent me to him!"

"Shh," I said.

"*Just to Hershorn, not that other-le!*"

"Shelley darling, shh," I said.

"Why? To bring him *Wonder Bread*? To take him jelly from the *A&P*?"

"Connie, shh, the neighbors."

"What neighbors?" my daughter demanded. "*What* neighbors, Daddy? Our neighbors are all dead. Oh, I hate this place! I'm so scared here! It's so grisly here! Why don't we get out? Why do you have to be the Rabbi of Lud? Why can't we move to a real town?"

"Shh, Connie, shh," I comforted. "You'd miss your friends," I said. "You really would. A lot of nice people have been very kind to you. Robert, for example. He taught you your Hebrew."

"Off *grave*stones, Daddy!" she said. "Which I studied off gravestones. On the big marble monuments in his yard. *Please*, Daddy," she said, "*please*. Let's *leave*!"

"That's absolutely out of the question," I told my daughter. "Shh. Shh."

four

HEY, I make a good living. Not what they pay in those big Riverside and Lake Shore Drive congregations. Not what I'd get along your Wilshire Boulevards, of course, or your Collins and Fairfax avenues, the spiffy, upscale, co-op, gone-condo neighborhoods where on even an ordinary Shabbes there are plenty of cops to help with the traffic and guard against the anti-Semitism and, on the higher holidays, the force's high-up Irishmen and brightest brass, captains and colonels sent from the Commish himself, in their ribbons, dress blues and white gloves, right down to the service revolvers in the spit-polished holsters you can't even see— to show the flag, to show solidarity and all the unsuspected, circuitous routes and ecumenical closures of good fellowship and called debt. Or those kempt temples where professional men's kids get bar mitzvah and their gentile partners go to so many affairs they own their own yarmulkes. Not *so* much. But enough. More than enough. We're not hurting. We're simple people of the clearing here. How much do we need? For the essentials we've got. The cardinals and paramounts. Even for the occasional fête champêtre and once-in-a-way skylark or dinner and opening night in NYC fifteen miles off.

So we're not hurting. Shull and Tober pay me forty-two thousand a year and lease my house to me for the taxes and

55

utilities. Also—this is privileged information—I do maybe another ten or fifteen K a year in tips. Don't misunderstand me, my hand ain't out. It's just that my pickup congregations don't always know the arrangements. How would they? Is a bill the decorous, proper place to stick in the overhead? Would the price of the electric be listed, what it takes to run the fridges and deep freezes, the cost of the fossil fuels burned in a good, roaring cremation? Why itemize the rabbi then? Certain things you assume. You weren't born yesterday, you know I don't come to you because the bereaved are good company. You figure something has to be in it for me, that solace and ceremony cost. So there's often a check already made out with a blank where my name goes, one or two hundred bucks maybe. Shull shuts one eye and Tober the other. *That's* the arrangement.

So I make a good living. What with one thing and another, my salary, my tips and my perks. But that's not it. Why I told my daughter that leaving Lud was out of the question.

The fact is, I have obligations. I'm in my rabbi mode here, talking ex cathedra. A fellow's family comes first. I've got the numbers. Three of the Ten Commandments relate directly to the family. Thirty percent. You honor your parents, you don't covet your neighbor's wife, you don't commit adultery. God Himself counts for another three, the graven image and name-in-vain bits, and the business about no other gods before Him. It's an even-steven split about the Sabbath day. So a fellow's family comes at *least* first.

I'm just doing my duty is the way this cleric figures it. Why I shush my dejected, scared-stiff, upset, importunate little girl, wave her from the room and go to put my arms around her mother. Family comes first and the wife takes pride of place. Husbands and wives before sons and daughters. Honor thy Mom and Dad, runs the commandment, not the other way round. If Lord-of-All-Worlds wanted us to honor the kids he'd have spelled it out. He's a don't-mince-words sort of God, a stickler. The *last* thing He is is reticent. He covers the material. "You shall not do any work," He instructs us re the Sabbath, "you, or your son, or your daughter, or your manservant, or your maidservant, or your cattle, or the sojourner who is within your gates." Doesn't He even spell out the dimensions of the ark itself down to the last cubit, God like a voice from the Heathkit?

It's a sort of sacrament then, what I'm doing, my husbandly obligation. I have to protect her from her nuttiness and outrageousness. Shelley would go crazy in a real congregation. So I *have* to condescend to her behind her back.

And they say a *little* knowledge is a dangerous thing. Do you know how much worse it is for you to be burdened with a lot? My heart goes out to the President and Joint Chiefs, to high-ups in the CIA and secret services, to everyone top-secreted, eyes-only'd. To editors with stories they dassn't break. To anyone with knowledge too hot to handle. Oh, it's awful, too terrible, and worse yet for the Rabbi of Lud. You think not? Are you kidding? Privy to the counsels of God? This is my rabbi mode. I don't fool around in my rabbi mode. This is straight from my studies, my lessons in the Forbidden Practices seminar with Rabbi Chaim on the atoll in the Maldives. From my practically pitch-perfect memory of those notes that we were not only required to destroy at the end of each class, but required to destroy in front of the bearded, sidelocked monitors in their long coats and ancient Polish gabardines, the Orthodox proctors of my offshore schooldays.

We don't tell you this stuff, the cruel, arcane orthodoxies that would scare you off and keep you out of Paradise— that it's forbidden to dip your right eye in an eyecup, that you can't be buried in your jewelry, no, not your wedding or engagement rings, not your locket with the picture of your kids, not even so much as a red paper Poppy Day flower or a tin button on your lapel from the Red Cross. That you mustn't look at an X ray or handle the vital organs of a woman taken in adultery. That you shouldn't wear contact lenses or shoes with lifts. That, strictly speaking—all of this is *strictly* speaking, of course—it goes against God's law to walk with a cane more beautiful than the leg it's intended to support or to use any prosthesis that improves upon the original body part. (Jews may place no hearing aid in their ears that corrects hearing acuity beyond what is considered normal in the population as a whole.) Left-handedness in an unmarried woman is a sin and, according to some interpretations of Talmud, a man may be denied his place with God if he can lift three times his own body weight.

You'd be amazed how much evil we do without ever knowing it.

But the family comes first and, after the wife, the consanguineous loyalties are clear. Husbands and wives before sons and daughters, but sons and daughters before brothers and sisters. Am I my brother's keeper? Of course not. Even old Cain knew it was a rhetorical question. The attenuate blood trailing away, thinning out and burning off till, if you want to know, the idea of humanity and the notion of universal love go up in smoke. God is no humanist, no One Worlder, and is hostile to the very concept of brotherhood. The fact of the matter is, even the *thought* of family, of family in its broader, metaphorical sense, is distressing to Him. He doesn't want His people to get too cozy. And in Isaiah? The wolf dwell with the lamb? The leopard lie down with the kid? The calf, lion and fatling together? Cows and bears feeding, and the big cats scarfing straw like the ox? This is theology? This is wish fulfillment. This is typos, bad translations, rotten scholarship. No? Give me a break. Are you kidding? Why did He give us zoos and cages then? Isaiah was a wuss.

To tell the truth, I talk too much. I don't have the character to be this Rabbi of Lud. Not twenty-five years out of the Forbidden Practices seminar and already I'm selling my teachers and proctors down the river. "Sure," I hear them saying, "go on, go ahead. Let everyone in on the cabala, why not? Tell them Lord of All Outdoors doesn't even need rabbis, that He knew what He was doing when He invented the Diaspora, Hansel'd and Gretel'd the Jews and lost ten tribes of Israel. Go on, go ahead, blow your own people's cover. Tell them, shout it from the rooftops, my yiddishe mama was a bad Jew, and chicken soup Hebes go against Nature. Go, ruin it for anyone who happens to believe Himself Himself is some big-spending Democrat, for the dole, disarmament, all the unilaterals, the A.D.C and other agencies."

Well, of *course* you can't look this up. It's privileged information. Why do you suppose we were sworn to secrecy, why do you think we had to tear up those notes?

Me, I don't agree with His politics. I happen to like and respect my fellow man. If it had been me, I'd have left Christ alone, and let him die our crowd's natural death, overweight, and all stressed-, smoked-, whitefish'd and cholesterol'd out, like anyone else in his early thirties.

Anyway, I love my wife. With me it goes beyond orthodoxy, duty, the slavish fear of hell. Constance is a fine daughter, none better, and I love her very much. But there's this glue in the glands for the Mrs. You have my word on it, I'd feel this way even if it weren't my religious obligation.

So you see the dilemma. On the one hand my Connie's everyday diminished fingernails bitten down to their bloody quicks while my nervous, heartsore child grazes beneath their gritty, jagged overhangs, waned moons and torn cuticles, settles in her anxiety and daily seeks fresh purchase, expert as some kid mouth-mountaineer contemplating the angles, all the flat, polished facets, approaches and billiard reckonings of face and, on the other, nutty Shelley, front-runner Poster Lady to the Loonies. I have to wonder. If she can do what she does for all dogleg kink, quirk and aberration just in little Lud, who *knows* what she might not yet get into, what marvels and wonders of the psychopathological she could work were she ever to come up to bat in the great world? There were my holy obligations and there was my good, old-fashioned romantic love, but there is also, I admit it, my heat-seeking curiosity, my blockbuster temptations. Because Eden ain't over, you know. We weren't thrown out of the Garden. We're still in it. All He ever really did was lock the gate. Eden ain't over. Beset we are by temptation, up to our fig leaves in it. So I have to wonder. And fear and tremble for the kid. But all I'm doing is speculating, talking momentary diversion, juggling the bright what-ifs. In the end it would be as it was in the beginning— no deal. The kid stays. The rabbi stands pat. The wife don't make a move.

Well, a *move*. It isn't as if she's under lock and key. She comes and goes as she pleases, in winter and throughout the school year chasing up and down the back roads and side streets of northern Jersey in her one-woman car pool the thirty-some-odd miles she puts on the car every day, rain, snow or shine, even on days when Connie is poorly, or some other child either, and has to stay home, and Shelley, operating under her screwy, self-imposed rebbitzin's rules of order, not only picks up the other kids anyway, but actually phones around, absorbing the city-to-city, intrastate tolls, to find an alternate, "so the seat-e-le shouldn't go wasted," every year trading in one big brand-new Buick station wagon for an even newer, even bigger one, some huge, gleaming Conestoga you wouldn't be afraid to cross the plains in (a station-wagon nuch, for an intimate little nuclear family of three!) because she doesn't want it on *her* conscience that a kid came to grief in any eensy, flimsy jalopy. So *move*. It's just New Jersey she can't leave, just, for more than her errands, Lud. Otherwise, she's all over the map, not only free to move but positively running with the pack.

I'm just getting comfortable again. (Now my erection is silenced, my meat withdrawn and chemicals subsided like clarity returned to cloudy tap water. In less time than it takes to speak, or speak to, the problems, my rabbinical conundrums not only unresolved but forgotten, my sins, and all, now my wife and I have had congress, and Connie's outside again, my cheese-it-there's-the-kid! misgivings forgiven.) When the doorbell rings like a cue in a play.

It's for Shelley. (And how, not being that kind of rabbi, not ever on call I mean, pulled to deathbeds or awakened and hustled into an emergency presentable enough to join the eloped religious in midnight matrimony or even, for that matter, hit up by salesmen in the Torah trade, how *could* it be for me?)

It was for Shelley and it was the girls, her sisters in an eight-lady group of musical Jews who entertained at various affairs in northern Jersey— showers, weddings, brisses, bar and bat mitzvahs, golden and other special anniversaries and do's. Shelley was one of the singers, though she sometimes accompanies herself on the tambourine. Only two of the women, Sylvia Simon and Elaine Iglauer, were trained musicians, checked out on guitar, mandolin and balalaika. The charter membership—Shelley is a charter member—was still intact after seven years but the group experienced odd cycles of popularity. They could be booked months in advance, then go through most of an entire season when, as Miriam Perloff, their manager and first soprano, put it, they "couldn't get arrested." Their bookings constituted a sort of sociological shorthand, which I supposed—I had a lot of spare

time—put them on the cutting edge of Jewish culture in New
Jersey. They were this really bellwether chorus and combo,
absolute musts for this season's showers and anniversaries, le
dernier cri for that season's bat mitzvahs and brisses. In a sort of
idle rabbi mode—I have spare time to spare—I figured it had
something to do with the baby boom.

They used *their* spare time for intensive, additional rehearsals and to experiment with the name of the group, thinking
perhaps that by adding to their repertoire or changing their
name they might goose up their popularity. They'd been "The
Sabras," they'd been "The Balebostes." Briefly they were "The
Mamas and the Mamas" but dropped that when they started
getting asked to kosher stag parties. Now, and for some time
past, they were "The Chaverot," Hebrew for members of a
kibbutz, or fellowship, and, in addition to Yiddish and Israeli
folk songs, standards like "Tzena, Tzena," "Havah Nagilah"
and "Ha Tikva," they specialized in vaguely Jewish songs—
"Those Were the Days," the theme from *Exodus*, "Sunrise,
Sunset," and other vaguely Hebrew-sounding show tunes.

Shelley had volunteered our house in Lud for rehearsals
and, in accordance with her special theories of good-natured
martyrdom, frequently arranged to pick these women up at
their homes and deliver them back again afterwards—two hundred sixty, two hundred seventy-five miles round trip, door to
door—but I didn't object because, well, frankly, I enjoyed having them in the house. They were Lud's only visitors not there
for death. They were crisp and affluent and gave off a snug
illusion of company, a suggestion of the rich, cursive icing on
coffee cake. They were all quite handsome and reminded me of
women shopping in department stores, elegantly stalking fashion like beasts doing prey, professional as pigeons pecking dirt.
In addition to Shelley, Sylvia Simon, Miriam Perloff and Elaine
Iglauer, the other members of the group were Fanny Tupperman,
Naomi Shore, Rose Pickler and Joan Cohen and, to be perfectly
frank, that's what I thought they ought to call themselves—
"Miriam Perloff, Sylvia Simon, Elaine Iglauer, Shelley Goldkorn,
Rose Pickler, Naomi Shore, Fanny Tupperman and Joan Cohen!"
That'd fetch 'em. It'd have fetched *me*, but then I'm my own
lost tribe, this exile, this standoffish, renunciated Jew. This,

I mean, time-on-his-hands outcast-in-waiting. Whatever it was I had for Shelley spilled over and I had it for these women too. (I'm in my macho mode now, speaking out of the sweet lull in my glazed-over blood, the drugged hypnotics of my engaged attentions, handled as a guy in a barber's chair.)

Meanwhile the women bustled about me, setting up music stands, rearranging chairs, turning our rec room into a sort of studio, and I was struck by the power implicit in their team-work. Women were not like this in my day. Then they were weak sisters, wimps, the beautiful nerds of time. Then they were without gyms, home fitness apparatus. Sometimes I think Shelley and Constance are throwbacks, designed to set a Sabbath table, bensch a little licht and, in the dark of their blindman's-buff-shielded eyes, make solemn, mysterious passes over the candles like thieves palming light.

Coffee was perking, chipper as rhythm, and Miriam Perloff, Sylvia Simon, Elaine Iglauer, Shelley Goldkorn, Rose Pickler, Naomi Shore, Fanny Tupperman and Joan Cohen were everywhere at once, pulling cups and saucers out of cabinets, spoons out of drawers, shuffling napkins, placemats, preoccupied as stagehands in darkness. Out my high kitchen window like an embrasure in a fort I could see two of their station wagons drawn up casual and unattended in my driveway as police cars on a lawn.

"Does the rabbi want milk and sugar with his coffee?" Elaine Iglauer asked me, coming into my study.

"He drinks it black, Ellie," Rosie Pickler told her. "Don't you, Rabbi?"

"That's so he doesn't have to worry about mixing dairy with meat when he's out at a function," Syl Simon glossed.

"Oh," said Miriam Perloff, "but that's so *in*teresting!"

"They teach us that in yeshiva," I said. "It's a trick of the trade."

"Yes," chorused Fanny Tupperman and Naomi Shore, crowding into my study with the others.

"But what about the sugar?" Joan Cohen wanted to know.

"It's only forbidden during Passover," I told her.

"I didn't know that," Naomi Shore said.

"Sure," I said, "black coffee is a bitter herb."

"The rabbi has a sense of humor," Rose Pickler said carefully.

"I speak for my people," I shrugged.

"Sometimes," Shelley said, glaring in my direction, "my Jerry likes to tease-e-le."

These women had been coming to the house seven years yet I was still a curiosity to them. People put us on a pedestal. Shelley, giggling, once told me they'd wanted to know about our sex life. "What did you tell them?" I said.

"I asked how they thought we got Connie."

"What did they say to that?"

"You could have knocked them over with a feather-le."

Yet I'd never doubted that they waged a kind of mass flirtation with me, even the dedicated fuss and bother of their preparations a pattern of honeybees, their hitherings and hoverings about our rooms some domestic cross-pollination. They treated me with an almost congregational deference which, if it wasn't patronizing, may have been a kind of actual tilting with God—guarded, circumspect Godtease. Women, and men too, are sometimes burdened by their pious curiosities. Mystery makers, what, they wonder, do priests do with their hungers? Were they so different from Shelley, turned on by her own awful wonder? Into my holy leathers, my phylacteries and parchments, as well as the garments, the shtreimel and kittel and gartel I did not even own (let alone wear), and embracing who knew Whom in her head?

As I've said, these women were all attractive and I could, I knew, probably have made time with them if I'd shown more interest. Miriam Perloff and Fanny Tupperman had been divorced and were now remarried. And, according to Shelley, Rose Pickler and Naomi Shore had had affairs. (As "The Sabras" they'd entertained at both Miriam's and Fanny's second marriages and, during the period when Rose Pickler and Naomi Shore were fooling around, it wasn't at all unusual for the group to work either Naomi's or Rose's favorite love songs into the program. Not wanting to abet immoral acts, Shelley, God bless her, was a little reluctant to go along with these practices even in the face of Sylvia Simon's argument that supporting these love-

sick ladies by singing their songs showed sisterhood. Shelley
was a sucker for argument, she loved pleadings—I was privy
to these proceedings, the rehearsals were held in my house,
Shelley's demurrers and Sylvia Simon's justifications came
through the thin walls of my study—and countered with an
argument of her own: "My dear girls," Shelley said, "of
course we would want to show support, to come when we
can to the emotional service of a sister in trouble. Why, in
Old Testament, in Old Testament, didn't Judith's very own
maidservant help her mistress chop off Holofernes' head?
Wasn't that sisterhood? To make oneself an accomplice? If
that isn't sisterhood I'd like to know what is. But some principles outweigh other principles. That's plain as the nose. So
I ask you, if, as Sylvia Simon suggests, we went ahead and
sang 'My Man' at Phyllis Levine's bat mitzvah Saturday, what
would that do to our artistic-e-le integrity?" Good old Shelley!)
Good old Shelley! No wonder I'm uxorious. Who ever had a
better, sweeter uxor?

   Though if those assorted Sabras, balebostes and chaverot,
the Fannies, Joans, Sylvias, Miriams, Elaines, Roses and Nao-
mis, showed an interest in me—I mean in the fascinated, spell-
bound sense of the word—why, I was no less interested in
them, all my powerful, exiled scholar's instincts alerted to their
own peculiar gynarchic routines. Joan Cohen shopped, one of
those lanky, elegant women who wore her boots and leathers,
suedes and woolens, their textures graduate as the gauge of
knitting or the finish on sandpaper, and all her colors flat and
dull as the shades on maps, as camouflage, as if fashion were
only a step from actual blood sport. It was as if, her tints
bleached by distance, you perceived her through binoculars,
some quick tweed movement in a field. She looked like someone
who could hold liquor. Because she seemed so efficient, she was
probably the least credible of the women in the group when she
opened her mouth to sing.

   Joan Cohen shopped and Elaine Iglauer moved. She was
one of those Jersey rovers—it's a phenomenon I've only observed here—who regularly changed houses, trading up or down
or even. Changing towns, following the school systems, following the country clubs, on the spoor of the fashionable syna-

gogues. Once, it's claimed, she actually bought a house because
the town it was in was reputed to have a good newspaper. In the
years we'd lived in Lud, Elaine Iglauer had lived in seven houses
in six different towns and, word had it, was now on the trail of
another.

But all these women—*good* old Shelley!—were on one trail
or other, hot pursuit a way of life. Joan Cohen's shopping
sprees, Elaine Iglauer's house hunting, Naomi Shore's and Rose
Pickler's romantic involvements, even, I suppose, Fanny's and
Miriam's divorces and subsequent marriages, and their flatter-
ing, collective forays into my (as the rabbi of opportunity)
customs—oh, oh, how they stormed my fort!—and secrets— the
question of sugar, the mystery of milk. The dietary proprieties
and pieties. For openers, for conversational spur-of-the-moment
ploys—a fishing expedition.

What, fishing myself, I might have told them!

That Lord-of-Kit-and-Kaboodle set Eve up, that He was
never any equal opportunity Creator, that He disdains women—
He doesn't like the way they smell, as a matter of fact, and
that's why He makes such a big deal out of the mikvah, the
ritual bath they're supposed to cleanse themselves in after their
menses—and why He never took a Goddess; that He isn't even
very interested if you want to know the truth, and never came
on to one as a shower of gold or swan or any white bull either,
and that the only books in the Bible named for women, Ruth's
and Esther's, are—what?—ten lousy pages. That He's this man's-
man God; that that's why He gave them periods in the first
place and relented only after He invented hot flashes and then
gave them those instead; that as far as He was concerned they
could stay in the tent barefoot and pregnant forever at the back
of the bus, and that *that's* why he made them beautiful, snappy
(looking at Joan Cohen) dressers, good (glancing at Miriam Perloff)
at real estate, interested (tucking my thumbs into my suspenders
and taking all of them in at once) in the big questions. That this
was why I had seen my Connie cry but never heard her whistle.

But this is what I thought, not what I would ever tell
them. I'm only the Rabbi of Lud. You go along to get along.

Telling them nothing and settling instead for the cheap—my
God, how difficult it is to have power, to be, I mean, however

adjunct, however peripherally, in the glamorous way— some idol of the amateur, a rabbi, *any* insider—thrill-a-minutes of any on-site, backstage reality. Giving them instead, Shelley's susceptible ladies, eyewitness, hands-on experience.

"Oh, *Con*nie," raising the window in the rec room where they'd been rehearsing, I called out sweetly, "*Con*nie darling." She was out front, risking the funeral corteges, which were the street's only traffic, rather than play in our backyard that looked out on Lud's biggest cemetery, gravestones floating on the level, becalmed surface of its unleavened earth like buoys. She was biting her nails, mauling her fingers with her mouth, drifting from station wagon to station wagon, aimless as a kid with a collection can at a red light.

"Connie," I called, "shouldn't we be doing Stan Bloom now? Come inside, sweetheart, and we'll get to him while we're both still fresh." As I'd promised Al Harry, I'd been praying for Stan Bloom's blood count, getting up Stan's prayers with my daughter like a kind of 4-H project. "Come on, darling, you'll play afterwards." I lowered the window again. "I've this very dear friend in Chicago," I told the ladies. "Connie and I have been praying for him."

"A rare blood disease. He was on his last legs," Shelley chipped in. "But Jerry thinks he may have caught it in time."

They trembled, I tell you, shuddered. A small seizure. The chill of awe. Because people believe in intervention, in salvation and influence like a fixed ticket.

Connie lumbered in, the little girl all bulked up in her resentment as if it were a kind of steroid.

"Go wash," I murmured.

"Ahh," quivered Elaine Iglauer, Sylvia Simon and Joan Cohen together.

"Excuse me," I told them, "I really ought to brush my teeth first."

"Hmn," vibrated Miriam Perloff, Rose Pickler and Fanny Tupperman.

When I came back I was wearing my yarmulke, I was wearing my tallith.

"Should we leave?" Naomi Shore asked.

"Not *me*," Shelley said.

"That's all right," I said. "We'll be in my study. Connie?"

"Here I am, Dad."

I began with a couple of broches, laid on a Sh'ma, then, before they knew what had hit them—I could hear their attention through the thin walls—I was into my theme.

"Teller God of Collections and Disbursements, of Bottom Lines and Last Dipensations," I prayed, "Lord, I mean, of Now-You-See-'em-Now-You-Don't— Your servant, Jerry Goldkorn here with his lovely daughter, Constance."

"Da-ad," Connie bleated.

"—his *lovely* daughter, Constance."

"Dad!" she scolded.

"Jerry Goldkorn here. Beseeching You from his hideaway in Jersey, Jersey Jerry Goldkorn. With my daughter at my side— the lovely Connie. As if," I continued, "You didn't know. Who knows everything. Eh, Old Sparrow Counter? Where we're coming from. Why we're here. *You* know what we're up to. I don't have to tell *You*!

"It's Stan Bloom's blood count again. Back in Chicago. In the the Kaplan Pavilion. A young man. In his early fifties. With a lymphocyte count of a hundred and fifty thousand bleaching his blood. To only seven or eight grams hemoglobin. Is this a way to do a young fellow? Fix my old pal's ratios, Lord. Bring that white smear down where it's manageable. Down to ten, fifteen thousand. Beef up his red count to acceptable levels— twelve, fourteen grams.

"We have not yet forgotten Hebe Heldshaft, the Yiddish Mockeybird, whose falsetto prayers raised up a melanoma on his vocal cords like a welt to Your glory. Or those other good lads from the minyan— Norm Sachs, Ray Haas, Marv Baskin.

"Do what You can, would You? Grant our prayer. Oh, by the way, this happens to be a challenge grant. The kid's faith is riding on it.

"Have you something to add, darlin'? Is there anything you'd like to say?"

"No," she said.

"Connie joins me in the Amen."

I could *feel* the frissons through the walls.

They so admire a rascal, other people's cynicism. I was their rascal of God. Only Constance did not admire me. Though I was doing this for her. Getting His attention for her. Only for her. I wasn't showing off for the women anymore. Not for Joan Cohen with all her wardrobe or Elaine Iglauer and her trade-up heart. Not for Naomi or Rose with their easy Valentine acquiescence. Or any other of those predisposed ladies, choir girls, songstresses for God. Not even for Shelley. (Though ultimately, I think, nearly everything I do is for Shelley.)

For Connie. Needing to impress Connie. Because I meant it when I said the blood count prayers were a challenge, that my kid's faith was riding on them. Even if what I really meant was her faith in me. (Though inevitably, down the road, *this* conversation— RABBI OF LUD: "Hey, kid, I gave it my best shot. You were right there beside me, you heard me. Weren't you? Didn't you hear me? The lengths I went to. All wheedle one minute, all smart-ass, up-front I/Thou confrontationals the next. Jesus, kid, I'm a licensed, documented rabbi. I was taking my life in my hands there." CONNIE: "He died? Stan Bloom *died*?" RABBI OF LUD: "I think prayer must be like any other treatment. I think the earlier you start, the more effective it is. Al Harry didn't even tell us about Stan until he was already down for the count." CONNIE: "He died, Daddy? You said you could pray him back to health and— Oh, Daddy, 'down for the count'! I get it. Oh, that's so *grisly*!")

Am I a buffoon? Some wise-guy, ungood Jew? Understand my passions then. All my if-this-will-go-here-maybe-that-will-go-there arrangements were in their service. What did *I* want? What did *I* need? To keep my job with God. To hold my marriage and family together. Who was ever more Juggler of Our Lady than this old rebbie? As much the God jerk as any chanteuse out there in my rec room tuning her instrument or vocalizing scales.

Because let's face it, I'm no world-beater. Lud, New Jersey, is not one of Judaism's plummier posts. It's hardly the Wailing Wall. Hell, it's hardly Passaic. I haven't mentioned it but it had already begun to see its better days. There is, for example, a small airfield in Lud, hardly more than an airstrip really. Its tattered windsock no longer waves more than a few inches away from its standard even in the strongest gale, and tough clumps of rag grass have not only begun to spring up through cracks in the cement but have started to puncture actual holes in the tarmac. The landing strip had been put in long before for the convenience of people who flew their own airplanes, wealthy, high-flying bereaved from all along the eastern seaboard, New York State and the near Middle West who didn't want to deal with the traffic controllers at busy Teterborough a dozen miles off, and who came in not only for the actual funerals and unveilings but with guests and picnic hampers for casual week-end visits to the graves of their loved ones, and who were willing, even anxious, to stay in the tiny hotel that the funeral directors had had built, also for their convenience. Now, however, the landing field was hardly ever used and the hangar was just a place where the gravediggers and maintenance men stored their tools and parked their Cushmans and forklifts in an emergency.

It's hard times.

Shull and Tober keep telling me so.

* * * *

"Rabbi Goldkorn," big Tober called out.

"Good morning, Reb Tober," I said, raising an imaginary cap. "Good morning, Reb Shull."

Sometimes, when we pass each other in the street, we pretend that Lud is this shtetl from the last century, this Ana Tevka of a town.

"Yeah, yeah," Shull muttered, "good Shabbes, l'Chaim. Next Year in Jerusalem."

"Is something wrong? What's wrong?"

Tober unlocked the coffee shop. It had closed its doors to the public long ago but its big stainless-steel coffee urn was still operational, its grill and freezer.

Shull stepped behind the counter. He looked oddly chic back there in his dark, expensively tailored suit. "You want something with your coffee, Rabbi? There's marble cake in the bell. We might have some fruit in the back. I could heat soup in the microwave. I could make toast."

"Coffee's fine."

"This was before your time," Tober said. "When the hotel was still open for business. This coffee shop had one of the finest kosher chefs in all America behind the counter."

"I'd heard that," I said.

"Talk about your funeral baked meats," Shull said.

"There just wasn't the business," Tober said. "We couldn't justify it."

"We had to send him packing."

"The Association hired him for the prestige and convenience."

Tober meant the Greater Lud Merchants' Association. Even the anti-Semite, Seels, was a member. Even I was.

"Then, when business dropped off . . ."

"That's the thing," I broke in. "I don't understand how business can drop off."

"That's because you're a scholar, Rabbi."

"Not so much a man of the world."

"You busy your head with the important things."

"Blessing the bread."

"The candles."

"The wine."

"Making over dead people."

"Making over God."

"Look," said Shull, "you don't have to worry."

"Your job is assured," Tober said.

It wasn't the first time I'd thought of my employers as some other rabbi might have thought of the people on the board of directors of his congregation. Trustees and governors.

They were not like the women.

They watched me like a hawk.

They listened to every word of every eulogy, professional as people at the rear of a theater on opening night, interested as backers, hanging on the sobs, waiting for the laughs and show stoppers.

"My job is assured?"

"If it'd make you more comfortable we could draw up a new contract."

"I don't think I—"

"Sure," Tober said, "we could stick in a no-cut clause, guarantee you four or five more years."

"Five or six."

"Sure," said Tober, "what the hell."

"But—"

"You know what keeps us going?" Shull said.

"The perpetual care," Tober said.

"The perpetual care and the exhumations."

"The perpetual care and the exhumations and the deconsecrations."

"The perpetual care, exhumations, deconsecrations and the deliveries of the disinterred we make out to the Island."

"The perpetual care, exhumations, deconsecrations and the deliveries of the disinterred we make out to the Island and up to Connecticut."

"Because this necropolis is dying on its feet."

I'm a fellow whipsawed between admiration and contempt, hard men and soft women, needful daughters and loony wives, God jerks and morticians.

"Think, Rabbi. How many graves and tombstones have we dug up this year? Just this year? How many times have you found yourself having to mumble deconsecration prayers over some watertight, concrete vault?" Tober asked, emptying his cup and rinsing it in the deconsecrated sink.

"Sure," Shull said, "*that's* what keeps us going."

"*Fashion!*" Tober grumped.

"Fashion and the interment customs. The laws and principles of the Funeral Code of the Great State of New Jersey."

"We live by checks and balances, Rabbi."

"And what if," Shull put in, "God forbid it should come to this, the fashionable Long Island or fashionable Connecticut funerary lobby bastards ever got to our Trenton bastards and made them do away with the points in the code which keep us viable?"

"Exhumation taxes."

"Fees for rezoning deconsecrated back into consecrated ground."

"The ten-buck-a-mile charge, point A to point B, to move the disinterred across a state line."

"All your prohibitives and pretty-pennies."

"Pffft!"

"Up in smoke."

"Gone with the wind."

"But it makes you more comfortable we draw up a brand-new contract."

"No cut for two or three years."

"One or two."

"Sure," said Tober, "what the hell."

Shull took an ice-cream scoop from behind the counter and hung over the open freezer, studying the flavors. "Hey," he said, "I'm going to make myself a frappe. Anyone else? How about it, Rabbi? You up for a frappe?"

"Why are you saying these things to me?" I asked Tober. "I don't know why you're saying these things to me," I told Shull.

"Listen," Tober said, "we're not the type to go behind your back."

"Of course not," Shull agreed. "Believe me, Rabbi, if we had a beef we'd be in touch."

"We perfectly understand your position," Tober said.

"We comprehend totally your point of view."

"It isn't as if we could reasonably ask you to fix up your eulogies."

"Good Christ, man, you never even *knew* these people!"

"By the time *you* see them they're already dead!"

"All you got to go on is what their loved ones tell you about it," Shull said.

"You going to trust loved ones at a time like that?"

"With all their special stresses and vulnerabilities?"

"Though you have to, of course."

"Even they tell you their daddies could fly."

"Stand around in the air like a guy on a staircase."

"It's the age-old story."

"Garbage in, garbage out," Tober said.

"We won't stand on ceremonies. What it comes down to is what it came down to the last time," Shull said.

"Arthur Klein and Johnny Charney have been asking about you again," Tober said.

"What with death moving further and further out on the Island and up to the bedroom communities in Connecticut, well," Shull said, "we don't honestly see how we can continue to protect you."

"I'm a rabbi," I protested.

"Of course you are. I'd come to you myself for spiritual guidance. Wouldn't you, Shull?"

"In a minute, Tober."

"I studied Talmud. What do I know about real estate?"

"Plots," Tober said, laughing lightly. "Not real estate. *Burial* plots. Real estate is something else altogether."

"They *tax* real estate."

"We believe in the separation of church and real estate."

"Posolutely," Shull agreed.

"It's Klein's opinion you wouldn't even need a realtor's license."

"Charney's too."

"Please," I said, rising to go, "I'm not your man."

"It isn't as if you'd be knocking on doors."

"Is that what he thought, Tober, he'd be knocking on doors?"

"Leads," Tober said, "you'd be following leads. Charney said to say."

"All you'd have to do is close."

"And collect the commission Klein says you're entitled to."

"I'm sorry," I said. "Thanks for the coffee." Again I raised my imaginary cap. "Reb Tober. Reb Shull."

It was always astonishing to me to see them work in tandem, zip through routines I knew had to have been rehearsed, the letter-perfect meeting of their minds, their rhymed intentions. Though of course this wasn't the first time they'd introduced the subject. For years they'd been after me to work part time at Lud Realty with Klein and Charney. Indeed, though they professed to be passing along Klein's and Charney's views—the business about the realtor's license, the commission, the leads— the idea of my selling cemetery lots had been theirs. They thought a rabbi would have extra authority with the customers.

Shull and Tober knew they were dealing in a depletable resource—not the dead; the dead, like the poor, we would have always with us, but the land, parcels of ground no bigger than the doorway to your room—and they were terrified. Always they were turning new ideas over and over in their heads. They entertained (and dismissed) a plan for a new, ecumenical cemetery, and offered at discount burial plot, casket, funeral and tombstone combinations that could only be purchased in advance. They worked out all sorts of schemes and drew up models of landscaping (like Simplicity dress patterns) that the men and women who would one day be buried there could not only preselect but were encouraged to tend themselves, like people working on their gardens. They would even sell you the seeds and rent you the tools.

So their overture to me in the coffee shop was not new. Even my guarded outrage reflected old positions, and each time they introduced the idea it seemed a little less outlandish.

"Goldkorn," said Tober, "think about this, please."

"I'm sorry," I said, starting for the door and stepping out into the street. "I really don't see what there is to think about."

"Goldkorn," Shull called, rushing to the door and shouting after me. "Hear me, Goldkorn! There are worse parishes than Lud! If this cemetery goes belly up you could finish your career in some condo on the Palisades! You could be The Bingo Rabbi, The Theater Party Rabbi! The Rabbi of Wheelchairs and Walkers! Is that what you want? Is it? *Is it, Goldkorn?*"

So they were terrified. It was those indivisible cubic feet of earth they knew they were stuck with, saddled with, the seven-or-so dirt feet by four-or-so dirt feet by six-or-so dirt feet— just those hundred-sixty-eight-or-so cubic dirt feet. Because they figured that all they really had to sell was the topsoil. Never mind that it had dimension, that it bottomed out at China. For these two, everything after those first twenty-eight-or-so initial square dirt feet was throwaway, pure loss leader, the mineral rights to which they could neither retain, sell nor give away. Hence the advance purchase plans, collaborative eulogies, all the layaway obsequies; hence the seeds and garden tools and elaborate landscaping arrangements. Hence their tandem, bicycle-built-for-two hearts.

But however alike Tober and Shull appeared to be in business, privately they were as different as day and night.

Emile Tober was the night.

Tober was a big, troubled, crafty and, on his own, secretive, taciturn and probably insane old man who was driven by a single goal— putting together enough money to guarantee that his son, Edward, once Tober was out of the picture—that's how he put it—would be provided for for life, a life, Tober was convinced, that would not only outlast his own and that of Tober's wife but the lives, too, of Emile's and Sonia's three other children, Edward's brother and two sisters, as well as their kids',

Ed's unborn nieces and nephews, should they ever *be* born, which, frankly, might never happen since they, the siblings, were not married yet and, so early were they enlisted into the service of their daddy's obsession, that they not only believed in it and shared in it but were actually given over to it as much as the father, and who (not even *counting* Edward), the funeral parlor guy's grown kids—ninety-six years old collectively, which was the only score Tober ever kept, and the only way he ever kept it, growing three additional collective years per annum which, should all of them live, would make them ninety-nine years the following year and one hundred and two the year after that one, only Edward getting the benefit of an individuated, customized, bespoke birthday— thirty-eight, according to his father, of the darkest, dizziest years in the recorded, concentrated history of man—therefore actively contributed to it, that hard-earned fund, store, reserve, hoarded, hope-chest and war-chest, nest-egg kitty, call it what you will, which, or so ran his dad's mad theory, would, if only it were allowed to grow big enough (if, that is, only God saw fit to allow all of them to live longer, if only He found them better jobs, kept inflation down, improved interest rates and guided them into safe, terrific investment opportunities), might finally permit—twenty-nine, thirty-two, thirty-five, sixty-one and sixty-four were their actual ages—one of them to die, so long, that is, as the rest of them didn't slack off and continued to chip in with their fair share, until, if God saw fit, they would perhaps have saved enough to permit another of them to breathe his or her last and thereby leave off putting by, so long, that is, as it was the surviving, least good wage-earner He took, and so on and so forth until the time, or so old Tober figured, that the nut was at last large enough to cover just about whatever might yet come up, leaving the by-that-time fatherless, motherless, brotherless-and-sisterless kid to all the devices in the armory of his protective attendants and retainers. Which had better be considerable.

Edward Tober had been blind since birth.

Which might not, considering all the possible curses and combinations of curses, have been so bad. There's leglessness and armlessness, hearing loss and a broad palette of the chronic and congenital that not only outruns, but will probably continue to outrun, however correct our priorities, strong our commitment or deep our pockets, however refined and elegant our solutions or frequent and prime-timed our telethons, our needs. And now we are up old Tober's alley, on old Tober's turf, somewhere along his twisted and complicated, infinitely long corridor and rich vein of troubles. There was just too damn much on Edward's plate.

He had been born without a labyrinthine sense. He had, that is, not only none of the blind man's comforting overcompensations but an additional and quite dreadful undercompensation with which he had to deal. He had perfect pitch, a keen, too keen, sense of smell, strength, a good heart, brains, common sense— all the attributes. Only a good sense of direction he did not have, or any sense of direction at all. He could not tell left from right, up from down, or even in from out. There he was, a loose cannon on the deck, apparently without the gift of gravity, unfixed as an astronaut. Thrown into a pool, or fallen into the sea, he would as likely swim to the bottom as to the top.

Because he was unable to see and had none of his labyrinthine senses, he couldn't learn to knot his tie, or tie his shoes, or dress himself at all. He buttoned a shirt by chance and main force, sometimes actually pushing—he was strong—the buttons through the cloth. He forced both feet into the same pants leg, blew his ear in his handkerchief and wore his hat rakishly on his shoulder. He could never learn braille, or even turn on a radio. He wouldn't be able to make love, of course, and I refuse to think about how he handled his bodily functions.

Yet Edward more than held his own in conversation, told delightful stories, had a sweet, equable disposition, and there was no one I knew whom I would rather go to for advice.

Shull.

Shull was the day, affable as sunshine. If Tober was driven to miserliness by his sense of the terrible consequences his death would bring to his handicapped son, Shull was hounded to earn by nothing more urgent than the pursuit of happiness. Not even happiness— pleasure. Though you couldn't tell it from his behavior during the long hours of his working day, which, until you knew him better, would have seemed to you not only full but frantic—the two and sometimes three phone conversations

he could conduct simultaneously, a telephone held like an ear-
ache between his inclined head and shoulder, and another in
each hand, shouting orders to his chemicals supplier in Philly,
discussing a floral arrangement with his nurseryman in Lud,
solicitous of some broken-hearted widow on the other end of a
third phone, and perhaps already catching the eye of some workman just then passing the open door to his office and signaling
with nothing more than directions jabbed out with his chin not
only where he wanted the workman to go but what he wanted
him to do when he got there—even his stomach-knotting,
ulcer-growing, stress-inducing activities a source of pleasure to
him (as almost everything was that he could feel— a sore throat,
a headache, an abscessed tooth, and his coffee and marble cake
and two- and three-frappe lunches too), though he perfectly
understood that what hurt him hurt him, was not, that is, good
for him, and betrayed nerve endings that might just as well be
used in a better cause than the destructive impulses and syn-
apses of masochism. Understood, that is, that if he was to be a
voluptuary, if he was to make his pleasures extend over a long
lifetime—he was already sixty-one, the same age as Sonia, his
partner's wife—then he'd better knock it off, get right with his
body. Periodically he gave up smoking, cut down on his drinking, traveled two to three times a year to the most expensive fat
farms, had himself checked by important specialists, elected
surgeries not covered by his health insurance, all the while
balancing, even juggling, the golden means of moderation in all
things, including his concern for his own health.

He spent what he earned. He could have been some dedicated, even obsessed, hobbyist or collector deliberately setting,
despite its cost, a final treasure triumphantly into place in the
collection. Yet he had no hobbies, no collection. His pleasure
was pleasure, his pastime was fun.

He'd once purchased a big-ticket, luxury item from a mail-
order catalogue and now he received catalogues from every
mail-order house in the country. These retailers, whatever they
sold, must have pictured him as some world-class yuppie and,
indeed, the stuff he sent away for was exactly the sort of
merchandise you might expect to see on the wish list of any
upwardly mobile, spoiled-rotten kid in the land. He owned

almost everything L.L. Bean and Sharper Image had to offer.
Banana Republic sent him pith helmets and commando gear—
sweaters, boots, compasses and flight jackets—from a dozen
armies. He owned a Swedish submariner's first-aid case, fuses
and assorted makings that might have been used by the PLO.
He owned an official knife from the Portuguese Fishing Fleet that
he used to loosen knots though it was designed to fillet fish. He
sent away for the best telescopes. He had an expensive home gym.
He owned a robot. He purchased state-of-the-art Camcorders,
audio equipment, edge-of-the-field cameras, rifles, Betamax machines, and alarm systems to protect all this shit. He gave
elaborate luaus and liked to charter planes on New Year's Eve
and fly his friends to mystery destinations. He hired symphony
musicians to entertain at his parties. They strolled among the
guests and took requests like gypsies in a restaurant. He flew to
Europe only if he could get reservations on the Concorde and,
though he did none himself, at parties he would lay, with this tiny,
special limited-edition sterling silver spoon beside it he'd purchased from the Franklin Mint, cocaine out on the coffee table
as if it were fruit. His measurements were on file with half a
dozen Jermyn Street shirtmakers and Savile Row tailors. A
Brazilian bootmaker had lasts for his feet. He had season tickets
to everything.

But oh, oh, infinite is the cash cost and list price of pleasure.
There seemed no bottom to the bottom line. He was always
strapped, as desperate as Tober to think up new ways to make
the funeral home pay off, to parlay the other guy's cancer and
bad germs into cash flow, additional ready for the general fund,
store and reserve, that hoarded hope-chest, war-chest treasury
and nest-egg kitty, that protective cushion, call it what you will,
that Tober wanted for the rainy day when he would be dead
and Shull to tide him over until the weekend.

Because he was a ladies' man, of course, a good-time
Charlie, an actual out-and-out Lothario.

I never met a more romantic-looking sixty-one-year-old. In
his camel's-hair coat, brushed Borsalino, suckling lionskin gloves
and soft Gucci shoes, he was the sharpest grandpa I'd ever
seen. I wasn't surprised to learn he'd once been Rose Pickler's
and Naomi Shore's lover.

"You see too much death in our business, Rabbi," he'd told me. "Well, you know, not *too* much, I don't mean *too* much, but all there is. I mean, what the hell, we don't rent the land out for picnics, do we? We don't use the organ for dances or pin corsages on the basic black. Jerry, Jerry," he'd moaned, "we're under the gun, we're working at knifepoint here. I memento mori morning, noon and nighttime too. It's all I ever think about. It makes me crazy and costs me money. Sure. Death makes me a big spender. It puts the glow in my cheeks and the stiff in my cock. Sure. Because I put a big day in at the office, all I'm good for is playing with my electric trains, trying on my new suits, easing the Jag out of my garage and putting the top down and taking her for a spin. I watch my weight, brush after every meal, and regard my pressure like I loved it. I'm aware of every organ, Rebbe. Not just my heart, lungs, guts and glands, but what covers them too, the hankie sticking up out of my breast pocket, the press in my pants. I'll tell you something. It's death made me cheat on my wife when she was alive. Because basically I'm a family man basically, or wanted to be, would have been. But you tell me, Goldkorn, you tell me— how you gonna keep 'em down on the farm? How, hey?"

"It ain't easy for me to get girls," he'd confessed another time. "Hell," he said, "it ain't easy for me to get full grown-up women. Pie bakers, widows, ladies with varicose in their veins, blue rinse in their hair, yellow in their underpants. It ain't even the immorality of it, that they know I'm this only recently widowered old man. You know what it is? They know I'm a mortician. How? It ain't the first thing I tell them. I think maybe they sniff it on my fingers. *Me*, who hasn't personally handled a stiff since to tell you the truth I don't even remember. *Handled?* Looked at in the casket even. Who can say? Maybe they smell the flowers on me, all that death grass. You think that don't make a difference? You think so? I'm telling you, Rabbi Jerry, I drive these ladies to their *own* bank accounts! An evening with yours truly and they're looking for the Neiman Marcus catalogue, the Henri Bendel. A night on the town with me and they're circling the item, checking off the size, choosing out the color, turning down the page."

"Hey, listen," he said yet another time, "it isn't as if I'm bringing you the news. You're the rabbi here. You're familiar with what goes on. Death's your speciality, so I know I'm not telling you anything you don't already know or haven't thought about plenty. Only, the way I see it, with you it's not so geferlech. There's even something spiritual about it, some natural order business, God's plan, that people like me don't even think about. Sunrise, sunset. Whatever. But personally, and speaking strictly for myself, and given the nature of the business even, I've got to be thinking 'Here today and gone somewhere else tomorrow.' Hell, that *is* the way I think. It's the way Tober thinks too, even if he comes at it from a different priority. So I'll tell you what's on my mind."

"I *know* what's on your mind," I said.

"Rabbi, please," he said, "give me a break. You know as well as I do it's all in the details."

"What's up, then? What is it?"

"This AIDS business is doing me in. I don't think I can handle it."

"AIDS? What do you mean? Who's got AIDS?"

"Not me. I don't know, nobody. It's a figure of speech, a sign of the times, just one more straw. I told you about the fingers, that maybe they sniff on me what I do? They go further. They flinch when I touch them. They're thinking, you know, the blood. God *knows* what they think. But they do, they flinch when I touch them. That's my stock in trade. Contact. Comfort. My hand on their arm. I lose that, I lose everything.

"They're terrified out there, Rabbi. They're shaking in their shoes. No, no, I mean it. They've soured on the venereal. Something's up. Something vicious and narrow-spirited that robs us of our consolations. Jesus, Rov, there ain't even tea dancing no more, *one* two three, *one* two three. What am I, a spring chicken? I'm an old fart. They look at me they've got to be thinking 'Do I need this? I don't need this.' I'm wrong they sniff it on my fingers, I'm wrong they smell the flowers on my suit. They breathe it in the *ground*, in the clods and clumps of my sanctified fields. It sticks to their nostrils, it goes to their heads." He leaned toward me, he lowered his voice. "There are eleven AIDS victims in the ground here."

"Hey."

"Eleven I know of, eleven that's sure."

"Hey."

"This mustn't get out. It would devastate business. We agreed," Shull said. "Me and Tober. We made a policy decision.

"Because," he said, "he saves his money like a miser and I spend mine like a drunk sailor. And because you just ain't doing your part, Rabbi. Content to call 'em as you see 'em, happy like a clam with all those Ecclesiastes checks and balances of your position, all bought into the goeth ups and cometh downs, the milchiks and fleishiks seasonals. Well, me too. Me too, Rebbe Goldkorn! *It's fucking now or fucking never!*"

"What are you saying to me? Why are you talking to me like this?"

"Ach," said Shull.

"Why would he speak like that?" I asked Tober when I saw him. "What's he trying to tell me?"

"Argh," said Tober.

"What do you want from me?" I demanded of both. "I do my job. Don't I do my job? Is it Charney? Is it Klein? Is that why you're pressuring me?"

"Phoo," they agreed.

"And what's all this about AIDS?"

"You told him?" Tober snapped.

"I told him a figure of speech, I told him a metaphor."

"You *told* him."

"I told him about eleven people," Shull said. "I never told him we're the Holy Faygeleh Sacred Burial Ground."

My God, I thought, they're crazy. Those multiple hundred-sixty-eight-or-so cubic dirt feet lots again. The policy decision. Burying AIDS victims their bold new marketing scheme!

• • • •

Tober came to the house. He was pushing Edward in a wheelchair.

"Hello," Tober said, "shalom."

"Hello," I said. "How are you, Edward?"

"May I leave him with you a minute?"

"Sure," I said.

"We're not disturbing you?"

"No," I said. "Of course not."

"Interrupting anything?"

"Of course not."

"I'll be twelve minutes."

"Take your time."

"He means well," Edward said when his father had left.

"Oh," I said, "he's a good man."

"He's a driven, self-centered, totally obsessive human being, but he means well."

"Well, Edward," I said, a little embarrassed as I often was with him, "you're looking fit."

It was true. For all his handicaps, his blindness and the fluids sloshing and tumbling in his inner ears like water in a washing machine, Edward was as poised and equable as a man with a pipe. He appeared to lounge in his wheelchair, like a fellow sitting up, taking his ease on a pal's hospital bed. Though it wasn't, you imagined one leg crossed smartly over the other. His opaque, fashionable glasses fit comfortably across his face like a dark, thin strip of style on the eyes of a musician. I knew that if he removed the glasses, the clear eyes behind them would seem intelligent, tolerant, amused. As I had before, I wondered again if he knew how elegant he was, how he'd developed—he evidently chose his own clothes—his graceful impeccables and flawless stunnings. He'd been blind since birth.

"In my dreams," he told me, "I'm someone else altogether."

"I'm sorry?"

"You remarked my appearance," Edward Tober said, "you said I looked fit."

"You do, kayn aynhoreh."

"In my dreams I am."

"That's terrific."

"I can see in my dreams."

"Really?"

"Quite clearly, in fact. Twenty-twenty the gnarled, brown stems of apples, the tight weave of wicker or the nubbing of towels. All twenty-twenty. Inches perceiving, acres and rods and nautical miles. Weights and measures, metric equivalencies.

The size of a pint. The heft of a scruple, the length of a dram. All calibration's ordered ranks, where the decimal goes, the bull's-eye's dead center, or where to put your nail to hang a picture on the wall twenty-twenty. The stain of the sky in a time zone, presented the hour, given the pressure, the weather, the wind. My dreams as matched to reality as pairs of perfectly teamed horses. I see in my dreams. The orange's blemished, unfortunate pores, its pitted sheen. I see in my dreams."

"Vai, such a megillah!"

"I do," Edward said, "I can. Things most blind men don't even know about, let alone see."

"The emes?"

"Freckles like a personal astronomy, suntan like the cream in your coffee."

"It's a miracle!"

"It is," he insisted, "it is. I see trees, their barks like rich textiles. Bolts of birch like sailcloth, and aspen like linen. Elms like a corduroy, and hickory like a patch of burlap. Quilted sycamore, I see. Silken cherry."

"Genug, I am fartootst!"

"I do," he insisted, "I *can!* I see plants, I see flowers. Not just art's abstractive, generical shapes, the wallpaper posies and the bouquets on ties, but trillium, cattleya, dahlia and quince. And see, in what even a blind man would recognize as the dark, the shaded mosses and shielded ferns— all drizzled ground's weathered cover."

"Ge*valt*, what a gesheft!"

"And shapes like a geometer— triangles, rectangles, pyramids, wedge. Cones and spheres, cylinders and tubes. The rhomboid, the quadrature, the octagon, the pill. All nature's jigsaw doings."

"And otherwise?"

"What, my balance you mean?"

"Otherwise."

"I walk across tightropes and stand on the flyer's narrow perch as lightly as the most casual man on the trapeze."

"Oh," I said, "the trap*eeeze.*"

"You don't believe me."

"Eddy, forgive me, you sleep in your bed with the rails up."

"I've no vertigo in dreams. I'm as surefooted as an Indian. Comfortable in height as a steeplejack."

"It don't make you nauseous?"

"It doesn't," he said, "it really doesn't. I'll be riding downhill on a bicycle. Untroubled by curves, negotiating the hairpin turns and spirals, the violent mountain switchbacks, momentum at my back like a gale-force wind. All derring do, all derring done. All will's and spirit's exuberant, unencumbered Look-Ma-No-Hands."

"And Eddy, if you fell, who'd say Kaddish?"

"Listen to me, Rabbi. You've known for years about my mazed bearings, my perturbed compass loose, free as a roulette wheel. I'm a guy who doesn't clean his teeth because I can't hold a toothbrush in my mouth, because it falls off my teeth. Because I lose track of where everything goes and gag on the bristles. I see, I *see* in my dreams. And not *only* see— I'm graceful."

"You have them often, these dreams?"

"Last night. I had one last night."

"Ahh," I said, dovetailing as expectantly into his tale as a psychiatrist.

"So I'm walking along beside this river," he said, as if breaking into his own story, "when suddenly I realize why those clouds are called 'cumulus.' Why, of course, I thought, it's for the idea of accumulation implicit in them. That's just what they look like— huge piles, great mounds, high white heaps of accumulated cloud stuff. I saw this reflected in the water— their dense, well-defined, straight-edged bases, their rounded, fluffy tops like the fluting on scallops. In the water, the imposed, accumulated clouds glanced off the current like a bunch of balloons.

"From the swiftness of the current in that latitude, and the light and color values reflected in the river, reduced, packed, tamped by the filters of the air and climate like an image in a lens, I judged it to be about one p.m. Time for lunch. And, indeed, I *was* starting to feel peckish, not outright hunger, understand, just the crisp snap and bristle in the throat and belly that is the beginning of appetite. I thought to bring it to the boil with some light exercise and determined to go for a swim before I ate. There was a very high, very narrow railroad trestle about a hundred yards ahead which I could probably climb by clambering up the sides of its steep ramparts. I pulled off my shoes and socks, placed them beside a low bush, and began my ascent.

"When I reached the top I heard a train. Well, no," he corrected, "I didn't hear the train so much as feel its vibrations on the tracks. There was a palpable shimmy, the rails, it seemed to me, like loose teeth, and swaying with what I could only hope were the factored, mathematical givens, the wobbled, engineered allowances of skyscrapers in a strong wind, say. Though of course I knew better."

Edward's voice was cracked now, dry, his tongue thickened around the story of his dream like spoiled meat. His handsome face had lost its poise, and I saw moisture collecting along the black rims of his dark glasses, spouting from God knew what pale and awful skin, tender, vulnerable and secret as a genital.

"It was a dream," I said dismissively.

"I looked around," Edward said, "trying to get my bearings."

"It was only a dream."

"By my best estimate I was maybe thirty-eight-and-a-half meters high. Throw in my height, I was probably forty-and-a-half meters from the surface of the river."

"It was just a bad dream, Edward," I told him.

"Light travels faster than sound. I could see the train, the locomotive, though I still couldn't hear it."

"Take it easy," I said, "you always wake up from these nightmares."

"I gazed down into the surface of the water. You have to do your calculations and make your allowances in split seconds. Two flattened piles of gray cumulus rushed toward the trestle and flowed under it. You know that moment when you look at something and can't tell whether it's you or the object that's moving? You know that instant of vertigo and confusion?"

"A dream, Eddy. A lousy dream."

"Is it hot in here? Did it get hot in here all of a sudden?"

"It *is* a little warm," I said, to reassure him.

"I could see the train, the locomotive, its black tatter of burned diesel tearing away from the engine like a dark pennant.

And heard it now too. And felt the vibration of the rails, and what weren't vibrations but the drunken sway and stagger of the actual wooden trestle. Did I tell you I had to scan the water, search beneath and between its surface reflections to determine its depth? I mean, I *knew* mine. Not my depth, of course, my height. A hundred and eleven feet—and, from the apogee of my dive, probably more like a hundred fourteen—above that taut, flowing skin of cloud-bearing, sky-bearing water. Searching, as the speed and weight and sight and sound, and smell now, too, of that train came bearing down on me, for the exact and singular depth between the reflections where it would be safe for me to dive into the river. And did I tell you I not only had to do all this, not only had to find those needle-in-a-haystack clearances almost half a hundred meters beneath me, but that I had to find them through my opaque, black glasses, because what with that charging locomotive and my straw-that-breaks-the-camel's-back weight on that flimsy trestle and all, there just wasn't any time to take them—"

"It was a *dream*."

"—off?"

"Edward, please, don't make a tsimmes. It was only a—"

"So I dove. Or danced. Or maybe just fell, my arms furiously pinwheeling, rotating about some imaginary axis that ran through my armpits— diving, dancing, falling, stumbling along that shaking perimeter of trestle. And recovered. And entered the water at the perfect angle, an angle so perfect, in fact, that if I hadn't felt the wetness climbing up my fingers as if I were pulling on a pair of gloves I'd have actually thought I was still diving."

And it was as if he actually *had* dived into that river he'd dreamed. He was soaked clean through now, what I'd come to think of as his relaxed, summery bearing, his picnic-hamper, seersucker demeanor ruined, soiled.

"After all that," he said, "*boy*, was I hungry!"

"You were?"

"Famished."

"Sure," I said, "all that climbing, the excitement, that dive that you dove. Who wouldn't be hungry?"

"And I didn't get out of the water right away."

"No."

"I went for my swim."

"Your swim."

"Fortunately, I'd been able to look around from the trestle just before I dived."

"I see."

"I'd spotted some wild strawberry bushes not far from where I'd left my shoes and socks. Though the bush in which I'd actually hidden my stuff was a lingonberry. I'm not partial to lingonberries. Too acidic.

"But even if there hadn't been those strawberries there'd have been plenty of other good things to eat. There were crab apples and plums and, near the poison ivy, a strain of breadfruit I'm rather fond of. There was iceberg, romaine, and good Bibb lettuce.

"So it wasn't any hardship for me to live off the land. What with the strawberries and the breadfruit and the fish I fried up, it was quite a grand lunch."

"You caught a fish?"

"Well," he said, "while I was on the trestle I happened to notice a kind of soil particularly hospitable to bait. I just dug down into it, carefully chose a worm—"

"*Carefully* chose?"

"—for texture, for color, I'd seen these perch—"

"Go on."

"—and fitted it to its hook like a stitch in crochet."

"Then what happened?"

He shrugged. "Nothing much," he said. "That's about it. I finished my lunch and dreamt I took a nap beside this weeping willow."

"Well, well," I told him, "that was quite a dream. You went for a walk, figured out clouds, had an adventure on a railroad trestle, observed nature, took a swim, went berry picking, fishing, prepared a first-rate lunch for yourself, and caught forty winks in the shade of the old weeping willow."

"Yes," he said.

"You did all that."

"That's right," he said. "Yes."

"What's wrong? Is anything wrong? Why are you crying?"

"In my dream," he said, "in my dream I was napping. Not dreaming a dream, only dreaming my nap."

"Yes?"

"Dreaming sleep."

"Yes? Dreaming sleep? Yes?"

"Dreaming the darkness. Dreaming the dark."

"Oh," I said, "oh."

"So I didn't know when I woke up."

"Oh," I said, "oh,"

"Because I'm without sight," he said. "Because I'm without sight and couldn't tell if it was the satisfied comfort of fulfilled coze and snug or only the dark, ordinary blackness of the blind."

"Oh, Edward," I said.

"So I had to try to turn my head."

"Oh, Edward. Oh, Eddy," I said, and didn't bother to echo his words this time or ask him questions. Because I was no longer interested—this is my rabbi mode now—in playing straight man, in feeding him lines, my faked incredulity and poised astonishment. It was too awful. He was making me uncomfortable. Because this is just ballast I do, only the dappered-up charm of my phony accommodation, ingenuous as a host on a talk show egging on a naive guest. Maybe, awash in my agog wonder, by playing to reason, I could make out I was playing to God.

"Or grab the safety rails of my raised hospital sides. I *had* to. To see if I'd throw up. To see if those liquids in my inner ear would move. And start the long rinse-and-tumble cycles of my spinning day. Help my father," he growled suddenly, his sightless, bobbing, handsome head loose on his neck as he sought a kind of random, flailing contact with me. "Work for Charney," he urged, "work for Klein. Help my father, help my brother. Help my mother and sisters put together an estate that will help me keep body and soul together after they're gone. Please, Rabbi," he pleaded, "provide, *provide!*"

•　　•　　•　　•

I got word my friend died and, when Connie came by for Stan Bloom's Get-Well-Soon prayers, I had to tell her it had been called off.

"He *died*?" Connie said. "Stan Bloom *died*?"

"We'll pray," I said, "for the repose of his spirit."

"He *died*?"

"Hey, Connie," I said, "it happens. People die. It's a fact of life."

I began the El moley rachamim.

"El moley rachamim," I prayed, "shochen bamromim, hamtzeh, menucho, nechon al kanfey hashchino, bemaalos k'doshim ut'horim kezohar horokeea mazirim, es nishmas Stanley Bloom sheholoch leolomoh, baavur shenodvoo z'dokoh b'ad hazkoras nishmosoh. B'gan eden t'hay M'nochosoh. Locheyn baal hor-achmim yastireyo beseser k'nofov leolomim—"

"He died?" she said. "Stan Bloom died?"

"—ve'itzror bitzror hachayim es nishmosoh—"

"Stan Bloom," she said, "Stan *Bloom* died?"

"Connie," I said, "hey, I'm praying here."

"He *died*?"

"What's all this about then?" I said, a little angry now, a little steamed. "He was *my* friend. You never even met him."

"He's *dead*?"

"Hey, kid, I gave it my best shot. You were right there beside me, you heard me. Weren't you? Didn't you hear me? The lengths I went to. All wheedle one minute, all smart-ass, up-front I/Thou confrontationals the next. Jesus, kid, I'm a licensed, documented rabbi. I was taking my life in my hands there."

"He's *dead*? Stan Bloom's *dead*?"

"Prayer's like any other treatment, Connie darling. Unless you catch it early enough . . . Al Harry didn't even *tell* us about Stan Bloom until he was already down for the count!"

"You said you could pray him back to health. You said . . . Oh, Daddy, 'down for the count'! I get it. Oh, that's so *grisly*!"

"Come on, Connie," I said.

"I hate it here," she said. "I hate looking out my bedroom window and seeing all those dead people."

"You don't see dead people. Why do you say you see dead people? You see markers. You see a few markers. It's like seeing a sign on the corner with the name of the street written on it.

Why do you say you see dead people? If we lived on Jefferson Street and outside your window you saw the sign on the corner, would you say you saw Jefferson? Would you tell me you saw Elm or River or Michigan or Maple? Be a little reasonable, why don't you? You see a few markers here and there in a field. Don't say you see dead people."

"I hate it here, I do, I hate it here, I hate it!" she said over and over with her hands on her ears to drown out my objections.

"Connie," I said, holding her, stroking her hair. "Connie Connie Connie."

"I hate it! I hate it! I hate it here, I hate it! I hate it!"

"Connie Connie Connie. Connie Connie Connie. Connie Connie Connie," I told my child.

"Please," she sobbed. "Please?"

"What, sweetheart? Please what?"

"Let's go away. Let's go away from here."

"Leave our home?"

"Daddy, our back yard is a *cemetery!*"

"It's beautifully landscaped."

"It's *perpetual care!*"

"Kids these days. I tell you, you can't put a thing past 'em."

"Stop *joking* me! I'm not a tough customer!"

"Can't you tell I'm teasing? Maybe I was giving you a little more credit than you deserve."

"I'm a little girl. Smoke rises from some of the chimneys here even in summer! You smell flowers all year round. Even out of season you smell flowers, even in winter! *Everyone is always all dressed up!* The florist and the man in the dry cleaner's. The barber wears a suit and tie, the man who drives the wrecker! I'm only fourteen years old. I shouldn't have to live around all this goddamn death!"

"It's all right to let me know what's on your mind once in a while," I said, "even if you talk back, but don't you *ever* say 'goddamn' to your father. I'm a rabbi, young lady, and don't you forget it!"

"*You're a goddamn fool!*" she shouted.

"*What?* What did you say?"

"*You're a fool!*" she screamed. "*You're a goddamned fool!*"

"*Please God*," I prayed suddenly, "*You-Who-Hear-Everything,
You didn't hear that!* It was a slip of the tongue. She didn't mean
it. She was having a bad dream, she was talking in her sleep.
Don't strike her dead tonight when she's just drifting off. And
what*ever* You do, don't You go disfiguring her, or crippling her
legs for life, so no man will ever want to marry her unless it's
out of sympathy, and the only job she'll be good for is sitting
outside in the cold against a tall office building selling pencils
out of her hat. CONSTANCE GOLDKORN OF LUD, NEW JERSEY,
would never have said a thing like that if she'd been in her right
mind, and she does *too* honor her father and also obeys some of
the rest of Your commandments."

"Oh," said my daughter, "you think you're so cool. You
think you're so cool. But you know something? You're just an
asshole."

I slapped her face but she was already crying.

My wife was in the doorway.

"What happened? What's wrong? Why is she crying?"

"She's got a fresh mouth."

"Darling," she asked Connie, "what is it, what's wrong?"

"She's got a fresh mouth. She called me a fool, she said
'goddamn.' She said I'm an asshole."

"Did you? Did you say these things to your father?"

"She sure did. I was saying the El moley rachamim for
Stan Bloom."

"I can't believe what I'm hearing," Shelley said. "Why
would you do such a thing? He was praying the El moley
rachamim for his old friend, Stan Bloom. Connie, he was talking to *God!*"

"Sure," Connie said. "That's when he prayed I'd be crip-
pled. That I'd lose my legs."

Shelley stared at me.

"That stuff she was saying, she really ticked me off."

"Just because I'm so scared here, Mama. Just because I'm
always so scared."

"Scared? You're scared here? What are you scared of?"

"I hate it here, Mama. I don't have any friends my own age.
They're afraid to come. The place stinks of dead people. Anyway,
it isn't as if he was a *regular* rabbi. All he does is bury people."

"It's where I work, it's what I do."

"You're really frightened?"

"Oh," Connie said, "it's terrible."

"You're lonely here?"

"Yes."

"You miss your friends?"

"How can she miss what she never had?"

"See?"

"That's not what I meant," I said. "I only mean—"

"He prayed God would disfigure me, that He'd throw acid in my face."

"I *never* prayed God would throw acid in her face. I never said that. That's not my style."

"Didn't you say about being struck dead in my sleep and that my face would be disfigured so no man would marry me?"

"No."

"He's lying."

"I'm not lying! I prayed He *wouldn't* do those things! Didn't I? Well, *didn't* I!"

"Well, yes, I suppose so, but that's not how it sounded, that's not what he meant."

"Oh, how it *sound*ed, what I *meant*! As if Talmudists don't spend entire lifetimes arguing over a comma, what's meant by whether something that happened happened on a hill or at sea level."

"Look," Shelley said, as no-nonsense, sensible and serious as I'd ever seen her, "I don't have a very clear idea of what's going on here. I don't even know if it would make that much difference if I did. All I know is that the two people I love most in the world aren't being very kind to each other." Connie had stopped crying but was fretting with some yarn that had loosened on her sweater. "*Listen* to me!" Shelley said sharply. "Do you know how it hurts me, how it *should* hurt *all* of us, or how disgraceful it is when people who are supposed to love and protect each other lose that kind of control? Well, do you?"

"I'm sorry," Connie said.

"So am I," I said.

"It's probably something to do with the misconceptions we have about what one another is thinking. Jerry," she said, "it's true I've made good friends here, dear and wonderful friends. The mothers of the children in my car pools. The girls in my group. Old Hershorn, the stonecutter. Reb Shull and Reb Tober. Others in the congregation. But it's not as if I was a hundred years old. I'm still young. You are too, Jerry. And if Connie's even half as miserable as she says she is—"

"I'm *twice* as miserable," Connie said.

"Well," said Shelley, "there you are. It isn't as if there's anything really *holding* us here. You could get another place. At least it isn't too late to start looking."

"You'd move? You want to move?"

Then, as suddenly as I'd shifted from one language to another when Connie and I had been quarreling, Shelley's finger was at her lips and she darted an anxious glance in our daughter's direction at the same time that she seemed to be warning me. "Life is too short. Stan Bloom's should have taught us that much. So then," she announced with conviction, "if that means we have to say good-bye to the good friends we've made here, pick up and leave Lud, I guess we'll just have to say good-bye to our friends, pick-e-le up and leave-e-le Lud!"

five

LEAVE *Lud*? Leave *Lud*? What were they, crazy? I'm *Rab*bi of Lud! It's like being Rabbi of Walden.

Anyway, I'd done it. I'd done it already. In '74. I was Chief Rabbi of the Alaska Pipeline from March 1974 to April 1975. The plan was, I was to take care of the spiritual needs of the Jewish construction workers, conduct Friday night services for the Orthodox back-hoers and forklift truck and heavy earth-moving equipment operators, and lead all those frum pipe fitters, drillers, welders, hod carriers, riveters, riggers, roughnecks and roustabouts through the long arctic Shabbes. When the pipeline was finished I was supposed to send for Shelley and the kid and try to get on at this shul in Anchorage.

Wasn't that a time!

With all the federal money and government contracts that were involved, the construction companies weren't taking any chances. Men and women were hired on from all over. All races and religions, all sexes, creeds, colors and appetites. There were Filipinos, boat people, wetbacks from Mexico. There was a rumor, and I believe it, that some Russians had managed to cross the Bering Strait from Siberia and that two or three of them, legendary in cold, in snow and ice, were actually promoted to gang foremen before they were discovered and repatriated back over the ice to Russia. I ask you, only in America or only in America?

But the scale of the thing! All that stir and drudge, all that hubbub and hustle! The sheer damn monumentality, I mean. Really, it was like we were building these pyramids of the latter-day.

Which didn't make me Moses.

•   •   •   •

I arrived in Alaska on March 27, 1974, ten years to the day exactly since the great earthquake that nearly destroyed Anchorage, moved the entire Chugach mountain range five feet to the west and sent Valdez and much of southern Alaska tumbling into the Gulf of Alaska. And I tell you that even in March's soapy, sluggish light I'd never had such an impression of distances. It was as if a mile were more profound than a mile, like those last few meters, say, compounding beneath the summits of great altitudes for mountain climbers. I'd not been the only passenger to gasp when I looked out the little porthole window of the plane as we came in over Anchorage to land and seen all that vastness and stretched space. (And it was the same on the ground, as if, in those steep, boggling latitudes, the fun-house principles took your senses, the near pushed farther off, middle distances moved to the horizon, and the horizon had somehow been pulled over its own edge and was already sliding down another side of the world.) "Mother of God, will you!" proclaimed one fellow, and "Sheesh!" another. And these weren't tourists, mind you, signed up for the sights, the points of interest. To tell you the truth, they scared me a little. I had been too long in Lud maybe, good, comfortable old Lud, too long among disturbed, distressed and distracted people, but *Jewish* disturbed, distressed and distracted people. These folks were like echt goyim, or no, not goyim, echt or otherwise, not anything religious at all finally, so much as just your off-on-a-tear, boys-will-be-boys, wild-oat-sowing, salad-day drunks, brawlers and killers. Like me, most of them had answered the Alyeska company ads in the paper to get here, but not half a dozen among them seemed to have left actual houses. They seemed like men airlifted off oil platforms. They came down from watchtowers in forests, a lighthouse's tight, spiral stairs. Sleeping in scaffolding, gantry, snug cement cubbies along the infrastructure of municipal industry— car barns, little rooms behind steel doors in subway tunnels. They lived on houseboats, or maybe in tents. They lived on sleds by sidings on railroad tracks, in converted buses, near mine shafts, in the wide cabs of trucks, and long trailers near high wooden fences on the rough, muddy, broken-glass-littered ground of construction sites.

"Boy," I told the guy sitting in the window seat when the hostess brought our lunch, "if I had a nickel for every tattoo."

"Yeah, what about it?"

"Well," I said, "I'd be a lot richer."

"What about it?"

"And maybe I wouldn't itch so much. Yours don't itch?"

But I was wrong to be afraid of them.

Though the plane had landed just after five, it was almost seven in the evening by the time I checked into the Travelodge. Anchorage wasn't much, not the city it is today, but the airport was a sort of no-frills O'Hare, booming, busy, unadorned as a discount department store and everywhere still under construction. Getting a cab was murder. Or rather getting out of the airport's two narrow, crowded lanes and into open traffic was. Virtually every four-wheeled vehicle in town had been pressed into service as a taxi. (I had to share a ride into downtown Anchorage with a fellow in some guy's metered wrecker, my two suitcases stuffed into the back with his duffel bag by the pulleys and chains, the big iron hook heavy as an anchor.) It was a kind of Marne, some Dunkirk of heroic gridlock.

I tried to call Shelley, couldn't get through to the desk, went, in my robe and pajamas, out to the lobby to a pay phone I'd seen when I checked in, but the line, which in the tiny motel lobby looked more like a milling mob—or even the deadlocked traffic in the streets—than anything as procedural as a line, was too much to deal with and I started back to my room.

"What's your name, honey?" a man asked who saw me in my bathrobe.

"Leave it alone, Spike," another man told him. "You forget it's Alaska? You ain't never heard of the high cost of living?

Wait till you put some of that pipeline graft into your pockets before you try to make out with the hookers."

"Ah, shit," the first man said, "what's money for?"

It was already after nine o'clock and too late to try to call Shelley in New Jersey. There was no room-service menu, the desk was still busy, and I was sure I wouldn't be able to get a table in the dining room, so I ate only what I was able to choose from the candy and soft-drink machines and went to bed with a sort of false satiety. This combined with the strange racket I heard in the streets—sounds of traffic, punches, the raucous camaraderie of drunks—and reminded me again of the Marne and Dunkirk impressions I'd had earlier. It really *was* like wartime. Like being in some sleazy R&R town away from the fighting. Also, there'd been that ribbing I'd taken in the lobby. It had been good-humored enough, but that's not why I was wrong to be afraid of them. Some were just kids—it was the beginning of the post-hippie era—intent on an adventure, out to pick up a trade, earn a few bucks and smoke some good dope under the aurora borealis, but that's not why I was wrong to be afraid of them either.

In the coffee shop the next morning it gave me a kick to see reindeer steak on the menu and I seriously considered having some with my eggs, but then I thought, Putz, you're in Anchorage, a thousand miles from the Arctic Circle, maybe two thousand from the North Pole. It wouldn't be fresh. And I laughed out loud, the joke being that it was on there strictly for the tourists, a tourist item, like all the Wisconsin cheese they tried to sell you as soon you crossed the state line from Illinois when I was a kid, or pecans the minute you hit Georgia, or Key lime pie as soon as you put your toe in Florida. And the cans of beer for two bucks a pop that they dispensed from the vending machines outside my room and from which I'd bought my dinner last night, the pony bottles of booze at five dollars apiece, and even the outrageous prices themselves, that was tourist stuff, too, local color, and it was actually reassuring, in the sense that I was on familiar ground, to realize that Anchorage was a tourist trap. It cheers you to get the lowdown on a place. It cheers you to be able to shift into the rabbi mode in unfamiliar parts of the world. But neither is that why I was wrong to be afraid of them.

After breakfast I went back into the lobby to phone Shelley and tell her I was all right. There was a line but nothing like the night before and, when I put my call through, I sat down to wait for the cab I'd called after I'd told Shelley good-bye. The guy who'd kibitzed me about my robe was there, though he didn't recognize or even notice me. And some kick-ass, shtarker types I'd seen on the flight coming in. They wore T-shirts and blue jeans, most of them, and looked in their colorless, climateless clothes rather like sailors. They were speaking a sort of quiet shop-talk that I suddenly, even unexpectedly, recognized as conversation and, without understanding why, I was moved and had to lift my handkerchief to my eyes to conceal the fact that they'd filled with tears. Maybe it had something to do with their jargon. As a rabbi, I'm a sucker for jargon, the sense it gives of community, solidarity. Or I might have been touched by my own, or all our distance perhaps. I was a long way from far-off New Jersey and I had a sense that they were even farther than I was. They were telling each other (and themselves, too, I thought) of their areas of expertise, throwing around the names of the various equipment they were checked out in, the rigs they were qualified to drive, the lengths of the fuses they were permitted to light, the tonnages they were ordained to bring down with dynamite, the acetylene power they were certified to spark, speaking of all their graduated tolerances as of recently inspected elevators, their earned sufferances and lenities— all their official, documented powers and strong suits, gifted in trowelers and dozers and yard loaders, the teamsters' knacks, the oilers' and operators' known ropes, their competencies and aptitudes, métiers and flairs, green-fingered in black top and carpentry and all the alchemies of poured cement. Yet a curious, even cynical subtext underlay their conversation. Much was bluff and some implied consent that it was all right to bluff. It had to do with the nature of the enterprise, as though they were enlisted men in furious us/them contention with Authority.

Was there a broche for laborers?

God spare these men, I prayed. Protect them from frostbite and snow blindness, don't let them fall through holes in the ice and keep their feet from stumbling into treacherous crevasses.

And where did *I* get off, I wondered, praying such prayers instead of pouring it on like any ordinary Jew with his customary mash notes and love letters?

"Uh-oh," said this guy from the night before, the one who'd reminded his pal about the cost of living in Alaska, "ain't that a company bus just pulled into the drive?"

"Big yellow mother?"

"I'd fucking say so."

"Who's the asshole coming off?"

"Honcho holding on to his faggot briefcase like a schoolgirl?"

"Cocksucker with the mincy-ass wiggle-waggle?"

"Guy looks like he's walking on his pinkie fingers?"

"Oooh, he thinks he's gorgeous. Doesn't he think he's gorgeous?"

"Spike thinks anyone in a suit and tie is gorgeous."

Spike smashed his left fist into his right palm. "Guy dressed like that is just asking for it. Like handing out an engraved invitation to the old bunghole investigation. This is what I believe."

The door opened and a well-dressed man with a briefcase came into the lobby of the Travelodge. The men snuffed out their cigarettes. Spike removed his dark woolen watch cap.

"I'm McBride," McBride said in an uninflected, middle-level executive voice, and took a paper from the pocket of his overcoat. "Acknowledge who you are when I call your name. —Ambest?" he said.

"Here."

"Anderson?"

"Yo."

"Jeers?"

"Present."

"James Krezlow."

"I'm your man."

McBride looked up from his list. "Look," he said, "why don't you just keep the Here's, Yo's, Present's and I'm-your-man's to yourselves? A simple 'yes' will save all of us time. —Peachblow."

"Yes."

"That's right, Peachblow. Schindblist. Is that right? Schindblist?"

"That's right," the cost-of-living man said.

"You're Schindblist?"

"That's right."

"Yes," Spike spoke up for him. "Yes, sir, he is."

McBride looked at Spike, whose real name turned out to be Jack Nicholson, the same as the actor's, then called out the rest of the names on his list. When he was done three people were unaccounted for and there was some difficulty about Jeers's credentials.

"We haven't got time to train you," McBride said. "Either you're checked out in jackhammer or you're not checked out in jackhammer."

"Ain't there a letter in there from my union rep?" Jeers said. "Geez, he told me he'd send it. Probably with how the mails are these days it might have been held up, but he sure said he'd send one, sir. He gimme his word."

"The union doesn't certify you," McBride said, "the company does."

"I been working in Alabama, Mr. McBride. I think it's a different statute in Alabama."

"You get on that bus you have to qualify. We'll give you a test at the camp but if you don't pass you have to get back here on your own. Plus you'll owe Alyeska for a bus ride."

"Could you just tell me what that test covers?"

"It covers jackhammer," McBride said. A few of the men giggled.

"Because I don't think it's fair to be checked out on a machine in one state and then have to be checked out on it all over again in another," Jeers whined.

"It's better than five hours to camp," McBride said. "Anyone has to go potty, he'd better make his arrangements now while I take care of the bill for the rooms. How do you like this, Peachblow?" he said. "Just like when we took that trip cross-country with the folks when we were kids. All right," he said, "America needs its oil. If I called your name and we understand each other you can board the bus."

McBride stepped to the desk and some of the men went toward the men's room while a few others started past me on their way to the bus.

"That is one hard-assed wonkie," Jack Nicholson muttered.

"Lord Fauntleroy? He's fucking Kitty Litter."

"He's catfood."

"He's pussy meat."

But they'd turned meek as lambs, sheep in blue collars, these drunks and scufflers of the night before. Why, I could have been their rabbi for them! I'd been out of the world, holed up in Lud, the familiar to too many mourners, their tamed rage and creped huff, and forgotten how many affronted hearts there are, the fat census of the peeved. If you took away their right to kibitz reality, what did you leave them? Jeers's makeshift injuries and whiney griefs were real, however inexpert he may have been with a jackhammer. He'd been led to expect. Never mind what he'd been led to expect, never mind who had led him to expect it. So I'd been wrong to be afraid of them because my fear made theirs redundant. This is what I believe.

Through the big plate-glass window I watched the men climb onto the Alyeska bus, its yellow oddly crusted and used up in March's dishwatery morning light. They looked vulnerable against the Travelodge logo— a teddy bear in a nightcap and nightshirt holding a candle in a saucer.

McBride turned from the desk and noticed me for the first time. "Are you—" He referred to the sheet he'd been reading from. "Just a minute. Are you Rodenhendrey or Cralus? Is your name Fiske?"

I shook my head.

They swaggered out of the men's room.

"Hold on," McBride said, put his hand into his pocket and took out a second sheet of paper. "Rabbi Goldkorn?"

"Yes," I said.

"You don't go up today," he said. "You fly out tomorrow with the bush pilot who's bringing in the Hebrew supplies."

"No, I know," I said. "I came a day early."

"You're a rabbi?" a man asked me who'd remarked McBride descend from the bus earlier.

"I am," I said, "yes."

"It's how guys talk," he whispered. "We don't mean nothing, Father," he said, and left to board the bus with the others.

•   •   •   •

This time the cab looked as if it might have been a bread truck in another life, a floral telegraph delivery. Like strangers everywhere I referred to the scrap of paper in my hand and pronounced the address to my driver like a question, as if we both knew such a place couldn't exist, that I'd given him the scam numbers and cross-streets of vote fraud. All he did, though, was simply nod, shift his truck into gear, and move it into the street. Cab drivers are wonderful, the tight tabs they keep on their communities.

After we left downtown where neon flared boldly against the ground-level windows of the bars and restaurants like bright shelving paper in a kitchen cabinet, Anchorage became a little less visible in the dusty light and began to look vague, muffled, some wood-frame, firetrap town.

The only totem poles I'd seen had been logos, their power drained out of them, like the sun or a mountain on a license plate, an explorer on a stamp. It had already occurred to me—the snap of reindeer steak sizzling on the grill, the sixteen-bit beers in the vending machines—that our forty-ninth state knew how to hype itself, and I'd begun to doubt it. To suspicion the neither-here-nor-there quality—it was March 28, we were only barely, only technically out of winter—of the light and temperature—it was colder in Lud—and to suspect that highest summer's midnight sun would, when it finally shone, turn out to be just another pale metaphor. Just as the Dangerous Dan McGrew types I'd seen in the Travelodge and had heard stumbling and singing their way out of the various Yukon and Klondike and Malamute saloons last night had turned out to be actors. Though, who knows? You can't argue with wreckers and bread trucks changed into taxicabs, or with men in suits springing for eleven-hundred-dollar motel tabs without turning a hair. There was this gushered and gold-rushed, ship-come-in and struck-it-rich feel to things. *Something* was stirring, some new bonanza shining through the chazzerei.

•   •   •   •

Rabbi Petch lived in a neighborhood that was familiar to me, though I couldn't think why. There was something mill-town to the texture of things, something peculiarly, even tragically, "American" about it. Then I realized why it seemed so familiar. It was the kind of place I'd seen flooded out on the news, the kind of place tornados touch down, or that gets evacuated in the dangerous wake of overturned freight cars from which clouds of poison gas are escaping. The irony, of course, was that the earthquake which had destroyed so much of Anchorage had left this neighborhood unscathed.

The houses weren't shabby so much as vaguely exposed, their pores open to the weather, the paint chipping and the metal chairs on the porches rusting out. It was a bungalow sort of neighborhood, raw and rugged, though I was under no illusion about what such places cost. Rabbi Petch had written me about the immense construction costs in Alaska, the high price of land. You could pick up a thousand acres in the wilderness for less money than you'd pay for a good used car, but it might cost you fifty to sixty thousand dollars for a small lot in a city like Anchorage where the sewers and electric and phone lines were already in.

And just who was this changed, charged-up guy, myself, I wondered, already worrying overhead, list price, living expenses, the price of beans—I'd rubbernecked the big red numbers in the windows of the supermarkets, chalked on the blackboards outside the gas stations, and tried to read how much the price of a ticket would set me back off the little sign in the cashier's cubicle of the movie theaters—just who was this new economic being, me, Spiritual Man figuring, comparison shopping, getting his estimates, counting his chickens? I hadn't had to think about this stuff since moving to Lud. Who was I kidding? I'd *never* had to think about this stuff. And why, I wondered, was I so perky? What was so awfully terrific about real life?

"Rabbi Petch? It's me, Jerry Goldkorn," I chippered at the man who came to the door and peered through the blinds at me.

"We don't need any," he said, and turned away.

"I've come thousands of miles. Rabbi Petch? Rabbi Petch?"

"Who wants to know?"

"It's me, Jerry Goldkorn. *Rabbi* Goldkorn? From Lud, New Jersey? We've corresponded."

He opened the door a ways, studied me for a minute, then stepped aside so I could enter. I put three fingers to my lips, kissed them, and touched them to the mezuzah on the door frame, seeing too late that it was a thermometer.

He stared at me. "Boy," he said, "are *you* religious! Never mind, it's an honest mistake in this country. Come in, *hurry*, come in, you'll let in the iceberg." He shut the door behind me. "Did you hear a weather report? Is it supposed to snow?"

"I haven't seen a paper, I didn't watch the news. But it seems pretty nice out, fairly clear, not very cold."

"Nice out," he said, "clear. Not very cold. Oh, boy, have *you* got a lot to learn! Don't stand *there*! What's wrong with you? Quick," he said, "go to the southwest corner of the living room!"

"The southwest—?"

"Where all the furniture is."

It was true. All the furniture in the rabbi's small parlor seemed to have been stuffed into a single corner. Even his books. It looked as if he were waiting for movers to come and put it all on a truck.

"I don't even bother taping sheets of plastic to the windows anymore, tacking felt strips to the threshold."

"You don't?"

"Nah," Rabbi Petch said. "What, are you kidding me? Insulate *this* place? Ol' Hawk want to come through, you think he let some itty piece of felt stop him? A dinky piece of plastic? Don't make me laugh. *Shit!* He huff and he puff and he *blow* the house down."

I gathered the rabbi was hipped on weather. He seemed to read my mind.

"I think about it more than I do about God," he said. "I *reflect* on it!"

"On weather?"

"What then?" he said. "Of course weather, certainly weather. You have to. You see anything else around here? You want to stay alive in this climate you have to."

"Actually, it's rather pleasant out."

"It can turn on you like *that*," Rabbi Petch said. "Storms blow up in a minute. A tempest, a blizzard. Gales, cloudbursts, the avalanche. Hoarfrost and rime. Lightning and thunder. All the inclements. There's no telling what could happen. The northern lights could melt your frostbite, take off your toes. A glacier could fall on your foot, sandstorms from Araby put out your eyes."

"Really?"

"Sure," Petch said, "absolutely. Spit, fire! Spout, rain! Blow, winds, and crack your cheeks! Rage, blow, you cataracts and hurricanoes! Hey," he said, "you want a cup of tea?"

"I wouldn't want you to go to any trouble."

"What trouble, I'm glad of the company. Go to the south-west corner of the room and sit down. Make yourself comfortable, I'll put on the kettle. No," he said, "push the piano out of the way. Try to squeeze your behind *past* the desk and sofa. Watch out for your knees, that wooden bench is murder. I think you'd be more comfortable in the La-Z-Boy. Just don't lean back."

I could hear him humming to himself in the kitchen, apparently as free of worry as any happy-go-lucky kid who'd never even heard the *word* "meteorology."

As I had reminded the rabbi, we'd been corresponding. He was listed under Alaska in *Who's Who in the Rabbinate*, and I'd first written him a week or so after I'd answered Alyeska's little classified in the *Times*. He hadn't mentioned weather in those letters and now I thought I understood why. He didn't want to scare me off. It was supposed to be a tradeoff. If things worked out. A good word from him to his board, a good word from me to Tober and Shull. (Who would have snapped him up, who even back then, in the seventies, weren't besieged by rabbis who wanted any part of their job—my job—who'd had to replace me with a kid still in yeshiva and, in return for my promise to return to Lud after a year, had permitted Shelley and the baby to stay on in that company house in that company town.) He'd been the one to introduce the possibility of my staying in Anchorage in the event I liked it up here. He'd made Alaska's frontiersmen Jews sound fascinating, hunters, fishermen, firemen, farmers— all busted stereotype, exotic, say, as black cowboys. In one letter he'd written that gentiles controlled the garment and jewelry store industries, that if you wanted to buy

your wife a mink coat for your anniversary or have a nice
cocktail ring made up for her birthday you went to guys named
Norton or Adams or Jones to get one wholesale. It made perfect
sense, he said. It had to do with the East India and Hudson's
Bay companies. It had to do with the L.L. Bean catalogue and
the deep, goyishe roots working the frozen soils of the mercantile.

"So," Petch bubbled when he came back with our tea,
threading the obstacle course of his cornered furniture without
ever spilling a drop, "so." He eased himself onto the piano
bench, set his burden down on the desk and, despite the fact
that he'd drawn his legs as far back as he reasonably could,
crushed his knees against the sofa. "So," he said again. "Cozy."

"Very cozy," I agreed.

"Yes," he said, "but it's hard sometimes to tell the difference between what's genuinely cozy and what's only cabin
fever. That's why I won't wear the sort of shirt you've got on."

It was a red-and-black checked wool Pendleton I had on,
and I didn't know what he was talking about.

"That lumberjackie stuff. You look like a wood chopper. It
gives me cabin fever just to look at you. Brr. I've got the chills.
Brr. My teeth are chattering. I can smell your long johns."

"They wear these shirts up here."

"More folks die of cabin fever in this state than they do of
cancer, than they do of the heart attack, shoveling snow. It's
why I wear a suit, it's why I wear a tie. It's why I go around the
house like it was Yom Kippur downtown. When they find me
I'll look like I put up a fight."

"Really," I said, "it's not that bad out."

"I know what I know," the rabbi said darkly.

"What do you do about services?"

"I call off services."

"They don't object to that?"

"I tell them it's a snow day, we'll make it up later."

"They stand still for this? Does everyone have cabin fever?"

"Everyone."

"Rabbi Petch," I said, "I'm drinking your tea, I'm eating
your biscuits. It's not my place to quarrel with you, but I've got
to believe you're having me on. That maybe this is something
you do up here. Some initiation thing, to see can I take it, do I

have the right stuff, as if I'd crossed the equator for the first time, or passed the international date line. To tell the truth, you're mixing me up. In your letters you made it sound attractive. Now it's as if you were trying to spook me. It's not necessary. We had no deal. I'm not moving in on you. The people in New Jersey don't even know about you. They don't know my intentions. I *have* no intentions. I told you what the position is, what my situation entails. That this was just supposed to be a break for me, to see how I worked out in the parishes, to see could I handle the pastoral parts."

"The pastoral parts," he said. "That's nothing. That's the least of it, the pastoral parts. Even the weather, that's nothing too. Even the cabin fever. What you've got to look out for are the Russian Orthodox. You're looking at me as if I was nuts. Russians *discovered* this place. They battled the natives years, some hearts-and-minds thing. Then they converted them. They did. The Russian Orthodox church is very popular with the natives. All those onion-shaped domes that you see. You do. You see them everywhere. In Sitka. In Juneau, the Aleutians. Up and down the Kenai Peninsula. Kodiak. Even right here in Anchorage. (You know there are scholars who believe the igloo is a serendipity? That some native was trying to build a little Russian Orthodox church out of blocks of ice and snow? Monkey see, monkey do. Who knows?) Anyway, watch out for them. You see any Russian Orthodox Cossack Eskimo momzers come roaring in on their dogsleds, waving their whips over their heads, hollering '*Mush!*' and thinking whatever the word for 'pogrom' is in Eskimo, in Ice, get out of their way because they're looking to beat the living shit out of you. Hey," he said, "they learned from the best. Free Soviet Jewry, yes, Rabbi? So that's another reason I don't go out, why I declare so many snow days."

"*Mush?*"

I swear I knew what he was going to say. I swear it.

"Ice for 'Jews.' It eggs on the dogs."

And let them pass, Petch's pensées. Only the distraction of the rabbi's high-grade cabin fever. Some distraction. Some only.

One of the disadvantages of being without a wife in company is that when it's time to vamoose there's no one with

whom you can make eye contact. Your body language falls on
deaf ears. One of you can't signal to the other of you that it's
time for the baby-sitter line to be offered up, the tomorrow's-a-
working-day one. I was on my own. There should be no hurt
feelings. He means no harm. Be polite with this all-cabin-
fevered-out colleague. I shifted my weight, I cleared my throat,
I tamped at the corners of my lips with my napkin, Ice for "be
seeing you," for getting the hell out of there.

"The deal's off then?" Petch said.

"What deal? We had no deal."

"You know," he said. "I can't come to New Jersey? We
can't trade? The prince and the pauper?"

"Rabbi Petch," I said.

"Listen," he interrupted, "I make a bad first impression. I
know that. I do. I'm paranoid. Hey," he said, "if Jews had
priests and bishops I'd be on the first boat out. They'd hang me
out to dry in the diocese's designated hospital."

"Please, Rabbi."

"No, please, come on. The way *I* talk? A learned man?
Listen," he said, and lowered his voice. Close as we were, I had
to lean forward to hear him. "Listen," he said, "they don't know
what to do with me. The congregation wants to be fair. They
come over. Machers and shakers. Boiling mad. Determined.
Minds made up. Once-and-for-all written all over their faces.
But you know? They're stunned when they see. Humbled. All
of a sudden the cat's got their tongue, they don't know what to
say. They're thunderstruck in the southwest corner. They can't
do enough for me. However they were feeling, whatever was on
their minds, on the tip of their tongues, it's forgotten. All is
forgiven. And I *know* what was on their minds, the tip of their
tongues. I could say it *for* them. You know something? Once I
did. I really did. I spoke their piece *for* them. From the tip of
my tongue to the tip of their tongue.

"'Rabbi Petch,' I said, 'how are you today? Cold all
better? Good, excellent, alevay! We were worried. As a matter
of fact, Rabbi, now that you're feeling so much better, it might
be a good time to tell you something that's been on our minds,
on the tip of our tongues. Some of the board members have
noticed that you don't quite seem to be feeling your good old

self of late. Not precisely a hundred percent, not specifically par value. Well, it's this winter, Sidney. It's been a terrible winter this winter. It's taken its toll from the best of us. Dan Cohen, for example. A shtarker like Dan. Heck, Rebbe, weather like this, unrelenting, you'd be a shvontz *not* to get shpilkes. We're *all* shlepping. Anyway, we had a meeting, we put our heads together, we had a discussion.'

" 'Loz im gayn. It's been a hell of a winter, he's starving for light.'

" 'Loz im gayn? *Loz im gayn?* Loz im gayn where? Sid's a widower. His brothers are dead, his sisters. All the mishpocheh got eaten up and picked clean in the Holocaust.'

"Someone said no, someone said yes. Someone said no again. Someone looked it up.

" 'Sidney. Sid. Kid. The long and the short. We made up a collection, we collected your airfare. We dipped into capital. We collected something extra. You'll be home for Xmas, Rabbi. Come April, alevay, you'll be searching for leaven, licking a hard-boiled egg, sucking parsley and charoses from between your teeth and having Pesach with your Aunt Ida in Arkansas hiding the afikomen from the pickaninnies. Next year in Little Rock, this is your life!'

"They never had the nerve. Even after I said it *for* them they never had the nerve. They went off biting their tongues, kicking themselves in the behind. So New Jersey was my idea. I can do what you're doing. Bury people, say a few words. They'd put up with me in New Jersey, with my ways. In New Jersey I wouldn't even have ways. Only here I have ways.

"I'm a spiritual, God-fearing guy. God-fearing? He scares the bejeesus out of me. I'm very impressed. Well, He makes an impression. All the ice and that darkness, the disproportionate strength of a bear. The whiteness of whales.

"Listen," he said, "go in good health, but promise me."

"Promise you what?"

"You'll keep an open mind."

"Certainly," I said. "I will. I promise. But now," I said, "if I could just use your phone. I'll call a cab. I have to get going."

He nodded in the direction of the telephone.

"You'll write me?" he said when I'd made my call.

"Write you?"

"From the pipeline. You'll let me know how things are?"

"Sure. I'll drop you a line. Well," I said, carefully making my way through Petch's obstacle course, "thanks for the tea. And thank you for seeing me." But he wasn't listening. He was peering out the window, looking hard at whatever it was he thought he could see in the gloom, March's short daylight already shutting down.

"Is it my taxi?" I asked him.

"What?"

"Is it my taxi? Has my taxicab come?"

"What?" he said. "No. I don't like the looks of it out there. Something's up. If I were you I wouldn't even try to go out this month."

●   ●   ●   ●

Remarkable. Wait. This is remarkable. What happened. Just remarkable. Maybe I should tell you— the guy? That I shared the ride with? In the wrecker? He turned out to be my bush pilot. Same guy. The law of no loose ends. What goes around comes around. The law of the return.

Well. We didn't have such smooth sailing. To Moose Lip. Or Bear Claw. Or Seal Shit. Or Caribou Dick. Or Wolf Tit. Or whatever other made-in-its-own-image totemics the municipalities, settlements, campgrounds and wickiups went by in those cold arrondissements along that booming Ice Belt.

We came down in trees. Sergeant Preston and the Rabbi.

"I want you to know," Skyking said, "I take complete responsibility for this disaster."

"You do."

"*Complete* responsibility. The FAA won't have to come up with any black boxes on this one."

"They won't."

"Pilot error pure and simple."

"You're some up-front guy," I said, shivering, jumping about, blowing on my mittens and pounding my hands together now we were clear of the plane.

"Mea culpa, Rabbi."

"Nobody's perfect, my son," I said, larky, in extremis the wiseacre.

"I just can't for the life of me figure what happened," he said, and launched into a song and dance I couldn't follow.

"We were never higher than five or so angels," he said. "Our attitude was always righteous and the artificial horizon might have been turned off for all the pitching and banking it displayed. We weren't below, and I never busted, minimums. We enjoyed CAVU weather straight up in the civil evening twilight. There wasn't any clear-air turbulence to speak of, and I never had to crab. I could have used some cultural features certainly, but what's a fellow to do, make them up? Heck," he said, "we even had eminence. And no use for a DF steer even if there'd been an FSS on our right wing. I didn't have to lean and seemed to be greasing it on. My Pop Teases Fat Girls. Everything going so smooth we could have joined the mile-high club if either of us had felt the need or been better looking. We were never close to issuing a pan pan pan let alone a mayday, and if we were even close to coming out of the envelope *I* never heard about it. I didn't red line or run scud or catch any lint in my transponder. I topped off in Anchorage so *that* wasn't it, and if we didn't get any pireps, airmets or sigmets, it's because there just *weren't* any weather conditions. True Virgins Make Dull Company? Perfect, A-OK. I wouldn't have said boo to them over the Unicom frequencies even if I'd had the chance. Hell, my V speeds were good, to say nothing of that nice VASI light effect I was catching from the ice. Red over white, pilot's delight. I never even needed VOR, and you were with me during the walk around. I've got good paperwork, Padre. I can't for the life of me figure what could have gone wrong. If anything even did. It's against all odds."

"Maybe we didn't crash," I said. He knew too many acronyms and mnemonics, a chap too talky for the stereotype I'd have welcomed. A man in his position, in charge of machinery that can kill you, owes it to the customers to be taciturn, reserved, to play everything close to the chest. To tell you the truth, I don't even like it when the first officer on a big commercial jet chats up the scenery. His eyes should be on the instrument panel or looking out for traffic. This guy, Philip, took me

too much into his confidence altogether. Even while we were
going down Philip was hollering information at me.

"Uh oh," he shouted as the plane swung out of control and
lost altitude, "something terrible's happening! If I don't get a
handle on this situation we're going to crash and die! The skin
of this aircraft's too thin, it won't stand up to a real impact. I've
got to get her nose up over those razor pines. See, in these
temperatures the needles on the trees are like swords. All we
have to do is just brush against them *gently* and they'll slash shit
out of our gas tanks. Then it's Pow! Bam! Fuck! I'll lay you
dollars to donuts we explode! We won't even get the *opportunity*
to crash! Goodnight, Nurse, will you just *look* at the glare on
that ice? It's curtains for sure now. It's too thin. Oh, it'd hold a
couple of good-sized boys and girls on sleds and skates, but
never the weight of a crashing, runaway airplane. The way I see
it, we've got this last-minute, split-second decision to make. It's
a question of whether we want to impact in the razor pines,
explode, catch fire and die, or go for the ice and drown. Those
are the alternatives, but we have to make our minds up quick."

"The ice!" I screamed. *"The ice!"*

And even though we came down in the trees, it was good
to know that I wasn't bad at the nick-of-time, last-minute,
split-second stuff. And terrified that what had occurred to me
hadn't to Philip. That the ice may not have been as thin as he
thought, and that even if it were there might still have been time
for us to scramble out of the plane to safety.

"Wow," Philip said, as we were set down, the plane's right
wing and tail cradled, resting, hung like a hammock in perfect,
miraculous balance between the heavy branches of two razor
pines, "did you feel that? A *thermal!* A save-ass, opportune,
eleventh-hour *thermal!*"

"God is a mensch."

"Tell me about it," the pilot said, "we were going down
for the count. Of course I was putting on the back pressure
trying to get the nose up, but that updraft came out of nowhere,
caught us and set us down again gentle as Mother."

"He's a baleboss."

"A *thermal!*" he said. "In Alaska! At *this* time of year!
We're sitting pretty in the trees. As if we were held in so many

palms." He started to laugh. "In *Alaska*! *Palm* trees!"

"He got de whole worl' in he han'."

Now, an hour or so into the aftermath, we were still cozy. We could have been soldiers before an attack, talking things over, our sweethearts back home, our plans for the chicken farm once the war was over. We could have been brothers sharing a bedroom, boys in a treehouse discussing the mysteries. We could have been crash victims. We could have been warmer.

The plan was to stay in the plane until it was light enough to see. Then, carefully as we could, we would try to extricate ourselves from the cabin, one of us looking out for the other and displacing his weight like a fellow leaning back out over the sea in a boat race.

What Philip had forgotten, and what I hadn't known, was that though we were only three or four hundred miles north of Anchorage, the threaded latitudes and longitudes of earth were already drawing together, coming to a point, light tightening, geography's diminished lattices and trellises, actually closing in on themselves, its patchwork weave of time and distance drawing together toward the perfect gathered pucker of the Pole. It was the old deceptive business of altered space I'd first noticed when we were landing at the Anchorage airport. Something happened up here. Time and space confounded each other. Tricks were played. At any rate, first light didn't break until around noon. We'd been caught in the trees at about six o'clock the night before, stuck in the small plane for maybe eighteen hours, peeing in thermos bottles, jars of instant coffee, pots and pans, like vandals pissing up a storm in your kitchen. And whenever the cramp in our bodies got too great and one of us had to move, the other watched him in the great concentrated dark and compensated for his movements, contracting as he stretched, shifting in mirror image. We were like people crossing a tightrope together.

"I'm yawning on three," said Philip.

"Go ahead," I said, "I'll swallow and cover for you."

Which stood us in good stead when it finally got light. And we saw just how precarious our purchase really was.

"Christ," I said.

"Jesus," said Philip.

We hung by a thread.

"The thing of it is," Philip said, "we don't want to go make any sudden movements that would tend to tumble this aircraft out of its tree." He was whispering. "The thing of it is, we'll be wanting to wait for a hard solid freeze to come up, then push the son of a bitch while it's still in one piece out onto the lake ice—see," he said, "it's just water—so's we can take off again someday."

"Where are we?"

"God," Philip said, "*I* don't know where we are. I'm all turned around. Lots of this country ain't ever been mapped. For all I know *we* discovered this place."

Making use of all we'd learned in the dark about each other, our close-order drill valences and physics (though neither of us mentioned it—we weren't the same height; I was taller, he was heavier—I could have told you Philip's weight to within half a pound; he could have told you mine), it still took us almost two hours to climb down out of the plane. He had lain an open toolbox on the seat and spread out various tools between us like a complicated run of cards. From these we chose iron chunks of ballast to stuff into the pockets of our parkas. Now we moved stiff as figures on a big Swiss clock. He opened his door. I reached for the hammer. He moved his head like a pitcher shaking off a sign. I picked up a wrench and leaned my head against my window. He raised his left leg and swung it slowly toward the open door. I put a hammer and jar of nails into my coat. I opened my door and turned both knees toward it. He reached back and took a pliers and screwdriver into his hand. I drew a file, he drew an ax handle. I picked up a knife. He picked up a chisel and a planing tool. "Can you reach your arm back behind your seat and get my duffel bag?" he said. "Watch it, it's heavy."

"Jesus, it is." I felt the plane rock.

"Wait," Philip said, "let me help." Together we brought the big duffel up over the seat and maneuvered it between us. We were practically back-to-back now, poised at our open doors. "All right," he said, "is that your briefcase back there?"

"About five or six pounds," I told him.

"Empty it," Philip said.

I pressed the buttons that released the hasps, overturned the briefcase and let its contents spill out. I handed Philip the empty case.

"Can you get my duffel?"

"I already have."

"That's gin then!" Philip declared, and both of us dropped out our opened doorways and fell the ten or so feet to the ground below.

Which is when he went into his rant about angels and attitudes and minimums that remained unbusted. His rap about crab, eminence, and the civil evening twilight. The old Alphabet Soup Rag— all CAVU, DF steers and V speeds. When he didn't red line or run scud and butter wouldn't melt in his mouth. Pireps, airmets and sigmets— *that* old black magic. Essentially good news his disacclamation of responsibility. Essentially music to my ears this music to my ears. I knew that by laying our mishap at the feet of magic, he was indicating we might just get out of this yet.

Though I barely heard him, was scarcely listening. Too taken with where I was. (I didn't *know* where I was.) Studying what I would probably be able to see for only another hour or hour and a half. The queer, mysterious, hidden sun not so much shining as somehow manifest behind a scrim of sky, its light like the stretched-out color of water in a cup. The endlessly repeated shape of the almost colorless trees that seemed, across the lake, to follow the steep curve of the otherwise featureless earth. I had thought of wilderness as a profusion of texture and color and life, some extravagant display, but this, this was what wilderness really was. I couldn't conceive of such emptiness. Did God know about this place? Maybe Philip was right. Maybe we discovered it. How could it be mapped? It was unmarked. No birds, I was sure, dwelt in its trees. Did fish swim in its greasy, unannealed water? Nothing lived here. Strike the earth anywhere here, with a pick, with an ax, and you'd crack soil permanently frozen, make a sound faintly brazen, some shrill chip of noise. God worked with the political, with the cantons and cities and principalities. With the nations and kingdoms. He needed a side to be on. Someplace populated enough to support a franchise. He's this through-and-through

City-Kid God and never took hold in wilderness. Which is why, counting pit stops in Sinai, it took the Jews forty years to cover the hundred and fifty or hundred and sixty miles from Cairo to Canaan.

Dear Rabbi Petch, I thought in my letter. How are you? I am fine. Who owns the North Pole? The whiteness of whales indeed! Yours truly, Jerry Goldkorn.

"Hey," Philip said, "we've got to figure some way to get that plane down from out of them trees before some big wind comes up and does it for us. Did you ever use an ax?"

I explained how certain classes of men contracted heart attacks just mowing their lawns.

"Oh," Philip said.

"Not me," I said. "I don't mean me. Did you think I meant me? Give me a break. I've split kindling and made little balls out of newspaper. I've built fires in fireplaces."

We chopped at branches and felled trees until full dark when it became too dangerous to continue. That night we lay together under the branches and pine needles for warmth.

And worked until dark again the next day and slept once more under our wooden blanket, developing in those odd, four-hour daytimes a curious, exhausting jet lag, time flip-flopped, bringing me awake at one and two in the morning with a terrible urgency to crap in half-dozen-ounce increments the twelve-ounce-per-person provisions it was actually state law in those days that pilots carry aboard their planes in the event of just such emergencies. Philip was different. He felt the urge as soon as it got dark at three-thirty in the afternoon.

And were at it again at the crack of noon on the fourth day too. Chopping until we had enough wood to make a six-foot wooden hill beneath the airplane and enough left over to build a blanket.

Then, close work this, we filed and sliced at the trees in which our plane was cradled, cutting away at boles and projecting branches like butchers trimming fat.

With long levers we carefully poked and pried the plane loose from out of the smoothly forked branches we had molded for it, and lowered it gently onto its new wooden base.

Somehow it struck me as a very biblical and oddly satisfactory solution.

Now, kept from the wind, we could sleep in the plane. Though I must be frank and tell you it wasn't easy that first night. We dozed on and off. We were, of course, both of us gamy. But that wasn't it. Though perhaps, in a way, it was.

Don't misunderstand. I'm talking here of some dark, masculine nostalgia. My sense that night of my own and Philip's rough stubble and all the soured perfumes of our decay. Each other's proximity a vouchsafe of the mortal. Oh, oh, this is hard. I'm looking for the clay equivalencies, some queer mix of broken exhalation and busted wind at close quarters on a haimish plane. The knowledge between us of our seasoned, salty flies and marked underwear. Never all night to be without the strange assurance that all men are fleishik and stand contrary to the principles of such a clean, inhospitable geography of raw phenomena, human finger-food in all that ice and in all that darkness against the disproportionate strength of the bears. Suddenly realizing the wind hadn't blown once during those four nights when we required calmness to keep the plane slung snug and orderly as a hammock in its trees. Yea, oh yea, I thought, grateful to a God Who answers the rough rabbinics of even unasked prayer, and wondered: *Hard? Hard? What's* so hard? There are no difficult davens. Ain't it just like I told Philip? Don't he do *too* got de whole worl' in he han'? Forgetting for the moment to remember where we were, where we were *really*, unconscious of all those raw, difficult, powerful phenomena— the tundra and temperature and true magnetic north. Out of my rabbi mode and chatting away with Philip, who couldn't sleep either. In the fetid cabin of the grounded airplane recruited yet once more into the sedated collegiality we'd shared after the initial excitement of the crash, Philip just beginning to tell me something about his duffel bag when both of us noticed that other wonder—the crack of the noonday dawn. To see—talk of mortality—that we'd been caught with our pants down.

The wind hadn't blown. It had remained calm, had it? Yes? God answers even unasked prayers, does He?

Two huge black bears, drawn great distances through the crystal neutrality of the calm, windless air, by our poor scat, stooped to sniff where we'd squatted on either side of the airplane; then, standing upright, looked up at the machine in which we were sitting and made a face.

"Oh, Jesus," Philip murmured. "Oh, Jesus Christ."

"Surely," I whispered, "they've seen airplanes before."

"Oh, Jesus."

"They *must* have."

"Sure," Philip said, "lots of times. Maybe what interests the sons of bitches is that they ain't never before seen one that could throw down one or two dozen razor pines, saw them up into manageable logs, knock them into a roost, then fling its shit out of the nest after it was done with it."

"They think we're a bird?"

"Do they think they can take us is what. Listen," Philip said, "Jerry, I've heard about this. Some clowns like to hunt out of airplanes. Hang a rifle out the window and potshoot anything that moves. Wild West antics. Like standing on the observation platform and offing the buffalos. Strictly illegal, of course, and a bush pilot would lose his license if he ever got caught, but it happens."

"Did you do this?"

"What, shoot? Hell no, I don't even fish."

"Fly the plane," I said. "For the hunter."

"Do you know what it was like up here before the pipeline? Oh, sure," he said, "now it's all boom town and gold rush days, but you come back in a few years, after it's done, and they'll have invented the Rough 'n' Tough industry. There'll be roustabout museums wherever you look. Nostalgia cakes. Maybe there'll even be a Bush Pilot Hall of Fame. And except for maybe something a little less than a tiny handful of World Canned Salmon Corporate Headquarters down in Anchorage, there won't be nothing else here. It'll be like it was before the pipeline. Because this country won't *ever* be civilized. I've got nothing to apologize for. I'm a bona fide pioneer. Pioneers do things. They'd do other things if they could, but they don't always have the choice."

This, it seemed to me, was inappropriate, improbable conversation to conduct while seated inside an airplane mounted on a heap of logs actively mistaken for a giant pterodactyl-sized bird by fierce bears in open country, but Philip, either propelled by guilt or driven by some idée fixé, had evidently hit upon his theme and was apparently content to explain himself to me at even greater length. Always while he spoke the notion never left my head that at any given moment he might become so exercised that the bears would mistake his passion for some loose atavistic theme that turned on the smell of rage and apoplexy and that then, out of simple, time-honored principles of self-defense and self-preservation, they would storm the plane and kill us. He continued.

"So don't charge *me* with breaching the codes or violating the folklore. The most they can get me for is unsportsmanlike conduct. What I did they don't even throw you in jail for. They can suspend your license, hit you up for a fine, but we're still talking the thin end of evil. I don't even *own* a rifle. Tops, I was an accessory. All I did was drive the getaway car. Do you know what it was like up here before the pipeline? Like some frozen fucking Appalachia, that's what."

"Hey, easy," I said, alarmed by his excitement.

"You want a statistic? That could give you the idea? Do you? Listen to this. In the fifteen years since they've been keeping records, you know how much money has been made from shoveling snow up here? I'm not talking about the highway department or the department of streets. You know how much? Clearing off snow? Counting kids, counting guys out of work? None. Zip. Not a nickel. They're an independent people. They shovel their own walks, put in their electric, their plumbing. You'd think there'd be odd jobs, that it'd be the odd-job capital of the world up here. The hell you say. Nothing doing. You got a plane, you do what they tell you. If either one of those mothers think I'm responsible that their relatives were turned into carpet or a trophy for the game room, let the record show I ain't the only one. There's plenty could be tarred with *that* brush!"

"Please," I said, "you're giving off frenzy. If *I* smell chemicals on you, what do you suppose those bears make of you?"

"I don't care," Philip said, "death's death. They're shot from a plane, they're picked off by some mug in the snow. Tell me the difference again.

"Anyway," he said, "I ain't any Lucky Lindy. I ain't no Red Baron. I couldn't pick and choose my jobs and ways. Not everyone gets to fly the medical supplies into the village or make the dramatic drop on the pack ice, the radio equipment, the flares and toilet paper. Even if I'd been a better pilot I could never get in with the right people, the environment monkeys and wilderness teamsters that run this place. It's enough they let you hang around to do the dirty work and odd jobs."

"You said there weren't any odd jobs."

"What odd jobs there were."

"What odd jobs were there?"

"What do you think?" he said. "I smuggled snow."

And this conversation improbable too, yet suddenly flashed back to the halcyon days when we were cozed comrades, the sedated collegiality of those predawn hours before it was over the top. While we were still boys in the treehouse chatting up the mysteries.

"Because there really ain't any economy," Philip said. "Not in any 'Hey, patch your roof for you, mister?' sense there ain't. Not in any 'Who'll take these caribou steaks off my hands for me?' one. Not even in any underground sense— stolen goods and tips and money passed under the table. The cash crop up here is wilderness itself."

"Tourism?"

"I'm not talking about tourism. I'm talking about climate, I'm talking about distance. It's a cold culture. I already told you," he said, "I smuggled snow. I was a snow smuggler."

"I don't know *what* you're talking about," I said impatiently.

"Rabbi, the morning I picked you up, did you have breakfast at the motel?"

"Sure," I said. "Yes."

"Can you remember what it cost you?"

"It was expensive," I said, "twelve or thirteen dollars."

"What we do here," he said, "—you, me, Alyeska, the cab drivers on their dogsleds and snowmobiles, the blue-collar help that flies in every day from the Outside, all them wilderness teamsters—is factor cost into the price of soup, jimmy profit and inflation into the price of doing business. We're *all* smugglers."

"The bears," I said. "one of the bears . . ."

"Don't make eye contact with the bastard. They see everything. They read lips. Nothing gets by them. Nobody can show them a poker face good enough. Let's just continue our chat."

"Tell me," I asked nervously, "you said you'd heard about this. Has it happened before?"

"What? You mean to me?"

"Yes."

"The silly gringo son of a bitch I was with, he had me fly in low so he could get a better shot. He mowed one down like it was Dillinger."

"With a rifle?"

"With a machine gun." Philip shuddered.

"What?"

"There were two bears. One got away. The Tlingits say bears hold grudges, that all animals do. That they pass their wrongs on in some deep, blood-feud way. I was just thinking," he said, "that what if what drew these two was revenge? That, I don't know, maybe they caught a whiff of 10w-20 up their muzzle and think they're on to us."

I glanced at this fellow with whom I'd been sharing the close quarters of the cabin for almost a week. We would probably die together. It hadn't occurred to me you could die with people you didn't much like. Clearly you could, however. One of the beasts, the one who'd been nosing around in my cold feces, began to swing its long head like a signal in the direction of the cockpit, pointing us out to its companion in some sidelong, ursine "Get this." As instructed, I bobbed and weaved out of range, refusing eye contact. "Is there anything else we can do?" I asked breathlessly.

"Like what," Philip said, "crouch down under our desks with our heads covered? Everything that can be done is being done."

Oddly, I was relieved to hear it, and, when I dared look again, the bears were gone. So now I'm convinced there's a certain amount of truth in what Philip told me. There's magic in lying doggo. And if this is a conclusion of ostriches and doesn't always work—there was difficulty, recall, when we resorted to it as a principle in warding off the Nazis—sometimes it does. As with most magic you have to pick your occasions. And know the beast you deal with, too, of course. But I was relieved as much by Philip's bravery as by anything else. On which I complimented him.

"Hell," he said, "if you can't be a wise man, you might as well be a brave one."

"Maybe you're a wise one too," I said. "You seemed to know your onions with those bears."

"Nah," he said, "wise men don't get into things."

"Like what? This little setback with the airplane? You'll get us out of it. I've every confidence. Sooner or later someone has got to pick up one of those radio messages you've been sending. We're as good as rescued."

"What? From this?" He spoke into the microphone attached to his headset. "Calling all cars, calling all cars. Be on the lookout for a blue Cessna 250 crash-landed somewhere in Alaska and mounted in pine trees like an egg. Shit, Rabbi," he said, "the damn thing's been on the fritz ever since before we even got into trouble."

"The radio? What's wrong with the radio?"

"Busted," Philip said. "Out cold. It runs on the power generated by the engine."

"We're going to die, aren't we?"

"Well," he said, "it's a question."

It was a blow against optimism.

"I'm a believer," he told me suddenly.

"You?" I said. "You're Jewish?"

"No," he said, "not Jewish. A believer. In God. In the services and ceremonies. In you guys. In, you know, middlemen. Men of the cloth. In your special relationships. In, no disrespect, the mumbo jumbo. In, forgive me, the voodoo, in smoke from the campfires. Like, you know, how one minute you can be knocking off a piece for yourself, all tied up in sin and on the road to hell, say, and how the next the preacher says 'Do you take this woman, do you take this man?' and everything's copacetic in Kansas City and the eyes of God too, and you can begin the countdown to your first anniversary. A believer. A couple drops of water spritzed in the cradle cap and—bingo!—you're baptized, your sins are washed clean and some baby's a brand-new citizen of God. With the right words you can exorcise a ghost or turn a wafer and a sip of wine into God Himself. Hey, you can bless bread, or people's pets, or the whole damn commercial fishing fleet if you wanted. You probably know the words to special prayers," he said, "*that could fix our radio and get us out of here right now!*"

Well, I thought, say what you will about old Phil, he's going to die with his faith on.

"Particularly," he said, "now we got all this special Jewish equipment I was able to pick up for you before we left."

"What special Jewish equipment?"

"In the duffel," he said, indicating the bag with his chin much as the bear had indicated us. "Man," he said, "the miracles you ought to be able to work with *that* stuff."

"What is this? What have you got there?"

He picked up the duffel and set it across his lap. "Let's see," he said, undoing its flimsy fasteners, "it should all be here." He looked hurriedly through the big duffel. "Yep," he said, "it seems to be. I think so. Wait a minute, where's the cutlery, the, what-do-you-call-'em, 'yads'?"

"What? What have you got there?"

He spilled the contents of the canvas bag into my lap.

There were three Torahs in parochets, their decorated velvet mantles. I recited a startled, quick, automatic Sh'ma.

"There you go," the pilot said. "You think she's fixed now?"

"You fool, what are you talking about?"

"Hey," Philip said, "Mister Rabbi, if it takes you more time to fix the radio, then it takes you more time to fix the radio. I'm not looking for miracles. Just don't go jumping down my throat is all. Or maybe you're hunting up that gold candlestick. It's there, I seen it. See, there it is."

He reached down and drew an elaborate menorah from the pile. He pulled a paper from his pocket and began, rapidly and audibly, to scan it. It was a page Xeroxed from the Old Testament. Exodus, chapter 25, verses 31 to 40. God's commandments to Moses like a page of specs. "Let's see," he said. " 'And thou shalt make . . . candlestick . . . pure gold . . . beaten work . . . its shaft . . . its cups, its knops . . . its flowers . . . six branches . . . three branches of the candlestick . . . three cups

. . . and three cups made like almond-blossoms in the other
branch, a knop and a flower . . . four cups . . . the knops
thereof, and the flowers thereof. And a knop under two branches
. . . and a knop under two branches of one piece with it . . .
Their knops and their branches shall be of one piece with it . . .
And thou shalt make . . . lamps thereof, seven . . . And the
tongs thereof . . . snuff-dishes . . . a talent of pure gold . . .
after their pattern . . .' That's got her, I think," Philip said,
"right down to the last cup and knop. Perfecto."

"Incredible."

"Oh, and look, there's them yads." He picked up three
solid silver pointers used under the tight Hebrew text.

"Astonishing."

"Right, and you still got you an ark of shittim wood,
two-and-a-half by one-and-a-half by one-and-a-half cubits, over-
laid with pure gold coming to you if you and God ever figure a
way to get us out of there and over to a proper Atco unit where
you can set it up."

"Stupefying."

"I hope to tell you."

"What's an Atco unit?"

"Well, the men live in Atco units. They're these big metal
trailers. All connected together. You'll probably have one for
your church."

"Synagogue."

"That's what I mean," he said.

"Where did you *get* all this?" Philip, pleased as punch,
smiled widely. Not having had a congregation of my own, I'd
never had access to my own Torah before. Suddenly I was in
charge of three of them.

"Didn't McBride tell you I'd be bringing supplies?"

"I thought yarmulkes. I thought Passover Haggadahs. I
thought maybe a tallith to throw over the shoulders of my
parka."

"I'm just the delivery boy," Philip said.

"No, no," I said, "I'm not criticizing. I'm overwhelmed. I
know how expensive this all is."

"Tell me about it. A hundred-forty-five thousand dollars
for the one in Sephardic script, two hundred thousand for the

Ashkenazic. The little reconditioned Sephardic was only ninety grand, but we're still talking almost a half million bucks' worth of Pentateuch."

"Half a million? Half a *million?*"

"We got the thirty-inch rollers."

"Listen," I said, "Philip, I'm no expert, but unless these Torahs are the work of historically important scribes, they couldn't cost more than—what?—fifteen or twenty thousand dollars *together.*"

"It's like everything else. The price of Torahs is higher in Alaska. It's like what it costs for your breakfast."

"And the menorah?"

"What about it?" he said. "You know what a knop, a cup, and a flower sets you back these days? Beaten gold?"

"Come on, Philip. What's going on here?"

"Or shittim wood by the cubit and half-cubit?"

"In that ark I've got coming."

"That's right," he said softly, slyly. "In that ark you've got coming."

"How do you do it? How is it done?"

"Hey," he said, "it's nothing. There's nothing to it. It's no big deal. It's not important like the kind of thing you do. It's only money. It's no big deal. It's like a value-added tax. We're a community. Everyone belongs. Whoever handles an item, whoever orders it, or makes it, or stocks or modifies or services it, or, like me, maybe just only even picks it up and delivers it, gets to goose up its price a tick. It's, I don't know, like a chain letter or the pyramid club. You know that sooner or later it's got to come crashing down around your ears, but in the meantime, so long as the balls are all up in the air and you make sure that the last to sign on is somebody else, it works. Or seems to anyway. Alaska is a scam, man."

"I don't understand your system," I told him.

"If I told you it's tied up with grants and subsidies and government dough and oil depletion shit and blind-siding the taxpayer, would it be any clearer to you?"

"No."

"That's because you're spiritual," Philip said, beaming. "I *knew* I'd thrown in with the right guy. I knew I wasn't making any mistake when I pitched my tent next to yours."

I stared at the small biblical fortune the madman had strewn in my lap.

"Go on," he said, "why don't you give her a lick? I can see you're just itching to try."

"Give her a lick? Itching to try?"

"Why don't you up and pray us the hell out of here? Use your powers! *Rub* that old God bag! Come on, I'll help you!" He picked up a Torah in a blue velvet parochet and began to spin between his palms one of the wooden handles around which the scroll was wound. "I wish I may, I wish I might, have the wish I wish tonight!"

"Hey," I shouted at him, knocking his hands away, "hey, hey you! What is this? What do you think you're doing? What do you think this is?"

"Who's that?" Philip asked suddenly. He nodded toward my side of the airplane.

Standing just where one of the black bears had stood half an hour earlier, there was an old man.

He looks so cold, I thought. Where, I wondered, were his shtreimel, his kopote? What had he done with his kittel? Why was he outdoors without his gartel, his tallit katan? What was the reason his payes had been shorn? And why was he snowbound, abandoned in wilderness like some lost, Jewish Lear?

(Because I recognized him at once. Here was Shelley's leathered, dreamboat Jew, her fringed, blue-banded, prayer-shawled Prince. And I hadn't even seen his face yet. In our steep pine roost, settled in our mounting like some bizarre cocktail ring, we were above him looking down.)

"Far out. Who's *he* supposed to be," Philip whispered, touching the Torah, "the genie from out of this bottle?"

"Hello," I said, the ordinary greeting as odd-sounding and queer to me under the circumstances as if I'd pronounced it "halloo," abrupt and vaguely frantic as someone in Shakespeare. As if to say "How now, my lord," or "Ho, by your leave!" or "Good morrow, cousin." Or thought to say, "Who's there? Stand and unfold yourself. I charge thee speak!"

"Welcome," he said. (And still hadn't seen his face or risen above my perception of his chill despite the knit cap he wore under his hooded parka, his insulated boots, ski gloves and scarf, his padded thermal bearing. Maybe it was just his being so isolated. So lone a figure in such stripped, lone elements might have looked chilled in desert too.)

Then he leaned back to look at us.

There's something wrong with the Plexiglas, I thought. There was a glare, a distortion. Some phenomenon of the thin, freak air, an anomaly of the light, like sunshine lasered in a magnifying glass. I shaded my eyes but failed to reduce the glare. "It's bright," I said.

"It is," Philip said.

"Wait," the old man said, and placed an arm across his forehead, shielding his eyes as a shadow covered the Plexiglas and things became visible again beyond the hard, clear glass.

And he wasn't old. His features seemed those of someone vigorously middle-aged, though there was something shrugged and bent about his stance, a sort of drawn, willful hunger (despite the well-fed aura of his arctic outerwear) in the way he arranged himself on the world, like the fierce, opinionated sufferings of an anchorite, some wandered-Jew quality to his ideas perhaps, even though I didn't know his ideas, even though I . . . I don't know. Maybe he was fifty. Maybe the length and fullness of his beard had given me an impression of age. (Though how could I have seen his beard before I'd seen his face?) Perhaps the sense I had of his singleness. Listen, look, I *don't* know. I'm in even deeper than my rabbi mode, or anyone's mode, rabbi or otherwise. Because what we're talking about now, the area we're into here, are spiritual sightings, the UFO condition. Two steady, responsible guys, one a family man, an official, out-and-out rabbi, the other a pilot, accredited, licensed to fly the more exotic air lanes, above the caribou herds and musk ox and seals. (And the sky is not cloudy all day.) Somewhere over the reindeer. People you'd trust with your credulity. Though one, granted, was an odds-on crackpot. (But religious. Hadn't he proclaimed himself a believer, and wasn't all his pilot's mumbo jumbo about angels and attitude, busted minimums, turbulence, eminence and the civil evening twilight, a sort of prayer?)

Listen, look, I told you I don't *know*. I *told* you this was different, and that I'm in even deeper and way past the ordinary rabbi mode altogether. All right, okay, listen. I'm backing and filling, I'm vamping till ready. *I haven't told you about his beard yet!*

It was made out of miniature flowers.

He was an old Jew with a beard made out of flowers.

A tight bouquet of daisies and irises, jonquils, lilacs, orchids and lilies. Poppies, roses, dahlias and dandelions drawn through a long green salad and lattice of stem. There was foxglove. Buttercups were in it, tulips, white baby's breath, blue bachelor's buttons, gladiolas, peonies, columbine. Flowers like rubies, like diamonds, like opals and sapphires. There were bright vermilions and blooms like a yellowed ivory the color of sunshine on snow. Pink carnations were mixed in, lavender freesias, sweet peas, nasturtiums, chrysanthemums, phlox. A gold-and-purple, red-and-emerald beard. A black-and-orange, brown-and-violet one.

(And I hadn't even seen it yet, not face to face, was still in the plane, kept from it by the Plexiglas, separated from it by the Plexiglas the way glass mitigates and intervenes vision in a jeweler's showcase. Still thinking, if you must know, of what Philip had been telling me about the cumulative, downhill-rolling snowball accretion of value in Alaska, wondering what an arrangement like that must have set the old boy back; speculating on the worth of such a nosegay of out-of-season, greenhouse-and-hothouse-grown posies which not only had have had to be shipped in from wherever in the lower forty-eight they'd been originally nurtured and then reshipped in Alaska to whatever lost latitude this odd old Jew had given them as an address, but had have had to have been packed and repacked each time in special protective, insulated, crushproof safety papers, and then carefully fitted by hand to his cheeks and chin by maybe the specially trained Japanese flower arranger and face-dresser who probably came with them. Adding the cost, too, of the extra blossoms, the ones that had made the trip only as a safeguard, the fail-safe flowers of sudden freeze and contingency, to say nothing of the hidden costs: what it would take to keep a first-rate, top-drawer high-priced Japanese flower arranger and face-dresser like this one would have had to have been, out of commission for a few days, to pick up the tab for his hard-to-imagine, special breakfast, luncheon and dinner appetites, what you must have had to have paid to send the plane back empty, first from the lost latitude, then from the found one, but quickly, no time lost, not at his prices, because at *his* prices you could go broke just forcing a plane to hang around an airport waiting on Nature for the fog to lift. So rounding it off at—what? we'll be conservative here—thirty or forty thousand dollars for him to do his devoirs, make his morning toilette. And I still hadn't really seen it yet.)

"*Can't you hurry?*" I hissed at Philip.

"Can't *you?*" he hissed back. "Grandma was slow, but she was *ninety!*"

Because we were both busy trying to cram the menorah, Torahs and silver yads back into Philip's big duffel before the wandered old Jew guy noticed something amiss. Noticed, I mean, that we were in possession of such things. So we locked once more into our old choreographed cooperation, bobbing and weaving, pecking like pigeons, doing our close-order-drill physics and valences, those practiced displacements and compensations and overcompensations.

"What are you birds up to in there?"

"Just catching up on our housekeeping," Philip said.

"Just tidying up is all. There," I said, "that's got her," and opened my door, swung my legs around and dropped down. Philip, on his side, did the same. Once I was out of the plane again I leaned over to rub my thighs and work out the kinks. "Boy," I said, "thank God you showed up. Hey, Philip," I said, "we're saved."

Philip, walking unsteadily over the loosely piled timber, came round to my side of the airplane. He looked down skeptically at the man in the pricey FTD beard. "You know a lot about the engines in these things, do you, old-timer?" he asked.

"No no," he said, "nothing."

"But you're not lost," I said, offering the punch line of the old joke.

"No," he said. "I'm not lost."

And looked up at me. Which is when I saw that they weren't really flowers, blooms, nothing vegetable at all in fact, no lush, tight-strung festoon, no garland like some actual hat or chaplet at a girl's head, but something deep and indigenous in his whiskers and hung across his chin like a fragrant tattoo.

"Did you see any bears?" asked Philip.

"Yes," he said mildly, "two great grizzlies, wide as passenger cars. They passed by me in the woods."

"He has," I insisted, "he's come to save us."

"They passed by you?" Philip said. "They let you alone?"

"Why not?" he said. "Why would they want to hurt me?"

"He's right," I whispered to Philip, "why would they? They need him for honey. We're saved. We're saved. We're money in the bank."

"I was drawn," he said, the wandered Jew guy, "by the almost human odor of your bowels."

"What kind of a crack is that?" Philip said. "What's that supposed to mean?"

I looked at the pilot and thought to myself, Boy, some people: Here's this Philip, a fellow who claims a certain standing for himself in the mystical community, who professes a belief in God's servants' services, in their mumbo jumbo and the smoke from their campfires, who doesn't recognize a spiritual power player, and maybe even the downright wandering Jewish miracle rabbi himself, when he not only runs right smack dab into one in what, since he didn't know where he was, he couldn't even call the middle of the wilderness, but has to crash-land a plane safely in the branches of evergreens and work out the most delicate, mysterious rapport with his total-stranger passenger, when it came down to gravity, wind shear, force vectors and the like, that they could almost have, the two of them, taken their act on the road, provided they were lucky enough ever to get even close to a road again, and not only that, but had had to withstand a siege by wild bears, wide, by the wandering Jewish miracle rabbi's own dispassionate testimony, who without incident had passed by them in woods and thus had had no need to lie, as passenger cars, sedans or maybe even limousines perhaps, he didn't specify, and who, at least momentarily, would have had to have stood right there before them with the produce and proceeds of what might well have been a to-scale, ordinary English garden, right down to the odd bit of crabgrass, wrapped around his chin and cheeks!

Only what made me so sure he was even Jewish? Not his accent. He might have been a disk jockey on some easy-listening FM station. And the fact of the matter was, I *still* hadn't had a really good look at him. What I've said here, all I've put down, I've said and put down as a kind of eyewitness. The details are there but are only impressions, the sort of things I might have told to an interested police artist. I will stand by them. Later, indeed, I confirmed them. I even have a Polaroid, although it was snapped months later, in October's weak light, when the season in Alaska was lowering like a shade, and the bouquet (which tended, he said, to fade in the late months, to shine in the early, seemed dead as flowers pressed in a book), frankly, looks blurred in the picture, all the remaining dull, calico colors run together, compromising the sharp, discrete blooms of my first bright impression. (But I, a rabbi, was never such a hot photographer anyway.)

All right. Not only hadn't (had a really good look at him), wouldn't!

Wouldn't look at his beard, avoiding it not as if it were some blight or handicap, a port wine stain along his face, say, or something not there at all, the missing tip of a finger or an absent limb; not finical, fastidious, or out of any ordinary, gracious civil deference, not *shy* I mean, unless we mean God-shy, or the way a kid primed to address his Santa Claus, to climb right up there onto his lap and tell him right to his face in the middle of the department store's toy department, with all the other kids waiting right there in line behind him and possibly flanked too by his, the jolly old man's, elves and helpers, will turn shy, either forget what he has to say or rather die than say it, let the cat get his tongue, humiliate himself, break down, cry. That's why I hadn't had my really good look yet.

Well, what do you expect? A guy tells you he was drawn by the almost human stink of your shit. This could be someone important. This could be . . . All right, this could be the Messiah. Or, for this little Rabbi of Lud at least, maybe just a big-deal, big-time genuine mystical religious experience. Anyway. Even if I wasn't absolutely convinced. That this was the man. I'm going to let some fourth- or fifth-rate pilot, who makes his living hustling Torahs and letting drunken cowboys from Texas strafe holes in the bears as he does bombing runs at them

or circles over their heads in holding patterns, pass remarks and
dish out shots to such a person?

So I looked him in the face. Stared him right in his beard.
All first impressions confirmed. This was him. As far as I was
concerned. And made a little welcoming curtsy in his direction,
losing my footing, almost dislodging the pines, only at the last
minute recovering myself, running in place on the logs like a
lumberjack.

"I was wondering," said the great teacher when I had my
balance again, "do you think there might be room for me in
your airplane? I'm not looking for something for nothing and
would make it worth your while. A wealthy man I'm not, but
I'm willing to pay."

("I've heard about this character," Philip told me. "There
are legends about him from Valdez to the Pribilofs. From Natchez
to Mobile, from Memphis to St. Joe. He scares the shit out of
the natives. Everywhere he goes there's trouble.") He turned to
the man. "Oh, sure," Philip said, "that's how we do it. We
collect our party as we go along like Dorothy loose in Oz. What
do we look like, mister, a taxi rank?"

"Philip," I cautioned him, and thought, My God, a fellow
like this, with heightened, sky-high senses that can not only pick
up men's scents but evidently rehabilitate them out of the very
air right back into the compost for his beard, this is somebody to
whom you give lip? "I am Rabbi Jerry Goldkorn of New
Jersey," I said, wiping my hand off on my parka, extending it.
"I am honored to meet you, sir."

"I've been meditating for almost an entire winter solstice
now. From ice field to ice floe. From glacier to iceberg. I'm
getting a little antsy—may Shaper-of-the-World, Blessed-Be-He,
take it in His Head to forgive me—waiting for spring to come
on." (So, I'm thinking, who is this guy? He seems to have ruled
out Shaper-of-the-World, Blessed-Be-He. Maybe he ain't God
either. And ha ha, I'm joking, relieved, because as I always say,
I/Thou or no I/Thou, you don't want to go one on one with
Him.) "Too much darkness just isn't good for you," he said.
"Let there be light. Know what I mean?"

"And what's all this 'almost human odor' of our crap crap?
He still hasn't said."

("Philip," I said, "please.")

"No, no," Philip said, "I mean it. I don't have to take this kind of garbage from a hitchhiker. Boy," he said, "you run into these guys every time you set your plane down in this country. I don't know where they come from. You could be lost, you could be behind the beyond, wherever, and there they are. Waiting for you. Cadging rides. Oh," he said, even more agitated now than when he'd lost control of the plane and we were about to crash, "always hair-trigger and up-front with their worth-your-while's and willing-to-pay's. But drop the fare off on his turf and you find out quick enough just what their worth-your-while is worth."

("Philip, please, did you see his beard?")

"A fad."

("Philip, his whiskers are *flowers!*")

"So? A passing fancy. Once crew cuts were in, then it was sideburns down to your lips."

"No," said the man with the beard made out of flowers, speaking as if he hadn't heard a word of Philip's pouted rant, my own whispered admonitions. As if they'd never happened. "So much dark . . . After a while you forget why you're out there. On the ice, on the glaciers, ice fields, ice floes and icebergs. Why you came in the first place. Exercising the fancy-shmancies, holy adaptations and dreamy propitiaries that it takes to live. The kill-only-what-you-eat commandments, practicing, I mean, all the waste-not/want-nots and wearing your food for fur and leather too. Doing the live-off-the-land economies— feathering your nest with the rare sea-bird's jewelry, the ptarmigan's, the jaeger's, the eider's cushy down. At one with the seal and musk ox, with otter and bear and whale modalities, recycling very calcium itself to scratch a scrimshaw into teeth, into shell and bone. Habituating yourself to all the conservationist's far-fetched recommended daily allowances, the cosmetics of environment, giving yourself over, I mean, to the elements— the flavors of air and temperature, the shading of salmon and the bushel-per-acre yield of the tundra."

"These are among my favorite things," Philip said.

(*Philip!*)

"But it wears you out," he said. "Concentration breaks down, breaks up in the dark. (The *dark!* Not some proper,

heroic blackness you could rub yourself against like braille.) You
can't *remember* color. You're too busy yogi-ing over your bloodstream and rearranging your metabolics so you can see what it
feels like to move at a glacier's pace, a few inches a day with the
wind in your face. Isn't this so, Rabbi?"

"Well, I . . ."

"Don't worry," he said, "it's so. I stake my reputation it's
so. So, when I caught that first, unmistakable whiff of what was
almost certainly ka-ka and quite possibly *human* ka-ka, I perked
up pretty quick, I'm here to tell you."

"Yeah, well," Philip said uncomfortably, making the first
shuffled, awkward cues of leave-taking, the preliminary guttur-
als and throat-clearings of departure, though clearly there was
nowhere to go in that wilderness.

"I started out three days ago," said the man with the beard
made out of flowers.

"Three days ago. You've been tracking our scent for three
days? That's some discriminating whiffer you've got."

"Well," he said, "I'm anxious to get back to civilization."

"Oh," Philip said, "*civilization*. Sorry. We're not headed in
that direction."

"Because," he said, "I'd had enough of darkness now, and
of found frozen shelters carved right out of the very bottom of
wind and temperature. Of my fur and leather ways and depriva-
tions and being perched in such high-up altitudes of the world
like a stylite on a column. So naturally when I first smelled your
feces, Rabbi Goldkorn"—he pointed to the side of the plane
where I'd been relieving myself—"and yours, Philip"—he pointed
to the pilot's little mound—"I asked myself: 'Human? Is it
human? Could it be human? It *smells* human.' Oh, there were
trace elements of digested fish and game, of course, but you'd
expect that up here. So I broke camp and started out. I followed
your trail and, sure enough, the closer I came the stronger the
spoor, until I thought I could make out the freeze-dried vegetables, cashew mix, dried, high-energy fruits, beef jerky and
chocolate of your emergency, survivalist meals. And, what do
you know?" he said. "Here we are!"

"That's amazing," I said.

"Tell me," he said, "Rabbi, you observe kashruth?"

"No," I said, "why?"

"Nothing. The Checkerboard Square's all right, but most other survival chow's trayf."

"We don't keep kosher even in New Jersey."

"Well," he said, "you're consistent. It's a point in your favor."

"That's good," I said.

"It depends," he said. "It's also a point against you."

"Are you," I asked, "are you kosher?"

"Oh, *me*," he said, "I keep house on an iceberg. Well," he said, "fellas, I'm looking forward to getting back. What's with the airplane?"

"We crashed in the trees," Philip said. "The engine won't turn over."

"Maybe the battery's dead."

Philip rolled his eyes.

"Give it a while. Maybe the engine's flooded."

"Sure," said the pilot, "and maybe it got all bent out of shape when we crashed. Here," he said, "look," and raised the cowl to reveal the bashed, stricken metal underneath. "That lake ice isn't firm enough to hold us anyway."

"Well," said the fellow in the flowers, "I won't say I'm not disappointed, but now there's three of us. When you're looking forward to civilization again, three at least is a beginning."

•   •   •   •   •

We were back in the plane. It was night and the man with the flowered beard was talking. Loading us up on Alaska, her legends and lore. (Without once alluding to the mystery right there on his jaw. That filled the cabin with fragrance, actual individual pulses of scent that flashed on and off like some code of the botanical. Freesia, rose, chrysanthemum, fern. Lilac, carnation, orchid and iris. Peony, jonquil, spearmint. How, I wondered, had he ever tracked us? Distinguished between the rival claims offered up beneath his nose?)

He told us of a night so cold fire froze. The flames, he said, were like icicles, you could break them off. And of a summer when the light was so intense that a little of it contin-

ued to brighten the night sky into the dead of winter. He related
a story about a muskeg swamp he once came upon in the tundra
country above the Arctic Circle where the moss was so thick
whole herds of caribou and reindeer were drawn to it, entered it
and remained there, unable to move in the deep, soft muskeg
(now effectively a sort of quicksand), feeding in place until they
died. And spoke of bonanzas you *don't* hear about—the great
salmon, king crab, fur, timber, musk ox (for its qiviut, its
remarkable underfur, four times warmer than wool but a quarter wool's weight), seal, scrimshaw, whale and totem-pole rushes.
There were tales of the Indian tribes: the seafaring Tlingits who
had amassed not only a fishing fleet but a navy as well, who had
first smoked salmon and discovered lox, the Haida Indians of
Prince of Wales Island, and of the Athapaskans, and of a tribe
whose men speak one language and the women another. He
spoke of the Aleut Eskimos and of their great bush pilots who,
as a matter of pride, not only refuse to use the radios, radar
equipment, and other navigational aids the FAA requires they
carry in their planes, but won't even refer to their compasses, or
even to the stars, to guide them, relying, to find their way, on
the simple fact that they are natives, that they were there first.

"Yeah, well, that's bullshit about the Eskimo bush pilots,"
Philip said sourly. "It's right up there with the crap you hear
about igloos. I've been in lots of them and never found a warm
one yet."

Which led to a discussion of Alaskan architecture, Philip
speaking of his preferences, the Quonset hut, the trailer, even
the sod house. "Something solid," he said, "more substantial.
That you know it ain't going to melt on you the first sign of
spring."

"I don't know," said the man in the flowered beard, "would
you really want to be tied down like that?" And began to tell of
his travels: of the summer he spent among millions of brood
seals on a beach in the Pribilofs, and of another summer, on
Little Diomede Island in the Bering strait, not two miles from
the international date line, contemplating time. He'd been to
regions where you could see blue glacier bears clinging to the
ice, wide and spread as rugs, embracing the sides of the ice
mountains with their powerful claws. And to great potlatch

feasts and ceremonials all along the Inside Passage and up the high Yukon where the host provided great quantities of grizzly and musk ox and moose meat.

"Tons," he said, "literally. All you could eat."

"Is that stuff kosher?" I asked. "Bear meat, musk ox?"

"Go know," he said.

And told of one spectacular potlatch to end *all* potlatches.

"It's the custom, as you know, that at the end of these feasts the host gives valuable gifts to his guests, and sometimes actually destroys his property just to show he can afford to. It's a lot like the beautiful, graven chopped-liver swans you see at some of our affairs. Well," he said, "but what do Indians really have? Their artifacts, of course, their gorgeous, custom duds and decorated furs. The whale's carved-up bones and etched ivories. Their blankets, certainly. Well, John Lookout, the founder of the feast I'm speaking of, was a particularly rich man. He even had, don't laugh, a refrigerator. (You've heard the saying— 'It's like trying to sell a Frigidaire to an Eskimo.' As far north as I'm speaking of, Indians too.) Though the village where he lived had no electricity.

"Well, let me tell you, Father Lookout decided to go all out on this one. And we all knew it, too. Just to give you an idea, the potlatch took place on a day that commemorated nothing, absolutely nothing. Not the opening of the canneries, or the liberation of the Indian slaves—oh, yes, the Indians kept slaves; for that matter so did the Eskimos—or some battle, defeat *or* victory, in the Russian and Indian wars of the early nineteenth century. It was no one's birthday. None of the Lookouts had made a rite of passage. He'd had an ordinary year, neither fat nor lean. Ordinary. The potlatch was neither to celebrate nor propitiate the gods of hunting or fishing. You couldn't even say it was a celebration of ostentation itself, because John didn't even bother to invite more than one or two people to come to it. Maybe it was the incense from his fires that drew us. The burning polar bears and king caribou, the greasy lava flow of shlepped blubber. Or the overnight skyline of the bright, patiently carved but hurriedly planted totem poles out there on his lawn like so many decorative flamingos or jockey hitching posts. Maybe just rumor.

"The food was like nothing anyone had seen before. The sheer amounts of it, I mean. Oh, what a spread! It could have kept entire villages well fed for a winter. And the drink! Not just the ordinary Black Label Scotches, imported beers and French champagnes, but sparkling reindeer blood, horned sheep ales and moose liqueurs, fermented lichens, spruce wines, and the cedar sherries.

"Oh, and that thermostated, G.E. frost-free, fresh-fruit-and-vegetable-crispered, makes-its-own-ice-, butter-trayed and egg-nesting icebox of his had been filled up with packaged white bread. (A great delicacy among the Indians, he was going to serve them toast for dessert.)

"So there we were, seated politely, our hands folded in our laps, mouths salivating, stomachs rumbling with hunger, our very noses watering from the delicious sights and wondrous smells of all that fabulous food, all the guests waiting for John to rise and make his toast so the feast could begin. He never made a move, and we might be sitting there still if some wise old man from a different village altogether hadn't somehow suddenly divined the point, risen, flip-topped a beer, and offered, off-handedly as he could— 'To Nothing at All!'

"That was the open sesame, all right. It was as if some movie director had called out 'Action!' All of a sudden the wines and boozes were flowing, and the platters of meats and fowl and tureens of soup were being passed around the tables as fast as the white men—yes, white men—John Lookout had hired could serve them. (Though it occurred to me that that village elder could have said anything, and the same thing would have happened. He could have said 'Here's mud in your eye,' or 'Permafrost Forever!' or 'So's your old man.' Anything. I could have started it myself with a bo-ray p'ree ha-gaw-fen. Then I thought it wouldn't even have taken that much, that it wouldn't have taken anything at all, maybe just one of the guests getting up from where he sat at the table, strolling over to the icebox and tearing open a package of Wonder Bread and pulling out a slice. Now I know it needn't have been a guest at all. One of the white hired help could have done it.)

"It was something, let me tell you. It was really something. It really was. There was ox bacon, there were bear chops,

there were caribou roasts. There were great Kodiak porter-
houses and sheep feet and walrus shoulders. There was smoked
lemming and barbecued musk ox liver. And the drinking? Like
there was no tomorrow! Well, you know— they're goyim. They're
Indians but they're goyim. Do I have to tell you? Goyim is
goyim.

"They were so sated and drunk by this time you'd have
thought he wouldn't have had the energy for what happened
next. It's what often happens. They fall asleep with their faces
in their plates and when they wake up the next day their heads
hurt so bad they're no longer interested in even the gift-giving
part, to say nothing of the host's destroying his property for
them—even if he still had enough left in him to do it. The taste
in his mouth alone is enough to make him wish he was dead.

"But I'd been watching him, John Lookout, the host. And
they'd been watching him too. He hadn't touched a thing.
Practically. He'd picked at his food. And though I won't say he
was on the wagon, he'd been abstemious, and seemed, well, to
have drunk only out of politeness, a sort of social drinker, to
make his guests comfortable. And that's what kept them interested, I think, helped preserve that last bit of alertness in them.
Gave them their second wind. Kept their peckers up.

"So they really didn't know *what* to expect. Even after he
rose and proposed that toast we had all been waiting for and
thought he was going to rise and propose at the beginning.

" 'I thank you all for coming, and drink,' he said, 'to your
healths, and ask, as a favor to me, that you accept a few lousy
tokens of my appreciation.'

"Whereupon he began to give away the store. You know,
the artifacts I was telling you about? His beads and his blankets,
his scrimshaw and tsatskes. But big stuff too, the stuff they use
to live by, the tools that earn their bread. The harpoons, nets,
rafts and kayaks. The paddles. The very machinery, I mean,
that made the potlatch possible, and not only that but his down
parkas, the qiviut wools that kept his family warm, the oil that
burned in his lamps during the long dark year.

"Then forced whatever the Indian equivalent is of the
doggy bag on them, pressing them with food that had not yet
been eaten, then with food that had not yet even been prepared.

"His generosity was shameless, and John's guests, both the one or two who had been formally invited, and those of us who, like myself, had merely been attracted—it was us, incidentally, who walked off with the biggest prizes; he was scrupulous about this—were beginning to feel more than a little uncomfortable. That kind of pride and ostentation went beyond tradition and custom and was starting to seem, well, destructive. Yet to refuse a gift was not only rude, it was taboo, a little higher than incest on the scale of things you don't do.

"When he had given away all the gifts he had to give, and disposed of all his food, he seemed physically to slump, somehow to collapse in the face as though he'd been rendered suddenly toothless, all expression fled from him. He seemed—we all felt it, I think—not only to have used up all his worldly goods and chattels, but all his ideas as well, all the hope he might ever have had for a future. This is important. I must make myself clear. Understand that he did not suddenly appear bereft or deprived. He did not seem desolated or stripped. No grief was in it. *Nothing* was in it. As if all the wise old man from the different village altogether who'd brought the potlatch to life by rising and proposing his toast to nothing at all had to do to see the toast bear fruit right before his eyes, was just stay awake long enough to see John Lookout's face at that moment. It was the empty, vacant, neutral face of someone not very interesting in pre-REM sleep.

"But just then, quick as it had emptied out, quick, that is, as a tire blown on the highway, it filled up again. Lookout jumped up, smacked himself in the head, ran out, and was back in a minute with an unopened case of French champagne. 'What's wrong with me?' he said. 'I'm all farblondjhet tonight. There's still some champagne left. Who needs a refill? How about it? How about it, Nanook?' Nanook, who looked as if he was going to throw up, groaned and covered his lips with his fingers as you might cover your glass with your palm to decline wine. 'You? Charley Feathers? No? How about you, Patricia Whalewater? No one? You're sure? No takers? You're sure? All right, it's going going gone then, everybody,' he said, and started to smash the bottles of champagne. He threw them against the walls of his house, he threw them on the floor. With all his might he threw them through his closed windows. He uncorked the last two bottles and emptied their contents over two handsome woven rugs he had apparently forgotten to give away.

"In the silence that followed we were not only too embarrassed to look at John, we were too embarrassed to look at anyone else either. I suppose that's why we never knew who the guest was that finally spoke, who broke the silence and pierced that tight ring of eyewitness shame we all feel when someone fails to bridle an enthusiasm that has passed beyond mere enthusiasm and spilled over into the red zones of lost control and flagrant zealotry.

" 'That is a fine icebox someone has sold you, John Lookout,' the guest said. To alter the mood. To save the party.

" 'Oh, do you think so?' John asked. Then he opened the door of his G.E. frost-free refrigerator and ripped it off. He removed its blue plastic crisper, set it on the floor and jumped up and down on it until it was in pieces. He did the same with the butter tray, tore out the wire shelves, destroyed the icemaker, and then went to work on the motor itself, being careful to spare, out of respect and courtesy to his guests, only those parts where the freon was stored.

"A stange thing happened.

"The mood altered once more. The zealotry retrograded back into enthusiasm again, and the enthusiasm re-metamorphosed into that ostentatious generosity which is the impulse and impetus of a potlatch in the first place.

"There was a *frenzy* of generosity. One Indian was so moved he gave away the lead dog of the dogsled team that had fetched him. The man he gave it to was so moved he shot the dog.

"Desperately they tried to part with the gifts they'd been given, and, when they couldn't, they destroyed them. And when they ran out of things to destroy that John Lookout had given them, they turned on their own property and destroyed that. Mukluks went, parkas. Snowshoes, canoes, curved ulu blades for gutting fish. Everything, everything! All were caught up in the spirit of the celebration. After a time, when there really *was* no more property left toward which they could demonstrate their indifference, they seized upon their own families. Braves beat their squaws, squaws hit their papooses, papooses scratched at their mosquito bites until they became infected. Even then that terrible nexus of generosity cum enthusiasm cum ostentation cum zealotry wasn't finished. When you thought it was over, something else would happen. Someone rose, for example, stuck his finger down his throat, and regurgitated the entire feast he had consumed just hours before. It was awful," he said, remembering, "awful. You couldn't know how they would ever manage to end it.

"It was the major trope of that particular potlatch, and the source of an important new Indian stereotype— the Indian-*taker*." He paused. "It was a sort of Black Thursday for them, you see, and effectively destroyed the Indian economy in that part of the high Yukon for years."

"How *did* they?" I said.

"Pardon me?"

"How did they manage? To end it."

"Oh," he said. "When I took out my ulu and started to shave off my beard."

It was stuffy in the cabin and I cracked open one of the plane's Plexiglas windows, surprised to feel the air, soft and dark and balmy as the sweetest spring. It was even a little warm, in fact, and Philip and I removed our outer garments. Flowerbeard seemed oblivious to the weather, and not only didn't take his parka off but hadn't even lowered its hood, which still covered his knit woolen watch cap. Indeed, he was talking again, launched, I supposed, into another tale, as oblivious to his audience as he was to the temperature.

He was speaking of the alienated Tinneh Indians, who are not only tribeless and clanless, but are without families, too. He was telling us how generation after generation of Tinnehs break away from each other, how parents divorce and children are placed in orphanages or live for a while with a mother or a father and then run off. (Identical twins, he told us, everywhere else handcuffed together by the genetic code, will, among the Tinneh, over time, burst their mutual bonds, drift apart, fall away, dissipate affinity, annihilate connection, disfigure resemblance, climb down some great, ever-attenuating chain of relation, and move from sibling to friend, friend to neighbor, neighbor to acquaintance, and acquaintance to stranger.) And how at one time they probably outnumbered the Tlingit, Haida and Athapaska tribes combined but were now reduced to perhaps a handful of individuals, rare in the general Alaskan population as Frenchmen. It was actually pretty fascinating. I know *I* was interested, and even Philip seemed to have lost, maybe even forgotten, his odd hostility to this man who was now clearly become our guest—I felt my host's role and offered to share the last of my portion of our survival biscuits with this queer Elijah of a fellow—and was concentrating on what he was saying as hard as I could. When suddenly he broke off. "Oh, look," he said, "the sun's up. Now we can work the plane down off these logs and get out of here."

"Oh," said Philip, fixing his hostility in place again, "and once that's done, how do you propose we take off? Seeing, I mean, as how the lake is all melted and more suitable for a toddler with a pail and shovel than for some bush pilot stuck in an airplane without a pontoon to its name?"

"Isn't it frozen?" said the wandered Jew. "Maybe it's frozen. I think it's frozen."

"What, are you kidding," scoffed Philip, "in weather like this? Like Opening Day in the horse latitudes?"

"I'll go check," the flower-bedecked man said and, limber as someone a third his age, was past my knees, had the cabin door open, was out of the plane and onto its wooden perch and dancing down the thick jigsaw of logs as if they were stairs. The next we knew he was leaping up and down on the surface of the frozen lake. "It's solid," he called, jumping. "It's frozen through. If it holds me it can hold the plane. I weigh thousands of pounds."

"I hate a showoff," Philip muttered.

"Shh," I cautioned.

"Yeah, yeah," Philip said, "nevertheless."

And before we could accommodate to the queer disparity of temperature between where we were situated in the plane and where, not fifty yards off, the lake existed in a different climate altogether, he had come back, shrugged out of his heavy outerwear (more, I guessed, for our benefit than his own), had signaled us out of the cabin and, clever as a moving man, was directing us in the this-goes-here/that-goes-there displacements and arrangements, furiously pulling the timbers away as if they hid children covered in a cave-in.

Maybe because there were three of us now. Or that one was a man with flowers in his beard. At any rate, we finished just as the sun was going down and were rolling the airplane out onto the ice when Philip offered his objection. (And me silently pleading with him: No, Philip, please. Not, Don't bother. Because that wasn't the point. The bother, the wasted energy. But because I was a theologian, even if only of the offshore sort. Because I was a theologian and knew that when you're sitting in the wilderness rubbing on a Torah's wooden handles and hocus pocus, lo and behold, who should appear but some stranger that he's got something as out of the ordinary as chin whiskers on him that look as if they might have been cultivated by the very folks who brought you the Garden of Eden, let alone trimmed at and mowed on by magic Jap floral arrangers, and the newcomer mentions he weighs thousands of pounds though he's light enough on his feet to jump up and down on water, you don't whimper and whine at him or make nag-nag at your human condition.) But the last thing this Phil is is shy. Something's on his mind, he lets you know. "I suppose," Phil says, "you have some special way of starting up a dead, battered-up engine that's seen its last days."

"Turn the key in the ignition."

"Right," Philip said, and we got in the plane. Before you could say abracadabra it was full dark, the engine coughed and turned over, and we were roaring down the ice to a blind, treacherous liftoff, Philip not knowing if he could risk pulling her nose up now or whether he still had some room left to muscle her a bit and maybe gain a little more speed and momentum before crashing into the razor pines on the opposite shore of the little lake, when at the last minute the northern lights came on like the bombs bursting in air and it was suddenly bright enough for him to see what to do.

"So," Flowerbeard says once we're at cruising speed and Philip's established radio contact again, "be it ever so humble there's no place like home. Even the sky seems familiar. It's good to be back. You know?"

And I'm thinking: Sure, if you live in the sky. If you live in the sky and your house is on fire. Because that old aurora borealis was blazing away in front of our eyes like a forest fire.

The primary colors at kindling point. At green's ground zero, at yellow's, blue's, red's. (It was like being in the center of the midway at a state fair among the garish, glaring, glancing illuminations and kindled neon of the rides, the blazing calliopedic centripetals and centrifugals of light, in altered gravity's dizzied sphere, hard by the game booths bright as stages. Or like hobnobbing among all the invoked wraiths of light and color like some Periodic Table of the Sun, the conjured avatars and possibilities of its bright erogenous zones and all the heightened decibels of heat, silent banging bursts of fireworks exploding like bouquets of semiprecious stone, amethyst, sapphire, topaz, garnet— the gem boutonnieres. Commanding the spicy savories of hot solstice and, oddly, remembering wicker, recalling bamboo, mindful of, of all things, summer's swaying, loose and ropy hammock style, the interlocking lanyard of the deck chair and chaise like a furniture woven by sailors, recollecting—most queer at this altitude—the littered life outdoors, stepping on candy wrappers, condoms, the sports pages like a dry flora and everywhere setting off the sounds of localized fire like a kindled shmutz, or the explosion of all our oils and fats and greasy glitter like stored fuel.)

Or, like flying directly into his beard.

"Well," I said, "bright enough for you?" And winced, frightened by my pointless nerve.

"Yes, sir," he said, "you start to look forward, you really do. Gone so long, in all that cold and dark, wearing the same mittens and snowshoes weeks on end, you forget what it's like. Civilization. The comforts and mod cons. And begin to believe God's all there is, and that all He ever made was weather, conditions to test your mettle, ice to suffer by and humiliate your character. But now spring's come and I remember all I've been missing— the amenities that make all the difference. Sterno, for example, simmering beneath good old-fashioned home cooking."

Philip confessed he was a news junkie himself, and told us that in *his* position, Bloombeard's, it was current events he'd have missed most, and that though he hadn't mentioned it while we were still technically crash victims, when 10:00 P.M. rolled around and the Eyewitness News came on TV, he couldn't help but wonder who had been raped, who had been murdered, whose house had burned down, who had been lost in natural disasters. He took some comfort, he said, from the fact that when we were out of radio contact with civilization, and he couldn't get the engine to turn over, we were something of a current event ourselves.

"Oh, current events," said the man with the beard made out of flowers dismissively. "The Four famous Horsemen of the Apocalypse— Mr. War, Mr. Famine, Messieurs Pestilence and Death. I've never been much connected with novelty myself."

Oh? I thought. Look me in the beard and say that. "But, Tzadik," I said instead in the rabbi mode, "isn't it important, particularly in these times of tribulation between ourselves and our Arab cousins in the Holy Land, in Eretz Yisro'el, for us to be informed and keep abreast of the developments? To search for peace? To seek, I mean, some equitable solution to our problems?"

He looked at me for a long while before he answered.

"You're one of these 'root causes of terrorism' guys, ain't you?" he said.

"Well . . ." I said.

"No," he said, "I can see it. You are."

To tell you the truth, I *was* a little troubled by some things the Israelis had been doing. The world was a complicated place. There were no open-and-shut cases. There was enough guilt to go around. Of course it was outrageous that the Syrians took pot shots at us from their vantage point on the Golan Heights, or that the PLO could lob shells into the kibbutzim along our northern borders wounding and killing our children, or that they planted bombs in buses and on supermarket shelves in boxes of detergent or mixed in with the oranges in the produce department. Certainly it was wrong to hijack airplanes and harm innocent civilians. But they had their grievances. There was no denying it. The Israelis were on the West Bank now, laying foundations, making it over, turning it into the new Miami. And the camps! For generations now the Palestinians had been crammed into rat-infested quarters open to the sky, forced to live out in the weather like a city for Lears. How different were these "camps" with their running sewers from the favellas of the hopelessly impoverished or even from the ghettos of our own people?

"Yes," he said. "I can see it all over you. You want to be fair."

"Well, it's their homeland, too. And, strictly speaking, they were there first, you know."

"Fuck them," he said.

"Please, Tzadik," I said, "this is not an argument."

"And finders/keepers *is*? Let me tell you something, kiddo. There are higher principles than finders and keepers."

"Hey," said Philip, "I think I'm getting a Fairbanks AM station."

"Because you don't kill someone over finders/keepers. A homeland? A homeland they want? What," he said, "they're imprinted to deserts, allergic to ice? Let them live on the glaciers. Let them have a go at making the icebergs bloom."

This was some rebbe we had here. Suddenly I was telling him all about myself, what I did in New Jersey.

"A rabbi is not a thoracic surgeon," I said. "He is not a proctologist or an ob-gyn man. He doesn't set your bones or flush out your ears. But all I do is say prayers over dead strangers. Tell me, Khokhem, is it right for me to specialize like that?"

"No, no," he said, "you don't understand. It doesn't make a difference if they're strangers. Or that you don't feel a genuine anguish for their loved ones. Grief is only a form, a kind of a courtesy. It's something we have to do. It's a sacrament. Not like sitting shiva or saying Kaddish or putting pennies on their eyes. Just grief. Grief itself. If you're properly shocked when you hear bad news. If you've got"—he waved his arms about at the invisible mountains of ice beneath and all around us—"sand."

And then, while Philip tapped his toes to the music coming in on his headphones from the Fairbanks radio station, Flowerface launched into the wisdoms. He told us how God did *too* create evil. "And you know something?" he said. "It's a good thing He did."

"It is?" I asked, surprised.

"Sure," he said, "it shapes our taste."

I lifted a headphone away from Philip's head, bobbing to the rhythms of Fairbanks radio. "What?" he said.

"Cut out the dreaming and listen to him. This ain't no sock hop. He's telling us worthwhile stuff. Go on, please, Macher."

He looked hurt, Philip. I regretted what I'd said and fumbled with his earpiece, trying to replace it, when Petalpuss stayed my hand and began to draw it toward his beard, guiding it into that luxuriant garden. "Be careful," he whispered, "of the thorns and thistles." I jerked my hand away as if it had been scalded. (Though I swear he let go first, his reflexes beating my reflexes.) Then he turned to Philip and apologized for me. "It's not what you think. He's a rabbi and has faith in lessons, the vicariousness of the heart's bright ideas. Incidentally, what was that song you were listening to just now?" Philip told him and he nodded. "I thought so," he said. "Sometimes, when the weather let up and it got warm enough to whistle, I'd whistle that one myself."

"Really?" Philip said.

"Oh, yes," said the man with the flowers in his beard. "It's a very catchy tune. It perks a man up who's been praying while the midnight sun goes down if there's a cheery tune to turn to."

"Really?"

"I just said so," he said. "But I have to tell you, it doesn't let you off the hook that we share the same taste in music. That's coincidence, not character, and don't redound to anyone's credit. Jerry was right finally to pull the headphone off your head. I'm only sorry he didn't catch your ear in his fist."

"Oh," I said, "no. I only meant . . ."

"You did your duty. It don't make no difference what you meant."

"He's right," said Philip.

"He is," I agreed. I turned back to the man with the flowers in his beard. "What else?" I asked him. Because, though I still had no idea where we were—Philip, when he'd discovered our coordinates, had passed them on to us but they hadn't meant anything—I didn't care. It was *all* wisdom now— how he'd spoken to Philip, to me, what he'd been saying. I knew there was plenty more where that came from and never wanted the ride to be over. Why, I was like a kid, staring out the window of a Pullman car berth, lulled by the mysterious geography of the night, seduced by the steel percussion of tons.

He spoke to us, instructed us, taught us, even Philip into it now, rapt, engaged as someone counting. Old Posypuss (because I didn't know his name, because he never said it, because I never asked) wising us up, even in English his voice cadenced as an uncle's aliyahs, like broches lilted as lullabies. One time he paused to ask if either of us had a cigarette we could spare and it seemed so out of character I questioned whether I'd heard him correctly.

"You smoke, Khokhem?"

"I butter my bread."

"Beg pardon, Tzadik?"

"What, I'm going to be killed by an omelet? French toast? A Carlton, a Vantage, a Lucky, a Now? They want me that bad, let the pikers come get me."

"Beautiful," I told him.

"Ah," said Philip.

"Sure," said the man with the flower-strewn beard, "a parable in every box. Philip, please," he said. "Watch the road. Look where you're going."

•　　•　　•　　•

We landed at Prospect Creek camp by the Jim River, thirty or so miles north of the Arctic Circle. It was full daylight and Philip took me over to Personnel, where I was photographed and issued an identification tag while he filled out Emergency Landing and Distress forms required by the company if he was to claim Distress and Hazard reimbursement, and which I, as his passenger, had to witness and sign.

"Hey," the clerk explained, "it's red tape but we have to have it. Otherwise these clowns would crash-land in just any old snowbank and loll around in the midnight sun building the old D-and-H to the tune of five bucks a day till their rations was gone and they *had* to lift off again."

"Five dollars a day? Why would anyone do something like that for just five dollars a day?"

"Hey," said the clerk, "you kidding me, Padre? Because it's an *angle*. Because it's another angle, and life up here is lived as if it was ge-fucking-ometry."

•   •   •   •

The clerk turned out to be right in a way, but missed the
real point, I think. (This isn't my rabbi mode now—I had, when
I was in Alaska, little occasion, as you will see, to fall back upon
my rabbi mode—so much as my apocalyptic one. —Ice. The
world will not end in fire—you can *see* fire; darkness was the
mode here—but in ice.) Which wasn't angles, not entirely angles
anyway, so much as a sense the men—we—shared of being
stuck along some infinite loop, embraced in the stifling bear hug
of a closed system. What that clerk called angles were only the
sharpish edges with which they meant to nick the system, to let
a little light bleed through. If they often seemed frantic as
children, on liquor, on pot, if they engaged, on days off or at
times when it was impossible to work, in endless tournaments of
round-robin poker, gambling for table stakes higher than any
ever seen in Vegas or my beloved New Jersey, it was because
they—we—were so caught up in our terrible doomsday cynicism. The impressions I'd had in Anchorage, of wartime, of
gridlock, of the sky's-the-limit life, and which Philip had explained to me up in our little wooden nest egg while we waited
for the weather to warm up so the lake could freeze over, as the
general Alaskan scam, were not only reinforced from the moment we touched down on the Prospect Creek landing strip (and
had to sit in the plane while the gas tank was refilled, at a dozen
bucks a gallon), they were raised from impressions to rules, the
forced, improbable etiquette of the North.

When I finished at Personnel the clerk handed me a map
of the Atco units, circled the useful addresses like the girl
behind the rental car counter at the airport (my quarters, Personnel, the Assignment office, the dining hall, the chapel, the
infirmary, the card room, the club, the camp theater), and
instructed me to report to the Assignment trailer after I'd eaten.
There were, I understood as I made my way along the corridors
and modules—it was a little like strolling through a troop train—
essentially two basic models the company had drawn upon
here— the Army, and the Starship *Enterprise*. After I unpacked
and had my meal—the food was marvelous, thick steak, wine,
lobster, and everything served on table linen the texture of

men's old white-on-white shirts—I reported to the Assignment office.

It was McBride himself who invited me to enter.

I'd seen him only once, at the motel in Anchorage the week before, and we couldn't have exchanged two dozen words, but it was like, I swear it, coming upon one of my oldest and dearest friends. Maybe it was the suit and tie, except for Petch's the last I'd seen since going down in Philip's airplane, or the voice, not only uninflected but smooth, without twang or accent, a reassuring sound of the civil. It could even, God help me, have been his briefcase, a signal of routine, of a world where men went to business each day and returned each night, late for supper if they'd been held up by traffic. The only discordant note in the ensemble was the yellow hard hat he wore, but even this could have been ceremonial as his suit or symbolic as his briefcase, a reminder to the men that, please, let's never forget it's still Alaska up here, we'll be blasting, working with heavy equipment, there could be avalanches, I love you guys, let's be careful out there. And he'd signed my motel chit (and reminded the men that it was like when the family had taken their trip cross the country). I'm no, God forbid, Eddy Tober but, no offense to Flowerface, a fella needs a father figure he can *rely* on once in a while.

So, as you can imagine, I was more than a little excited to see him.

"Mr. McBride," I greeted him, "how *are* you! I guess you heard about the trouble we had. It was touch and go there for a while, but Philip kept his head on him—he's a good man, Philip is—and we had a couple of very lucky breaks there, which I'll tell you the truth I figure we had coming in view of the near-*tragic* stuff we went through. Anyway, all's well that ends well, and here I am, a week late but rarin' to go. Oh," I said, "which reminds me. Did Rodendhendrey ever show up? Did Cralus? Did Fiske?"

"Who are you?"

"I'm your rabbi, Mr. McBride. I'm Rabbi Goldkorn, sir. We met at the Travelodge? In Anchorage? I have to laugh. You didn't know me then either. You thought I might be Fiske. Or Rodenhendrey. Or maybe Cralus. It's just that I'd never been taken for a Rodenhendrey or Fiske before. I suppose a Cralus. Cralus is one of those names that could be anything really, but Rodenhendrey? Fiske? No way. That's why I have to laugh. Though I want you to know I'm reassured you don't *have* these preconceptions. It makes me more comfortable, it puts me at ease."

"You're at ease?"

"Well," I said, "we've been through some rough circumstances, the pilot and me. There were times we both had to wonder whether we'd make it. I guess I'm just relieved, maybe a little nervous."

"You're my rabbi? Sure," he said, "now I remember. You arrived a day early. You were flying up the next day with the Hebrew supplies."

"That's right."

"Sure," he said. "I remember. I recognize you from your ID tag."

"I wasn't wearing an ID tag. I didn't have one then."

"No," he said, "of course not." He was looking at my shirt, and I suddenly realized he was the sort of man who never forgot an ID. What people looked like on their driver's licenses and passport photos. It was his business, I guess. When he saw me in Anchorage, he didn't so much see me as my picture, reduced and laminated, what I'd look like behind plastic. "Hey," McBride said, as if he were reading my thoughts, "it's a good likeness."

"Thank you."

"And the supplies? You have what you need?"

"The supplies? Oh, you mean the *Hebrew* supplies. Yes," I said, "they're fine. I locked them in my room in the duffel. They'll be all right there, won't they, till I find a safer place to store them?"

"Oh, sure," he said, "why not? You'll find that people don't so much steal up here as get into the more violent crimes. There's lots of cheating at cards, so naturally there's a certain amount of killings and beatings and stabbings. Crimes of passion, too, of course, because even though there's ladies on our crews, there's not nearly enough to go round. That's why we try to keep it a lot like downtown Saigon."

Of course. Downtown Saigon. Not war so much as the behind-the-lines life, the R&R one. Which would explain my Anchorage impressions, my instincts here since we landed. Which would explain the thickness of the steaks, the wine and lobster, the drawn butter, rich and yellow as the yolk of an egg, and understood at once that anything goes, that probably everything did, and knew—and feared—that my work was cut out for me, that there'd be, good Lord-of-All-Worlds, Jews to save! (Resisting, kicking and screaming in my head: Hold it, hold on there, I'm Rabbi of Lud, only some offshore ordained justice of the peace, really. What did *I* know of sin, what did *I* know of evil?) Of half a mind to protest to McBride right then, right there, that I didn't bargain for this, that, like everyone else, I was there for the history of the thing, the visionary once-in-a-lifetime opportunities of boom. That, oh, yes, if some welder's, or blaster's, or heavy-equipment operator's kid suddenly wanted bar mitzvah'ing, I was prepared to handle it, or even a shotgun wedding, say, and certainly I could pronounce a nice eulogy at a moment's notice over the body of some poor unfortunate come to a bad end in an avalanche, but that, well, what I didn't know about heroin and dirty needles, cocaine and prostitution, high crimes and misdemeanors, could fill a book, and that perhaps he really ought to get somebody else— a priest, say, and that I would understand. Of course I held my tongue.

Though I hadn't forgotten I was in the Assignment office, and looked at McBride waiting for him to tell me what to do. He didn't speak, and looked at me as if I had him stymied, this fellow who never forgot a face on an ID.

"Well," I said finally, "if you could give me some idea of my duties . . ."

"Your duties?"

"It's a long pipeline," I offered by way of a joke.

"Oh," McBride said, pulling open a drawer in his desk and referring to a sheet of paper he took from it. "It's not Rosh Hashanah, is it?"

"No."

"Yom Kippur?"

"No, of course not."

"Succoth? Shemini Atzereth? Simchas Torah?"

"No."

"Is it coming on Chanuka?"

"Not till Christmas."

"Chamish' Osor b'Shvat? Purim? Pesach? Lag b'Omer?"

"Chamish' Osor b'Shvat? Lag b'Omer?"

"Shavuoth then, Tisha b'Av."

"No, I don't think so."

"Hey," he said, "smoke if you got 'em."

So, on the principle that we'd once been in the same motel lobby for a few minutes back in Anchorage, and were all in this together, I asked about Spike. I asked after Ambest and Anderson, and about old Jimmy Krezlow. I wanted to know what had happened to Peachblow and tried to find out how Schindblist was getting on.

"Did Jeers ever qualify?"

"Jeers?"

"Guy said he was checked out in jackhammer but didn't have the certification to prove it."

"Yeah," McBride said, stroking his jaw, remembering, "yeah, Jeers. No," he said, "we gave him a test. He flunked. We let him wash dishes and work the grease trap till he earned the fare back to Alabama."

I'm next, I thought, thinking of the half-million-bucks' worth of Pentateuch back in my room under canvas and hasp. I'm next, I thought, thinking of that small biblical fortune in sterling silver yads and eighty-seven-thousand-karat beaten-gold menorahs and the shittim-wood arks.

"Was there anything else?"

"Yes. Well, no. I mean, well, what am I supposed to, you know, *do*?"

"You're the rabbi. You're on call. You sit in the rabbi trailer and chat up the Jews."

Sure enough. There it was. Right on the map. With my other useful addresses. However could I have missed it? If it'd been a snake it would've bit me. The rabbi trailer. To which, once I'd settled in, I repaired.

·   ·   ·   ·   ·

I posted regular office hours and, at least for the better part of the first two or three weeks, scrupulously observed them, almost as if they—the hours—were themselves a claim of conscience and comprised a set of canonical hours I solitarily kept, a squeezed matins and lauds, a concentrated prime and terce and sext and nones, the vespers and compline of contractual duty. (More often than not reminded of the flower-faced man, whom Philip had flown off with the next day, depositing him, so I was told, in Fairbanks, from which town he meant to make his way to Anchorage, perhaps by glacier, moving at the glacier's pace, a few fast inches a day with the wind in his face.) No one came.

I had the use of Alyeska's secretarial services and duplicating machines, and had notices posted on the bulletin boards announcing my presence at Prospect Creek camp. No one came.

And, after first reserving them with the authorities to be sure the Atco units that served as the club for Prospect Creek camp would be available when I needed them, I put other notices up— for dances, for get-togethers, inventing affairs, making the coffee-and-Danish arrangements, inviting our singles to come together in Jewish sock hop—high times for one and all. Again, of course, nobody came.

If, I figured, the mountain won't come to Mohammed . . . And visited the sick in the infirmary. All I accomplished was to make those who were well enough nervous, and those who weren't, terrified.

And it wasn't as if there were no Jews at Prospect Creek. There weren't a lot, but there were some, Jews of a different color, as the Catholics and Prots and even the Eskimos and Indians there were of a different color, order. Pipeline, they were pipeline Jews, there to make a wonder of the world. No back seat to God, they seemed to say. Oil or nothing! Valdez or bust! And proceeded to live some specially dispensated, tall-story life of the body and mind, their attention focused somewhere around the speed of sound, the speed of light, richocheted, caromed off the forces and their unleashed, hopped-up pagan energies.

I'm telling you, pally, like goyim they were.

So here's what happened.

Piecemeal, I stopped being so scrupulous about office hours and came later and later to open up and sit inside my rabbi trailer. And closed shop earlier and earlier, too. Some days neglecting to drop by even to check the mail (letters from Shelley were delivered to my quarters), Alyeska's endless series of internal memos, bulletins, clippings, pledge cards (for blood drives, for the Prospect Creek branch of the United Way), newsletters, notices, press releases, announcements ("Commencing the first of the month the laundry's new hours will be from . . .")— all that purple correspondence, as I came to think of the company's impersonal, one-size-fits-all mimeography. And stayed indoors (as I came to think of the Atco unit where I lived), watching, in those old, pre-dish days, two- and three-day delayed editions of the *Tonight Show*, Merv Griffin, Dick Cavett.

In all fairness, what else could be expected of me?

In all fairness, nothing at all, but I knew that what I'd undertaken, to serve a sort of sabbatical year (to pick up extra bucks, to shop around for a congregation, to see how, or if, Alaska would suit, and send for Shelley and the tyke if I discovered it did), was become, for me, a time of trial. Prospect Creek, rather than the week or so I'd lived with Philip and Poseypuss in the crashed airplane, was quickly becoming my time in the wilderness. In Lud the dead were my congregation. I cheered for them and rooted them on the way St. Francis was said to do for the birds and the animals. Here, on the pipeline, I had no one at all.

You want to know something? You want to know what the Rabbi of Lud started to do with his hands now that he had so much time on them? That's right. A grown man. A rabbi. Playing with himself like a bar mitzvah boy. True to Shelley at first, but getting out on the town more, at least in my head, gawking the cleavages and pupiks, underthighs, calves and asses on Carson's, Griffin's and Cavett's guests on three-day delay, old Goldkorn placing shlong to palm for a little shvontz tug and putz pull.

It was an effort even to go to meals.

So I pulled myself together.

I went to meals. I went to meals and spoke when I was spoken to. I went to meals, spoke when I was spoken to, and passed the salt. I went to meals, spoke when I was spoken to, passed the salt and offered the bread basket. Piecemeal, I'm saying, in fits and starts, I fell in with them.

You have no idea what money was like in those days, what it meant, I mean. How easy it was to come by, how difficult it was to save. Generosity became a way of life. A way of life? A competition, an Olympic event. (Don't think I wasn't put in mind of the man with the flowers in his beard, of the tale he told us of John Lookout's spectacular potlatch, of the competition among his guests to outshine, outspend and just generally outright outdo Lookout's incredible example.)

One of the reasons, I think, the pipeline took so long to complete as it did, is that we fell victim to each other's parties. We were beneficiaries and legatees, and went surety for one another's benders and hangovers and lost weekends. We strung each other out, I mean, and put each other on the nod on the arm. Wasting and blazing our brothers and sisters. (We? Absolutely we.) There was a custom in those high-kicking, free-wheeling, last-of-the-go-to-hell-goddammit days, for someone to come into a saloon and "six-pack the house," by which was meant that one withdrew three hundred dollars or so from his billfold, laid it down on the bar (not slapped, laid, set down, though it must have started with slapped, started, that is, with noise and showbiz and only gradually, or maybe not so gradually, slipped into a quieter though even more ostentatious— reminded this time that there's nothing new under the sun, reminded, I mean, of the flashy discretion and noisy circumspection of my bar mitzvah days, when people slipped money into my hand and into open places in my clothing—mode), and purchased half a dozen beers for everyone in the tavern. (It may have been a sign of the season's excessiveness when the three hundred dollars became four and five hundred dollars, or even more, because the sports were offering not just six beers this time, but six actual mixed drinks. And it was *certainly* a sign when the four or five hundred dollars was no longer even laid on the bar, when the six-packer was entirely unknown to his devisees and annuitants, and all you needed to know that a treat was in store, was the sound of a phone ringing behind the bar, the sight of the saloon man answering it, the look on his face as he agreed and nodded into the telephone. And surely the final sign was that not one dollar, not *one*, was ever lost by a barkeep for his willingness not only to extend credit over the phone, but to extend it to someone who because there wouldn't be any credit in it for him—in the generosity sweepstakes, in those great give-and-let-give games—if his name ever got out, not only refused to give it but often wasn't even asked!) It was like when Moses came down from Mount Sinai and found the Jews trying it on with the Golden Calf!

You want to know how bad it got? Would you believe me if I told you? Probably not. They never do. I'll tell you anyway. All right. Here goes.

I was on fabled Alaskan Air Flight 265, Fairbanks to Juneau, the night that word got out that someone—his name isn't just lost to history, it was never known to it—was going to six-pack the entire plane.

When I heard that I knew it was time to get right with God.

And, unfastening my seat belt, I rose at my seat and, raising my arm and extending my glass, toasted first class, toasted economy class, toasted smoking and nonsmoking, toasted the crew, the folks in the lavs. Thinking: the look, the look, the proprietary smirk. *Hold* that look. Whatever it was that platformed the heart and smugged the senses and leant to a guy his survey-or's instincts, like a fellow on horseback, something at once possessive and hospitable. Something father-of-the-bride, say, founder-of-the-feast, chairman-of-the-board, leader-of-the-band. Something maître d', master-of-ceremonies. Something patrician, the long, deep bloodlines of first families and old dough. *And something underneath, something villainous and wicked, something You'll-Get-Yours!*

As if to say to them: You see? You see how hard-core the greed is behind this, behind all the joke anonymity—Look who says he's anonymous—and grab-bag glee. And might have brought it off, right then right there have ended all the big-shot posturing (which was already beginning to spill over, which was already beginning to spill over and leave mere just money behind holding the bag, which had already, I mean, started to cost actual lives—in mad heroics, in throwing sound bodies after broken ones, good lives after bad, in all the leap-before-you-look strategics of futile, crazy kamikaze), and might have brought it off. Closed down the bidding right then, right there. If at that moment the stewardess hadn't come up to me and within the hearing of at least nine or ten passengers told me she was grateful I'd identified myself because there'd been a mistake, that Alaskan Air apologized for the delay but the ground crew in Fairbanks somehow hadn't gotten the word and had failed to lay on the requisite additional liquor they would have needed for me to six-pack a sold-out 747. She said she'd notified the captain and he'd made arrangements with the tower in Anchorage to set down and take on supplies though she was afraid there'd be a several-hundred-dollar landing fee that I'd have to pay and that after I gave her the green light she'd have to clear it with the rest of the passengers anyway.

Too late it occurred that I hadn't thought all this through but had engaged in some pretty fair leap-before-looking kamikazics of my own. Too late it occurred that the real founder of the feast may have been on board, sitting back, watching me, waiting on my green light before springing through his. To *jolt* my Hebrew ass. But then I realized that spurious mercies was what it was all about in the first place, and took my chances.

"Folks," I said, collecting their attention, "folks?" And cupped my hands to shout our situation to them through. Concluding, "FAA regulations require a community decision on this one. Who wants to divert to Anchorage? May I see hands?"

Relying, you see, on the kindness of strangers. On their generosity ransoming my generosity. Which, of course, in those flush times, it not only had to do but did. The nays had it, and forty minutes later the pilot turned on the Fasten Seat Belt sign and was about to illuminate the No Smoking one in preparation for our landing in Juneau when the real six-packer stood up and identified himself. "Go back," he demanded, "go back to Anchorage. Turn this fucker around and let's go *get* that liquor! What say, fellows," and, pointing at me, said, "my friend here is thirsty!"

And this time the ayes had it. Because of the *fuel* situation. *Because we just might not have had enough to make it back to Anchor-*

age, and risk and foolhardiness were generosity too, a sort of princely
largesse and lavish bounty when what you're giving is your life!

Never mind my humiliation. My humiliation wasn't even
in it. Not at these prices. Not for those stakes.

In all fairness, did I say, what else could be expected of
me? In all fairness, did I answer, nothing, nothing at all?

What could I do?

Well, I could become a missionary.

I became a missionary.

Taking advantage of my company plane privileges, and
sending my posters and announcements on before me, the purple mail I didn't bother to go in for myself when it turned up in
the rabbi trailer, I began to fly to the other crew camps. I flew
to the camps at Prudhoe Bay and Toolik, Galbraith Lake and
Happy Valley. I flew to Dietrich and Coldfoot camps, to 5 Mile
and Fairbanks. And though I was gone from it now more often
than I was there, Prospect Creek continued to serve as the base
camp for Mother Church. Except for the topography (and even
the topography was more or less the same, the guiding principle
of the pipeline geologists being, I suppose, to lay as straight and
low a line as possible Prudhoe Bay to Valdez, sea level to sea
level), the camps could have been gas, food and lodging stops
just off an interstate.

Preceded, as I say, by my purple mail campaign, that
one-sided indigo correspondence based on all those already failed,
in-house missives I had for model— the memos, bulletins and
announcements I insisted (as those I myself received, and which
I not only ignored but, if I saw them at all, regarded merely as a
kind of neutral fallout, like dead leaves in a gutter, say, dry and
past their color, are a neutral fallout, looking on such sad-ass
stuff as mere second-per-second hype, insisted they would mine)
would change, though I didn't even know them yet and only had
their names off Alyeska's Address-o-graph machine, their lives.
Borrowing (though I don't believe I knew this) from my Christian
friends the mystic possibilities, coming on strong with joy for joy,
arms opened wide in forgiveness. Ahead of my time in the forgive-
and-forget department, wiping their slates of incest and child
abuse, fornication, drunkenness, wife bashing and all the rest
of the seven deadlys, inventing customized, Jewish, no-fault sin.

Signed Jerome Goldkorn, Chief Rabbi, Alaska Pipeline.

And climbed down from my airplane at Prudhoe, at Toolik, Happy Valley and Galbraith Lake, at Dietrich, at Coldfoot, at 5 Mile, at Fairbanks, not only ahead of my time but out in front of theirs, too. Or what would have been theirs if there'd been enough Jews waiting out on the tarmac for me or in the presecured Atco units, the card rooms and chapels, dining halls, clubs and theaters to constitute a them. It was all right, I told myself, Rome wasn't built in a day either, and went off to look for them in the infirmary, tracked them down in their trailers, or out on site where they worked. If you're going to judge only by—what? —the sock hoppers I managed to sign up or got to agree to go on retreat or come to services, I don't suppose I was much of a success (although Alyeska had no cause for complaint and, I'll say this much for them, they never did, and this much for myself— I worked my ass off), but I was planting the seed, laying the groundwork, showing the flag, and when I returned, dropping like Santa out of the sky, I had food for them, the recipes for which Shelley gave me over the phone and which I passed on to Alyeska's bakers and chefs.

"Here," I would say, dispensing mandel bread, dispensing kugel, dispensing kishke, kasha and varnishkes, holding putchah out to them (a sort of jellied calves' hoof), thermoses of full-fledged chicken soup, gefilte fish made from arctic char and salmon, dispensing macaroons, "from the kitchens of Prospect Creek! Enjoy, enjoy! Will we be seeing you come Chol Hamod? Can we count on you this Lag b'Omer?"

If anyone had actually liked this stuff I guess it would have constituted a kind of vote fraud.

But, as I say, I wasn't much into corruption. I had taken (because I couldn't afford not to up there) a Christian's view of things, forgiving their debts as they forgave their debtors, and willing to go them, the Christians, one better, forgiving even the sin of final despair. Though who asked me?

To tell the truth, no one. Asked or was expected to. It wasn't my job. No, my job was organizing the picnics and volleyball games, the Jewish retreats and Jewish discussion groups (where we would talk about what we always talked about— "The State of Israel," "The Palestinian Problem" [there was none], "Anti-Semitism" [rife, it existed everywhere, under the bed, out in the hall, wherever people gathered, wherever grown men strolled by themselves down country lanes, everywhere], "Hebrew Education," "Cross Marriage," "Marriage and the Family," "Judaism: Race or Religion?"). But they knew me now. And if I accomplished nothing else I'd accomplished that at least. I taught them, that is, their rabbi's name.

I made a nuisance of myself. Hey, no problem. It pays to advertise.

Because by now, even if they weren't showing up for actual services, I'd begun to put together a small cadre of kapos, little Hebrew helpers, Jewish or not, you see them everywhere, dressed to the nines in stockings and heels behind their aprons, female or not, volunteer minutemen, male or not, smoothers of the way, chipper chippers-in and general all-round good sports who not only supervised the music, lettered the signs, put up the crepe-paper decorations, prepared the eats and mixed the punch, but stayed on afterward to return the records to their jackets and, hunching the state of the treasury, lay by money and string to turn economies right and left, taking the crepe paper down and folding it, pouring the punch out of the bowl and into a jar and, waste not, want not, making up doggy bags from the uneaten scraps. Then, God bless them, they went over the signs and erased the words and dates they deemed it unlikely we would be using again.

I had Karen Ackerman, I had Milton Abish. I had Bill and Miriam Jacobson, Debbie Grunwald and David Piepenbrink. Arnie Sternberg and Howard Ziegler from the motor pool were with me. These were my good Jewish sports from the early days. These were the folks who knew me when.

It was time.

I'd had my second brainstorm—my personal Marshall Plan, the food giveaway, was my first—and it was time. (It was obvious, really. If it had taken the kindness of strangers to get me off my duff in the first place, that infectious, killer generosity that I took to be the hitch and hinder, blemish, chink and defect that flawed their characters and made seconds of their souls, why hadn't I also seen that if epic profligacy was what got you *in*to trouble, wasn't it only poetic justice then that what ought to get you out of it again was more of the same? A taste of their own medicine. A hair of the dog. Which was when I stopped the flow of just ordinary purple mail, all those announcements for parties and invitations to kick the Jewish issues around, and started to send out barefaced pledge cards, requests for money, pleas for bucks, your outright give-till-it-hurts pressures and appeals. The money *poured* in.)

So it was time.

I gathered my prayer books together—I don't understand it, but for a people of the Book we Jews use our Torah less cost-effectively than any religion I know of uses its own scriptures; strictly speaking, it's not required at all, really, save on Monday and Thursday mornings, on Shabbes and on the holidays—and flew to Coldfoot where I conducted Friday night services for those by this time good old boys Arnie Sternberg, Dave Piepenbrink, Karen Ackerman, Debbie Grunwald and Milton Abish, among my kapos only Howard Ziegler and Bill and Miriam Jacobson no-shows and holdouts. I knew, however, that when next we met (in Prudhoe Bay the following week), I would have not only Ziegler and the Jacobsons in the congregation but a considerable portion of the Alaska pipeline Jewish population as well.

Because it was easy now. Because it was like shooting ducks in a barrel. Because it was Prudhoe Bay, the farthest north of Alyeska's camps, and they would have to inconvenience themselves, put out money, and charter a plane to get there (and it had been a difficult spring, the weather foul that year, powerful storms, high winds, low ceilings, lousy visibility).

Even more successful than that. More successful than I had any right to expect. Because once the word got out, and the non-Jews learned that the Jewish Jews had found a whole new way to six-pack the house and dispose of money, the gentiles dropped by too. And actually even volunteered a collection when they saw I was not going to take one up myself!

"No," I objected. "No, no," I protested, "you don't understand. I'm quite well paid. The company pays me. Alyeska does. I've a quite good rating. As high if not higher than the most highly skilled laborers among you."

And when they overrode my objections and insisted I keep it anyway I told them, well, oh, all right, if they wouldn't take no for an answer, I'd hold on to it and donate it in their honor to the Trees for Israel Fund.

"*What*," someone shouted, "*there's a Trees for Israel Fund?!*" and wrote out a check right then and there for two hundred dollars. It was Jack Nicholson, the man I'd seen in the motel that first day, the one they called Spike. Peachblow was there too, and Ambest. The money *poured* in.

"Building the tip," I think they call it. Building the tip. Whatever you do to create interest, demand. The dancing girls in their scanties in promissory, there's-plenty-more-where-this-comes-from undulation outside the tent. The you-ain't-seen-nothing-yets. The no-obligation-examine-in-your-own-home-for-ten-days-frees. All that primed-pump, water-cast bread that gets the juices rolling. Free sample. Words to the wise.

I was building the tip. That's all those Friday night services were to me. Who had this hunch (not even articulated) that real Judaism consists not of the ingrained and the daily, the taken-for-granted, steady-state ritual attentions one pays to God, but comes in jolts of enthusiasm, in fits and starts, in great waves of stored-up sanctity and the piecemeal pious. In feelings released—released? escaped, exploded; I hadn't been a burier of the dead all these years for nothing—on great occasions. Not just on any ordinary Sabbath like a magazine you get once a week in the mail, but on our most sacred holidays, our movable feast days and festivals.

I would have come before them heavy-laden, burdened as a priest, a doctor, blackly bagged, making a house call. I would have brought them, I mean, the jeweled tools of my trade, the branched candelabra with all its official, thou-shalt-made cups and knops, set up my shittim-wood ark like some holy swing set knocked together, and hidden—wrapped like a mystery in the velvet, masculine mantle with its great, rampant, appliqué lions and weighty crowns—the Torah there, and spread my heavy cloth before them on the bema, the sterling silver yad like the major piece in a place setting. Above the ark I would have burned whale oil for them in eternal lamps.

So it's a Shavuoth I'm shooting for, a Pesach, a Purim, my Friday nights only God's little loss leaders, as Mother's or

Father's Day, say, are only your jerry-built festivities of the historically lackluster months. And what I'd really like to have given them was something spectacular, honored the creation of the world, say. (The reason, I think, Christianity has the numbers—though I'd be the first to tell you it's not numbers alone that make a great religion, ideas have something to say about it too—is that Christianity has heavier holidays. Real concept occasions. What's Christmas but your birth of God, Easter week but those seven action-packed days from the time he first pulled into town to the time he got killed and resurrected? Succoth, which is only a harvest festival, pales in comparison. Chanuka, our famous festival of the lights, which commemorates a victory of the Maccabees over the Syrians, does.) There are marvelous untouched holidays there for the plucking. I myself could have come up with a dozen new reasons to praise God. We might have celebrated heart bypass operations, Chinese take-out, record-setting Wall Street rallies. The Festival of the Cruise we could have. The Feast of the Successful Children. Yes, and heart-breakers too, heavy and solemn as anything Christians put on—The Fasts of Auschwitz, Dachau, Bergen-Belsen. The Festival of the Holocaust, say.

It was Shavuoth. Now Shavuoth is a fairly important holiday. It commemorates both the revelation of the Law up on Mount Sinai and the celebration of an ancient wheat festival. Something for everyone, Shavuoth is. That year it fell on June 6, so I picked up D-Day too.

It wasn't as if I was surprised at the turnout. The factors were all there. They were in place, I mean. Well, I'd been building the tip. And there was the money thing. (Did I say how I was reminded of the engraved-invitation revolution back in the forties? The construction of the pipeline was a little like that.) And then, of course, when you weren't actually working there wasn't a whole lot to do. So church—I speak generically—became your entertainment. As lots of other things did. (I remember reading, for example, that in the seven major Alyeska camps the men pumped over a million dollars a month into the pinball machines. Of course, that was at Alaskan prices. A game was a dollar, a free game cost you fifty cents.)

So of course I wasn't surprised. The other way round, really. I would have been surprised if they hadn't shown up, if

all those Tshimian and Athapaskan Indians, if all those hunters
and fishermen and totem-pole carvers and ivory scratchers from
King and Little Diomede islands hadn't shown up. If all those
blasters, heavy equipment operators, jackhammerers and acetyle-
nists hadn't. What, and miss Shavuoth? Frankly, I'd have been
less surprised if Karen Ackerman, Milton Abish, Debbie
Grunwald, Dave Piepenbrink, Arnie Sternberg, Howard Ziegler
or the Jacobsons failed to show. But that's a figure of speech. Of
course *they* were there. Dave Piepenbrink met my plane. He was
waiting for me out on the 5 Mile camp landing strip. (The
different camps had begun to submit sealed bids to see who
would host the services, proceeds to the Trees for Israel Fund.
You have to understand something, none of this was my idea.)

"Good yontif, Rabbi."

"David."

"You had a pleasant trip?"

"Very nice, thank you, David."

"Thank God! Alevay! Kayn aynhoreh!"

"Could you lend me a hand? The makings for the ark are
still in the plane, the Torah and accessories."

"The Torah? You brought a Torah on the flight with you?
Oh, let me carry it. Please, Rabbi, *please*. I'll give you a hundred
dollars for your trees if you do."

"Enough with the trees already, David."

"*You* said trees," Piepenbrink protested. "Trees for Israel
was *your* idea. I *never* thought trees was a hot idea. Trees is just
another place for Arab snipers to hide themselves and take
potshots at us. So tell me, Rabbi, if not into trees, where then
should we put our money? You're the rabbi, you tell me."

"Nowhere. It was a bad idea. But everyone's so hipped up
here on throwing their money around. On being a good sport. I
shouldn't have to charge people to get them to help me out. I'm
not selling indulgences. Of course you can carry the Torah. It's
in the duffel."

I took the smaller duffel, into which I'd transferred a
Torah out of Philip's duffel before I left Prospect Creek camp
that morning, and held it out to Piepenbrink. He'd lost his
enthusiasm. Oh, he carried it, but now that it wasn't costing
him anything all sense of ceremony had gone out of it for him,
even decorum. He practically brushed it along the ground.

"Hey," I said, "watch what you're doing. That's a Torah in there. You don't shlep it along like it was a bowling ball."

"Yeah, yeah," he said, and hiked his burden up a few inches. "I'll bet you're one of those guys who thinks he can get a ticket for flying a torn flag."

It was true. I *did* think I could.

Karen Ackerman, Abish, the Jacobsons, Debbie Grunwald, Arnie Sternberg and Howard Ziegler were already setting up the chairs for services the next morning.

"I don't know," Debbie Grunwald said, stepping back, considering. "You think it'll be enough?"

"Oh, sure," Milton Abish said. "Hey, there's three hundred chairs here. For Shavuoth? Three hundred chairs? Sure it's enough. What, are you kidding me?"

"I don't know," Bill Jacobson said, "we were out at the airstrip earlier and there was an unusual amount of traffic landing for a Monday morning. Isn't that right, Miriam? Didn't you think so?"

"I sure did, Bill."

"We could always put more out if we need them," Arnie Sternberg said.

"Absolutely," Howard Ziegler agreed.

"Well, I'll bet we *do* need them," Debbie said.

"I'll take that bet," said Miriam Jacobson.

"All right, big shot," Debbie said, "what are the stakes?"

"For every chair we need *over* three hundred I donate ten dollars to Trees for Israel. For every chair under three hundred *you* donate ten dollars."

"You're on," Debbie Grunwald said. "Who holds the money?"

"Why don't we just put it down on the ground here where it can blow away?" Miriam Jacobson asked triumphantly, as Debbie Grunwald, knowing she'd been both set up *and* outsported, blanched.

As it turned out, Debbie Grunwald would have had to pay Trees for Israel a hundred and twenty dollars if I hadn't disallowed the bet.

It was just the sort of thing I was up against, the point of my missionary's message to them. It was sin. Such pride and vainglorious strut and vaunt and bluster. Put brag by, friends, I would have told them. Put by swagger and swank and grandiloquence. Knock it off with all swelled-head big britchery, all that high and mighty of the soul and hot air of the heart. You don't six-pack God, smarty-boots, I would have told them. I *would* have. In my sermon. If I'd gotten that far.

Because I *wasn't* surprised. It was Shavuoth. I *wasn't* surprised. I practically almost expected not only that just about a third of those two hundred and eighty-eight seats would be filled with Athapaskans, Tshimians and other assorted fisherfolk, hunter-gatherer and totem-pole types, and that ordinary blue-collar Baptist, Methodist, Adventist and Mormon drillers, drivers and sappers would take up still another third or so—it was Shavuoth, after all; it was Shavuoth, come one, come all—leaving another ninety-six for the outright Jews in attendance. I *wasn't* surprised. I *counted* on it. It was those Russian Orthodox Cossack Eskimo momzers up on dogsleds with whips I hadn't figured!

Because this was June, for God's sake. D-Day. (Could they, I wondered, be opening up some second front?) There wasn't even any damned *snow* on the ground! Yet there they were. In full fur. Mukluk to parka in the June heat. Tricked out with their harpoons and ulus by their sides, the sharp, curving knives the women used to gut fish. The dogs, sprawling on the ground in their complicated harness, seemed at some lazy, cere-monial equivalent of parade rest, but at a signal from their masters, some tug of the reins, I suppose, which rolled along their gear like a wave, they rose to a sort of attention. I made some announcements, called out the preliminary blessings (thank-ing God for restoring the body, for dressing the naked, for opening the eyes of the blind, for freeing the captives, for giving the rooster the intelligence to distinguish between the day and the night, and for making me—I couldn't keep my eyes off those Eskimos—an Israelite), and began the service.

I'd just finished the Akdamut, the ninety-verse alphabeti-cal acrostic praising the greatness of God and the excellence of Torah (and concealing the name—Meir bar Rabbi Yitzchak—of the poem's author and father) you recite on Shavuoth before you open the Torah.

I went toward the ark. I proclaimed the Sh'ma. "Hear O Israel," I announced, "the Lord our God, the Lord is One," opened the ark, withdrew the Torah, took the silver crowns off its wooden handles, undid the soft, fine cords that bound it, removed the velvet parochet that covered it, and laid it down on the bema. Since this was a Torah that had never been used, all its slack was taken up. The scrolls were set at the beginning, like a rental cassette from a video store. I would need someone to help me roll them to the portion for Shavuoth, and I beckoned David Piepenbrink to come up beside me.

"What?" he said.

"This is a virgin Torah," I told him from the side of my mouth. "I'm laying a very high power aliyah on you here. You hold on tight to the left side while I roll up the right. It should be about a third of the way through." He started to say something. "*Don't*," I warned, "don't you *dare* mention money."

"The dogs," he said.

"What?"

"The *dogs!*"

The huskies, urged on by their Cossack Orthodox Russian Eskimo masters, were pulling the heavily laden sleds over the dry, stony ground. "Quick," I told Piepenbrink, "take up the slack. *The slack!* We've got to save the Torah from them. Quick, Piepenbrink, this is an even higher honor than that first one I gave you."

"What," he said, "protect this? It's a *crib*, a trot. It's a pony." He was speaking conversationally now, all the nervous, customary stage inaudibles, the directions and quiet, cryptic promptings that flow back and forth between a rabbi and a bar mitzvah boy, say, and which ordinarily aren't heard in even the first row—why is this, I wonder, what special physics protects our grit-teeth, iron-jaw arrangements?—his voice normal, audible, clear, punched up as a broche.

"What do you mean, a crib?" (And my voice normal too, as clear as Piepenbrink's.) But I saw what he meant. I'm *such* a lousy rabbi. When I'd chosen the Torah in the black velvet mantle to bring with me to 5 Mile, I didn't even look at it first. It wasn't Hebrew but a phonetic transcription of Hebrew, a transliteration in English. It was Wolfblock's work. It was old Rabbi Wolfblock's work, the man who'd written out my tiny haphtarah passage in English for me when I was bar mitzvah, the shortest of the year. I'd have recognized his printing anywhere.

And all they ever meant, the Eskimo Russian Cossack

Orthodox momzers, was just to come closer, and the dogs too
very likely, who were probably called, someone suggested later,
when I sang out that Sh'ma!

•   •   •   •

I went out again, on Tish'a b'Av. McBride was there, but
not an Eskimo, who were gentlemen, was to be seen.

Tish'a b'Av commemorates the destruction of the first and
second temples, and also the expulsion of the Jews from Spain.
The year I'm speaking of it fell on Thursday, August first, and
I'd chosen Toolik camp, maybe two hundred miles above the
Arctic Circle, as the venue for our services. The Jacobsons had
dropped out, Dave Piepenbrink of course, Arnie Sternberg,
maybe a quarter of the Jews. Of course Tish'a b'Av was never
your most popular holiday anyway. What's it got going for it?
All negatives. Two acts of high vandalism and the blackballing
of an entire people from a major country. That's Tish'a b'Av.
What's to celebrate? To tell the truth, I think it should be taken
out of the canon altogether. Too defeatist. Why, it's like cele-
brating the date the first Jew wasn't admitted to a country club,
or the first time his name showed up in an ethnic joke. And the
destruction of those temples? Commemorate swastikas painted
on the walls, why don't you? Crosses burning on your lawn.
Also, it always falls in the hottest part of the summer. People
are out of town.

It was a packed house anyway. Gentiles and Indians made
up for the defection of the Jews and Eskimos. And Deb Grunwald
was there. Shlepping chairs, offering her optimistic body counts.

"You'll see, Rabbi," she told me the night before the
services, "there'll be an even bigger turnout than last time."

"Sure. They're coming to see how I'll screw up."

"No," she said, "really. They never heard such davening.
Once you found your place, you whizzed along like a champ."

"I read from a crib, Deb."

"Who knew?"

"After Piepenbrink stepped down? Half the congregation."

"It was beautiful."

"Well, you're kind," I said. "Thank you."

"Tell me," she said, pointing in the direction of the ark, "did you happen to get a chance to look over . . ." The question trailed off.

I'd chosen the blue-mantled, hundred-forty-five-thousand-dollar Sephardic job, I recall Philip pointing out, but no, I hadn't looked at it, hadn't rolled it yet to the appropriate portion, hadn't even removed its crowns or undone those tasseled ornamental cornsilk cords that loosely bound its twin cylinders. (Because I was working on the theory that it was Fate, God's hand, that it was up to Him, that if He still wanted me chastised and publicly shamed practically a quarter of a century to the day after some overripe Chicago bar mitzvah pisher went head-to-head with Him over something as insignificant—to a child, remember, a little kid—as the thickness and shape of the letters in what was apparently the Father Tongue, if He, that is, could hold a grudge—or should I say Grudge, your Majesty? —every last second of every damned minute of every single one of those twenty-five years, just because I happened to be learning-disadvantaged in the Hebrew department, if all that His vaunted Mysterious Ways came down to was moving Jerry Goldkorn by way of Lud, New Jersey, all the way past the Arctic Circle so he could make asshole/asshole before a bunch of folks who weren't too nuts about His Chosen People in the first place, then who was Jerry Goldkorn to sneak a peek, or look up the parchment skirts of some multimulti-K Torah?)

"No, Deborah," I told her sweetly, "I didn't happen to find an opportunity."

As I said, and as Debbie predicted, the house was packed. Standing room only. I delivered my announcements to the bare quorum of Jews and approving goyim and unsmiling redskins, giving all of them the times for the next Jewish Singles' Happy Hour (Alaskan corned beef, Juneau pastrami, rye bread flown in from magnetic north), and began the morning prayers. I thanked Him for redressing grievances, for being a Settling Scores kind of God, finished the prayers, told the congregation that we would read the Torah portion, declared the Sh'ma, and summoned Deborah Grunwald beside me to join me on the bema. Together we went toward the ark.

"Not," I told her, speaking in my normal voice now too, in

that customary pitch of conversation which, if it wasn't audible
in the first rows, was a proof of God's existence that just by
raising the volume a few ticks it was clear as a bell in Heaven,
"because, counting Shavuoth and all those Friday night services,
you must have set up the better part of a couple of thousand
chairs for me by this time, and I owe you. Not even because"
—our backs to the congregation as we moved toward the precious shittim-wood cabinet that contained the scrolls, I wasn't
even ad-even addressing her out of the side of my mouth, but
was speaking flagrantly, profile to profile, like people in public
seen from behind—"you're a special favorite of mine, Rabbi's
pet, say, or something, well, lurid. I'll tell you the truth, Miss
Grunwald, lurid ain't on my palette. I know how it goes in the
world, how some-times it's the priest gets the girl just because
he *is* the priest. Not just the celibacy thing but because he has
God's ear, a line on the mysteries. That's impressive to girls.
Look, break in anytime if I'm out of line here, because, well,
chances are I could *be* out of line and not even know it. See, I'm
this Garden State rabbi and as much at a loss when it comes to
the mysteries as everyone else. I mean, *I'm* impressionable too.
Innocent beyond my years and trade. A rabbi who never had a
proper congregation, who just says words over dead people for
living people who don't have the hang of or calling for it themselves. So it shouldn't come as a surprise to you I'm the kind of
shaman ladies don't usually take a shine to. I regard myself as
eligible and red-blooded as the next guy, but you've got to
admit, the death of the next-of-kin doesn't normally put someone in the mood. Widows never fell all over me, I guess I'm
trying to say. So of course I never had much op-portunity to fall
all over them back. So it isn't because of the likelihood of either
of us having a crush on the other. *It's because I need a witness and
you happened to ask the question is why!*"

We opened the ark and took out the Torah. We removed
the silver crowns and stripped the mantle from the loosely
bound parchments. We were unrolling, separating the scrolls.

It was a little like waiting for a strip of leader to play out
on film or recording tape. And at first, not distracted by the
thick, black Hebrew letters, which always look, with their diminished, left-leaning hooks and finials like the spiky flourish on
custard, as if no one not right-handed could ever have made

them, it was easy to imagine that the hundred-forty-five-thousand dollars Alyeska was said to have paid for it may in fact have been its actual price.

The story of Creation came up, Adam and Eve, Noah, Abraham and Isaac, Miriam, the Tower of Babel, Moses and the Exodus, Joseph and his coat of many colors, the Ten Commandments. The Sh'ma, the Mi Hamocha with its apostrophe to God— "Who is like Thee, O Lord, among the mighty? Who is like Thee, Glorious and Holiness, awe-inspiring in renown, doing wonders?"

And then its gorgeous parchment, the true, smoothly shaven, lime-buttered, chalk-rubbed skin of a sheep, abruptly ended, went the blank, vague, smudged and ancient ivory of a window shade.

"We missed it. Quick," I told her, "roll it back, take it up. We missed it." I fed her slack off my spool. Mi Hamocha went by, the Sh'ma. The Ten Commandments, Joseph, Moses, Babel. Miriam. Isaac and Abraham. Eve and Adam. Creation spun by and was furiously swept away back into blankness, the thick yellow light of the empty parchment. "It's not here," I told her, "it's gone. Tish'a b'Av dropped out." I looked at Deborah as if she might have taken it herself, like the Grinch who stole Christmas. Then we rolled it carefully in the opposite direction, the Torah bound on its wooden poles like newspapers in a European coffee shop. It was the same thing. The dietary laws were gone, the Korh Rebellion. It had all dropped out.

"Do you read Hebrew, Miss Grunwald?" McBride, some of the Indians leaned forward. I think they could hear me now, as if, with my question to Deborah, I had started the services up again, resumed the prayers. As, in a way, I had. "Do you know what we have here? Do you know what this is?" Deborah shook her head. So I gave them fragments from the story of Adam and Eve, selections from Exodus, a piece from the Tower of Babel, a bit from the Flood, throwing in all I could remember, whatever I had by heart, of the story of poor old God-bedeviled Job.

I assume the gentiles never noticed, nor the Indians. Maybe even some of the Jews.

Because what it was, what we had here on that authentic, lime-buttered, chalk-rubbed, hundred-forty-five-K sheepskin I was so taken with, were the Old Testament's Greatest Hits!

•   •   •   •   •

The next, the last time, it was blank.

It was Rosh Hashanah. Deborah was gone too now. Which I might have expected. Which I did expect. What I *hadn't* expected was that Howard Ziegler, Karen Ackerman and Milton Abish, on whom I counted to be there, if only out of the same goodwill and curiosity they shared with Arnie Sternberg, Dave Piepenbrink and the Jacobsons before *their* defections, didn't show up either. I set up my own chairs, but I didn't care about that. That was all right. I didn't mind that part. What I minded was the other thing, the sense I had of having actually *lost* souls.

It doesn't require much telling, this shouldn't take long.

McBride was there again. I recognized Spike and recognized Ambest. I spotted Anderson, I spotted Jim Krezlow. And picked out others whom I'd first seen in Anchorage. Peachblow and Schindblist. Jeers, who had failed to qualify in the jackhammer and been flown back to Alabama, had evidently come up to snuff and was being given a second chance. (Or perhaps not, maybe he was just there to see me.) There were Indians who looked familiar, and others from earlier fiascos. There were almost no Jews at all.

Rabbi Petch, with whom I had thought to trade jobs, was there. At the Jewish New Year's solemn beginning—it was early October; we were at Crystal Creek camp; at this latitude the fierce fall had already begun to drain the light, suck at its sparkle and leach its golds and yellows, tamping it flat, white, thin and dull as skimmed milk—he sat dressed in the hot woolen suit he'd been wearing when I'd last seen him, at the dead center of the congregation, not its southwest corner, but in its actual bull's-eyed nub and nucleus. I was certain he huddled there for protection, as though maybe there were two neutral corners in the natural world, one for indoors and another for out.

Well.

This was the little reconditioned one, the short-handled, twenty-four-inch, ninety-thousand-dollar Sephardic. Or which would have been Sephardic if it hadn't been blank. Which could be—who knew?—Sephardic yet, if all we needed was to get some specialist, someone checked out in the Sephardic hand the way old Jeers was checked out in jackhammer to go to work on it and copy down Pentateuch (which, considering the losses so far sustained, and providing the new guy was willing to work for nothing, would still come to something just over a hundred thousand bucks a teuch). Or could be if we didn't have to fly in some extra-holy type first (the flower-bearded fellow, say) to re-deconsecrate the hoaxed-up sheepskin, reconsecrate it again and just set the scribe loose.

But that was something that would have to wait.

First I had to get through Rosh Hashanah.

I began by asking the Four Questions.

"Wherefore," I chanted on this brisk Alaskan autumn morning six or so months after the Passover in the only Hebrew, with the exception of my haphtarah passage, a handful of broches and poems, and a few prayers for the dead, I had ever memorized, "is this night different from all other nights?

"On all other nights we eat either leavened or unleavened bread; on this night why only unleavened bread?

"On all other nights we eat any species of herbs; on this night why only bitter herbs?

"On all other nights we do not dip our herbs even once; on this night why do we dip them twice?

"On all other nights we eat our meals in any manner; on this night why do we sit around the table together in a reclining position?"

When I finished I looked up from the empty parchment, looked down again quickly, and hurriedly started to recite my haphtarah passage before the remaining Jews, McBride, the other gentiles, the redskins, and the Anchorage Seven.

I might have gotten through it, too, the first Chief Rabbi of the Alaska Pipeline ever publicly to re-bar mitzvah himself, when I felt someone beside me. It was Petch.

He took over for me, going through the service without a single mistake. Though why anyone should take *my* word for this I can't say. He even had a shofar with him and sounded it, the dark, mottled, polished ram's horn, glazed as tortoiseshell, summoning the New Year through its harsh, amplified winds like a sort of spittled Jewish weather, brusque, gruff as phlegm. He finished the morning part of the Rosh Hashanah services and started up again in the afternoon. Then again at sundown. From the Torah that never was. I stood beside him on the platform and, properly cued, even participated by chanting the broches, reading them off the blank parchment by following the silver yad that Rabbi Petch moved along the missing Hebrew.

Through the long, prayer-filled day we carried on one of those mysterious conversations inaudible to the congregation.

"I heard about you," he said.

"I guess everyone has."

"Is that what you want? To be famous?"

"No. Of course not."

" 'Thou, O Lord, art mighty for ever. Thou quickenest the dead. Thou art mighty to save.' "

"I'm sorry about all this," I said.

"You should be. This is the first time I've ever been so far from Anchorage."

"What do you think?"

"Barbarous. Worse than I thought. Will you look at that raging river? I think it's going to bust its banks and take the bridge out."

"That's Crystal Creek," I said.

"I'm taking my life in my hands. How are the Eskimos around here?"

"Very tame. Gentlemen, in fact."

"A lot you know."

"Yeah," I said, "there you have me. I'm a bumpkin." I wanted to make him understand. "Because I never took it seriously. The proposition that roughnecks could ever get into any of this. Or that God would take their disengagement seriously either. On my side in this, though why I should assume so I don't know."

"God's opinions?"

"That's right."

" 'Now, therefore, O Lord our God, impose Thine awe upon all Thy works, and Thy dread upon all that Thou hast created, that all works may fear Thee and all creatures prostrate themselves before Thee.' "

"Since," I said, "there was going to be an Alaskan pipeline anyway, and all the red tape and Title Nines and Tens and whatever were already in place, I thought it was a good time to get out of Jersey, put a stake together, and, if things worked out, maybe trade congregations with you."

"Out of the question," Petch said. "No deal. Deal's off. You aren't serious. You were never terrified enough. I wouldn't give a plugged nickel for your stake," he said suddenly. Then, softly, "Someone must stand between us and the Eskimos."

Though it was humiliating to me, I can't say I wasn't at least a little relieved. Here was Petch with his phantom Eskimos and chimerical natural disasters ready to throw himself into the breach, to intercede on man's behalf for God, or God's for man's, whichever came first, like a limited warranty.

"Maybe," I told him, "I *wasn't* terrified enough. Though by any normally terrified guy's standards I'm pretty terrified."

" 'Let all the inhabitants of the world perceive and know that unto Thee every knee must bend, every tongue must swear. Before Thee, O Lord our God, let them bow and fall.' That's why . . . What's his name, McBride?"

"McBride, yes."

"That's why McBride don't fire you. You ain't scared enough yet to blow in a whistle, you're not quite afraid to make a wave. That's why he'll probably let you play out your contract.

"Oh," he said, "by the way, is it true? Were the others like this?" He touched the yad to the godforsaken parchment.

"One contained highlights. One was written out in English."

"No swastikas but? I heard swastikas."

The scrolls were covered and placed back in the ark.

"No," I said, "of course not. You think I would have sat still for swastikas?"

"A bold, stand-up guy like you? Why not?"

We finished the services. Then we shook hands and each heartily wished the other might be inscribed in the Book of Life for another year. Everyone did. McBride and the Indians. Jeers and the gentiles.

I walked Petch to the airstrip where his bush pilot was topping off the fuel in the gas tank and listening to music coming in over the plane's radio on an Anchorage AM frequency.

Next week was Yom Kippur. Petch offered to come up, but I told him there was no need, I'd use the transliterated version.

"Ballsy," he said.

"Why do you have to go? You don't have to go. Stay over, go back in the morning."

He looked up at the calm, perfectly cloudless sky. "Better get out," he said darkly, "while the getting's good."

"Don't you think you're imposing a skosh too much awe upon His works? Is it necessary to dread *all* He created?"

"Sure," he said, "everything."

"Safe trip," I told him.

"Wise guy," he said and turned to the pilot. "Excuse me, you're not afraid you'll wear out the batteries?" He pointed to the plane's radio, turned high, pushing its tinny music through the headset on the pilot's seat. Philip also liked to use his radio for purposes for which it was never intended. I recalled how upset I'd been when we were airborne again and he'd tuned in to listen to a Fairbanks station, perhaps the very one that was playing now. Only now I understood what was happening. It was the same instinct that drove them to six-pack the house, that same sporty waste and recklessness lifted to a kind of code. You started with the realization that you only lived once. Then you modified your behavior to spite the bad news. (I had a sudden hunch about the stake all of us were supposed to be putting together up there, that it was a myth, more chimerical and dreamy than any of Petch's disasters.) Maybe that was what was so unamiable and cynical about the idea of the potlatch. Maybe it was what Petch objected to in me. Life was *so* difficult, being good, respecting God. Dread and awe, I was thinking, were hard in such an awesome, dreadful world, and I began to pray that Rabbi Petch and his pilot be inscribed in the Book of Life for another year, then that Shelley and my daughter Constance were, Spike and Ambest and Krezlow and Anderson and Peach-blow and Schindblist and Jeers, and all the names of all the people I could remember meeting up there— the Jacobsons, Dave Piepenbrink, Arn Sternberg, McBride, Deb Grunwald, Howard Ziegler and Milt Abish and Karen Ackerman and Philip, the bush pilot who'd almost gotten both of us killed. Which is just exactly when the song ended and they broke for the news and the announcer came on to say that there'd been a plane crash on a small island in Cook Inlet. His two passengers had survived, but the pilot, Philip Kutchik, a Fairbanks resident and Tinneh Indian who flew for the Alyeska Corporation, had been killed instantly.

• • • •

I went to Phil's funeral. A busman's holiday, you're think-ing, but that's not it at all. I hadn't been to the funeral of anyone close in years. Not since my mother's, not since my father's. Living in New Jersey, in that queer, Jewless, almost unpeopled town, there'd been no occasion. Shelley and I had only a few friends, and none of them, knock wood, had died. So I went to Philip's funeral. Though we were hardly friends and I thought him a bit of a jerk, we'd certainly been through a lot together. We'd hacked out a nest together. We'd broken hardtack, shared the last of our jerky, displaced each other's weight—I'd bite a fingernail, he'd spit out a window. I *shouldn't* go to his funeral? My God, we were besieged by bears, found out by the wind-wafted tang of our mutual excrement. We weren't close. That was only proximity in the plane, but I *shouldn't* go to his funeral?

And a good thing, I thought at the laying out. Because except for one or two pilot chums (there, it turned out, as official Alyeskan delegates), and the crash's two survivors (who stood by the casket—which, to my surprise, was open, Philip's face having escaped injury, its only wound being in the sud-denly paid attention of his expression—and told everyone who came near, myself, representatives of the funeral parlor, who they were and that, but for the grace of God, it could have been them there in that coffin instead of the poor dumb, jargon-spouting son of a bitch with his attitudes and minimums, civil evening twilights, eminences, DF steers, pan pans and A-OKs who lay there now), no one showed up.

I had rented an automobile and drove in the three-car cortege (the hearse, my rental car, a bright yellow Alyeskan truck) out to the cemetery. The two survivors had decided not to come, but the man with the flowers in his beard was outside the funeral parlor when I came out, and he rode with me in the rental car.

"They seem a little faded, Khokem," I said. I think it was the first time I ever referred to his beard to his face.

"Yeah, well," he said, stroking it lightly, "you know. October. The last leaf, same old story."

"It's good to see you."

"Next time it should be a better occasion."

"Well, of course," I said, shamed and chastened as I always am whenever anyone pulls this line on me. "It's awful about Philip. Just awful."

"Terrible."

"I felt I had to come," I said.

"Of course."

"Though we were hardly friends and, to be perfectly frank, sometimes I thought he was a bit of a jerk, we went through a lot together."

"Certainly," he said. "I understand."

"That plane crash. All the time we spent living in that airplane. Remember that nest that we hacked out of pine trees?"

"I do."

"We lived out of survival tins and broke hardtack together. We shared dried jerky."

"I had some myself."

"That's right," I said, "you did."

"Sure."

"We learned each other's weights and measures. I bit my nails, he spit out the window. He tutored me in the intricate Alaskan economy. My God," I said, "we were besieged by bears!"

"I remember that."

"I *shouldn't* come to his funeral? I *shouldn't* come? He was like a brother to me."

"To me too," he said.

"I know," I said, "I know, Tzadik," and wiped my nose with my handkerchief. " 'Every man is a piece of the continent, a part of the main. . . . Any man's death diminishes me, I am involved in mankind.' "

"No, no," said Flowerface, "you miss my meaning. He *was* my brother."

"Phil was your brother?"

"We were identical twins. Here," he said, "look," and removing an old black-and-white photograph from his wallet, he pushed the snapshot toward me. In the photo a fifteen- or sixteen-year-old youth, who bore a substantial but, considering the face I'd seen in the open casket, fallen-away resemblance to the Phil he had become, stood next to someone who might have been his mirror image. Both boys were beardless and, near their left temples, where, back in the plane in March, their heads had been covered by parka hoods, each had a tiny birthmark like a corporal's chevrons. I saw the tzadik's where he tapped at his temple. "Hmn," he said, "hah? Hmn?"

"He was your brother? Phil?"

The falling away had occurred on both their parts, as if Phil had come to resemble a distant, younger cousin who would always look youthful, while old Posypuss, tricked out in his now fading flowers, was an actor, well cast but unrelated, carefully prepared by Hollywood makeup artists, to look like a relative, an uncle, say, even a grandfather, of the kids in the photograph.

"We were Tinnehs," he said. "It's the way with Tinnehs."

"Beg pardon, Khokem?"

"Tinnehs. Tinneh Indians? I told you. In the plane? How the Tinnehs are tribeless, clanless. How they—we—break away from each other. Generation after generation. Highest divorce rate in Alaska. Alaska? The world. How the children are placed in orphan asylums when the parents run off? That picture was taken in the orphanage. Don't you remember? Why don't you listen? You think I talk for my health? Identical twins, I told you how even identical twins drift apart."

He *had* mentioned identical twins. Phrases came back to me. They would, he'd said, "dissipate affinity, annihilate connection." They moved, "down some chain of relation from sibling to friend, friend to neighbor, neighbor to acquaintance, and acquaintance to stranger." And remembered his saying how once the Tinnehs outnumbered all the other tribes put together but were now "rare in the Alaskan population as Frenchmen."

Now I recalled how interested I'd been, and the moment when the sun came up and he couldn't finish his story because we had to take off.

We were back in Fairbanks, parked in front of the hotel where he was staying. I had to drop off my rental car at the airport before my flight, I told him.

"Well," he said, "it was good seeing you."

"Next time," I said carefully, "on a better occasion."

"Yeah," he said, and put his hand out to open the door.

For the first time I noticed the mourner's band on the right sleeve of his coat.

"Listen," I said, and touched him on the shoulder, "I'm sorry about Phil. I can't tell you."

"Thanks," he said. "But you know something?"

"What's that?"

"I don't know," he said, sloughing off my condolence, "we like drifted apart."

Then he opened the door and got out. I started to turn the key in the ignition, but the man with the flowers in his beard was rapping on the window for my attention. I leaned across to roll the window down on his side and he pushed his big head into the car.

Up close, straight on, the beard seemed lopsided, lifeless. I caught the pinched, stale scent of mold. "Ain't no murracles," old Posypuss said, "I dud wished dey would was, but dey ain't."

•   •   •   •

As Petch had predicted, McBride let me play out my contract. As a matter of fact, he wouldn't let me resign and *made* me play it out. I guess he thought I was pretty well seasoned by the time of those Rosh Hashanah services and didn't figure even Alyeska could afford another greenhorn rabbi until the fiscal year ran out on the one they already had.

He never mentioned the Torahs. McBride, like the Eskimos, was a gentleman too.

Which isn't to say I could ever stop thinking of Flowerface out there in the dark. Out on that iceberg, in that proper, heroic blackness he rubbed against like braille, yogi-ing his bloodstream and rearranging his metabolics and contemplating not the ways of God or even Man, but figuring red tape, the long odds of Corporate Life, how the Feds would probably require affirmative action, Prots and Mackerel—snappers and even Jews demanding rabbis, Torahs, the works, and what all this could mean to him at Alaskan prices, till he saw what it felt like to move at a glacier's pace, a few fast feet a day with the wind in his face.

six

"WHERE," I asked, "could we go?"

"Shh," Shelley said afterward as we lay in each other's arms in the dark. "Shh."

"You told Connie we'd leave Lud. And do what? Where? How?"

"Shh. Shah. Ay le lu lu."

"Where, Shelley? What would I do?"

"Later-le."

"Later-le's too late. Right-e-le now."

"Leave-e-le now?"

"Talk-e-le now, ask-e-le questions afterward."

Because it's one thing to calm your kid down with easy promises, but I'm not talking about eat your greens, sweetheart, we'll go get 31 flavors. Connie's no fool. She had real problems, even—I say it—legitimate gripes. Not all that death prattle, of course, ghosts in the drinking water, phantoms in her pants. Not even my failure with God in the Stanley Bloom affair, nothing metaphysical. She had flawed birthrights, I think. A misser-out on the gemütlich circumstance, the curled and comfy lap-robe life. I don't know, maybe it would have been better for her if she'd had an aversion to the four food groups, better if we could have done business, traded and bribed her, appetite for appetite, taken her to the mall more, kept her up past her bedtime, made nests for her in the back of the car and driven her home in the dark. Maybe we should have turned the radio low and shifted from texture to texture for her on the highways, playing the percussives and hypnotics of different road surfaces like some long, cozy organ, the dash's soft glow and the averted headlamps of oncoming cars like light skimming along the walls and ceilings of dark bedrooms. But still her stinted birthright. She was an only child. She had no grandparents, no cousins, no uncles, no aunts. Was this mild orphan of relation. ("I'm the last of your line," she told us once. "When I marry there'll be no more Goldkorns," she'd said, and burst into tears. "Please don't cry," Shelley said, "I'm the same as you are." "Me too," I said, "the fall of the House of Usherkorn.") But another thing altogether to offer to change their life.

Which is what I'd been trying to impress upon Shelley.

"What?" I asked. "Where?"

"Anywhere," she said drowsily.

"Anywhere. Shell?"

"Mnn?"

"What?"

"Anything-e-ling-e-ding-e-ling-e," she murmured and then, I swear it, actually yawned in that pidgin Yiddish or whatever the hell else it was she thought she was speaking.

"Shelley, wake up, we've got to talk." I shook my wife.

"What," she said, "what is it?"

"A couple of days ago you told Connie we'd leave Lud and she believed you. Jesus, Shell, *I* believed you. All right, the kid hasn't made a fuss, she hasn't even brought it up again, but I see her watching me. Yesterday I told her I hadn't had time to type up my resume yet but that I was working on it. Working on it. It would take me ten minutes! Two minutes to write and eight to find the envelope to stick it in, address, and drink the glass of water to get rid of the bad taste in my mouth from sealing it and licking the stamp. Only I'll tell you, Shelley," I said, "I'm fresh the hell out of ideas."

"Poor Jerry."

"Shelley, you don't know."

"Poor Jerry. So much on his head."

"I mean really," I said, "what experience have I had?"

"Thinking about Talmud all day. Talmud Talmud Talmud."

"A man my age. It's worse than being fired. Really," I said, "it is. It really is."

"Tch tch. Should I say something to Connie? I'll say something to Connie. You want me to say something?"

"No," I said, "the kid's got real problems. You think I'd go along with any of this if I didn't believe she had real problems?"

"She said 'goddamn.' She said 'asshole' to her papa."

"They lay you off, at least they offer to retrain you. They teach you computer programming, give you a hundred dollars and a new suit."

"Everything's going to be fine. You worry too much."

"Talmud Talmud Talmud."

"I know," Shelley said.

"So here's what I've come up with."

"What's that?"

"We emigrate to Israel. They'd have to take us in. It's the Law of the Return."

"Emigrate? To Israel?"

"Sure," I said. "It won't be so bad. They set us up in a suitable kibbutz."

"We emigrate to *Israel*?"

"I thought you'd be pleased. You'd be an Israel-e-li."

"But Jerry," she said, "all we have to do is move to Fairlawn."

"What?"

"Or Ridgewood."

"What?"

"Or any of dozens of towns. We've got all northern Jersey to choose from."

"Jesus," I said, "northern Jersey!"

"Sure," Shelley said, "I asked one of the girls in The Chaverot to be on the lookout, to tell me if she heard of a place. Elaine Iglauer?"

"Elaine Iglauer. The one who moves. Yes?"

"You should have heard the leads she came up with just off the top of her head."

"Sure," I said, "she knows her stuff."

"She really does."

"You're telling me," I said. "Seven houses in six different towns."

"Oh, you're behind. They've just closed on their eighth."

"That's wonderful," I said. "That's marvelous, that's really wonderful."

"Of course we'd have to buy," she said. "We wouldn't have the kind of deal we have here."

"Utilities and taxes? No," I said, "are you kidding? Who could expect to? Not me."

"Joan Cohen said she'd shop around for a temple once Elaine's found a place for us."

"Joan Cohen," I said. "The one who shops."

A person's so single-minded. When Shelley told Connie we'd leave Lud, I thought . . . But a person's so single-minded. Our problems were solved. If it cost us a few bucks then it cost us a few bucks. Hey, you don't get *all* the way through life on the arm. Who knew better than I? Wasn't that what so many of my eulogies were about? Sacrifice? Being there for others? I had no problems with that. Anyway, hadn't we been able to put a little something by? Weren't we okay in that department? No mortgage payments, no rent, living scot-free years in a big white Colonial, 5 bdm, 3½ bth, lg lvng rm w/fr plc, rmdld kchn, scrnd brzway, rbi's stdy, grg, patio & swmng pl, convnt to grvs, crpts, tmbs & mslms? Of course it would take a hefty chunk out of the savings to replace something like that, but I could always take Klein and Charney up on their offer. In fact, I *would*, and decided to call them first thing in the morning. No, to call them that night and leave a message on their machine, to call Shull and Tober, too, and leave a message on theirs, that they could start drawing up the fancy new contracts with the no-cut clauses. (Of course a person has to sacrifice, but if he plays his cards right he might not even have to dip into capital.)

And hadn't I, misunderstanding or no misunderstanding, and despite my relief—my relief came afterward, a solidly come-by, legitimately earned relief—already shown that *willingness* to sacrifice which ought, if it already wasn't, to be all that God ever actually outright required of anyone—*vide* Abraham, *vide* Isaac—just that momentary glimpse of the revealed soul like a private part? Hadn't I already fixed it in my head to go to the wall for my spooked daughter? Even unto such lengths that I was going to uproot everything I knew or was good at, as if everything I knew or was good at were some tainted husbandry, the rotten fruits of a bad season, and the wall was the wailing one. Next *month*, say, in Jerusalem? So never mind I was relieved. I knew what was in store for us if we emigrated. To humiliate myself and endanger my family. Jersey Jerry Goldkorn, the Klutz of the Kibbutz like a court jester, terrified of incoming on the northern border, terrified of incoming, period. Suspicious of ancient Arab ladies and gentlemen on the buses, suspicious of *everyone*, innocent-looking kids, the more innocent-looking the guiltier, as if an entire population had become suspects in a mystery, everyone, rabbis and shamuses and balebatish providers, a potentially turned Jew, trust and belief vitiated until all that there was left to believe in were the up-for-grab loyalties, some remarkable shifting double agency. (Besides, I was an American and not only had no use for terrorists but no business in politics. An American's politics is his standard of living, and I say God bless him for that. Money and comfort. All else is vanity.)

I got out of bed, left the sleeping Shelley, and made my calls, but instead of leaving a complicated message on the machine about having finally decided to take Charney and Klein up on their offer to push grave lots because we were thinking of buying a house and would need the extra income, I simply left my name and asked if they could get back to me in the morning.

I couldn't get over it. A person's *so* single-minded, so committed to one avenue of thought he really *can't* see the forest for the trees. Shelley'd told the kid we'd pick up and leave Lud, and I'd thought she meant it was all up with me in the rabbi business, that I couldn't be Rabbi of Lud anymore. I couldn't get over it, I really couldn't. I'm thinking life after Lud, she's thinking Ridgewood.

And so I'm lying there beside my sleeping Shelley, all stimulated and pleased with how things work out and, if you want to know, actually looking forward to the new duties I'd be taking on if we were to avoid being kicked in the head financially. And kicking ideas around in *my* head, things I could say to the people I'd be dealing with, the folks whose names Klein and Charney would have given me as leads. For openers—I'd have on my yarmulke, to show the flag, you know?—I'd say, I'd say, oh, "Shalom, shalom. How are you today, Mr. Fishbone? Mrs. Fishbone? I'm Rabbi Jerome Goldkorn, the Rabbi of Lud. Mr. Charney suggested I speak with you. Mr. Charney? Charney and Klein? Realities? What, did I say 'realities?' I meant realtors, but face it, it's realities we're really talking about here, isn't it?"

Working variations in my head, versions of the instructions they dictated to their machines, reprises of the messages I had left on them, until, one thing leading to the other as it does in the act of drifting off, I lost my place and fell asleep.

And when the phone woke me the next morning and I heard Emile Tober's voice, it was as if it had been a perfectly seamless night.

"Yes, Emile," I said, "thanks for getting back to me. It's about—"

"I *know* what it's about! Just what in the hell is wrong with that lunatic daughter of yours? Has she fucking gone *crazy?!*"

seven

BECAUSE she's as single-minded as I am. Single-minded on my behalf, taking an even more single-minded view of things than I did. Not figuring the kibbutz into the equation, not figuring Ridgewood or Israel or the Law of the Return or any other loophole. Too single-minded for that, her single-minded eyes focused on one single-minded principle— Rabbi of Lud or nothing. *More* single-minded. (Because with me there was never any question of stealth, but then—give the devil her due—she wasn't her father but only the helpless kid in the affair, so maybe she felt she had to. Well, of course she *felt* she had to, obviously she *felt* she had to, though—though this is the father in me talking—it was a perfectly reasonable, perfectly honorable stealth, like that famous letter hidden right in front of your eyes in the story— a sort of *purloined* stealth. Getting Shelley to drive her to all those libraries that spring and winter and even, when she was over the limit herself, to check out extra books for her on her card. And we worried because no matter how much work she did it didn't seem to get reflected in her grades. To say nothing of the three or four hundred dollars she was able to put away by never volunteering to return the change we had coming to us, or by saving ten or eleven bucks out of the fifteen we gave her each week for her allowance. The little dickens.)

This is what she said in the deposition:

I, Constance Ruth Goldkorn, being of sound mind and body, do solemnly swear and attest that what I am about to affirm is the truth, the whole truth, and nothing but the truth, so help me God.

I didn't know who she was. When I saw her that first time I didn't recognize her from Adam and would have hurried away as fast as my legs could carry me, but of course I didn't, and probably couldn't, even though I wanted to because when I saw her that first time it was a snow day and the sidewalks and streets were all covered with ice and snow and it was very slippery out, which is the reason, she said, the schools were closed and our paths happened to cross in the first place.

I told her excuse me, that I was on this errand for my mom, and started to walk away from her, and that's when she started to cry.

Which I thought was very curious. Not that she was crying because it was very cold out, ten or fifteen below maybe, and there were tears in my eyes too, only the tears in my eyes were because of the cold weather, that like icy stinging you get in your eyes when it's real cold and you almost feel your eyeballs are going to crack, or those sharp, sticky pains that you get in your temples. I'm a little embarrassed to tell this next part, but my attorney, Counselor Christopher Rockers, says that a deposition is a testimony taken down under oath for use in court, although in this case there's not going to be any trial or anything and I'm making this deposition only because I want what happened to go on the record. Anyway, the point is, the lady was not only crying but crying so hard she had this runny nose too. (I was raised in a cemetery, I know about Nature. I don't get the giggles if a boy cuts a fart. I don't go all squeamy when it's that time of month. I know that bodily functions often have nothing to do with whether a person has or has not got bad manners. I'm like a kid on a farm in that respect.) Anyway, what was so curious was that the tears were pouring out her eyes and running down her cheeks, and the mucus was dripping out her nostrils just exactly as if she was crying indoors in a warm, toasty room and not outside on a cold, blustery ten- or fifteen-degree-below-zero snow day. That's the sort of tears and mucus they were— soft, room temperature tears and mucus.

My father, Rabbi Jerome Goldkorn, works for Shull and Tober Funeral Directors of Lud, New Jersey, and even if I am only fourteen years old, I've been around enough unhappiness, sadness, sorrow, gloom and grief in my time almost to be able to tell the difference between them (and, if you ask me, I think it was all five), and certainly to swear that whatever it was that caused all that weeping didn't have anything to do with weather.

Though you'd almost think it could have because all she had on was this—I don't know how to describe it exactly— not a kimono or shroud, more like what those ladies wear in Middle East countries so men can't look at them, that they wrap around them like a shawl and that covers their heads too—big blue gown like a housewife who's locked herself outside her own house.

Now this next thing is embarrassing because it's on me. I don't have a whole lot of friends. My father thinks it's because of where we live, and there's some truth in that because there certainly aren't a whole bunch of kids around here to play with. Anyway, even if I don't have a lot of friends, those kids who do get to know me, the kids in my car pool, for example, or some of the people who know me from class, will tell you I'm shy, that I keep to myself and like to mind my own business. I'll give an example that comes to my mind. Last year I graduated from Junior High and there was some foulup at the printer's about the school colors—they're brown and white, not green and red—and our yearbooks all had to go back to the bindery and we didn't get to see them until after we actually graduated. What happened was, they sent us this announcement that the yearbooks were ready and that we could come to the gym and get them if we brought our receipt along to show that we'd paid. Only I had a bad cold the day we were supposed to pick up the yearbook and didn't get to the school until three days later. They had to open the gym especially for me (which as you can probably imagine was pretty embarrassing just in itself), and Mrs. Sayles, the lady from the office who opened the gym, went to the table where they'd put all the yearbooks. "It's too bad you had that cold, Connie," she said, "or you could have written in your friends' yearbooks." Then she said, oh, well, at least mine had been inscribed, that she'd seen to it herself that the kids wrote something in all the kids' yearbooks who couldn't pick them up on the regularly scheduled day they were supposed to. Well, after she told me that I never got up the nerve to even open my yearbook. Because she'd made them write something in it, you see. I'm shy. I keep to myself. I mind my own business. It would have been like reading someone else's mail.

That's why I didn't ask her anything. Like why she was crying, or if she was lost—I'd never seen her before—or cold in just her thin blue wrap, and made out like it was perfectly natural to find someone in the street on the coldest day of the year, crying like a baby with stuff coming out of its face, and even—and I'm *really* embarrassed about this part because shyness and keeping to yourself and minding your business are one thing and only part of a person's particular makeup, but this was something else altogether, not just disposition but character— that people around here were free to behave like they want to behave, as if letting someone suffer was democracy in action or something and not asking them if anything's wrong is a plus, rather than the cruel minus I knew it was even then. And wouldn't have even if she hadn't turned the tables on me, making out as if it was me and not her standing out there in the street in this summery lightweight with the wind tearing at my head, and the temperature banging my blood to a standstill.

I've already mentioned how I'm this agony expert. I wasn't boasting. I wasn't even trying to suggest that it's a natural gift. I think it's just what a person is accustomed to. If I'm able to tell which one is really in mourning and which one is probably only putting on a show, I don't think I should get extra credit for it. As I say, it's what a person gets accustomed to. You live and learn. I just happen to have this sort of perfect pitch for heartache. It's unusual in a person of my years, I admit, but I come by it honestly. Anyway, that's not the point. The point is that if I thought *I* was good at different shades of misery and grief, it was because I'd never seen this lady before. She made me feel insensitive. She made me feel like, well, some tone-deaf piker.

But this is a deposition and that last part, while it's true as far as it goes, isn't really what I was paying a lot of attention to at the time. I mean I really wasn't into whether I was feeling insensitive or worrying about losing my perfect pitch for the

somberness of the heart or not. Anyway, I hadn't. Lost it, I
mean. I could read hers, the somberness of *her* heart. And I was
scared. Because what I saw there, in her woe, in her wracked
heart, was the deepest mourning I'd *ever* seen. It was for me.
She was in mourning for *me*!

I'm shy. I keep to myself. I mind my own business.

"Who are you?" I demanded.

She said, "I am the holy mother, Constance child."

"What do you want? Why did you come? Why are you
here?"

"For the harrowing of Lud's cemeteries. For the harrowing
of Pineoaks and Masada Gardens. To rescue the poor lost souls
of righteous Jews."

Well, maybe I am afraid of Lud, maybe I *am*. Maybe I *am*
bothered by having only dead people for neighbors like my
father thinks, or hurt because kids won't play with me, who
won't even visit even though my mom drives the car pools and
would not only go out of her way to pick them up in the first
place but would bring them home too, even though I try to
make my folks think that shyness and a solitary spirit and
minding my business are part of my nature and not just these
add-ons to my character like those cardboard cutouts in which
you dress your paper dolls. (Because I'm not shy *really*. And
don't keep to myself by choice, or mind my business like some
miser in his counting house in love with his ledger. No. Really
I'm like some cheerleader and could name things even in Lud
that swell my pom-pom heart and fill me with pride. Our
monument carvers and landscapers, for example, are the best
there are!) *But even if I am, even if I am afraid to live here, even if I
secretly agree with the kids who make fun of me because of what Lud
stands for, I'm no anti-Semite!* I'm no anti-Semite, and my first
reaction was that the woman in blue was probably Seels's wife.
Seels is a vicious anti-Semite who probably felt exactly the same
way the woman did. Only he wouldn't have thought *poor* and he
wouldn't have thought *righteous*, and he wouldn't have wanted to
rescue them.

So, given the bite-my-tongue probables of my reputation,
I did the only thing I could have done. I excused myself.

"Wait up. Hey, Connie, wait up," said Holy Mother.

And, again given the house odds of my character, did. Like I might have waited on a girl friend, if I'd had one, who offered to walk me home. (I've seen them. Waiting for my mother, sometimes I've seen them. Boys walking boys, girls walking girls—they could almost be sweethearts, they could almost be sweethearts putting off for as long as they dared some significant curfew—as if, so long as they never quite reached their destination, or no, so long as they never stopped *moving*, shuffling in place, in front of their own addresses maybe, in motion like people treading water are in motion, wearing the pavement like mutual convoys in mutual seas. Waiting for Mom I've seen them make two-and-a-half round trips— and filled in, or at least wondered about, the others— that half or trip-and-a-half or even more that would have permitted them to come out even, as friends should. Or with one friend still graciously owing the other, or the other as graciously owed, the extra half trip that could always be made up tomorrow. Just speculating here as I—the other kids in the car pool off to one side—waited for my mother to come pick us all up, doing the even-steven, double-entry bookkeeping I thought was all there was to friendship.)

Did wait up. And strolled, just as if we *were* girl friends, Holy Mother and me, to the corner and back. (I'm fourteen-and-a-half years old but I've never had a sleepover or even been. So I don't know what happens, if they're more like camp than birthday parties, or closer to overnights in the woods than either, or treats after sports, say, the station wagon pulled up outside McDonald's and the team piling out. Do they talk about boys? Who's cute, who's gross? Do they talk about how far they've gone, do they talk about who's done it? Is it okay to go if it's your time of month?) Walked to the corner with her and back to Sal's, where my dad gets his hair cut. Walked to the corner, turned around and went to the florist's and looked in Lou Pamella's window and admired the flowers and Holy Mother said to me, "Oh, Connie, look at the lilies. Aren't they gorgeous? I've always been partial to lilies." And walked to the corner and crossed the street, and then we stopped outside Klein's and Charney's but neither of us said much and soon we were walking again. Despite the difference in our ages, or that she was divine and I was only this mortal female teenager, and just as if it wasn't ten or fifteen below out, two best friends, chatting about life and stuff and harrowing Lud's long main street.

Though you mustn't think I'd forgotten that "rescue the poor lost souls of righteous Jews" remark.

I even called her on it, but she was real surprised, insulted I think, and explained how her family had always been Jewish, that she kept Shabbes even on the evening of the day her son got crucificated, busy as a bee, too busy to think, rushing around, so busy she didn't have time to think about the neighbors, whether they'd remember to bring something, not to bring something, so she and the Magdalene doing it all, preparing the body, preparing the meal, the soup and boiled flanken, quick kasha cholent, kugel and sponge cake (though to tell the truth she wasn't real hungry, no one was, or, if they were, they were too ashamed to admit it, and made the excuses people do at such times, that they were watching their diets, or it was too hot to eat, though she couldn't think of anyone who'd come empty-handed— dishes of all sorts, dishes of all kinds, for every appetite—knishes and blintzes, latkes and noodles and farmer's chop suey, challah and strudel, cabbage soup, beet borsch, lentil and barley bean), then lighting the candles like on any other Friday night. "It was a waste of good food," said Holy Mother, "a sin with kids going hungry," and then somebody suggested they go find some Roman soldiers who might still be peckish after eating their pound of flesh and maybe offer *them* some of the food, and Holy Mother saying how she knew that the person speaking meant it as a joke, but that she didn't happen to be in the mood for joking right then (and added how she didn't know at the time, telling me how you could have knocked her over with a feather, how, quite frankly, she would have thought you were a cuckoo clock if you'd have told her that two days later her son would be out of His tomb, gone, pfffft, just like that, and up in Heaven having the last laugh, or she wouldn't have snapped at that fellow who made the joke about giving the soldiers some of the food, and that she might actually have gone out and done it herself, or invited them in, and that, who knows, it might have made better people out of them because didn't they say you are what you eat, and would anyone in his right mind honestly argue that good kosher cooking wasn't better for your disposition, personality and character than having to live on dry hardtack and stale Roman rations, but that seriously, it was a shame she *hadn't* known, that not only would it have bucked them all up to have known what was what, but just to have had a sign, *something*, that remark to the gonif on the cross—"You will this day be with me in Paradise"—what, this was a *sign?* this was something you said to a child to calm it down), and that believe it or not, of all the things that happened that day, this was what she regretted the most, her rudeness to the fellow who'd made that remark about feeding the soldiers, that—and here she asked if I could keep a secret, and, oh, if ever there was a time for me to think, Well, good for you, Connie, that's just exactly what best *friends* say to each other! that was the time for me to think it, even though I know that by going on the record like this I'm not keeping it—she personally had a very particular problem about hurting people's feelings, what with all her husband Joseph was put through and suffered because of her. I didn't know what she was talking about but understood just from the way she said it that it was something really important. I suppose I was testing her friendship, but I asked her flat out. She told me what had happened. "Oh, wow!" I said.

But I still wasn't sure of her story, or even that she was really who she said she was, or believed her after I asked why she'd looked so sad when she first saw me and she said it was because she knew I had no one to play with and that Jesus had no one to play with when He was my age either, that once He went into the temple and answered all those questions the rabbis asked Him, how no kid His age ever went near Him again, that they called him "egghead" and "stuck-up brown nose" even though nothing could have been further from the truth (although even if she *was* His mom, she didn't see how He could have failed to be at least a *little* conceited, knowing who He was and all, and the connections He had). And then she said how I only *pretend* to enjoy keeping to myself, and even told me about the yearbooks. But she could have gotten that stuff anywhere. Robert Hershorn knew (a man I know who has Alzheimer's and that I tell my troubles to) and *he* might have come out of his fog long enough to say something, even to that vicious anti-Semite, Seels. I still couldn't *really* be sure.

Holy Mother must have read my mind or something because she suggested we walk down to the cemetery together. (I was plenty terrified of what we'd see. Even though she'd explained it to me a couple of times already, I still didn't have a real good idea of what "harrowing" was exactly, or what it might look like. I thought everything would be all dug up or something. Even if it was just the graves of people she'd already rescued it could still have been pretty grisly. *And it was!* At Pineoaks, in the new section of the cemetery near the landing field, there was a cluster of terrible gashes in the ground, the broken earth wet as fresh wounds. There was a smell like, and I guess I almost cried out. Didn't, but almost. And would have run off if Holy Mother, who was *very* smart—that's the thing about her, that she's so smart as well as so nice—hadn't put her hand on my arm, not in the way you'd catch a person's sleeve and hold them there, but as if you were just reaching out to help them with their balance, and told me hush, don't cry, that they were only fresh graves, not even graves yet actually, just holes for the Povermans, graves where they'd go when Daddy buried them tomorrow. Then I asked what's that smell, and she said it was just what deep, fresh dirt smelled like in cold weather, a little like steam rising off of manure. I suppose I looked a little surprised when she said that about manure, but Holy Mother just smiled and said I mustn't be priggish, it was bodily functions that kept us alive in the first place, and didn't she just get through telling me how after the Crucification she and the Magdalene prepared his body—and that Son of God or no Son of God, *that* was no picnic—and then just rinsed off afterward in the river with a little ash log soap and went in and made supper? But I depose that even if those holes *were* only for the Poverman family, two kids and their parents killed the day before in a tragic accident where no one wore their seat belts, harrowing was pretty grisly anyway, probably all the more so because *nothing* was disturbed— not the graves or the gravestones or the perpetual care. There weren't even any footsteps in the snow! "The only way," Holy Mother said, "anyone could tell I was even here is by the little stones and pebbles I left underneath the snow on the tops of the markers and monuments." Which made me, though I suppose I ought to be ashamed to admit it—and really am, *now*—a little suspicious, because there she was, talking about lentil soup and boiled flanken and farmer's chop suey and steam rising off manure and bodily functions and washing the dead one minute, and sneaking little stones and pebbles in under the snow so you couldn't even notice where they'd been slipped in the next. It was grisly. It was a contradiction. I told her it was a contradiction. "Lord love you, child," said Holy Mother, "but didn't you know that eating and drinking, sleeping and moving your bowels are bodily functions, and that magic and faith and seeing to it your soul is saved are bodily functions too? I swan but you're a funny little girl. You're a funny little girl, I *do* declare.")

Maybe I just didn't get the hang of harrowing.

"Think of it as a good, brisk spring cleaning," Holy Mother told me.

But I still didn't get it, didn't get it *really*. When she said that about the good, brisk spring cleaning, all I could think of was moving the dead people out of the way to vacuum their pillows and coffin linings, or polishing their caskets with Lemon Pledge.

"Think of it as a legal loophole, as an ambiguity, or outright omission in the wording of a contract. As a means of escaping a difficulty," my counselor, Christopher Rockers, just put in.

But I meant then. Now I get it. I'm saying what I meant then.

So we came to a part of the cemetery where I was walking with my dad just this summer, the part where his old friend Jacob Heldshaft is buried, the one who used to sing in the minyan with him, that they called all those funny names— "Puffy Pisher," "Yiddish Mockeybird," "So-and-so Canary." The part where Samuel Shargel is buried, who my father told me was related to a man in the slipcover business, and Ira Kiefer, that Dad says used to be this big-time uncle with ten nephews and nieces that Mom invited to come swimming over at our place after the funeral. The reason I remember all this so clearly is that Holy Mother happened to mention that Jacob Heldshaft had been harrowed because he had such a wonderful voice and Jesus wanted him not so much for his righteous soul as for his beautiful falsetto.

Which I really didn't think was fair.

"Pshaw, child," Holy Mother scolded, "*fair*? Don't go getting started into *fair* or we'll be here all night." She looked around the cemetery. "I need this? All my people have been Jewish," she said.

"These people are Jewish."

"Sure," she said, "and I have to roust them. What am I, a bouncer?" She confessed she didn't like being away from Joseph, and she started to giggle.

"What," I asked, "what?"

"Nothing," she said.

"No, really," I said, "what?"

"You'd have had to have been there."

"No, really, come on," I said, coaxing. (Because in all the time I've lived here, Holy Mother is the closest I've come to having a best friend, or any friend at all.)

"Well," she said, "it's so hard for him, he's always been such a good sport about it." Holy Mother had the giggles real bad. It was good to see my friend laughing.

"What?"

"Well, he says he doesn't know what to call Him."

"Who?"

"Jesus. God. Either one." She was really laughing now. It was the second time that day I'd seen her in tears. "He calls Them, he calls Them— his mahuten! He calls Them his moketenestah!" And her nose was running too. From laughter. From pure joy. She wiped her eyes, then blew her nose in a Kleenex I gave her. "Oh," she said, recovering, "oh. I can't remember when I've had such a good laugh. Well," she said, "what were we talking about? Oh, I remember. You were mentioning about what was fair. Don't come to *me* with such notions. Is it fair that one man gets hauled off to Heaven because he sings falsetto and another like Ira Kiefer over there should die all alone not only without a wife or children to mourn him, but not to leave *any* relation behind, even a niece, even a nephew? Or Samuel Shargel, what about him? Everyone in his family a miserable failure, everyone, *never to have had even a distant cousin in the slipcover business he might have been proud of!*"

I dusted snow from one of the monuments.

"What about this one?" I said, pointing to the stone, to some big Hebrew carving from which poor old Mr. Hershorn had taught me to read. "Did she get harrowed?" Holy Mother looked in the direction I was pointing and squinted.

"I can't read, child," she admitted.

And I'm ashamed of this part too.

Because I thought for a moment my friend was a phony. If she couldn't read, how did she know who to harrow? Or did she just run helter skelter through a cemetery, harrowing at will? Or how did she know who Shargel was? Or Kiefer? Or the Puffy Pisher?

"I just do," she said softly, reading my mind, "I just know," and she began to cry.

When I asked why she was crying she said it was because I doubted her, and that when she was my age it was unusual for a girl to learn to read and that if she did, ninety-nine times out of a hundred it turned out she was a witch and she'd had enough trouble just trying to explain Immaculate Conception and the virgin birth without being called up for being illiterate too. This must have brought back some pretty bad memories because she started weeping harder than ever, so I fished around in my pockets and found another fresh Kleenex and gave it to her.

"Oh," she said, glancing down at the Kleenex I'd handed her, "I've wiped off my stigmata, haven't I?" She touched her dry eyes. "I've rubbed it all away."

I didn't know what stigmata were.

"Usually blood, usually wounds and sores," said Holy Mother. "But tears and runny noses too. Even a rash, even gas. A statue on an altarpiece puking."

Then something unusual happened. I noticed I wasn't cold anymore. I mean I hadn't been conscious of the cold for a long while anyway, but now I was *aware* I wasn't cold. And of how beautiful everything is if only the weather doesn't get in your way. I mean a rainy day if you don't get wet, or a bright, sunny summer afternoon if you aren't hot. Well, that goes double for the ice and snow when the wind is howling and the sky is leaden and the temperature is hanging around negative ten or fifteen. I guess winter would be just about the most beautiful season there is if it wasn't for the cold. People are pretty perky in it as it is— having snowball fights and going skiing and putting on ice carnivals and making snow forts. And all of a sudden I wanted to frolic, had this incredible urge to frolic, and felt this just *tremendous* burst of energy. It was all I could do to keep myself from scooping some snow off poor, sad Samuel Shargel's grave and popping Holy Mother with a snowball. I guessed what I felt was the opposite of stigmata. Joy like a sort of brush fire. And knew even then that I'd *better* resist my impulse, not only because it would have been disrespectful not to, but because with all I was feeling, the joy and high energy, I would have knocked Holy Mother halfway into the middle of next week. (But knew, too, that it *wasn't* all I could do to keep myself from packing a snowball to fling in her face, that with all *I* was feeling I could probably resist anything, any temptation, *any* pressure or urgency, the very heat and cold I was suddenly so conscious were no longer factors in my life.) ("A state of grace, yes," Holy Mother said, breaking into my thought.)

But had to do *something*, and felt myself pulled by a stronger force than even my own high spirits toward poor old Sam Shargel's tombstone and, before I knew what was happening, reached down toward the snow. Which I pulled off the marker, brushed off the marker.

"I'll teach you."

"Oh, Connie, no."

"I will."

"No," she said, "you don't have to."

"I'd like to. I want to."

She saw I meant it and let me.

I, Constance Ruth Goldkorn, of 336 Main, Lud, New Jersey, do hereby depose and affirm that I taught Holy Mother how to read a sort of Hebrew for Beginners off the clean, snow-swept tombstone of Samuel Shargel, 1921–1973, one school snow day in Pineoaks Cemetery. We used his epitaph, reading the big Hebrew letters off the marble slab like Moses calling out the Ten Commandments. As I say, it was how Mr. Hershorn taught *me*.

Mostly we worked on learning to recognize phonemes and blends, her syllabication skills, homophones, consonant digraphs, hard and soft *c* and *g* sounds, and reviewing vowel patterns, affixes and suffixes.

If I gave her a report card I'd have said: "Holy Mother works conscientiously and completes the assigned work with consistent effort. She takes pride in organizing the material and cheerfully accepts constructive criticism, and is always on task. She was a joy to work with this semester."

As a matter of fact, I think she enjoyed it too. She told me it was very moving and that she hadn't had such a good time since Christ knows when. She said I reminded her of the Juggler of Our Lady.

I remarked how she was such a natural scholar it was a shame they didn't have women's lib back in her day.

"Well, I don't know about *that*," said Holy Mother.

"But it is," I said. "A mind is a terrible thing to waste."

"Oh, Connie, my dear," she said, looking around Pineoaks, looking across Lud and over to Masada Gardens, "a soul is an even *more* terrible thing to waste," and she invited me to come along as she completed her rounds. (Which it turned out weren't so grisly after all. There's really not very much to harrowing. It's one of those words that sounds worse than it actually is. Like a dog whose bark is worse than its bite. We'd be going along and Holy Mother would just pause by a grave. What took all the time was having to stop and brush the snow off the monuments so Holy Mother could practice her reading. I wasn't a bit cold. It was still ten or fifteen below out—it had quit snowing, but the sky was grayer than it had been earlier and the wind was blowing more forcefully, so it may even have been a bit cooler—but I didn't feel it. I still had all this energy left over from my state of grace. It could have gone down to absolute zero and it wouldn't have meant any more to me than if I'd opened a window on a fine day in spring.)

When she suddenly pulled up and stopped.

"You harrow this one."

"Who, me?"

"Yes, dear."

"Oh, but I couldn't."

"Certainly you can."

"But I wouldn't know how."

"There's nothing to it."

"I don't know what's involved."

"Didn't you ever have a birthday party?"

"Yes."

"Was there a cake?"

"Certainly."

"Were there candles on it you had to blow out?"

"Of course."

"Well, there you are then."

"I blow out the candles?"

"You make a wish."

It was scary. I mean, so much was riding on it. It wasn't like teaching Holy Mother how to read. Suppose I made a mistake? It meant that the person wouldn't be rescued, that his lost, Jewish soul would never see God. It was so *grisly*.

"Go on," Holy Mother said, "go ahead."

I shut my eyes tight. I took a deep breath.

"Harrow Harry Jacobson," I wished.

"Well," said Holy Mother, "I guess that about does it."

"I'm finished?"

"I think so, yes."

"How many souls of righteous Jews did we rescue? How many did there turn out to be?"

"Counting the ones I did before I met you?"

"Yes."

"Oh," said Holy Mother, "seven or eight."

When she left that evening she thanked me for teaching her to read and said what a pleasure it was to have met me. I told her likewise I'm sure, and that she'd been like a friend, or at least a big sister. I already missed her by the time I got home.

And couldn't stop thinking about them. The dead. The poor souls who remained unrescued.

Because if there were righteous souls then there must be *un*righteous souls, too.

The earth of Lud stocked as any lake or river. (My dad this Johnny Appleseed of the damned. Sowing the not-just-dead but downright unacceptable. Scattering and casting, tilling and turning with some special sorry husbandry, pitching his seed and vegetive milt into all the imponderables and mixed variables of the foreclosed earth, its busted topsoils and clays and unknown weathers— moisture and light and temperature. With blind abandon shifting from one medium to another without even knowing, offering to the soil what was the water's or sky's.) All Lud a ruined continent, a land of drought and blight. Each plot this failed farm.

And how do you think *I* felt? Second-guessing Daddy's handiwork, not wanting to but mixing in anyway? Already, for that matter, mixed in from the minute I first ran into Holy Mother window shopping along Lud's main street? My sympathies shot. All that loose grief I'd felt all my life, or at least for as long as I'd understood where I was living, suddenly altering from one state to another like those solids and liquids and gases they tell you about in school and which are always in some perpetual tumult of rearrangement. That grief. That loose grief. Now you feel it, now you don't.

Because what they kept in those coffins, besides mere personal effects, I mean, the jewelry, eyeglasses, hip wallets, watches, snapshots and belt buckles, and just sheer meltdown of the remains, all the corrupt soup of their spoiled biodegradables, was some hot elixir from which, in time, anything could grow except a serviceable soul. (Coffins, I supposed, would slosh if you shook them.) Plus that other, impersonal effect, their nonviable souls like counterfeit coins or rotten teeth. (Though something about them at once animate and doomed as cut blossoms or dime-store turtles.)

My niggled, watered, here-today/gone-tomorrow griefs downshifted as some truck on a steep grade to something more like sorrow than grief, and then taken down another tick or two to sadness, say, or even gloom. Until it wasn't even unhappiness anymore (though I couldn't stop thinking about them, I mean worrying), was out of *that* spectrum altogether and had entered some new stage with which I, for all my power to take melancholy's measure and my perfect pitch for heartache, was unfamiliar.

Until it came to me. Until what bothered me so came to me. Just came to me. I hesitate to say with the force of revelation. (I mean I've been there. Hadn't I spent almost an entire snow day with Holy Mother? Didn't we hang together? Weren't we pals? Best friends even? Hadn't she already told me some fairly intimate stuff about her immediate family that wasn't even in the Bible—I know, I looked it up—and that would probably be worth a small fortune to me and set me up for life if I could just get to the right people with it? Hadn't I, for that matter, taught her to read? Anyway, the point is, revelation isn't forceful at all. It's subtle as sunlight, spotty and gradual as shade.)

It was taste. What I felt for those unrighteous souls in Pineoaks and Masada Gardens and everywhere salting Lud's earth, turned out to be just a question of taste. It was a matter of civic, or even of hometown pride. Maybe not even taste finally, maybe nothing so grand as taste—didn't I already tell you I'm no anti-Semite, and isn't it already in the record that the big thing I got out of the time I spent with Holy Mother was chiefly to do with the joy parts and not much to do with religion at all, because I mean, what the heck, hey, I'm still a kid, there isn't any Song of Bernadette going on here or anything—maybe only good old-fashioned boosterism, more like who I might want to win the Homecoming Game than anything as serious and important as God. And maybe in back of taste or boosterism or hometown loyalty I was just my mother's little girl running on pure baleboste instinct. Maybe that's the real reason I wanted them harrowed. As baleboste as Holy Mother herself. Wasn't she the one who'd told me to think of it as a good, brisk spring cleaning?

I went to Pineoaks.

It was easier this time without the snow to deal with.

"Harrow Simon Fingerweiss."

"Harrow Philip Pfeiffer," I said, weeding the garden.

"Harrow Rose and Frances Feldman."

"Harrow the Mitgangs, harrow the Blooms. Harrow the Helfmans and Goldstones."

"*Stop!*" shrieked Holy Mother. "What do you think you're doing?"

"Oh," I said, "you scared me."

"*Just what do you think you're doing?*" she demanded.

"Nothing," I said. "I was sprucing up a bit. Did I do something wrong?"

"Oh, child," she said, "oh, my poor child."

Let the record show that I make no claims. Let the record show I'm no better than the next person. Let it show I make mistakes too. That just because the Holy Mother revealed herself to me and once chose to spend the better part of a day in my company doesn't entitle me to go all hoity-toity, or get a swelled head, or lord it over the next guy. It didn't give me any rights in the swanks and swaggers, high-and-mighties, or holier-than-thou's at all. Where do *I* get off throwing *my* weight around, I mean?

Well, I don't. I just don't. Because it's one thing to whine and complain and criticize the way your dad might do a certain thing, and another altogether to go and do it any better yourself. I'm only sorry for whatever confusion or inconvenience I may inadvertently have caused the Mitgangs and Helfmans, the Goldstones, Feldmans and Blooms. I'm only sorry if I got Philip Pfeiffer's or Simon Fingerweiss's hopes up. Though I perfectly understand that it's too late and can make no difference to their families, I would like the record to show that none of this was my intention when I undertook to harrow their souls. I hereby apologize to Heaven, too.

On the other hand, how was I to know? Any more than my father? I'm not trying to set myself up as any big-deal Bible scholar or anything, but it's my opinion—and soon I'm going to show how I got the wherewithal, as it were, to back this up—that the reason I fell into this trap is the old business of the forcelessness of revelation. (It's already in the record how it's subtle as sunshine, spotty as shade?) Rome nor anything else worth bubkes wasn't built in a day. My experiences with Holy Mother have taught me *that* much, at least! (Don't feel bad, Daddy. Those evangelists on TV have no more authority than Jews in this respect. "Accept Jesus, accept Jesus," they cry. "Let Him come aboard your hearts." As if that was all there were to it. As if Jesus has no say in the matter. As if all you have to do is declare the war and the day is yours. When it's got nothing to do with stand up to be counted, sit down, Bingo! you're saved. *Because what it's really got to do with isn't just declaring the war but laying the siege!*)

"Oh, oh," groaned Holy Mother, "my poor, poor, sweet lost child," and took me in her arms and guided me to one of the benches where she sat down and drew me onto her lap and held and comforted me, undone and forlorn, crooning "poor child, sweet child," over and over again above me like we were figures in a Pietà.

The next day she started sending the saints. Because, make no mistake, this was *her* siege— Holy Mother's. She went to a lot of trouble with me. An all-out effort.

(A footnote should go here, what, back when I was learning how to write term papers last semester, I was taught to stick beside an asterisk and write N.B., Latin for nota bene, or note well—a sort of disclaimer, a sort of alarm. My footnote has to do with the disinformation there is concerning the so-called supernatural "visions" or "manifestations" made by the saints and even the Godhead when It chooses to present.

(I understand this is only one girl's experience, and how if anyone appreciates that there might be more than one way to skin a cat it would certainly be God, but it all seemed so direct and straightforward a procedure, I find it almost impossible to believe it's ever, or ever very often, otherwise. I acknowledge it could be, and agree there are historical instances when it probably was, but I'll lay you dollars to donuts those precedents were rare exceptions. For one, there's the forcelessness-of-revelation thing. By which I never meant feints and codes, riddles and misdirection. Put yourself in Heaven's place a minute. Walk a mile in its golden slippers. The name of the game is communication. Why revelation is forceless has less to do with the subtlety of the message than with the stubbornness, or even stupidity, of the person for whom it's intended. Didn't I already say I'm still a kid? So even if I'm wrong about the forcelessness of revelation, tell me, who's more set in her ways than a kid? Who takes more convincing? Anyway, the point is, it's always one belief looking to take over another belief. That's the reason for the hard, though forceless, sell, the constant repetition. That's the reason they kept coming at me from all sides, the reason it was always a little like Rush Week.

(So let the record show, and let me begin by laying to rest, some misconceptions.

(Ready?

(Divine agency does not work through the medium of barely legible images showing through certain kinds of paint in certain lights at certain times of day. It doesn't rub itself into the warp and woof of cloth. The Shroud of Turin, for example, is no Polaroid of Jesus. I showed Holy Mother a picture from a magazine and asked her directly. You know what she said? "What, *my* Jesus? How do people come up with such mishegoss? This fella? Where's the resemblance? This isn't Jesus, this is just some stubby little gypsy."

(And statues of saints neither weep nor bleed. They don't wink or perspire or pull a long face. They never move their lips or open their mouths to speak. God doesn't use ventriloquists' dummies to make His points. Neither does He rely on Nature. Oh, He splits the Red Sea if there's a need, or throws a Flood, but in the piecemeal One-on-one of a conversion He doesn't like to disturb the topography. He'll hesitate to pull a river from a rock, say, or lay down an instant copse of trees onto the barren earth like you'd put up a fence.

(Holy Mother explained this, too. "He doesn't like to scare you. He's very gentle. Didn't He send the Angel Gabriel to explain what was going to happen to me? And, after it happened, after the Lord had already been with me and I'd begun to show so people could see, didn't I concentrate and study on it as hard as I ever concentrated or studied on anything in my life to try to figure out just when it could have happened, and all I could ever come up with was just this thin memory I had of a draft I happened to be sitting in when I was sewing a few garments together one time for my dowry after Joseph and I were already betrothed. So He's gentle. Whatever else He is, He's gentle. Even though He's only ever satisfied when His arrangements uproot and change the world!"

(No. The last thing that bunch is is shy. Gentle, yes, but persistent. They have something on their mind they let you know about it and don't nod at you from the woodwork or send you signals from the plaster of Paris. I'll tell you what they're like— Scrooge's ghosts.)

My first visitor was a young woman who looked to be maybe seventeen or eighteen years old. At first glance she could have been my older sister. Holy Mother introduced us.

"Hi."

"Hi," St. Myra Weiss said.

"St. Myra Weiss?"

"I thought so too," I told Mr. Rockers. "I was really surprised. She looked too preppy to be a saint. But Holy Mother vouched for her. She must have been legit."

"Go on."

"She was the patron saint of kids whose dads get transferred and have to relocate in a different city."

"Wait a minute," the attorney said.

"I know. I was surprised myself," I told him. "When she said what her job was I looked right at Holy Mother and rolled my eyes. I think I offended her. St. Myra. She got kind of defensive."

"Not army brats."

"Beg pardon?" I said.

"Someone else handles army brats. St. Captain Ralph R. Sweeney."

"Hold it right there, young lady. Do I have to remind you that this is a deposition and that you're under oath?"

"I know that. Don't you think I know that? Don't you think I know how ridiculous this is going to make me look when it gets out? I *know* all that. Did *I* make it snow? Did *I* lower the temperature so everything would freeze and they'd have to declare a snow day at the exact time Holy Mother was going to be in my neighborhood and practically guarantee that we'd run into each other? *I* didn't do that stuff. What do you want from me? It's God's plan."

"All right, Connie, that's all right. Calm down. You can calm down now. Here's a Kleenex. All right, you've got your own hankie. That's fine."

She was the patron saint of kids whose dads get transferred and have to relocate in a different city.

I told her in that case I thought she might have the wrong party.

"Aren't you Jerry Goldkorn's daughter?"

"That's right."

"I have the right party."

Her father was an executive in Coca-Cola Bottling's corporate headquarters down in Atlanta, Georgia. St. Myra was born there. "I was a Georgia peach," she told me, smiling, looking down. "It's true, I was. A Georgia peach. Oh, I loved Atlanta, loved my friends, our life there. Loved our club. You know my parents had to bribe me to get me to agree to go off with them to Europe in the summers? They promised that after I graduated high school I wouldn't have to go East to college, or any further away from Atlanta than Agnes Scott College for Women in Decatur.

"I was as happy with my lot as any sixteen-year-old girl in America. Because I was best friends with nineteen dozen other kids just like me. Who were as happy with theirs. Who had the same credit cards for the same malls and department stores, who got the same clothing allowances and took their lessons from the same piano and ballet and figure-skating teachers and worked out at the same fitness centers and had children-of-paid-up members' privileges at the same country clubs. Who went to the same humongous open parties on weekends in each others' houses when our parents were out of town and then went on to meet at the same fast-food drive-ins when the parties got busted at midnight. Who got our learner's permits at the same time, and our licenses, and, by default, the same second or third or fourth family car, till we'd get, for graduation, or some special birthday, the same cute red or yellow convertible of our very own and who couldn't wait to be yuppies!"

"But you said you—"

"I am. I'm telling you. The patron saint of kids whose dads get transferred and have to relocate in a different city. It's just that I was always such a good sport.

"Daddy called me in in the summer of my seventeenth year when I was on the cusp of my junior year in high school.

" 'Coca-Cola's just bought out this blockbuster diet soft drink company in the Midwest, sweetheart, and they want your dad to head it up. Now I know, I know, the only home you've ever known has been right here in Atlanta, and that you're very happy here, and that it's a little unfair to ask you to leave your friends, and normally, well, normally, darn it, I wouldn't think of asking you to make that sort of sacrifice, but the soft-drink business is entering a new phase. It's expanding and changing right before our eyes, and if we don't expand and stretch and change right along with it, well, sir, we're going to be left at the starting gate and there won't *be* any money for balls and country clubs and Junior League revels. I'm not asking now. I have too much respect for you for that. I'm requesting. If you say no then it's no, and you and Mummy and Bubba and me will just have to stay put right where we are. If it were your senior year rather than the junior year you're entering I wouldn't even be requesting, or inquiring either for that matter, but as I see it you'll have two whole years to settle in and put your life together and get yourself a gang as close to the one you have here in Atlanta as, given the demographics, you can get in Milwaukee.'

"It was the most disagreeable decision I ever had to make. I assented at once, of course, and even made out that I was getting a little tired of Atlanta anyway and actually looked forward to the move."

"But you *loved* Atlanta."

"A patron saint of kids whose dads get transferred and relocate in a different city must be as devoted to her father as she is to that generation of children for whom she is the earnest, supplicatory object of appeal."

"I see."

"Milwaukee was a disaster."

"You couldn't duplicate—?"

"Kids our age are a demographics unto ourselves. Of course there was to be had in Milwaukee what was to be had in Atlanta. Doesn't Milwaukee have malls and country clubs, doesn't it have roadsters and fitness centers, the children of the CEO classes, credit cards, cotillions, open-invitationed weekend bashes by the pool when the folks leave town for a few days? Doesn't it have fast-food hangouts and not only those places you can go to for a fake ID, but those other places you can go to where they will be honored? Of *course* there is to be duplicated in Milwaukee anything that had already been imprinted upon you in Atlanta."

"Then what's the big deal?"

"Because I was a Georgia peach. Because when I opened my mouth to speak they laughed and called me names and said, 'Hey, get her, she talks like a nigger.'

"Because they always think they have to draw a line some-where, so they draw it around you, or around themselves in some tight-knit, gerrymandered circle. Because there's always this eleventh-hour, last-ditch, last-minute exclusivity among any given nineteen dozen best friends, Atlanta, Milwaukee, New Orleans or Paris, France, either."

"Tell how they martyred you, dear."

"They martyred me by pretending to capitulate, Holy Mother."

"They betrayed you."

"Yes, ma'am. I was invited to one of those Friday or Saturday night parties that they didn't have to bother to invite anyone else to because no one else ever even had to be invited. One of them called out to me after our ten o'clock French class.

" 'Myra. Myra Weiss. Myra, hold up.'

" 'Chapters eleven and twelve,' I told her. 'Mademoiselle says we're responsible for the subjunctive and all the idioms with "coup" in them.'

" 'No,' she said, 'not that.'

" 'Monday. The quiz is Monday.'

" 'Not that either, silly. I know when the quiz is. Clyde Carlin's folks are going out of town this weekend. He's throwing a party. Around nineish.'

" 'I know that.'

" 'He wants you to come.'

" 'He does?'

" 'He asked me to invite you, didn't he?' "

But when she showed up at Clyde Carlin's house that Friday at around nine she didn't see any cars in the driveway, though all the lights seemed to be on on the first floor. St. Myra could have kicked herself for coming so early. In Atlanta, too, these things never started on time. "Well," she told herself, "*some*body's got to be first," parked her car, and went up to the door and pulled on the bell.

Clyde Carlin's little brother, Ben, opened the door.

"Hi," he said.

"Hi," she said, "I'm Myra. Your brother asked me to come to his party."

"Myra Weiss?" Ben said.

"That's right."

"I'm Ben," Ben said, "Clyde's brother. Clyde told me to tell you that our parents changed their plans and didn't go out of town this weekend after all, and that our party's called off but Suzy Locke-Miller is having one at her house instead."

He gave her Susan's address and precise instructions how to get there. She knew something was wrong, but it was already the middle of the spring semester, nine months since they'd moved up from Atlanta, and this was the first time they'd ever even *seemed* to open their ranks for her. She couldn't take the chance. So she took the carefully drawn map Clyde had left with Ben to give to her and started out for Suzy Locke-Miller's.

Where the same thing happened. Only this time it was an older sister who came to the door.

"Yes? What is it?"

"Does Suzy Locke-Miller live here?"

"Who wants to know?"

"I'm Myra Weiss."

"Sooz went off to a par— Weiss? Hold on a minute, she left a note."

And left the girl in the hall and went off to find it. It was so apparently hurried and scribbled it might almost have been what it purported to be, a hastily written apology, an explanation Myra couldn't quite follow saying there'd been a change in plans, that the party had been moved again and that Myra must come to Franklin Bradbury's house. She gave the address, and directions how to get there, and even put down a number Myra could call should she get lost.

She knew what was what now. What they were doing to her. But she kept on going anyway. She had to. Because she was into her martyrdom now, she said. She was on this scavenger hunt for her martyrdom. At one house it was the parents themselves who sent her on to the next place where the putative party was supposedly being held.

She drove from house to house, really seeing Milwaukee for the first time, reminded, in those pricey suburbs, how much like Atlanta it was after all.

It was when she was on her way to the seventh or eighth house that she became momentarily blinded by her own tears and missed the curve and swerved off the winding street and ran into a tree on the lawn of the very house where, ironically, the party they had been hiding from her actually was going on. It was Clyde Carlin himself who heard the crash and was the first on the scene. When he saw what had happened and who it was it had happened to, it took his breath away. The girl from French class came running up to him.

"*Qu'est-ce que c'est?*" she said.

"Don't look," Clyde said.

"No," she said, "what?"

"Great goddamn," Clyde said, "it's the nigger. It's that Myra. She's gone and crashed the damned party!"

"But that's not my problem," I told St. Myra. "My father wasn't transferred, he hasn't relocated in a different city."

"It's still a question of being lost where one is," St. Myra Weiss said. "Of becoming separated, locked from some Palestine of the heart's desiring. You're *already* relocated. I'm your man."

So she sold me a candle.

"She *sold* you a candle? *She* did?"

"It's how they live. You take money for depositions, don't you? It's how *you* live."

"Go on."

There's not a whole lot more to tell. More saints came marching in. Holy Mother thought we should become better acquainted. So both sides would know what they were dealing with. It's pretty specialized. More than a Jewish girl raised on the notion of Moses and monotheism would have guessed. I told Holy Mother.

"Land sakes, child, is that what you think? That God doesn't have helpers, that He's this Workaholic Who thinks He has to do everything Himself or nothing would ever get done? No, hon, that's not what He's like at all. He don't only love us, He trusts us."

She must have brought on more than a dozen. They just kept coming. Before I knew it I'd run out of money to buy their candles from them, but they kept coming anyway. Saints of shopping for a birthday present when you've been invited to a party at the last minute and the stores are all closed. Saints for throwing an outfit together when either they've seen everything you have, or what they haven't seen is at the cleaner's and you've got nothing to wear. Acne saints. Saints for your period. Saints of the S.A.T.'s and the Minnesota Multiphasic Personality Inventory tests. Saints for split ends, for limp or oily hair. Brittle nails saints. Saints for putting in your contact lenses, or finding them again when they pop out in the grass.

"What's that? What's that smell?"

"It's all right, Counselor, he's had an accident. Mr. Hershorn? Mr. Hershorn, it's Connie. That's all right, no harm done, you've had a little accident, Mr. Hershorn. I'll have you cleaned up in a jiffy."

Then I interrupted my deposition and asked Counselor Rockers where the rest room was. I excused myself and led Mr. Hershorn off to make him more comfortable.

While Mr. Hershorn and I were in the washroom, Holy Mother appeared to me one more time. She watched what I was doing without saying anything. Then she said I would probably be a saint myself one day. When I asked of what, she just shrugged and said she didn't really know but possibly of incontinent old men, and when I told her that didn't sound like such a hot job to me, she allowed as how that might be so but that somebody had to do it.

This is the sworn deposition of Constance Ruth Goldkorn of 336 Main, Lud, New Jersey 07642. Present in attendance were Elizabeth Packer, 1143 Hapthorn St., East Orange, New Jersey 07019, Certified Court Reporter and Notary Public within and for the Township of Lud, New Jersey; Christopher Rockers, lawyer of 4 Rosewood Ct., Passaic Park, New Jersey 07055, and Robert Hershorn of the Hershorn Monument Company, 105 Main, Lud, New Jersey 07642.

This deposition is for immediate release to all northern New Jersey newspapers, TV and radio stations, school districts, synagogues, churches, hospitals, funeral directors and to the Archbishop of the Archdiocese of Newark.

eight

"Don't *think I don't know what's going on!*" I shouted at her. "I *know* what's going on! Oh, *boy*, do I know what's going on! I know what's going on better than *you* do!

"You're looking to discredit me. You're looking to get me fired. Always the short view. Always the short view, hey, Connie? Go, run to the bishops, run to the papers. Go run right up to Elaine Iglauer herself, looking in Fairlawn, looking in Ridgewood for a house for us while you're out there playing in the street with Holy Mother! *Ha!*

"Well, my friend, you ought to know just a *leetle* bit more about your religion before you go barking up *that* tree! We're this Sins of the *Fathers* people visited even unto the third and fourth generations. Where is it written, you tell me, where does it speak *any*where in Torah about the Sins of the *Daughters*? Can you answer me that, Buster Brown? *No!* Because it doesn't work that way. It ain't any two-way street we ride past each other with the windows rolled and the top down flipping hexes and trading calumnies.

"So I *know* what you're doing, little missy.

"You're not afraid of any ghosts. You're looking to drive a wedge. Why don't you own up? You think you can trade your meshuggina mishegoss for your old mother's. Bingo bango! Moishe

Kapoyr! Moses reversed! But what *you* don't understand, my fine-feathered friend, is that husbands and wives cleave. I'm a cleaver, kiddo. So's Mummy. We're the whither-thou-thither-me chosen people, your mother and I. The Bible tells us so. Go," I told her, "you can look it up!"

nine

I TELL YOU, it was like a siege those first few days. We couldn't leave the house to buy groceries without having some reporter jump out from behind the bushes, or paparazzi we couldn't even see take our picture through a telescopic lens a mile and a half off. Once a guy waited for us in the driveway, sitting in our own car. They were after us. We were scoops and exclusives waiting to happen. All I ever gave them, however, was my silence, never even the brisk "No comment"—that sounds so defensive—they'd have been all too pleased to run.

The phone rang off the hook with people not so much requesting interviews as demanding them. And not just major papers but the free community papers too, sunny neighborhood weeklies up on the lawn with their ads and deep coverage of girls' public league basketball. There were calls from a couple of national tabloids that wanted to buy our story. And not just the papers, radio stations too, TV stations Connie'd alerted, and the networks it hadn't even occurred to *her* might be interested. Everyone itching to bounce us off his satellite and offering to wring our images through his fiber optics. The rabbi, they promised, wouldn't even have to leave the comfort of his study. They'd come turn it into this hi-tech mini-TV studio and he could just sit there hugging a couple of Torahs or maybe poring over the Dead Sea Scrolls with a jeweler's loupe hanging out one eye like a long black tear. If we switched to an unpublished number, inside an hour they would crack the code and the phone was ringing off the hook again.

Shelley, God bless her, was a little soldier. She didn't give them any more satisfaction than I did. She'd step outside to put out the garbage and they'd pop up, materialized all over her with all the breezy clarity and force of Holy Mother herself, poking their tape recorders and microphones under her nose and shouting questions into her face as if she were a candidate for high office or someone under indictment. "No comment," she'd tell them, smiling, holding her humor. "No comment, thank you, gentlemen," she'd say, slyly, as if it was a joke they shared. I think she liked it. Her "no comment's" spoke volumes.

But I'll tell you the truth, it wasn't my wife they were interested in, or even our daughter. It was me, my rabbi's opinions they sought. Looking, the momzers, to stir a little trouble between the Judaeos and the Christians. Though I have to admit, not all the phone calls were for me. Some were for Connie from incontinent old men. "Connie's not here," I told them. "She's still alive," I said, "call back when she's dead."

I tried to contact the Archbishop of Newark. He wouldn't take my calls. Neither would Shull, neither did Tober. School was supposed to open in a few weeks and Shelley started to phone up some of the mothers in the car pool. They thanked her and said other arrangements had been made.

And suddenly I'm thinking: This is bad, this is just compounding the problem. Our silence hasn't done us any more good than Connie going public in the first place. And it occurred to me that while I still had their attention (which was beginning, I'd noticed, to slack off), I ought to agree to an interview, or at least try to get a statement together which, without airing all our daughter's problems in public, might, one, put forward the notion that a lot of this was just kids-will-be-kids, or, two, at least put Connie's extravagant bobbe myseh into perspective. It was a problem of dignity, it was a question of taste. I threw out any idea of appearing on television or going on one of those radio phone-in talk shows. No, I thought, we

were the people of the Book. The Word was precious to us. I
would go to the papers.

Dismissing the idea of a hoax—I didn't want it to seem
that Connie had played a joke on the Christians—I rehearsed a
carefully worded, balanced, entirely neutral account of what
might be *any* teenage girl's motivations for inventing the events
my daughter described in her deposition.

"Excuse me, Rabbi," said the man from the *Newark Star-
Ledger*, "are you saying she made it all up? That Connie doesn't
believe she saw those saints?"

"Of course not."

"What about Holy Mother? Does she believe she saw the
Virgin?"

"She doesn't even believe there *is* a Virgin."

They ran the story in their Saturday edition on the religion page under a picture of Connie and an even larger one of
me. Mostly it was background information—which I'd supplied—
about our life in Lud, accompanied by a rather sensationalized
restatement of my daughter's original claims, everything topped
off with a cunningly placed, incredibly damaging "No comment!" taken out of context and attributed to me.

I phoned John Charney.

"Sure, the offer's still open," he said. "Nah," he said,
"why would I have to check it out with Artie? Artie's already
signed on. It was Artie's *idea*, for goodness' sake. Klein's the one
with the vision in this outfit. He's our Columbus and our Queen
Isabella too. Of *course* I'm sure," he went on, continuing to
supply answers to questions I hadn't asked, insisting on con-
ducting the conversation as if he were an actor on a telephone on
a stage. "No," he said, "no. It's not of the least consequence to
either of us that you're in the doghouse just now. Shull's and
Tober's loss is Lud Realty's gain. Well, frankly," he said, "because if anything, we stand to gain from the publicity. What do
you mean how do we know? We *know*. That's how we know.
Certainly. Of course. Look," he said, "burying people, making
holy holy over them is one thing, and we're the first to admit
that, rabbi-wise, the two old frauds are entirely within their
rights to put you on hold and send you to Coventry. It's
bad enough people have to die in the first place. That they

should have to put up with the additional indignity of some compromised offshore yeshiva bucher getting in the last word for them is out of the question. At a time like that they got a right to expect the best and not have to worry whether they're going to end up in some chop shop with some sad-ass, on-call chuchm that's fighting for his life from a flakey kid to stand between death and New Jersey for them. They have this right. They have *every* right.

"No," he said, "I'm *not* holding you up to scorn. I'm not. I *said* we want you in, and I *meant* we want you in. What do you mean the real reasons? All right, okay. You're nobody's fool. That ought to be real reason enough right there, but all right, you want real reasons I'll give you real reasons. I'll spread the cards out on the table. A, you're a rabbi. B, you're famous. C, death, impending or otherwise, is at *best* a grim business and we happen to think that maybe that little extra aura of laughing-stock you give off might just lend you a sort of cachet. At the very least it ought to get your foot inside death's door for you."

Then Tober called. I was still under a contract that had fifteen more months to run on it, he reminded me. And since not many people would want me to bury their dead for them anymore, he and Shull had seen fit to sell my contract to Lud Realty. He understood, he said, that that probably wouldn't be a problem for me since I'd already been in contact with Charney about a job anyway. He softened his tone. "Hey," he said, "I'm sorry. Really. You think I'm trying to save a few bucks off your grief? Not off your grief," he said. "Never off the grief that comes from children. I appreciate what you must be going through. Just thank God she's healthy. Thank God she can see. Thank God she's kept her sense of balance and that she don't fall off chairs when she crosses her legs." He lowered his voice still further. "The fact is," he said, "I'm not getting any younger. In less than a year I'll be sixty-five, an age most men see fit to retire. Sonia was sixty-two last week, and our daughter's birthday is just around the corner. The family's almost two hundred and twenty-four. We're getting up there, Rabbi. How much longer can we hold on? Edward's only thirty-eight. The cash has got to be there for him when we're gone. Everyone knows it costs more to maintain a shitty, feckless life than the life of Riley."

Shull called to apologize.

"I'll tell you the truth," he told me, "don't think I bought into this pursuit-of-happiness thing because I value pleasure any more than the next guy. I'm just this overachiever. I can't help it, Rabbi. Forgive us our debts as we forgive our debtors, you know? The fact is, I happen to be entering a particularly heavy cash-flow cycle just now. Something's been missing from my life. There I was, the man that had everything, a glass of fashion, a mold of form. My shoes and suits, my shirts, coats and ties are on the cutting edge. I have furniture and tsatskes they ain't even shown yet in the witty, high-budget films. I drive fast cars and run around like a fleet that just put in. I've everything money can buy. What else can my money buy? Then one night I wake up beside a woman she could be a world-class spy or the girl from Ipanema, and it comes to me like a bolt out of the blue: Schmuck! What are you, a spring chicken? You won't see sixty again! You should be married, you should have a family, obligations. Jerry, it was so *clear*. When it's that clear you don't even think about it, you just do it. I know this widow, a lovely girl. I proposed and she accepted. She's in her forties. Oh, her biological clock ran out on her years ago, but she married a little later than most and still has these five teenage kids, three still in high school, and twins, just entering college. It will be my privilege to support *all* of them. *That's* what else my money can buy!

"And a leopard can't change its spots, you know. I don't kid myself that I'll be settling down. A leopard can't change its spots, and you don't teach an old dog new tricks. I'm under no illusions. This is the way in the animal kingdom. I'll still hit on the ladies. You're a spiritual, you may not have thought these matters through, but it costs a married man more to fool around than a single guy. The price of a hotel suite, tips to the door-men and bellhops, what they get from you for room service these days.

"Anyway," he said, "now you know why I need to scrape up more dough, and that it's nothing personal we sold your contract right out from under you and traded you to Lud Realty in your darkest hour. Or that you're going to have to earn back the cost of your contract before you ever see a nickel from the commissions on the grave plots you sell."

It must have given them a kick to chat me up. Over and above whatever business they may have legitimately had with me. I honestly think so. No matter what Tober told me about hanging back from a parent's privileged grief, it's exciting after all to have an opportunity to yell "What in hell's wrong with that lunatic daughter of yours?" into her dad's ear and ask if she's fucking gone crazy. It lent spice to Charney's day to put humbling questions into my mouth and then provide the devastating answers to them. Even Shull, who'd run through all the pricier pleasures, was not above the cheap ones. And those reporters, don't tell *me* they were just doing their job. The *Star-Ledger* guy runs an innocent "No comment" out of context! I wish I *had* gotten through to the Archbishop of Newark. His refusal to take my calls made him seem classy.

Understand, please. I'm not a cynical man. I haven't turned sour. I repudiate no one. I honor God, I cheer His Creation. The world's a swell place to be, and Humanity is a jolly good fellow. But don't it give a person just that little something extra to hang around grief, to rub himself warm near its hearth?

The town's other funeral director, Billy Zimmerman, called. He was genuinely sorry, he told me, but he already had a real rabbi.

"Who asked you?"

"No, really, Mr. Goldkorn," Zimmerman said, "I'd like to help you out but I run a strictly Orthodox show. You'd be lost. What could you know of the hesped? Washing the body, the chevra kadisha? Of the shomrim who guard our Orthodox dead? What would you make of the tachrichin, all death's white-linen laundry, or the kittel like a kind of body bag? Would you cry out the kriah, would you remember *that* rending? In the cemetery, in the cemetery, would you make seven stops to recite seven psalms? Would you splinter your finger on a plain pine box? Could you take up the shovel with everyone else? Or remember to wash your hands with the mourners? What would you bring to the meal of consolation?"

"The salt from my eyes, you bastard."

"Yes," he said, "I'm sorry for your trouble."

"Well," I relented, "thank you, then."

"Tell me," he said, and I could almost hear him bunch his shoulders, hunch forward, lean into the telephone, "you think the child may have a dybbuk?" Why, he was like the guy from the *Star-Ledger*.

Sal Pamella called. He told me it was all off. Even the barber's bogeyman wouldn't let me near their dead now— all those Jimmy Hoffas of his fix-is-in imagination.

Still, I bore no grudges. Connie I forgave outright. She had her father's wholehearted, up-front blessing. If I'd roughed her up with my tongue after I saw her deposition, why, I was only having my say, as a dad will with his kid, a Jewish Judge Hardy.

I couldn't understand why Shelley wouldn't allow me to sleep with her, why she had set up separate rooms for us, as if we were two fighters returned to our neutral corners.

"What happened to us?" I asked.

"Scissor cuts paper."

"Scissor cuts paper?"

"Rock smashes scissor."

"What are you talking about, Shelley? What are you trying to say to me, sweetheart?"

"Scissor cuts paper. Rock smashes scissor. Paper covers rock."

"Two out of three, Shell."

"Two out of three? Two out of three? 'Husbands and wives cleave,' you told Connie. Husbands and *wives*? Mothers and daughters. Scissor cuts paper, rock smashes scissor, paper covers rock. And mothers, mothers cleave to daughters! That's who cleave! *There's your two out of three!*"

"This is all your fault," she said another time.

"*My* fault? *My* fault?"

"It isn't your fault? It isn't? Why do I drive all the car pools? Why do we own a car that accommodates nine people? *Why do we own a station wagon at all?* What do we even *need* a family car? We could get by with some two-door subcompact with a little lever on the bucket seat so she could climb into the back! Why do I bring her to libraries or take advantage every chance I get to put more miles on the car? If I were a pilot I would have had thousands of hours in the sky by now. It *isn't* your fault?"

"How come you don't talk Yiddish anymore?"

"So that I might at least lend her the illusion we were a family. So we might pretend for as long as it took to get us from one destination to the next that she might even be on her way to lessons— swimming, piano, tumbling, dramatics. Locating her gifts— baton, figure skating, beginning ceramics, beginning ballet. On all the bespoke errands—weaving and tennis and aerobics and tap—of any ordinary childhood. (Yes! Chasing her gifts. We could have been on a scavenger hunt.) Turning up the volume on the FM and going the long ways, choosing the routes with the most traffic signals to them so that when were stopped on red Connie could scout out the cars with the real mothers and the real daughters, sometimes offering an actual nod of recognition or even just that shy, tangential, enigmatic, secret sidelong Mona Lisa glance of acknowledgment from one teenager to another in that mysterious freemasonry of girls."

"You've *had* thousands of hours in the sky."

"Or our shopping expeditions. As if it weren't Connie herself we were dressing but some bright Connie avatar, some inconstant Connie of a thousand forms and faces— Connie as matron, Connie as bride. Enrolled for showers, registered for gifts. Handling the china, fingering the forks. Browsing in Maternity or picking baby's clothes. In Women's Wear indifferent to sizes but examining the racks of suits and sweaters and dresses and coats and choosing from them as one might first pick out and then return a novel to its shelf at the public library, out of pure random instinct, some deft, unprincipled inspection. Trying on a hat or holding, hanger and all, a blouse out before her in front of the three-way mirror, then bringing it next to her body, brushing it against her with her arm. Looking toward me for an opinion, as if we weren't just mother and daughter but any two females, related or not, even acquainted or not, in any boutique, shop or department store in the world. 'With brown accessories? You think so?' 'With such a high heel?' Not House we were playing but Other People."

"Why hasn't she? Why *hasn't* she taken ballet? Why *hasn't* she signed up for those classes?"

"What friends would she have taken them with? We live too far out. She'd have had to have dropped the illusion of those seven playmates in the car pool."

"Why didn't you? Why *didn't* you buy her more clothes?"

"Where would she have worn them?"

Well, la de da, I thought, watching her closely, just look at her, just listen. In her own rabbi mode for once. Talk about your avatars. Shelley the rebbitzin, Shelley the vamp. Shelley the wronged and Shelley the miffed. Holy Shelley Mother dealing all her Shelley shell games like three-card monte in the street. (Sometimes, in old and, often, better days, I'd come upon her in the kitchen, pulling stuff out of the cabinets—plates, a glass—and drawers—knives, teaspoons—and darting from the refrigerator to the kitchen counter with food in her hands, talking to herself like one of those chefs on TV. "This afternoon," she'd say into the wall telephone by the kitchen table, "we're going to prepare a lox sandwich. For this we'll need a bagel, some cream cheese, lox of course, and this lovely Bermuda onion for garnish-e-le.")

"If you should happen to hear anything," she abruptly said, and turned and went to her room.

Because she kept to herself these days, camping out in the spare bedroom like a self-conscious guest. Suddenly she wasn't there anymore when I pulled my modified Shachris just before breakfast. Recalling other occasions, I pretended she didn't want to disturb me at prayer, excite me, I mean. Stepped back, removed from the energy field of all that cumulate prayer like the politic, insistent-signaled clamor of traders, say, on some bourse of souls (as she might step around some just recently waxed floor), I told myself I guessed she didn't want to stir stuff up. I guessed, or told myself I did, she meant to clear my air, help me get through, not break God's radio silence.

It had been a while since I believed Shelley believed I still lay t'phillim. So one morning I got all dolled up. I strapped on my phylacteries, attaching one to my forehead and binding the other about my left forearm, girding myself, a Jewish Crusader.

"Get out," Shelley said. "Don't touch me."

"No," I said, "I'm praying. Honest. I am. I'm going at it for all I'm worth."

The odd thing was that the talk about us had already begun to die down. We'd stopped hearing things even before that column appeared in the *Newark Star-Ledger*.

I was following Klein's and Charney's leads now. Geniuses, those two, ahead of their time, with probably a couple of the greatest noses for death in the business. Bloodhounds of the terminal who could sniff out serum cholesterol, plaque, decay in urine, the dark spots on X rays, maybe even suicide— a thing for all the gamy pheromones of death.

Maybe because I'd been a rabbi too long and not only hadn't kept up but had bought into some picturesque little peddler myth of the Jewish people, some one-on-one, door-to-door notion of intimately pressed spiel, all the pulled-stop oratory of insistent last-stand need, was overextended, that is, in some outmoded sweatshop/piecework notion of economics and salesmanship. Progress caught me unawares, unprepared, I tell you, for life as it's lived, civilization as we know it. I mean there I was, thinking they were actually going to send me door to door, have me make calls on sick folks in genuine hospital rooms, or, at the very least, on their relatives grieving in waiting rooms or hanging about ICUs biting their nails and preparing themselves for their five minutes at a loved one's wired bedside. (And me, a rabbi too long, recall, actually ready to do it, having talked myself into it, having sold myself this bill of goods: "Well, why *not*? Ain't you how many times already in your career been Johnny-on-the-spot with your professional ordained consolation, and faced down genuine article, fait accompli, real-thing death, and not just the—admittedly—high-risk, long—admittedly—odds actuarials of the merely terminally ill? So what could one more lousy time into the breach mean to a fella like you? Haven't you, I mean, been there already, sent out on all those sorrow sorties where we stuck our noses in? And anyway, isn't it true that where there's life there's hope? Or that old Holy Holy Holy could always change His mind at the last minute? And what if Connie's right, or at least on the right track, and there are, if not saints, then angels, all sorts of them, cancer and coma angels, bum-ticker angels, angels of the broken

spirit, maybe even murder angels? So, if you can find words for
the already bereaved, it only stands to reason that you ought to
be able to come up with a little snappy patter for the simply
only just apprehensive, tenterhooked, on-call, bedside-vigil ex-
pectant." And *this* bill of goods: "Well, *why* not? I could tell
them that if worse—God forbid—came to worst and we were
faced with a bona fide, signed, sealed and delivered death-
certificated corpse, what would be so terrible if the family were
prepared? If it didn't have to concern itself with those literally
last-minute details, if it already had a plot picked out, taken
whatever small—admittedly—advantage it could of prospect,
access, and the rare shade tree. No one must be in a hurry to
die, but it's a first-come, first-served world, and just plain good
husbandry not to buy more grief than you have to. 'Who's,' I'd
have asked them, 'more entitled, more deserving?' ") Or utzing at
them in the dayrooms of old peoples' homes, on their cases from
somewhere in the gridlock of walkers and wheelchairs that was
like a metaphor for the very plat of the cemetery I had set up on
an easel for them as a visual aid. But what did *I* know?

Because the world, it turns out, always takes you by
surprise. It's always one step ahead of you. If you look away for
even a minute, and often even if you don't, you have to be
retrained.

They didn't want me *near* sickrooms. Or doing my hovered-
buzzard number in any dayrooms or otherwise, in nursing or
retirement homes where this twenty-four-hour service or that
twenty-four-hour service, or any damned service you could
think of, including the one I was prepared to render, was
constantly on call. I had no access to an official list of telephone
numbers of even the merely widowed or widowered or bachelored
or spinstered elderly, people living on their own who got called
every morning by concerned volunteers ringing up just to see if
they could still get to their telephones. They didn't, I mean,
want me where I might, even reasonably, become unctuous.

And had other plans for me altogether.

There are these seminars conducted in motels, sessions on
tax shelters, positive thinking, how to get rich in real estate with
no money down. Experts advise on ways to increase your word
power, build your memory, bulk up your portfolio, and offer

instructions on avoiding probate. Any number of transcendental arrangements take place in these ballrooms, hospitality suites, and private, sectioned-off dining rooms of the country's leading motels. This—motels were only rarely the venue—was the aura— places where Kiwanis met, the Lions' Club, the Jaycees. The scrubbed and neutral geography of profit and community service, some vaguely fraternal sense of the benevolent and secret.

Halls I mean. The card and game rooms of great condominium structures on the Palisades. Chambers of the hired-out and interchangeable. Though occasionally in the auditorium— never full—of a Jewish Community Center, and sometimes in an actual temple on an actual Friday night. These were the places that usually booked me, Lud Realty's designated speaker. And where I came to them, Lud Realty's booked and bookish man.

"Shalom," I'll begin. "Good yontif to you," and sweep into my theme, speaking, except for the commercials, much as I might have spoken to them at their funerals:

" 'We owe God a death,' says the poet, 'He who pays it this year is quits the next.' Yet we dassn't rush to die, ladies and gentlemen, but must take our turn, and wait till the last minute.

"But you know something, friends? We are owed to earth, mortgaged to dirt, in debt to the very ground we walk on, up to our ears in arrears to the planet. God holds our note. This is the reason for sickness, this is the meaning of pain, why He duns us with sniffles, eczema, germs. Why He claims us with rashes and toothaches. Why He forecloses with tumors and strokes.

"We must never forget obligation. This is why it's all right to smoke and stay up late, de rigueur to dance and carouse. Yet we must never forget obligation. It's *good* God ties a string round our finger with troubles. It's *good* He favors us with envy and ambition and plants needs in us in perpetual shortfall to our means. *Thank* Him for cancer and kidney disease, for our preoccupation with money and the kids who break our hearts. He gives us our renewable thirst and programs our hunger. He sets up our lives like a memento mori. Praise God from Whom all blessings flow.

"Is this harsh?

"We must never forget we're gifts He gives to Himself, that it's His *right* to move us about like lead soldiers, to run us around like a set of toy trains. The world's only this box where He puts away His things. Is this harsh? This Nutcracker view of Creation? Is this harsh? No, in thunder, says the Sugarplum Fairy. It's delightful to be God's bauble, this human doodad knickknack of the Lord's.

"And that's why we mustn't get too big for our britches, mustn't forget what's what. Prepare to die. Let's just get it over with, I say. Make our arrangements, I mean. Turn our thoughts to the time when we have to get back in our boxes, fluffed up in our deaths like pillows, mounted in our caskets like jewels or bright gewgaws. *Never* put off till tomorrow.

"Hey," I'll tell them, "I'm selling cemetery plots here. It's your *duty* to ground yourselves in ground, that obligatory seven-or-so dirt feet by four-or-so dirt feet by six-or-so dirt feet— just those hundred-sixty-eight-or-so cubic dirt feet of clay and dimension, that closes out your indenture like a valedictory 'Yours truly' above your signature in a letter.

"Is this *harsh?*

"Because the alternative to Nature is Nature— flora, fauna, beauty, geology, corrosives and temperature. Floods and avalanches, forest fires, tidal waves and the Richter scale. We're human beings. Is this harsh? We're human beings and weren't raised to be salvage. We're human beings and weren't created to become party dip for the vultures and buzzards. Or lie about on the lawn like the Sunday paper. *Is this harsh?* We're human beings, and He didn't make us to bob the high seas like flotsam or, random as jetsam, wash up on the shore.

"Come on," I'll tell them, "cemetery plots, cemetery plots here! Get your cemetery plots! I'm the ashes-to-ashes man, the dust-to-dust kid comin' at you! Get your cemetery plots!"

And while they look up at me, staring, wondering (no longer recalling—last month's talk now—exactly whose father I'm supposed to be) about me, maybe even a little frightened, gentle Jews unaccustomed to the stench of brimstone, more used, at least the older ones, to the odor of cooking, the smell of vaguely camphorous stews and briskets in the hall, family people (or why would they be here in the first place?), no use for mishegoss, impatient with it but too polite to say so, unapocalyptic altogether, I'll finally tell them something that strikes a chord, that actually rings a bell.

"What, were you brought up in a barn? You weren't brought up in a barn.

"Look," I'll say, "it's like this:

"Who dies? Your children die. You die. Everyone dies. Your parents and uncles. Your cousins and aunts. Your wife and your husband. No, no, don't you *dare* say 'God forbid.' What, God forbid God? I'm not telling you anything you don't already know. He *wasn't* raised in a barn. It's how He picks up after Himself. Death's just the way He keeps up His housekeeping. He's a balebatish kind of God. He's neat as a pin. He makes us natural disasters no insurance policy in the world would cover us against, but He forbids us to lie in the rubble. It's simple as that, ladies and gentlemen. It's simple as that, my good friends. From the beginning. It was always as simple as that.

"Didn't He guide Noah, didn't He instruct Moses right down to the last cubit of the chore? Ain't that His wont? Ain't God in the details? Well, then. You think He'd trouble with the minutiae of weights and measures and then fail to ordain those hundred-sixty-eight-or-so cubic dirt feet of His holy metrics? What, you think so? Get outta here!

"Because the reason there was a Diaspora in the first place was just that Canaan's soil was too sandy ever to hold a grave steady! Why do you suppose He jerked the Jews around for forty years in that wilderness? To prepare them, to get them ready. Because if you can scratch out those hundred-sixty-eight-or-so cubic feet and bury your dead in just sand, you can bury them anywhere!

"It's that important. It's that important to Him. And that's the reason for markers. (Didn't I tell you we die? Didn't I mention that everyone does?) Because how could He find us otherwise? That's why it's important we bury our dead, His dead. Why none dast break the chain of relation. Just so He can find us again if he should need us!

"Plots here!" I'll hawk. "Cemetery plots here! Get your plots here! Nuclear and extended-family cemetery plots here! Get 'em while they last! Get 'em while *you* do!"

And they did. The harder, more outrageous the sell, the quicker and more eager they were to take me up on it, as if as long as they had to die anyway I could somehow sanctify their passage, or at least make the absurdity of their death le dernier cri, lending just that in-the-swim spin of flair and style and currency to it. I might have been that season's caterer or society band leader. Nothing would serve but that they have their little plot of death from the Rabbi of Lud. I was good for business.

It didn't last long. Probably no more than four or five weeks. So it didn't last long. It couldn't have. (Though if it had lasted even a little longer I'd probably have started to earn my commissions.) Anyway it didn't, and the talk, already dying down when Tober and Shull traded me to Klein and Charney, had ceased now altogether. The archbishop, had I tried to get through to him—which I didn't—would probably have taken my call. So either the talk had died down, or it no longer made a difference to anyone that my daughter used to receive Holy Mother socially. People were asking to have me at their funerals again—Sal called to tell me it had got back to some people he knew what a good job I did—and Klein and Charney, suspecting, I suppose, if not the staying power of such campaigns then the staying power of such campaigners, proposed trading me back to Shull and Tober.

It was about this time I heard from Al Harry Richmond in Chicago.

"I'm sorry about Stan Bloom, Al Harry," I told him. "I gave her all I got."

"Sure," Al Harry said.

"I did," I assured him. "I tried my best. I went after her tooth and nail. But you know how it is," I said, holding my hands up for him almost a thousand miles away. "The old gray mare."

"You saying she ain't what she used to be," Al Harry said.

"That's right. That's so."

"Goddamn it, Goldkorn, she never was."

"Oh, yes, Al Harry," I said. "Don't you recall Wolfblock and our charmed lives? We couldn't get arrested, or come down with a cold."

"I recall a thousand Kaddishes. I recall all that grief and remember thinking it's a good thing death ain't contagious."

"Oh, no, Al Harry, that was some minyan, that minyan of ours. We were the ten musketeers. I even got a vocation out of it. And that was some Wolfblock, that Wolfblock of ours. What a character! I miss that old man." But couldn't get a rise out of him, or catch him up in my nostalgia, or any other of the historical sympathies who'd already, it seemed, let bygones be bygones. "Gee," I mused, "ain't it odd? Your turning out to be our sort of social secretary and all, the one who keeps up. I mean, I'm the one that came to New Jersey and turned out to be the rabbi, and you're the one who stayed in Chicago and turned out to be the pope."

"There's one in every minyan," Al Harry said. I listened to the contempt he couldn't keep out of his voice.

"Listen," I told him, "you only heard one side of the story. Ain't you learned yet that anybody can make a good impression with just one side of the story?"

"A good impression? A good impression?" Al Harry shot back. "With her punim on matchbooks and milk cartons? On coupons to Resident offering half off on film, on tools and detergent? A good *impression*?! I wasn't even struck by the god-damn *likeness*! Tell me, Rabbi, how come you didn't give them a more recent photograph?"

"I didn't have one."

"Ahh," said Al Harry.

"Al Harry," I said, "it's not what you think. Connie shies out of pictures. Literally. Really. She does. She jumps out of focus the minute you snap. Or ducks under parallax quick as a wink. She leans her head into shadows and wards you off with one hand to the side of her face, or a hankie she's pulled out of the sky you didn't even know she had. They don't make ASA ratings or shutter speeds fast enough to catch her. She thinks," I confessed, "she's homely."

"Oh, Goldkorn. Oh, Jerry."

"I'm a different person now," I told him. "You don't judge a guy by the length of his haphtarah passage."

"She's flying into Newark," he said. "I'll call you when her plane takes off."

"God bless you, Al Harry. Thanks, thanks a lot. Oh, and Al Harry?"

"What is it?"

"That picture of Connie that they ran in the *Star*? That didn't come out until after the matchbooks and milk cartons had already gone to press."

"Oh, Jerry," he said, "oh, Goldkorn."

"You don't know the half of it."

And he didn't, of course. Because how could he? Because it's just like I said. No one can know the other side of a person's life.

ten

HANGDOG. I was hangdog. Shelley was sheepish. Connie was like a little jellyfish. We seemed, come together outside the gate in the Newark airport where the TWA flight from Chicago had just landed, like characters in a fable, a little bestiary of the wishy-washy. Like embarrassed Animal Crackers.

"Uncle Al Harry signed me up for their frequent flyer program," Connie said.

Sure, I thought. Just in case. "How was the flight?" I asked.

"Fine." She was holding a stuffed animal I didn't recognize. Al Harry must have given it to her.

"Did you eat on the plane?" Shelley asked.

"I ordered a kosher snack."

I wondered if it was an apology.

"How was Chicago?" Shelley asked.

"Chicago was fine."

"Did you go to the museums?" I said.

"I went to the Natural History Museum with Beverly and Diane."

"Who are they?"

"Uncle Al Harry's their grandfather."

"Al Harry has grandchildren?"

"He has *three* grandchildren. Seth lives in Ohio."

"Was it boring for you," I said, "having to be around babies?"

"Diane's almost thirteen. Beverly's eleven and a half and tall for her age. Both kids are taller than I am."

Shelley looked as if she'd been slapped. Long red wales appeared on her cheeks, without depth or texture, a blushed stigmata.

"Where else did you go?"

"We went to the Art Institute."

"Did you get a chance to go to the Museum of Science and Industry?"

"Yes," said Connie.

"Yes," I said, "that's a good one. That was always one of my favorites."

"Do you have any bags?" my wife asked, and suddenly we couldn't look at each other, a kind of mortification glancing off our eyes and wildly strafing the carpet, the passengers still coming out the jetway, the entire lounge area. It was the first allusion we'd made to Connie's having run away. Until now it was as if she'd come back to us from a vacation.

"Yes," she said, "there's the duffel I took to camp that time," and burst into tears.

•   •   •   •

Shelley had hurriedly removed her things from the spare bedroom, overlooking a tortoiseshell comb, a set of matching brushes. Connie brought them to her.

"Oh," Shelley said, "I've been looking all over for those."

She brought a porcelain lion Shelley kept on top of the dresser.

"Oh," Shelley said, "thank you, sweetheart."

She brought a small case in which Shelley kept her jewelry.

"Well," Shelley said, "imagine that."

"Guess what?" Connie said.

"What?" Shelley said.

"Cousin Diane has a boyfriend."

"You told us she's not even thirteen years old," said Shelley.

"A boy in her Hebrew school class. Guess what else?"

"I don't know," I said.

"Mom?"

"What else?"

"Beverly's on the swim team at her middle school."

"That's not all peaches and cream," I said. "Every morning you have to get up early for practice. Her hair could dry out. Her ends could all split. She probably smells of chlorine."

"Guess what?" she asked at the dinner table.

"What?" Shelley said.

"They belong to a health club. The East Bank Club. It's very exclusive. They have a family membership and go whenever they want. I was their guest. There was this cosmetologist, there was this hair stylist. I had a makeover. They gave me a facial with collagen, the skin's natural moistening conditioner, and taught me to use eyeliner, to start in the middle and go to the outer corners instead of starting from the inner corners. That opens your eyes and makes them look bigger. Guess what?" she demanded.

"What?"

"You have to pat it with a Q-tip to make it less harsh."

"Connie?"

"Because my face is so round she showed me how to use blusher to bring out my cheekbones. She put apricot scrub on my skin to clean out the pores. I had a cellophane wrap. I lost three pounds."

"Connie?"

"Guess what?"

"Connie?"

"Guess what?!"

"What?" Shelley said.

"They gave me a shampoo and washed it out with herbal rinse. They conditioned my hair, they styled it. They gave me the layered look. Guess what else?"

"Connie."

"Go ahead, Dad. You can guess too. *Guess what else?!*"

"What else?"

"Marvin? Diane's boyfriend from Hebrew school? Marvin likes me. That's what they told me at the slumber party. They said he got this crush on me when he saw my new makeover. They said he means to write me. And guess what else?"

"What else?" Shelley and I said together.

"They get clothing allowances. All the girls get clothing allowances. My colors are autumn. Forest green, deep orange, the browns. Guess what?"

"No, you guess what, Connie! *You* guess what," I shouted at her.

"'What?"

"*More St. Myra Weiss? More with your St. Myra Weiss?*"

"You don't believe Marvin likes me? He *likes* me all right! You think I made that up? You think I'd lie about something like that? You just wait until he starts writing me letters."

"Connie," Shelley said.

"Connie," I said, "Connie, sweetheart."

"Or that they *don't* get a clothing allowance? Well, they do too."

"Connie," said Shelley.

"Connie," I said.

"*And* they belong to the East Bank Club! It has Nautilus. It has free weights. It has aerobics and jazzercise. It has Jacuzzi and whirlpool and sauna and racquetball. It has an Olympic pool and a natural juice bar where they'll mix you a cauliflower or spinach cocktail or anything else you want, or squeeze out the juice not just from organically grown fruit, melons and oranges or bananas or whatever, but from right out of the peel too. And they bring it right to your table. I had this cauliflower cocktail on a dare? And you know something? If you chug-a-lug it, it's not half bad."

"Connie, calm down."

"No," she said, "you calm down. *You* calm down!"

"How can I calm down," I asked reasonably, "if I'm not the one who's excited?"

"Well, you *should* be," she said. "You *should* be. *I'd* be excited if I were you."

"What's that supposed to mean?"

"It means what it means."

"You hear this?" I asked Shelley. " 'It means what it means.' What's that supposed to mean? Now she talks in riddles."

"She's telling us about Chicago-le."

"Oh, *stop* that!" Connie said.

"Don't talk that way to Mama."

"Oh, *please*," Connie said.

"You're a little cranky," Shelley said. "It's probably jet-e-le lag-e-le."

"That's old, Mother. That's so *old*."

"Don't you criticize your mother," I warned. "Who do you think you are? Don't you *dare* criticize her!"

"You think I don't know what's going on? You think I don't know you don't even sleep together anymore? You think I don't know that?"

"We sleep together, dear," Shelley said. "Really," Shelley said. "Honest. We do."

"Why do you answer her? Why do you give her the satisfaction?"

"Really," Connie said. "I suppose your comb and brushes just happened to *walk* into the spare bedroom! I suppose your lucky porcelain lion did! *And* your jewelry case that you never leave lying around *any*where and always keep in the bottom drawer of your bureau under your sweaters! Oh, *sure*! Tell me another, why don't you?"

"You spy on your mother? You search out her little secret hiding places?"

"I decided to move some things around without going to the trouble of rearranging the furniture," Shelley said. "To see how it would feel, you know? You were visiting in Chicago and I had some time on my hands."

"I wasn't 'visiting' in Chicago, Mother."

"Of course you were. You were visiting your uncle Al Harry. You were visiting your cousins."

"He's not my *real* uncle. Don't you think I don't know he's not my *real* uncle?"

"No," I said, "Al Harry's *not* your real uncle, and you *weren't* 'visiting' in Chicago. You were on the lam because of all the trouble you caused."

"And you and my mother don't sleep together anymore."

"I already explained that," Shelley said. "I already told you what that was all about. There's a saying: 'A place for everything and everything in its place.' I was a little bored. The sheets with the sheets, the tablecloths with the tablecloths. My jewelry case in the bureau drawer under my sweaters."

"Oh, yeah? Then why'd you put it all back?"

"It was too hard to find things. I couldn't remember where anything was."

"Oh, sure, oh, right," Connie said, crossing her arms and glaring at her mother. *"If you couldn't remember where anything was, then how'd you know where to find the things you forgot so you could put them back where they belonged?"* she demanded triumphantly.

"Aha," Shelley shot back, trumping her triumph, "but I didn't! *You* found the brushes, *you* found the comb! *You* found my jewelry and lucky lion!"

"What is this? What's going on? What's this about?" I asked, sliding into my rabbi mode. "What's all this fireworks between my two best girls?"

"Because if there's one thing I've learned, young lady," Shelley said, "you must never, but never, go to bed angry. Your father and I never go to bed angry."

"Mother, that's gross."

"Because we're no different," Shelley told her suddenly, ardently. "Connie, dear, you have to understand this. We're no different. We're not. You aren't different. I'm not. What, just because we live in a funny little town? What's that? It's nothing. Or any of the rest of it either. All that peer baloney you think you missed out on. It isn't anything, Connie sweetheart. Really. I promise you. It's nothing at all, Connie dear."

I looked at my serious, even solemn, wife, in her rabbi mode once more. I'll be, I thought. I'll be damned, but you never know where your succor is coming from next. I'll be, but my redeemer liveth. I thought we were all about to embrace each other.

"If he was my real uncle, or Diane and Beverly were my real cousins, I could never look them in the face again, especially Diane," Connie said softly, suddenly, her point dipped in a sort of quiet, come-hither hostility.

"What's this, a new riddle?"

"I'd be too ashamed," she said.

"Connie?" I said.

"You don't do that to real cousins."

"You don't do what to real cousins?"

"Who've taken you in. Who trust you."

"This isn't some new St. Myra Weiss thing we haven't heard about yet, is it, Connie? Something like Gold Cards or individual retirement accounts and living wills of their very own for teenagers? It's about Keoghs for kids, isn't it, Connie?"

"No wonder she always goes to the papers first," my wife said. "You pick on her."

"Another county heard from."

"You don't? You don't pick on her? You're not sarcastic? You don't poke fun?"

"He seduced me."

"I'm out of line?" I said, wailing my woe, to Connie, to Shelley, to the room, to all the living and dead in Lud. "I guess maybe I'm out of line I turn a phrase on a kid she tries to tear up her daddy's career, who has a problem with the neighborhood she runs to the press with handouts and bulletins, who practically cleaned me out with my own wife." I turned to my daughter. "Guess what? Guess what?" I demanded. "I sold Klein's and Charney's dirt for them. I gave up my nights and weekends and flogged cemetery real estate to the trade and came home to an empty bed. *What do you mean he seduced you? Who seduced you?*"

"I couldn't help it," she said. "He swept me off my feet. He turned my head."

"*Who* swept you off your feet? *Who* turned your head? What are we talking about here?"

"All he does is just stand next to me and I hear music playing."

"Music," put in Shelley, my wife the entertainer.

"Marvin made me feel like a woman for the first time in my life."

"What Marvin? Who Marvin?"

"Marvin. Diane's boyfriend from Hebrew school. The one with the crush on me they told me about at the slumber party. He taught me how to play miniature golf. He wined me and dined me."

"He's twelve years old!"

"He's tall for his age."

"I'm going to kill her," I said.

"You're upsetting your father," Shelley said.

"I'm going to kill her."

"Jerry, calm down. We'll gather our thoughts, we'll find out exactly what happened. Connie," Shelley said carefully, "Connie, dear, when you say he 'seduced' you, just what is it you mean exactly, sweetheart?"

"I surrendered my cherry to him."

"Your *cherry*, your *cherry?!*"

"He promised to write!"

"That's why you did it, so you'd get *mail*?"

"No," Connie said, "of course not."

"Of course not," Shelley agreed. "Let her explain."

"*Explain what? What's there to explain?*" I yelled.

"Oh, you think it's so easy for two people who want to get it on, one of whom doesn't even *live* in Chicago but is only staying at her uncle's place (who isn't her real uncle anyway) until some stuff blows over in New Jersey, and the other of them not only has no car but isn't old enough to drive one yet even if he did, or even old enough to have a learner's permit so he might at least have access to one so long as there's a licensed driver or even just a person old enough to have *her* learner's permit beside him in the death seat when the cop stops him. Or if they *had* the car. Even if they *had* the car, where could they go to be alone? To her cousins'? Even if one of them was off practicing swimming at the East Bank Club in the Olympic-size pool, what about the other one? What about Diane, whose boyfriend he actually was supposed to be? Even if neither *one* of them was at home? You think *that's* so easy? How would you handle *that* one?

"I'm sorry, but it's not the easiest thing in the world to be young and in love and from out of town and not have access either to a car or an apartment.

"Oh," she said, "it's all right, I guess, during the courtship phase, when you're at the movies, say, and he's sitting there, holding the tub of buttered popcorn between your Cousin Diane on the one side and you on the other and you reach into the box and accidentally brush his hand. Or you don't, you put your palm out and he places the popcorn into it piece by piece. Or when you're both guests at the East Bank Club and you're both in your bathing suits side by side at one end of the pool holding the stopwatch between you and timing laps and flip turns for your cousin Beverly.

"So don't think it was so easy for us. Because what they say is so. The course of true love *doesn't* run smooth. Or when we were at the Art Institute together standing in front of the nudes. (That's when we knew. That's when we first actually realized we were going to need either a car or an apartment.)"

"What is this? What am I listening to here? I'm your father. I'm her father," I told my wife. "Why is she talking to me like this?"

"So what do you think he did?"

"What do I think he did? He took your cherry. That's what I think he did."

"*Jer*ry!" Shelley said.

"Come on, Dad, guess what he did."

"What did he do?"

"Marvin's got a friend, Larry. Larry's big brother works at this motel in Skokie. (It turns out we didn't even need a car. We decided to take the bus. It took three buses and two transfers to get there. People worry for nothing.) He's the one who let us into the room. We had our own key and everything. We could use the TV. We could use the air conditioning. He even said we could use the telephone. So long as we didn't call out and only used the phone to check the time with the motel operator. The only thing, the only thing we weren't supposed to do was take the spread off the bed, and when we finished we weren't allowed to use the shower. Because the maid had already made up the room? But it worked out okay. Guess how?"

"You found an extra blanket in the closet and laid it over the bedspread. You decided to use the shower anyway and cleaned up the bathroom yourselves."

"That's *right!*" Connie said. "What did we do about towels?"

"You used that extra blanket. You wiped each other off with it. Then you wiped up the inside of the tub. Then you wiped up the floor."

"Guess what we did afterward?"

"After you surrendered your cherry and cleaned up the bathroom?"

"That's right."

"You thought about calling room service, decided it was too risky, and got a couple of candy bars and some ice and Cokes out of the machines instead."

"That's *right!* Then what?"

I wasn't trying to be a wise guy and, though she was my daughter, it's not that I even had any very particular curiosity about it. It was simply clear to me, plain as the nose. As if, yes, this is what a couple of underage twerps would be doing at a time like this. This is how they would kill the time until their embarrassment settled and they felt calm enough to go home.

"That's right," she repeated. "Guess then what?"

"You dialed other people's rooms. You found the motel's writing paper and envelopes and wrote love letters to each other. You wrote Diane and Beverly postcards and circled your room on the front. You read them out loud. He said 'Wish you were here' on his. You laughed but were too frightened to send them and tore them up."

"Oh, yeah? Oh, yeah?" she said. "*Then* what? *Then* what?"

"You got more candy out of the machine and watched HBO on the television."

"Uncle Al Harry told you all this."

"Al Harry *knows* all this?"

"Cousin Diane told him."

"So," I said. "Your cousin found out what you did. Sure," I said, "Larry's big brother. He's the one who told Larry, Marvin's friend."

"She's not my real cousin."

"Larry told Diane about your boyfriend." I was tired now. A seance really takes it out of you.

"He's not my real boyfriend," Connie said. "He told her himself."

"Oh, Connie," Shelley said. "Oh, my poor dear Connie. Do something, Jerry. Can't you see her heart is breaking?"

Do something? Do something what? My daughter was stretched across her mother's lap, the two of them composed like the little Pietà of Connie's deposition, Shelley stroking Connie's madeover, layered hair and crooning her There-theres and consolations.

"That's right," she comforted, "it doesn't. It *doesn't* run smooth. Of course not. Not for anyone. How wise you are. Isn't she, Jerry? Isn't she wise? How *proud* we are, sweetheart. What a level-headed heart you have on your shoulders! Such a love detective! Isn't she, Jerry?"

"Sure is."

"To have learned what you've learned? At fourteen? And to have found out our secret? Your father's and mine? Not back in the house an hour and you discover we're not sleeping together anymore. That Mother moved into the spare bedroom the minute you left. Wasn't that clever of her? Wasn't it, Jerry?"

"Absolutely."

"Yes," Shelley said. "And we thought we could fool her."

"No way."

"Well, tell her," said Shelley.

"Hey," I said, at once exhausted and as suddenly and frightfully free as a man who has just been in a stupid and devastating accident, "we're happy to have you back in our funny little town where death drags down the neighborhood and kicks shit out of the property values."

"Really?" Connie said.

"Hell, yes," I told her, "cherry or no cherry, we're just pleased as all get-out to have you back where you belong."

eleven

BUT NO, I had to end it on a sour note. No sense
of timing, when to get out. If I'd—so to speak—turned off
the lights when she got to the part about the real uncle, real
cousin, real boyfriend business, we could all have kissed and
made up. Even if we'd brought down the curtain when the big
lummox, all tragic and cozy, was crawling up and down my
wife's lap, we might still have been able to bring it off, music,
swelling, up and out. But no, I had to hit the kid with my
cherry-or-no-cherry speech. I just don't know when to get out.
Or where I get off.

So instead of all is forgiven, nothing was. Shelley huffed
and puffed, fussed and bothered, preening her car-pool temperament and conscientiousness like nobody's business. The very
picture of a mother right down to the last detail. As, before
Connie came along, she'd been the very picture of the brand-
new bride and, after, the perfect picture of a wife and lover. Or,
throughout, had the rebbitzin, if not letter-perfect—I never
said Shelley was letter-perfect—down pat, at least in the sensi-
bilities. And, as now, she had become some vehicle of born-
again reproach to me. We *didn't* sleep together. Oh, we shared
the same room, even the same bed, but we might, absent and
yearning, have been in different cities. It wasn't even as if she

felt a sexual antipathy toward me. (I know my Shelley.) No, this was the judgment of the court. She was serving time, waiting until the next down-to-the-last-detail down-pat picture came to her.

Connie, God bless her, harassed me with attitude while she—I thought—thought up new ways to go public. I asked if she meant to run away again, and she said, "Where would I go?" Sealing the ménage. Locking us, forever could be, into her tight, airless little game plan.

And me? What about me, the Rabbi of Lud?

Well, to tell the truth, I was in love at the time and couldn't be bothered. I don't know, maybe it was my problems at home made it happen, one of those cause-and-effect, chicken-or-egg deals that make you crazy trying to fathom. Connie had already revealed God's plan for her in the scheme of things, split Lud, and sent Shelley off packing into the spare bedroom with her jewels and lucky porcelain, so I was probably already half a goner anyway when I ran into one of my wife's singing sisters in the hospitality suite of a nearby Best Western when I was working the interment circuit for Klein and Charney. Of all the musical Jews, God knows she was the one I'd always found the most attractive.

It was Joan Cohen, the one who shopped. The tall, elegant Chaverot in the suedes and knits who, in her wool autumnals and graduated rusts and yellows, looked like camouflage, and seemed, as I've said, some quick tweed movement in a field, fashionably earthen as a saddle or the burnished stock of a rifle, a step from blood sport. She could have been poster lady for the National Rifle Association. Joan Cohen was like moonlight in Vermont, autumn in New York.

Oh, oh, Joan, Joan, it wasn't just the leaves you set ablaze when you stepped up to fill the brisk fall air with your smoky, musky chlorophyll, but whole heaped piles of my heart. You were aristocratic and as full of gorgeous, solid presence as some handsome, tweedy lady sensibly shod. Foxy Joan Cohen, do ye ken John Peel?

I don't know, she made me feel, well, Church of England, as though I had a "living," two hundred a year, say, like some curate in a country parish on a great estate in a novel. Jerry

Goldkorn, Rabbi of Dorchester House. Well-met we were in that Rutherford, New Jersey, Best Western.

"Yoicks! Is that Joan Cohen?"

"Rabbi, it is," she said. "Shalom."

"Hail! Halloo! What cheer?"

"I read about your Connie in the papers."

"My," I said, "what a beautiful sweater. Shetland, is it?"

"Kids," she said, "go figure them. A bunch of nudniks."

"Lightweight, but I should think it keeps one quite cozy astride a good, strong jumper taking the hurdles and hedges of a brisk morning."

"They haven't any sachel."

"Would it also come in a herringbone jacket, do you suppose?"

"All chutzpa and shpilkes."

"Pinched at the waist and flared at the hips? With little leather patches at the elbows?"

"To say such awful things? To strangers? A shanda! What? No," she said, "I haven't seen it in herringbone."

She was there, she told me, to check out the acoustics for the Nathan Nizer bar mitzvah. She'd heard I was selling grave-yard properties and happened to have seen my name on the special events board in the lobby. Was my seminar over already?

"No, no. It doesn't start till seven."

"It's twenty to eight."

"Sometimes they're a little late."

"Oh?"

"Sometimes they don't show up."

"Oh," Joan Cohen said.

"I give them a couple of hours."

"Oh."

"Then I'm out of here."

"I see."

"Oh, yes. Two hours. Then I'm history."

"Are those brochures?"

"Hmn?"

"On those chairs you set up. Are they brochures?"

"Well, yes, in a way they're brochures. They're cemetery plats. They describe the services we provide. The different perpetual care options you can choose from. The legal height you can have your monument. Examples of the sort of thing we do. What, would you care to see one?"

"Oh, yes, please. May I?"

"I don't see why not."

She took a piece of literature up off one of the empty chairs and appeared to study it.

"Well," I said, "what do you think?"

"It's very interesting," Joan Cohen said. "I like Plan D. Creeping euonymous is my favorite ground cover. I love a dark, shiny leaf. And it's green all winter. It never drops off."

"Well," I said, inspired and suddenly ruthless with desire and decision, "I'll tell you something about Plan D and your creeping euonymous."

"Oh?"

"It's a forbidden vine."

"Really?"

"Strictly. You didn't know that?"

"There's forbidden ground cover?"

"There's trayf fruits and vegetables."

"Really?"

"French fries. Guavas and papayas are outlawed fruit, certain kids of nuts and grains."

"I never heard that."

"A good rule of thumb is, Only what grew in the Garden of Eden is kosher."

"Oh, Rabbi," she said, "you're teasing me."

"Yeah," I admitted, "I am. The jury's still out on the french-fried potatoes," I whispered.

"Oh, Rabbi."

I really believe she meant Shelley no harm, that it was her piety did her in, her fervent, terrible, swift Godbent. We did it right there in the paid-up hospitality suite.

"Oh, Rabbi. Poor, sweet Rabbi Goldkorn."

She said my name but I was just the surrogate, the middleman, her humble conduit to the Lord. Hey, it's lonely at the middle, let me tell you. What else can it mean, a lady comes and she screams, "Oh, oh, Rabbi, oh, you're giving me the suntan!" That's what she told me. That I was giving her the suntan. Reflecting glory, glamour. Spritzing sperm and wonder. She couldn't get enough of my insider's wowser connections, this God-juiced, God-foreplayed lady. My inside info a turn-on. Treating me to her giggled deference and excited by all the landmined, bedmined, riskwrath. God was my copilot *that* night, let me tell you. And hers too, into all the holy sacreds, and embracing, as I say, who knew Whom in her head. Just as I, in mine, the both of us naked in that Rutherford Best Western, made love to some idea I had of her clothed in her own forbidden ground cover. Until, Godspent, she shoved out from under me. "Hallelujah," she sang, "is that all there is?"

It was. We didn't see each other again.

Though at night, alone in my bachelor's bed or, afterward, when Connie returned from Chicago, alongside Shelley but still alone, her image continued to inflict me. Displayed in all her crisp, beautiful golden basket tones like some woven woman or a girl made out of plaid, appeared in my consenting head in all her gorgeous barks and browns, the tarnished hues of open, airing apples, come dressed to kill, got up in all the muted splendids of Joan Cohen's fall and fallen fashions.

• • • •

As always, as I walked along Main Street, I felt cheered, my heart lifting, lifting, lifted by the pink Federal-style buildings all around me like so many small banks. I opened the door to Sal's barber shop and stepped inside, tripping the modest tinkle of Sal's prop bell. Someone was lying back in one of Sal's three chairs, his torso covered by a barber's cape, his face by a hot towel. The bell must have startled him awake because the minute I entered he sat bolt upright, tore the cloth from his face and, the cape bunched in his fist, looked about wildly.

"Easy," Sal said, "easy there, Bubbles. It's only our skullcap. It's only the rov."

The fellow stared at me a moment, then relaxed back into the chair.

"It's cold," he said of the still-steaming towel.

Sal resettled him under the barber's cape, fixed another towel he lifted from the sink with tongs and laid it across the man's face like a cloth over a bird cage. And with something like the same effect. In seconds I heard a light, companionable snoring. Sal grinned at me above the man's heaped absence and, reaching in under the back of the hot towel, began to massage Bubbles's hidden scalp, vaguely working him like a magic trick.

"I can come back," I said.

"No, no, I'm practically done," Sal said, motioning me to a chair. "Sit, he's a pussycat."

"That's all right," I said.

"No, really," Sal said, "I don't cut his hair, I don't give him a shave. He already had that forty-dollar manicure on his hands when he came in. That's so, ain't it, Bubbles?"

"People notice your hands. It's the first place they look."

"Bubbles has his priorities straight," Sal said.

"I'm here for the shmooz and hot towels," Bubbles's voice said behind its wrappings, and he sat up again, at his leisure this time, fastidious as an actor as he picked the linen cape off his suit and peeled the towel from his face. "Yeah," he said, studying himself in a hand mirror, "that's good, Sal. That brought the blood up good." He turned to me. "What do you think? How do I look? Sally's tip rides on what you tell me."

"You look fine."

"Yeah?"

"Hey, Bubbles," Sal said, "hey, Bubbles, come on now."

"That's all right," I told Sal.

"Sure," Bubbles said, relenting, holding open palms up at the level of his lapels, a broad, innocent "Who, me?" smile on his face. "No more shop talk."

"Next?" Sal called out nervously, and I took a chair different from the one Bubbles had just vacated. The two of them did some business at Sal's big brass register and then Bubbles left. " 'Next,' " Sal said, "you know how long it's been since I said that?"

"Business is bad?"

"Business is booming," Sal said, watching Bubbles cross the street and get into a car. "He brings his own *towels*," Sal whispered after Bubbles had started the car and driven off.

"Who is he?" I asked.

Sal didn't answer. He pointed to some loose locks, clipped fur-balls of different-colored hair scattered about the floor of his shop. "That's off of dead people," he told me. "*I* put it down there. To make the place look lived in. What do you think? Too much?"

"It's nice."

"Yeah? Maybe I'll get a darky with a push broom. Give me shoeshines, fetch me coffee. Hey," Sal said, "you were safe there with Bubbles. You think I'd jeopardize a pal? He's a wise guy. So how is it having the kid back? Is it great? Kids," Sal said, "you can't live with 'em, you can't live without 'em. Hey," he said, "she came in one time, asked me some stuff about Jesus. Said it was for a report she was doing for her school. I told her what I know. I don't know much. Did I do wrong?"

"Who is he?"

"I said," Sal said. "Just some wise guy. Hey, those birds don't shoot you for kicks, you know. There has to be something in it for them. Sure," he said, "the hardest guy in the world to rile is a professional hit man. You can give him lip, butt in front of him in line, spill soup down his pants, he won't lift a finger. I don't know, it's a professional pride, something."

"Sal," I said, "I saw his *gun*."

"A calling card, a trademark. Like my barber pole, like that shit on my floor." Then, urgently, he leaned toward my ear. "All the years you been coming into this shop," Sal scolded, "did I ever hold out on you? Wasn't I always up front? Didn't I already tell you fifty-sixty times about the American way of death? What'd you think that stuff was I was feeding you? Folklore? It was hard information. Jesus, Padre, show me a guy brings his own towels, I'll show you a fuck working hard on his image! And he ain't shy, that one. Or even like I was in some need-to-know relation to him. Hell," Sal said, "I'm a dime a dozen with a man like that. We all are. He's got barbers all across New Jersey, throughout the entire tristate viewing area. A hot towel here, a manicure there, a haircut somewhere else. Dropping hints all over. 'Here, Sally,' he says, 'use my towels instead.' Fucking showboat."

"It's a sickness," I said. "Some people are terrified of germs."

"He don't give a shit about germs. It's in case they shoot him while he's in my shop. He says he don't need it on his conscience he's the one responsible for ruining my towels. Who the hell does he think he is, Anthony Anastasia? Fucking showboat! How do you want it today, Rabbi, the usual?"

"What hard information did you ever give me?"

"Oh, come on," Sal said, "what more did you need?"

"What hard information?"

"Oh, please," Sal said.

"No," I said, "really."

"What do you want to see, Rabbi, a bill of lading? You want to look in a body bag? Come down to the basement of the business parlor with me. We'll look in the one Bubbles brought in."

"What are you talking about?"

"No, no," Sal said, "we'll check him out against the death certificate. You'll see for yourself."

"What will I see for myself? What are you talking about?"

"No, no," Sal said, "don't take *my* word."

"Boy," I said, "who is it this time? Jimmy Hoffa?"

"You already did Jimmy Hoffa."

"Then who?"

"I don't know. Some guy who's connected."

"He couldn't have been too connected," I said.

"They disconnected him."

"Sure," I said.

"I seen him, Rov. What they done to him. He looks like Beirut."

"Watch out, Sal, the goblins'll get you."

"Probably," Sal said. "Yeah," he said quietly, "they probably will."

"Come on," I said, "what's this? You can't really be scared. This is more shmooz and hot towels, right?"

"Right."

"Talc and toilet water."

"That's right," Sal said.

"A little hair oil and stickum."

"Why do you think they tell me?" Sal demanded suddenly. "Why do you think he showed off in front of you? Why do you think they let us know their business? What's wrong with you? If they didn't want to make certain we were going to protect their secrets, why would they let us learn them in the first place? Guys like that? Like him? God *damn* Tober's goddamn Edward! God *damn* his sporty poster kid who can't tell here from there, up from down, in from out. God *damn* Shull's fucking goddamn needs. God damn need itself or whatever else it was stole shit from the gods and brought it to goddamn Lud!"

"Hey, easy," I said, "easy there, Sal. Easy."

"Like Beirut. I swear. Like he was in an earthquake. Jesus, Rabbi, he looks like a fucking act of God!"

"Who, Sal? Who does?"

"Who *knows* who does?" Sal said, and showed me a death certificate. "The guy, the special delivery in the business parlor, but who *knows* who does? He could have been anybody. They bring them in from all walks of life. Guys behind on their payments. Insider trader guys from Wall Street whose inside information didn't pan out. He could have been anyone who ever disappointed them."

"This has a woman's name on it."

"So," Sal said, "I guess they'll be wanting a closed casket then, hey, Rabbi?"

•   •   •   •

Our own odd version of the car pool—sillier than ever, I suppose, since Connie would no longer permit her classmates to ride with her—had started up again. She was adamant about the point, even though some of the mothers had begun to call, making overtures, devising schedules, proposing ways to divide the labor. She was too humiliated, she said, and told us that the only reason the kids were willing to start up a car pool with us was her notoriety, that she'd become a character. Nor, for the same reasons, would she agree to ride in the school bus. I tried to reason with her, but she had put her foot down, made up her mind.

"The only one you're punishing here is your mother," I said.

"I'll run away if you make me ride to school with other kids," Connie said.

"It's all right," Shelley said. "I don't mind driving. Really. Real-la-le-lee."

"This isn't fair," I said. "Do you think this is fair, Connie?"

"Whoever said life is fair?" Connie said.

"No one," I said.

"I don't even mind if life isn't fair," Shelley said.

"Hey," Connie said, "no sweat. I'll run away."

"Go ahead," I said. "Go ahead and do it."

"I'll turn tricks on Forty-second Street for a couple of weeks. What have I got to lose? It's not as if I still had my cherry or anything."

"Go ahead," I agreed, "run away and turn tricks on Forty-second Street. It's not as if you still had your cherry."

"Sure," she said, "I'll lick some dick for a couple of weeks, put a few bucks together, then come home for a visit."

So the strange car pool started up again, on the road again in the brand-new season's one-woman show in that year's late-model, big new traded-up Buick station wagon, an open door speaking to them for company, an unfastened safety belt, a still-engaged emergency brake, a tank low on gas or an unnecessary light, all the machine's articulate parts nagging at them for attention. More ridiculous than ever, Shelley more like a chauffeur than ever, Connie more like the poor little rich kid, no matter what they did or where my daughter sat, beside her mother or way behind her, deep in the boondocks of the huge automobile, looking more than ever as if they had already arrived at the end of whatever journey they had been on, even as they were pulling out of the driveway, as if everyone else must already have been dropped off or, peculiarly, as if the car had been hired. It seemed a sort of Air Force One, some company jet, I mean, vaguely conspired, tax loopholed, as if, if you came right down to it, it was no one's station wagon at all, or a station wagon under some Bahamian or Liberian registry. And though their route no longer required them to make doglegs and detours to pick up anyone else, it seemed as if the car might accumulate mileage by the simple fact of its existence.

Despite what it may sound like, Shelley and I had settled into a sort of truce with each other. As if not just the station wagon but we too had settled beneath some flag of convenience, pulling our testiness, our neutrality a legal fiction. Whatever else, we were each of us relieved to have somehow made it through the summer.

And, whatever else, we had.

I said nothing about Sal. I never mentioned Bubbles.

We went almost directly from summer into Indian summer that year. There was a blustery Labor Day weekend when a sudden, fast-moving front lay down cold, withering, hard-driving rains during the nights like sustained blasts of heavy incoming, and left the days out to dry in a thin, heatless sunlight. This was followed by a week or so of damp, stalled cold weather, bright, freezing days alternating with nighttime cloudbursts and record lows. (Resorts in the Poconos and Cape May and Atlantic City and Greenwood Lake screamed blue murder over their lost profits.) Then, suddenly, a few days after Rosh Hashanah and before Yom Kippur, the front moved out to sea, and New Jersey looked washed, fresh in the new, immaculate weather like God coming out. The foliage flamed on the trees and then some of it began to fall, laying a torn, bruised cover over the yellowing fields, motley as pizza.

I would have come clean too, the troubled tzadik, I would, the muddled chuchm, and went off to Tober's to burst Bubbles's bubble. I meant to make it up to Shelley, too, for my infidelity, and balance the books with Connie.

But the boys weren't in, were off on some errand and, when I got back, Shelley was crying.

"What?"

"Joan Cohen," she said.

"Shelley, I'm sorry."

"Elaine Iglauer told me," she said. "I picked her up after I dropped Connie off. We were going to look at a house in Oakland." She spoke—and wept—in griefless tones of shock in some register beyond outrage.

"Shelley, I'm so sorry," I said. And I was, and cursed my lousy timing and wondered how I could have allowed them to beat me to the punch and why it had never occurred to me that Joan Cohen would ever share Rutherford with anyone. Meanwhile thinking, the sons of bitches. Thinking, kiss and tell, kiss and tell. Thinking, base kissers; thinking, base tale bearers. "Shelley," I said, emotionally toed-in as a child, "if there was anything I could do . . ."

"I know," she said, and laid her hand on my arm. "Elaine

would have been with her. It was only because we had this appointment."

"I'm sorry?"

"To look at the house. In Oakland. Because the agent who normally shows it had to be somewhere else. So she let Elaine have the key. Well, they know her. Well, they do so much business. Or Elaine might have been killed too."

"Killed?"

"Yes, that's what I'm telling you."

"Killed?"

"If Elaine hadn't already promised to go with me after I dropped Connie off at school."

"Killed?"

"Sure," Shelley said. "That's why she had to tell her no when Joan invited her. Because we already had this appointment to look at the house."

"Invited her."

"To go walking," she said. "In the woods. Near the lake. She wanted to try out her new boots. Elaine saw them. She said they were gorgeous, that they looked beautiful with that new fawn skirt she was wearing. She would have gone, too. Such a lovely, crisp day. After all this rotten weather we've been having. Elaine Iglauer says I saved her life."

"*Killed?* Joan Cohen?"

"Yes," Shelley moaned, "isn't that what I've been saying?"

"Who killed her?"

An image of Bubbles came into my head, twenty dollars' worth of manicure clutching a hand mirror, examining his face, the blood Sal had brought up.

"Rangers found casings," she said. "They think it was a hunter. They think it was a hunting accident."

Sure, I thought, of course. What else? A hunting accident. Do ye ken Joan Cohen? It was hunters jumping the season must have bagged her.

twelve

IT FELL TO ME to do the honors.

All these years in the business and—touch wood—there'd never been anything personal before. No one—thank God—had died on me. (Well, there was my little stillborn boy, but he didn't even have a name, and we didn't have the koyach to bury him.) What I'm saying is that, well, for me, kayn aynhoreh, it had *all* been in the rabbi mode. Not that any man's death doesn't diminish me too. Sure it does. It does. If a clod be washed away by the sea, isn't Jersey the less? This is a given. Still, there's loss and there's loss, there's death and there's death.

They came the same bright, crisp afternoon of the day she was shot, Fanny Tupperman and Miriam Perloff, and assured me they spoke for the surviving Chaverot, for Sylvia Simon and Elaine Iglauer, for Rose Pickler and Naomi Shore, even, they said, for Shelley.

"My," I told them, "such a vote of confidence, but surely, wouldn't it be better if her own rabbi performed the service?"

"*You* were her rabbi," Fanny Tupperman said.

"What's Judaism coming to?" I deplored. "No one belongs to a temple nowadays? *I* was her rabbi? *I* was? I rabbi the dead.

I minister the fallen away, the caught out and caught short in New Jersey."

"That's Joan all right," Fanny Tupperman said.

"I don't know," I said, "if I'm up to it. A grotesque, off-season hunting accident. Listen, I'm still in shock."

I was. I was a draikopf, and couldn't keep it straight who knew what and when they knew it. *I* was her rabbi, singing Fanny Tupperman had enigmatically piped. Plus there was the truly false light into which I would be plunging my wife, and daughter, too, for that matter, who would probably take a day off from school and martyrdom to hear the family's other religious, her dad, recite his holy bygones-be-bygones above Joan Cohen's gamy remains. A tall order for a guy who for most of his professional life had tried to maintain a low profile. Plus the fact of my own real, adulterous, grief. Which was unresolved and would make, along with the visions I continued to access in my head of Joan Cohen's doelike leaps to errant, risky freedom, all that tragic dodge and cut-and-run (because surely she would have picked up his scent even before he—the killer poacher, man-eating, deer-stalker hunter—would have picked up the visual equivalent of hers— that quick tweed movement in the field, that flash of leather boot or hoof), any words of mine of no avail, of never any glimmer of avail. (Who would still think "doomed" the moment I remembered the moment she proposed to Elaine Iglauer that they go walking in the woods. And still ask God-*God!*—"What would a woman like this be doing out on a day like that anyway? Tell me, what could You have been thinking of?" Or scold, *scold* her memory. "Running such risks! Practically inviting every trigger-happy, redneck, rifle-bearing yahoo in this neck of the woods to take a potshot at you! You were asking for it. You almost *deserve* to have been killed!")

I tried to tell them I was the wrong man for the job and marshaled all the fool-for-a-client arguments I could think of. They looked at me closely. "It's just that I knew her," I told them lamely. "I couldn't be objective."

"Those other times," Fanny Tupperman said, "those were *objective* funerals?"

Shelley asked me to do it. "If not for me, then for Joan Cohen. She'd have wanted it that way."

"Boy," I said, "every Tom, Dick and Harry knows what dead people have in their heads, what they've got up their sleeves and would get off their chests. Why do they draw up wills? What do we need lawyers?"

"Jerry," Shull confided, "I'm picking up the expenses on this one. The deluxe mahogany. Down stuffing in the satin lining. I'm going all out."

"What, you are?"

"My pleasure," he said.

"Your pleasure? That's very kind, Sam."

"No, no, you don't understand. My *pleasure*. I dated her."

"I see," I said.

"Twenty grand I must have spent on that woman. At *least* twenty grand. I was the one who put her into all those suedes and Harris tweeds she wore. The tiny pinstripes. I dressed her for success. What the hell? What's a few thousand more? Still, well, you know, if we had to bring in another rabbi . . ."

•   •   •   •

That she'd never married. That she left no survivors. That was the angle I meant to punch up. Working her childlessness, working her spinsterhood, working the theme we were all her survivors.

Her singing. I'd bring in her singing. Her musical Judaism. And sketch her, powerfully clapping, bounding round the campfire, draw her generous kibbutz heart. A cheerful, reliable, companionable sort, her soul in the backpack with the provisions. This echt Sabra, some maiden Jewess, say, who might have been there with Moses on the long voyage out from Egypt to the Promised Land. Some slim, dark au pair of the wilderness who kept an eye on the kids and helped with the tents. Though this, of course, was not how I really saw her. (Oh, how I *really* saw her! Never mind how I *really* saw her!) Though you know? In a way I did.

Her good-sport mode, I mean, and elegant outdoor ways. Which got her killed for her trouble, slaughtered for her style. And led her out into the very fields and locales where models posed for their pictures, out into the unfenced surreal, that deer-stalked, fox-hunted, cony-catchered bluegrass where you could almost have anticipated the sniper would be.

And that's not how I really saw her either.

One time—this was two years ago—Shelley came to me, very excited.

"We've got a gig-e-le."

"I'm sorry?"

"A gig-e-le, a booking. It's a show biz-e-le term."

"Who does?"

"We do, the girls. The Chaverot."

"Oh," I said, "that's nice."

"It is," she said. "Jack Perloff finally popped the question. Miriam doesn't have to be a divorcee anymore."

"Well, that *is* good news," I said. Jack Perloff had an automobile dealership in the Oranges. He and Miriam had been seeing each other for years. There was a question about his intentions. Until Shelley's announcement it was understood that, officially, they were only "going steady."

"They're getting married in Philadelphia. His parents live there. Miriam wants the Chaverot to entertain. Of course, we couldn't think of charging anything. It's a professional courtesy."

"Of course you can't charge them," I said. "It will be your wedding present."

"Oh, no," Shelley said, "we have to get them a *gift*. Anyway, we're all invited. The Chaverot spouses too. We could go down on Friday. The wedding's Saturday night and we can drive back Sunday. The ceremony's in this wonderful new hotel, which is supposed to be very nice. They have a weekend special. Miriam says the groom's people will make all the arrangements. Can we, Jerry, can we?"

Why not? Every once in a while every now and then you have to make a weekend of it. I say this in my rabbi mode.

So we drove—the Chaverot colleagues, the Chaverot husbands—the eighty or so miles down to Philly in three of our big cars and checked into the hotel. The Barry Bernstein bar mitzvah was posted on a black hotel reader board in the lobby, Lou and Gloria Kaplan's Silver Wedding Anniversary was. An announcement for the Mindy Weintraub Sweet Sixteen party was up on an easel. (Shelley was right, I thought, it *was* a wonderful hotel. Understand me, when I say that every once in a while every now and then you have to make a weekend of it, I don't mean you must get away. The opposite, rather. You have to go back. You must ground yourself in the familiar, settle back in the thick, sweet old gravity of things.)

There were a dozen of us, five men and seven women. Miriam and the lucky man had gone down before us and would be staying with the Perloffs. Fanny Tupperman (divorced, she was Fanny Lewis then) shared a room with Joan Cohen, who was also single. (I'd never met Joan's husband, and until that weekend hadn't realized she hadn't any.)

We'd hardly unpacked when there was a knock on the door. It was Jack Perloff, big in the doorway, rubbing his hands, kibitzing, bullying welcome. "How is it," he asked, stepping inside, "is it all right? Is it going to be big enough? Oh, yes, it's a *nice* size. Jesus, you could sleep three in the front and five in the back in here," the car dealer remarked amiably. "What about closet space? Got enough? What's this, a walk-in? Oh, yeah, terrific. Swell threads. Gorgeous gown, Shelley. Am I marrying the wrong chick, or what? Hey, how about these soaps? That's some classy odor. Very delicate. You don't have to use 'em, you know. Take them home if you want. With the shampoo and the shower cap. Souvenirs. Call the desk, say the maid didn't leave you any. Have them send up some more. Wait a minute. Something's amiss here. Where's your rose? There's supposed to be a long-stemmed rose in this room."

"That's all right."

"The *hell* it's all right! It's part of the deal. Listen, you don't have to do a thing. When I'm in the lobby, I'll speak to the concierge. There won't be any trouble. Oh, wait a minute. You got the fruit. Some get the fruit, some get the flower. Would you rather have the flower or would you rather have the fruit? I know the Iglauers got a rose. Maybe you could trade. There's your TV. Look, they've got a movie channel. If you're still up at three, they show an X-rated film. If you slipped the kid a fin, I bet they'd probably run it for you now. Sure, all they do is throw it up on their VCR and just plug you in. You're too shy, I'll say something on your behalf myself, Rabbi, and give him the finif, too, for that matter."

"Thanks," I said, "that won't be necessary."

"You're not offended? I didn't offend you?"

"No, of course not."

"Hey, just because old Cupid stings *my* toches with his arrows I think *all* blood is boiling. I shouldn't be that way. I'm too romantic."

"Perfectly understandable."

"Yeah?"

"Certainly."

"Miriam and I are delighted you came, Rabbi and Shelley," he said gravely, "and only hope that this weekend will be as memorable for you as I know it's going to be for us."

"I'm sure it will be."

"Thank you," Jack Perloff said. "Coming from a rabbi, I'm going to regard that as a blessing."

"That's how I intended it."

"Thank you, Rabbi."

"Jerry, Jack."

"Jerry," he corrected. "Hey, I almost forgot," he said, and opened a door next to the desk. "It's our hospitality suite," he said. "It's for the wedding party, but I want everyone to feel free. Mi casa, su casa," he said, and just then we heard his intended in the hall.

"Knock, knock," Miriam said in the open door.

"Hi there, sweetheart."

"Just a minute," she said, and moved a foot or so back out into the corridor. "On the count of three," Miriam called down the hallway. "One!" Jack stepped up to a door at the side of the television set, and turned the little whoosis in its round, recessed fitting. "Two!" she proclaimed. "*Three!*" she sang out. Jack opened the connecting door and, on their side of the wall, the Picklers did the same. Rose Pickler stood at the threshold between our two rooms. "Hi, stranger," Rose, grinning, greeted Jack, "how you doin'?"

"Come here, Miriam," Jack Perloff said, "will you just look at this, will you?"

Shelley and Jack and Miriam and I crowded around the connecting doors. Through some repeated suite, double, double, suite arrangement peculiar to the hotel, we could see down the entire length of rooms. I looked past Rose and Will Pickler in their room, and Al and Naomi Shore in theirs, beyond the Iglauers where Elaine held her rose, and beyond Ted and Sylvia Simon to where, at the distant end of the queer railroad-flat configuration, Fanny was handing Joan Cohen a piece of complimentary fruit.

And *that's* how I saw her.

And later, after dinner, in Perloff's hospitality suite, where we had gathered to shmooz and tell jokes, to play cards and listen—and some of us dance—to the music on the FM, and watch the lights of downtown Philadelphia, and pick from the bowls of nuts, and nosh from the platters of food Perloff had had sent up (not so much without appetite or edge as somehow ahead of it), and drink from the bar he had stocked, lying about, secure, lulled by the movements of the ladies, by the sweet, soft music of their commentary like a kind of vocalizing, brought back to some ancient, lovely treehouse condition, that's how I saw her, too. Then, later, after Perloff had left with Miriam, and some of the others, tired out, had mumbled vague goodnights and gone back to their rooms (actually too tired to leave the hospitality suite, too tired or too reluctant, and choosing the shortcut, returning through the inner corridor, through our rooms, through the Picklers' and Shores' and Iglauers' and Simons'), and then a few more did, and then the rest, until, deep in the dark Shabbes, neither of us speaking and the volume turned low, only Joan Cohen and I were left to watch the X-rated movie when it came on at three.

Because I saw her all sorts of ways. (I couldn't *stop* seeing her. Should I try to put that in?) How she danced at the wedding. With me, with the others. Sensing some distant availability in her, something game and something ready. Up for a frelach, leading a hora. Maybe there was nothing more to it than her bachelor-girl pluck, the simple, ordinary honor of the privately led life. And I could bring in how gorgeous she looked in a lobby. Jesus, she did! Never *mind* the fancy Philadelphia hotel where the Perloffs tied the knot. In the Rutherford Best *Western* even. How she shined *there*! They could just imagine what she must have looked like, how she must have been, set off against all that Philadelphia Bulgari and Pucci, the high glitz of all those

upscale outlet stores! I'm a rabbi, a teacher. I leave nothing to
the imagination. If they were to get a last good glimpse of her
during that brief, last patch of time before I consigned her to
earth forever, then I would have to lead her to them up through
the murk of seance and memory. Presented like a girl on the arm
of a pop. Handed off like a deb, handed off like a bride.

I'd certainly have to tell them about the lobby. I couldn't
keep my eyes off her. I would *have* to tell them about the lobby,
occupied by that vast guest population, guests not just of the
spiffy Philadelphia hotel but by the guests of those guests,
invitees to all the showers, weddings, parties and anniversaries,
all the affairs and mitzvahs, floating their generous mood like a
kind of collective weather, and packing their gifts like handguns.

People checking in, people checking out. (And didn't I
wish I could stay there forever? Held inside the gold parameters
of the handled, splendid atmospherics of the place? Didn't I
just?)

We sat near one of the hotel's bars and breathed the lovely
alcoholic spice lofted out over the lobby, and watched the richish,
sporty, middle-aged Jews importantly lounging, guys in crew
necks, guys in gold, guys with a bypass under their sport shirts
and a hint of Sunday brunch on their breath, Wasps in a Jewey
register. Except that I felt almost like some pale, poor relation
beside them, thinking, Oy, the savvy Sabbath motley of our
crowd.

I could repeat our conversation for them, explain the conditions—I mean the context—in which it took place— Shelley
gone back to the room after the late breakfast we took with the
rest of the wedding party—our last collective act before it broke
up and we went back to New Jersey—to see if she'd left anything behind, to try to move her bowels.

"Well," I said, "it was a lovely wedding."

"Yes, it was fun. Everyone enjoyed themselves."

"I'm glad we decided to make a weekend of it."

"Yes, it was nice."

"I like this hotel. I'm glad we stayed here."

"It's lucky Jack's parents live in town and knew about it."

"Oh, I know," I said. "It's an advantage when you're not
familiar with a city if someone you know is."

"Philadelphia's so close. It can't be ninety miles."

"Sure," I said, "but New York is closer. New York's where we go when we go out to dinner."

Joan Cohen chuckled.

"What?"

"Nothing," she said. "The way those rooms were connected."

"I know," I said.

"That was cute."

"Look, that girl brought those people drinks from the bar. How about a drink, would you care for a drink? They serve you right in the lobby."

"After last night? No, I don't think so. But you go ahead if you like."

"Who, me? No. Drinking's not one of my vices."

"It's not one of mine either really. Though I guess you wouldn't be able to tell that from last night. I was pretty pissed. Oh," she said, "excuse me."

"I say 'piss,' " I objected. "I say 'piss.' I say 'shit.' "

"You do?"

"Hey," I told her, blushing, looking down, "I watch the X-rated movie channel." And try to explain to them the sense I had of her hand above my head, feeling some hypnotic, unheard tonsorial snick-snick in my hair, some tingled attraction, the energy of her fingers, of her rings perhaps, doing tentative passes. I don't know, a gravity, an electric pleasure, some gentle force field of flesh. "Well, that one time anyway," I said.

"Yes," she said, "me too."

"You think people do that stuff?"

"I suppose some people do," Joan Cohen said. "I suppose some people do everything."

"Others don't do anything at all," I said. "I guess most of us go our whole lives without ever getting a blow job," I said.

"Or giving one," Joan Cohen said.

I could put this into my eulogy, how Joan Cohen and I talked about blow jobs, how it came up naturally. In the course of the conversation.

"Did you see all those things he shoved up her behind?"

"Yes, I did," she said.

"That was probably trick photography," I pronounced in the rabbi mode. "Don't you think?"

"I should certainly hope so."

"It sure wasn't responsible sex."

"That's for sure."

"Not when there's AIDS."

"Certainly not," Joan Cohen said.

"I think I *will* have a drink," I said, and signaled the girl where she stood in the bar's broad, open entranceway. "There's something about the sharp smell of a highball in these places."

"So what is?" she asked me.

"What is what?"

"If drinking's not one of your vices."

Her curiosity. I could put in about her curiosity. How we discussed sin, vice, good and evil in the lobby of that Philadelphia hotel while we waited for Shelley to come down with the floral arrangement she'd taken from our table the night before. Just a rabbi talking shop with an interested, dead, lone congregant untimely taken, prematurely plucked out of season.

"Oh, I don't know," I said. "Doesn't one of the commentators tell us that the last thing a man knows is himself?"

"I love it when you talk religious," she said. "But really," she said, "if you had to guess."

"I can't," I said. "I don't."

"No, of course," she said. "You don't *have* to, but tell me," she teased, "*what*? That you haven't any will power? That you don't exercise regularly? That you can't stick to a diet?"

"Do I look out of shape? You think I'm too fat?"

"No," she said, "they're examples. I'm poking around."

"I really *don't* know," I said. "Maybe that I try to lie low."

"Oh," she said, "what a *good* one."

And pick this moment to bring in something of the stunning mystery of death. This was just two years ago. Two lousy years! The day before yesterday, for God's sake! And I'm rounding it off. What would that be in terms of seasons? Two or three wardrobes? Six or seven shopping sprees? How much hose, how many leather accessories? What naps and wools, what hides and knits and fine finished fabrics? All that chic, organic cloth, all those hues like altitude tinted on maps, pale as sea

level, amber as mountain range. Her blood-sport wraps and
fashionables, her swift kinetic tweeds.

Of death more mysterious than life. Because death is harder,
I'd tell them, or what are we grieving for here? (Though life's
pretty mysterious too. Come on, two people chatting each other
up in a hotel lobby, and one's got the hots, and chances are the
other has too? All this while the one's wife of twenty years is
upstairs, possibly humming a tune or sniffing stolen flowers?)
Bringing in God. The mystic extrasensories and supernaturals.
Because ain't it just at this point that the heart did its tap dance
while the head figured all the possibilities like a good gambler
counting cards? And the *body*, don't forget. What's all this
terrible new energy, these sweet swoopswoons and tickles, these
pit-of-the-stomach accelerations and acrobatics like a belly lifted
in an elevator? Come on, two people side by side in a hotel
lobby. Sharing a couch but not even touching. Heart rates up.
Palms moistening. (I mean, it was all I could do to hold on to my
highball!) What, this *isn't* mysterious? This isn't a sort of mind-
reading, this isn't some kind of out-of-the-body travel, or bend-
ing nails without touching them? This ain't God loose in the
lobby? Tell it to the Marines.

"So what about you?" I asked. "How is it a girl like you
never got married?"

"You sound like my parents."

"How is it?"

"Maybe I'm just waiting for the right man to come along."

And stick in here about her character, her qualities and
virtues. Her righteous probity and defense against temptation
as if she were protected by fire retardant, or Scotch-Gard,
say. Her loyalty, for example. What she said next. "Not
you," she flashed. "Shelley's my friend. She's only your
wife."

I could tell them I underestimated her, and go on, pushing the landmarks and saliencies, the highlights and points of
interest, putting her together, too like a police-artist's sketch.

"Did you misunderstand me? Oh, you misunderstood me,"
I objected. "No, I'm just curious. A nice Jewish girl. Intelligent,
attractive. It just seems to me that someone like you would have
no difficulty meeting fellows. Perhaps at your temple. In your

job where you work. I'm told that sometimes, if you take your
wash to the laundromat . . ."

"Oh, I meet plenty of men," she said. "That's not the
problem. Last night."

"I'm sorry?"

"Last night. After the ceremony. After the dinner. During
the dancing."

"I'm sorry?"

"It was so stuffy. I was all overheated."

"Yes?"

"I needed some air."

"Some air. Yes?"

"So I came down here."

"Down here."

"Well, I was on my way out."

"Outside you mean."

"Yes, out. Outside for fresh air."

"I see."

"I was crossing the lobby and got as far as that bar, and
suddenly there was this Japanese man. He was quite good-
looking. And, well, *he* hit on me."

"He *hit* on you?"

"Well, it was no big deal. He asked if I wanted to have a
drink with him."

"You'd gone into the bar?"

"No," she said, "I was crossing the lobby, I was going out
for some air. He saw me crossing the lobby. He was in town on
business, I guess. He was alone. I mean, he wasn't *with* anyone.
Colleagues or customers, a woman, a friend."

"He just asked if you wanted to have a drink with him."

"That's right."

"Just like that."

"Yes."

"So what did you tell him?"

"Well, I'm afraid I wasn't very nice."

"I can't believe *that*."

"I said, 'How come the sport coats you guys wear always
have all those lines and bars and look like blowups of a computer
chip?' "

"Goodness," I said, "that *was* a little rude. It was sort of a racial slur, wasn't it? What did he say then?"

"He was hurt, but I made it up to him," she said. "I bought him a drink. Then, afterward, I took him up to the room."

"Oh?" I said. "Yes?"

"I didn't go outside after all."

"So you never did get your fresh air."

"We opened the windows."

I would tell them . . . And just then remembered. Her parents. She'd mentioned her parents. They would be there. That's it, I decided. And destroyed my notes. Just ripped them up. Just threw them away. All my notes. Toward my eulogy for Joan Cohen.

•   •   •   •

And decided to play it straight.

The place was packed. Joan Cohen's bewildered parents sat in the front by themselves, rent strips of grosgrain pinned to their clothing like black campaign ribbons. The Chaverot were there, their Chaverot husbands and children. Musicians I recognized from bands that had played at their affairs. People I'd never seen in my life.

I read selected passages. I read "O woman of valor who can find?" from Proverbs. I read the twenty-third psalm. I did other selected passages while Shull's and Tober's people set up additional chairs for the latecomers. I did "I lift up mine eyes unto the hills" and "Praise Him with the sound of the trumpet; praise Him with the psaltery and harp."

Then, scanning the faces of the mourners—Shelley glared; Connie, seated beside Hershorn, was openly snarling—I waited until the last seat was taken, and began.

"Joan Cohen never married," I said. "Raised in the values of the traditional Jewish family, she never chose to indulge herself as a 'single parent,' and so remained childless. Save for her beloved parents, of course—and it's typical of Joan how, as a good daughter, she was ever conscious of her mother's and father's worries for her (incidentally, one of my fondest memories of Joan is how once, in Philadelphia, she confided in me as her rabbi and spoke of exactly this subject— their concern that she meet Mr. Right, settle down, and make a good Jewish home)—she may be said to have left no survivors.

"Yet there are so many here. How crowded it is! Additional chairs have been set up to accommodate the overflow. And *still* people stand at the back of the chapel and along its walls. So many, so very many, heedless of ordinance, in defiance of the safety codes, willing to put themselves at risk! Why? In order to pay Joan our last respects? A childless, single woman who never married and left as survivors only her grieving mother and heartbroken father? So many? So *much* respect?"

Shull was weeping. (What this must do to his pleasure, I thought absently. How it must play hell with it. How many thousands it will cost him just to break even again.)

"As you know, Joan was a talented musician. Her group was called 'Chaverot,' Hebrew for 'fellowship,' and what a jolly good fellowship it was! I see her fellows in the fellowship here. I see other musicians, bandsmen whose privilege it may once have been to accompany Joan.

"But can you *all* be musicians? And who are we talking about here anyway? A Beverly Sills? A Barbra Streisand? An Eydie Gorme?

"Of course not.

"We're talking about someone barely and scantly professional, who made, in the psalmist's inspired words, her 'joyful noise unto the Lord,' and who praised Him not 'with the sound of the trumpet,' nor 'with the psaltery and harp,' nor 'with the timbrel.' Well, maybe with the timbrel, that's like a tambourine. But not 'stringed instruments and organs.' Nor 'upon the loud cymbals,' either. So, with the possible exception of the timbrel, what *was* Joan's instrument? Her person that she went to so much trouble to keep kempt and was always such a pleasure to look upon, if only to watch the fall fashions that she preferred and never seemed to tire of wearing, as if autumn were her season of choice, like a winter snow scene, say, kept in a crystal? Was it her style, then, that was her instrument? Her elegant outdoor ways? Which led her into the very fields and unfenced vastnesses where the deer stalker and fox hunter and cony catcher wait for their prey?

"Or was it some cheerful, heady exuberance we caught from her when she raised up her voice in song? That powerful clapping I can almost hear now? Was it some sense we had of her bounding 'round a campfire, leading the singing from the bottom of her generous kibbutz heart? Because she had the energy of a counselor in summer camp and could have been this echt Sabra, a maiden worthy of having been there in the days of Moses, pitching in, helping out, this slim, dark au pair of the wilderness.

"But so *many?*"

I've never been particularly proud of what I do. I do it well, I think, and give fair measure. But, as I say, I'm this professional comforter, like one of those who tried to talk Job out of his grievances and, as on occasions like this, often too much in the rabbi mode. Practically speaking, I'm an unmoved mover. Today, though, even I was a little moved. (What the hell, I knew her, Horatio.)

Most of them were weeping now. Tober's son, dapper behind opaque glasses, wept blind tears. (Sure, I thought, she taught him to dress.) Anyway, most of them were weeping. It was no time to let up.

"*So many?*" I demanded. "A woman without children? An unmarried woman who, except for her parents, leaves no survivors? No sisters or brothers? Not an uncle, not an aunt? A distant cousin even? With no mishpocheh to speak of save the general, at-large, human family we all of us are?

" 'Ah, then, Rabbi,' you say, 'then *we're* her survivors.'

"Well, yes, but so *many?* Lud's not such an easy place to reach if you've never been here before and don't know the way. What's today, Tuesday? An ordinary day of business. But think, *think.* Rosh Hashanah wasn't a week ago even. Yom Kippur's four days off. Two days you closed the store. Four more and you lose another day. Is business so good then? So *many?* Why? You know, tell me why.

" 'Well, but Rabbi,' you say, 'she was in her prime.' "

All of them were crying. I swear it. All of them were. (Not old stony-face Connie. Not my wife, not Shelley, even if she was one of the Chaverot! Oh, no, not Connie and Shelley, who seemed, in their bubble of smugness, distanced as Hershorn. But the rest of them, yes.)

"Of course she was. And it's a terrible thing when you're cut down in your prime. Well, it is. It happens, but it's terrible.

"Think," I coaxed, "what is it we say when we hear of the death of someone we did not ourselves know? What do we ask? After we question the circumstances? What do we say? 'How old was this person?' And, if we're told sixty-eight, sixty-nine, anything within shooting distance of the biblical threescore-and-ten, we say, 'Well, at least they lived a full life.' Shaving a year or so here, there, up, down, plus or minus, but still in the ballpark. And it's true. Sixty-eight, sixty-nine, is within the parameters. Low-normal perhaps, but God is kept honest. This is the acceptable numerology of death.

"Joan Cohen, cut down in her prime, did *not* live a full life.

"Or was it the *manner* of her death, then? That she was shot? Not in the course of things, not, I mean, violently. Not in a rape or holdup, not in a serial killing or to keep her from testifying, but in a straight path on an ordinary day in a green pasture beside still waters in a valley of the shadow of death— taken out out of season in a grotesque hunting accident.

"But tell me, what death, shaved point here, there, up, down, plus or minus, *isn't* grotesque? Is there a doctor in the house? Tell me, Doctor, what death isn't? You tell *me*.

"Still, so many?

"Or doesn't it matter how she died? Isn't it rather *when* she died? Isn't that what it comes down to? When all is said and done?"

There wasn't as much crying as before. Here and there a few were still inconsolable. Joan's parents, of course. Fanny Tupperman, Elaine Iglauer. (And Shull was still sobbing at a pretty good clip.) But most of them were quiet now, interested. Behind their sharp looks and open glowers, Shelley was, Connie.

"Because what's today, Tuesday? Because Rosh Hashanah wasn't a week ago even, and Yom Kippur's four days off.

"*Because she wasn't inscribed in the Book of Life, and that scares us*. It sure scares *me*.

"Because Rosh Hashanah was Thursday. Because Sunday's the Day of Atonement. Because she had ten days. All the ten days of Teshuvah. Because she had ten days of repentance

before it was sealed. The Book of Life she prayed and petitioned
a loving and forgiving God to inscribe her in. Who wouldn't do
it. Who heard what He heard and *still* wouldn't do it. Who *must*
have heard her. Who heard her, all right. You recall what
yesterday was like, the crisp weather, Monday's fine, clean,
clear, open air. You could have heard her yourself.

"Here's the picture:

"All Teshuvah she had, but this was the first good day,
and even if the pastures weren't all that green now—you know
what the weather's been like—still, the foliage was fine, and the
still waters. And she must have been feeling pretty good—what
was there to fear? it was a clear day; you could see forever—and
may even have brought a bit of picnic to nosh—say an apple, a
hunk of cheese, say, say a heel of bread—to restore her soul, to
dull her appetite if she became peckish.

"So she put forth her argument, laid out her reasons, her
bill of particulars, covering the ground like a Philadelphia lawyer, pulling out the stops, actually appealing to His sense, if He
had one, of shame:

" 'But I'm not even married, O Lord our God. I *want* to
settle down, I *do*. I *want* to settle down and make a good Jewish
home. I'm still waiting for Mr. Right. Too many marriages end
in divorce nowadays, O Baruch-Ataw-Adonoi. I want mine to
work. And I'd make a swell mom. As I've tried to be a good
daughter.

" 'And what *about* my parents? It would kill my pop, and
that would kill my mom. They're great people, they never hurt
anybody. Why drag two innocent people into this? For what?
What for, O Blessed-Art-Thou? What could possibly be in it for
You? What would You be getting? A woman without children?
An unmarried woman who, except for her parents, leaves no
survivors? No sisters or brothers? Not an uncle, not an aunt? A
distant cousin even? With no mishpocheh to speak of save the
general, at-large, human family we all of us are? What do you
need it?

" 'Oh, and I have a nice voice, Thou-Art-God, and know
many songs, and this year resolve to learn more.

" 'Oh, oh, and I keep myself kempt, and am still in my
prime, so how about it, Holy-Holy-Holy, inscribe me in the

Book of Life for another year. How about it, what do You say, Lord-Is-My-Shepherd?'

"He said 'BOOM!' And 'BOOM!' And 'BOOM!' again, and Joan Cohen dropped where she stood like a load too heavy to bear any longer.

"We spoke of keeping God honest? *Honest?* Because don't think this is like your car breaking down the minute the warranty runs out. This isn't like that. This was yesterday she died. New Year's was Thursday. Today's Tuesday. The Book of Life isn't sealed until Yom Kippur. Yom Kippur is Sunday. So what did she have? Until Sunday. Counting from Rosh Hashanah, He'd already given her five days. He'd split the difference. She was midway. In a sort of time warp. The warranty hadn't even started yet. She hadn't even driven it off the lot!

"So *honest?* My God, my friends, He's positively *fussy!*"

Shull had stopped weeping. Elaine Iglauer, Fanny Tupperman. Even the Cohens. In their absolute grief these five had been a beat or so behind the rest of the congregation all morning, vaguely aged and weighted, like actors unsure of their blocking, or as if they moved chest deep in water. As for the rest, they weren't just interested now, they were fascinated and couldn't wait to hear what I would say next. Except for Shelley, except for Connie. And me. Except for me. The Rabbi of Lud. I was weeping. *I* was. Not fascinated, not even interested. Only penitent, only asking for my atonement, and began to recite bits of prayer I remembered from the Yom Kippur service.

"We have trespassed," I prayed, "we have been faithless . . . we have spoken basely . . . we have done violence . . . we have forged lies . . . we have counseled evil.

"For the sin which we have committed before Thee under compulsion, or of our own will.

"And for the sin which we have committed before Thee in hardening of the heart.

"For the sin which we have committed before Thee with utterance of the lips and the folly of the mouth.

"For all these, O God of Forgiveness, forgive us, pardon us, grant us remission."

I'd forgotten a lot, but spoke the fragments I remembered as best I could. So, I thought, here I am, a rabbi myself now, and still pull—my sculpted, fashioned, modified Yom Kippur—the shortest haphtarah passage of the year. And went on with my tally.

I prayed to be pardoned for open sins and secret sins, for sinful meditations of the heart, for sins of evil inclination.

They stared at me.

And prayed to be forgiven for contentiousness and envy, for being stiff-necked, for tale-bearing, for vain oaths, for ensnaring my neighbor, for breach of trust, calling them off indiscriminately, guilty of some but not of others. Apologizing for slander sins and sins in business. (I remembered all I'd been told of Lud's contraband dead.) And prayed to be let off for sins of scoffing, for wanton looks, for causeless hatred.

Some were irritated, stirring, grumbling. Charney and Klein were whispering together. Sal, God forbid something should happen in Lud and he not be in on it, moved closer to them. A few of the mourners looked around for their things.

"Hey," I urged, "wait. We're not finished," and specially, suddenly, pled:

"For the sins we have committed against Thee by grandstanding," I tried. "And the sins we have committed against Thee by seeking to lie low and maintain a low profile," I told them, and had a vision of Rabbi Petch cowering behind the furniture jammed together in the southwest corner of his living room in Anchorage. And looked about, excited now, my sins as much in the public domain as if my fly were open. "And the sins we have committed against Thee by the hanky panky of the heart and flesh," I rushed on, though even this didn't cut into their murmuring. I wasn't drunk, or crazy, or even much of a crank, but try telling *them* that.

"For the sins which we have committed against Thee by living in the wrong communities," I said.

That wasn't it. It wasn't even more like it.

"In which we raised our children," I amended.

"Our daughters," I revised.

"*My* daughter," I atoned, not quite grieving but getting warmer and aware of the immense, twisted tonnage of complex grief in the world at any given time, in any given place, some tight amalgam of woe and rue and complicity and fear. Grief like a land mass, like the seas, complicated as weather seen from high space or the veiled, tie-dye smudge of the alloy earth itself.

But why couldn't I let them go? What was I up to, the offshore yeshiva bucher with the tiny haphtarah passage? What was I up to with my spilt-milk penitentials and public-domain regrets and all my deplored, gnashed-teeth, learned-my-lessons? With my sullied sympathy, giving out quarter like a drunken sailor? Pushing off my easy, condolent affections on them, laying on all my outstretched formulas of finessed sensibility and participatory grief, plea bargaining the world, fending God off with my sorrys and sorry-fors— sorry for Shelley, for Connie, the Cohens, for Shull and for Tober, for Charney, for Klein? What was I up to who had enough on my own plate, more than enough, all I could handle with just my own grievances, *forget* my swooping, all-embracing, crash-course sympathetics?

Several were standing now, edging toward the exits. I couldn't let it bother me. There wasn't anything *I* could do about it.

So, thinking of Connie, thinking of Shelley, and playing with Him for time, I prayed that we all be inscribed in the Book of Life for one more year.

I was calmer now, but just before I said the El Moley Rachamim for Joan Cohen, I recited some special blessings I'd learned in yeshiva. I offered the broches you say when you see a rainbow, when you eat ripe fruit, when you hear good news, when you laugh out loud, when you buy new clothes, when you kiss a woman, when you repair an appliance, when you touch a giant, when you smell sweet wood.